# Caerule

By Lauren Hemphill

Caerule



ISBN 978-1-7325866-1-1 (paperback)

ISBN 978-1-7325866-2-8 (hardcover)

ISBN 978-1-7325866-3-5 (kindle)

To everyone who told me to keep writing, and to my biggest fan,
who never let me quit.

Please be advised that this story is intended for mature audiences and contains the following:

Gore, foul language, sexual situations, sexual assault reference, suicide reference.

Events to Remember:

After an event heralding her as a hero, Jade Cavvar is kidnapped by enemy forces and smuggled deep behind their lines. There, she discovers the Thrax—her sworn enemies—are not all that she thought and finds that many of them are not the bloodthirsty beasts she believed. As she forms a bond with their prince, Thaddeous Malkov, she soon discovers that his sister, Voshell Malkov, is the infamous Mad Queen, known for butchering Blues and Reds alike in explosions on the battlefield. Furious, Jade lashes out, and King Daxgor of the Thrax takes this as a sign that she cannot be trusted to broker a peace for both sides. This opportunity soiled, she and Thaddeous must act quickly to stop Voshell from using a superweapon that she claims can kill the entire Exuro Empire. In a desperate attempt to show his father what Jade is capable of, Thaddeous sends A'doxia Calavar, known torturer of Jade and subject of many PTSD hallucinations, to attack her, resulting in the reveal and understanding of Jade's Helix.

Hurt and betrayed, Jade strikes out on her own against Voshell, cutting off the woman's arm, but ultimately failing to stop her as Voshell beheads Thaddeous and flees with the weapon. Jade steals a ship with A'doxia, who swears to aid her, and sets off to save Aris, who is stationed on the planet of Sobek. However, Aris has had her own struggles while Jade was gone, which lead to uncovering many secrets within the Opes, including that of a monstrous creature kept on the neutral planet of Sypher. Something has changed Aris, and as Jade arrives to insist they run away together, Aris strikes the woman down.

Terms to Remember:

Helix: A supernatural power connected with the color of eyes a person has.

H-Blade: Heated-Blade; primary weapon in the galaxy, made up of a folding blade that retracts and extends from the hilt; a small generator heats the edge and allows for the weapon to cut through most materials.

Exuro Empire: The empire Jade hails from, which wars constantly with the Thrax.

Opes: The term for the Exuro Empire's military branch, which is often looked down upon; otherwise known as Blues.

Thrax: Otherwise known as the Reds, these are the enemy of the Exuro Empire, all of which have red eyes.

Vix: Term for the galaxy's primary deity.

Ghawor: Term for the galaxy's primary devil.


People to Remember:

Jade Cavvar: Green Demon; (former) Corporal of the Opes.

Aris Sell: (former) Friend of Jade Cavvar; Opes soldier.

A'doxia Calavar: (former) General of the Thrax.

Thaddeous Malkov (deceased): Brother of Voshell Malkov.

King Daxgor Malkov (deceased): Father of Voshell Malkov.

General Kasaar: General of the Opes; was aware of Jade's eye color.

Salene Vyrr: Retired Opes soldier.


Societal Structures to Remember:

Class structures are constructed by the eye color someone has. A child is born with the eye color they are predisposed towards, but this is malleable and can change as maturity continues. However, after the eye color is set in adolescence, it is seen as a traitorous act for eye colors to change again.


Exuro Social Classes:

Golds: Highest in the Exuro Empire; run all the major government systems.

Plurals: Those with two different colored eyes; often seen as angels who hunt Greens down to the death.

Browns: Civilians.

Blues: Opes soldiers; often looked down upon.

Hazels: Retired Opes soldiers; seen as traitors due to the eye color change.

Greens: Demons; only one can exist in the galaxy at a time.

Thrax Classes:

Reds: All classes.

Greens: Angels of great change; have the power to end the war.

Plurals: Seen as helpers to Greens.


Galaxy Species:

Humans: Though their origin is unknown, they have quickly spread to most planets throughout the Known Galaxy.

Kodarians: Leather-skinned with horns and tusks, these sentient beings often stand taller than an average human and take pride in their horns.

Snippers: Previous stewards of Nevar, these arachnid beings have multi-pupiled eyes and two pairs of arms; small hairs cover their entire bodies.

Syphers: Small, fleshy beings with four legs; these beings often remain on their homeplanet of Sypher and are great inventors—if not great con-artists.

Halos: Canine sentients that stand four to five feet tall; instead of fur on their hands, halos have water-resistant feathers and often come in snow-patterned colors.

Victers: Avian beasts with sharp beaks and deadly talons; thin membranes from their wrists to their ankles allow them to glide; are regarded as highly dangerous and incredibly dim.

Planets to Remember:

Nevar: Main homeworld of the Exuro Empire; overpopulated and choking with fumes that block out the sun and stars; capital city is Nanza City.

Soldar: Main homeworld of the Thrax; an entirely mechanical creation that houses the dwindling population of its people.

Sobek: A planet made of floating islands and currently under contested rule by the Empire and the Thrax.

Taotar: A planet made of desert sands and orbited by a small second sun; location of Jade's torture at A'doxia's hands.

Sypher: Neutral planet; home of the sypher people, who sell items to the highest bidder; nigferra, the metal used in most weapons and armor, is found in the mountains here.

Hallow: Currently ruled by the Thrax; home of the halo people; made up of a broken world covered in ice and spotted with hot springs; has a seasonal warming that thaws the frost.

Daoth: Split planet; small skirmishes dot the surface but is not actively fought over; home of Jade and A'doxia.

Ferges: Neutral planet; home of the vicious peoples named victers; unknown territory.

# Part One

# Chapter 1

Aris planted her feet in front of the Gold council, a severed arm in a jar to her right. It floated in a clear liquid, bubbles suspended and frozen against its flesh. A human steward held it with his copper-colored hands, discomfort written on his face with downturned lips and a scrunched nose. Freckles spotted the arm in containment, calloused fingers limp and unmoving within the glass. It had spilled most of its demonic blood upon the wanting Sobek dirt, but Aris had seared the edge of it with a hot blade, cauterizing the wound that rewarded her with a most valuable prize.

Jade's right arm.

*No,* she reminded herself. *The demon's right arm.*

"You saw it plummet into the water?" the kodarian asked, her voice harsh and dry. Small, golden eyes stared sharply from leathery black skin, scrutinizing Aris' form, searching for a weakness in her resolve, her posture, her success. But she—no, the entire council—would find none. Aris was sure of it.

"Yes, councilwoman," Aris replied, her eyes moving to meet the kodarian's. Her name was Silva, and age creased the ebony flesh around her eyes and particularly around her horns, which dripped with gold jewelry. They caught the light from one of the many windows nearly eleven feet up the wall behind the council members. The smog-covered morning of Nevar drizzled through them and neon signs stained what little sunlight the planet received with blues and purples.

"The demon fell into the waters," Aris continued. "From such a distance, the fall itself would've broken its back. But if it did somehow survive, there are plenty of carnivorous fish. They would've eaten her before she bled out from her wound."

"*It's* wound, general," Silva replied, the slitted nostrils above her eyes flaring with aggravation.

"Forgive me," Aris said, bowing her head, strands of her golden hair falling from her bun to frame her face. "I admit it is still difficult for me to drop the façade of its humanity."

"The demon was alone, then? There was no one there to help the monster struggle on?"

"No, councilwoman," Aris said, her voice even, just as she had practiced. She looked up at the kodarian, ensuring unflinching, guiltless eye contact. "The demon was completely alone."

The woman sighed and leaned back in her chair, her golden eyes flicking towards the rest of the council on her left of the semi-circle table.

"The galaxy is safer for it," she said, her voice little more than a whisper.

"It was wise of you to bring what remained of this monster back to us," said the snipper, sitting on the other side of the table. Councilman Hassar, with greying pinprick hairs covering his arachnid body. The pincers on both corners of his mouth tapped idly.

Aris gave him a curt smile. "I am glad to have been able to find it for you all, councilman. I hope you're able to discover the root of such a creature's existence."

"Let us not forget that it is because of you that this monster existed within our city's borders," growled the human, who sat directly in front of her in the 'u' shaped table. His name was Dameon. "You were the one who put us all in danger by not reporting the monster sooner. It could've snapped here and taken out numerous civilians."

Aris kept herself from smiling. *Look at you, so caring. Who would have guessed a Gold would love civilians so much?*

"I do hope that I am able to make up for my risky decision," Aris replied. His rage was thick like sweat against her skin, making the other council members peer quizzically at him.

*What's the matter? Aren't you proud of me?* She knew he wanted her to let it slip, to say *something* of their relation. But she wouldn't. She was just a lowly Blue, doing her duty. That's what he wanted, wasn't it? A demon slayer. A general. The first Blue to have housing on the hundredth level of Nanza City.

Or did it bother him that a Blue had done so much and he so little? She suppressed the humor bubbling up in her throat, fearing it might rumble out if she spoke too soon.

"Forgetting that," said Hassar, waving Dameon's concern away with one of his four hands, "who is this creature you've brought to our shores? Can we bring it in?"

The guard behind Aris turned and opened the massive wooden door. It swung easily, hardly making a sound. Aris didn't look, not even when the beast's fleshy, hoof-like feet thumped against the marble tile. His tail brushed along the floor behind him, the scales that made up his ebony exterior sending a whispering sound through the room. He came up beside Aris, his hood pulled over his face, his eyes downcast, and the rest of the cloth falling over his shoulders. It was opened in the front to allow the nostrils on his collarbone to breathe—and to display the ivory tattoos that decorated his body. Even in the short amount of time knowing the creature, Aris was aware of his pride in his tattoos.

"Vix," Silva gasped, her eyes widening. "The thing is huge!"

Aris allowed herself to peer at the ten-foot… *man* to her left. The creature's tail swung idly, continuing the strange, unearthly sound of scales dancing over the stone floor. She had to arch her neck just to see his profile.

"Kuroda," he spoke, his voice heavy with weight and tinged with an odd, internal echo that stained each word he uttered. His large hands reached up and grabbed his hood. He pulled it down to show off his face, but instead of gawking at the strangeness of his anatomy, Silva screamed, leapt to her feet, and sent the chair clattering behind her.

"Its eyes are *green!*" she screeched. "Guards!"

"What is the meaning of this?" Dameon demanded, slamming his hands on the table. "You slay one demon to bring us another?"

"Council members, please," Aris said, sparing a glance over her uniformed shoulder to see where the guards were. They remained at their posts beside the exit, though their H-blades were now drawn, the crimson hue of the metal prepared to slice anything with a simple flick of the wrist. "He is not here to harm us. He's here to ask for a place of refuge!"

"*Refuge?*" Silva breathed. "For a Green? It's a monster!"

Kuroda dropped to one knee, his cloak billowing up around him to show off his thickly muscled legs. He pressed his fist to the ground, while the small arms on his chest—no longer than his forearms—spread out in a gesture of welcoming or surrender.

"Peace," he said, his voice storming through the room and making Aris' teeth ache. "Peace."

"Calm yourselves," Hassar said, his golden gaze situated curiously on the newcomer. "He is nothing we have seen before. Blues are not known for their cunning, I'll grant you that, Silva, but I doubt even a Blue would bring something to us she did not think was safe."

"The Blues are treacherous," Dameon insisted. "Surely we cannot allow this *thing* to remain here."

"He," Kuroda growled. "Kuroda he."

"I apologize for the surprise, council members, but I thought it imperative to bring him to you," Aris offered. "If I am not mistaken, his eyes are different than that of the demon's. I am unaware of the others from past documentation—did their shade of green vary? Or were they all bright like the one I slew?"

She waited as the trio peered at each other. Hassar sighed, his pincers tapping together in a thoughtful manner, bone on bone swallowing the silence.

"Where is it from?" Hassar asked.

5

"From a planet outside the Known Galaxy, councilman," Aris answered.

"Impossible," Silva whispered. "*Impossible*—no one can get through the asteroid field."

"His ship was badly damaged, councilwoman. I suspect he did not make it through unscathed."

"He looks quite unharmed," Hassar noted. "He must be rather sturdy. How far away from home is he?"

"Year," Kuroda replied. He kept his head down, his four mandibles flaring as he spoke, a green tongue flicking behind rows of carnivorous teeth. While each mandible was rather malleable, replacing the sections of his face where cheeks should be, they still had a difficult time reproducing certain sounds from the Os language. His 'r's and 'o's were particularly bad, often filled in with hearty exhales, leaving the listener to decipher what he attempted to say.

Hassar's brows lifted with surprise. "A whole year?" He looked from one council member to the next. "How did you survive all that time?"

"Sleep." Kuroda said, the word coming out more akin to "slee-bah."

"You slept the entire journey?" Hassar pressed. "That's quite curious."

Silva looked around, saw that her fear was garnering her no sympathy, and turned to pick up her chair. The sound of her movements and the dragging of metal across the stone filled the pause in the conversation, but once she was seated, Hassar spoke again:

"You said he was a refugee, General Sell? You do not wish to go home, strange… creature?"

"No." Kuroda used his smaller hands to gesture to the ground. "Stay. Make safe."

"Make safe?" Hassar repeated, tilting his head.

"That does not change the fact that it is a *Green*," Silva insisted, her eyes watching Kuroda as she spoke. "It is dangerous."

"I am peace," Kuroda said.

"You are *violence!*" Dameon snapped. "This is insane—he should be sent out immediately!"

Kuroda let out a rumbling sound from his chest, an uncomfortable hum of uncertainty as he glanced to Aris. The white markings that lined his body drew her attention, as they always did. The intricate lines across his face encircled his eyes, indicating some sort of status among his own people. A crescent shape sat higher up on his elongated, shield-like face, appearing as if a moon was dripping down towards his pupils.

She tore her gaze away and faced Dameon, not allowing herself to get lost in the curving strokes and curious meanings that tattooed Kuroda's blackened scales.

With her focus back on him, Aris noticed Dameon's fine tuxedo now looked as if it was collecting sweat along his neckline.

*Are you angry with me?* she thought, amused.

"He holds no Helix," Aris said evenly. "And while this was the case for the Green before as well, you will find that he came from outside the realm of a demon's domain, where indeed, many green-eyed creatures live."

"A whole *race* of them? Surely letting this beast stand here is a danger to us all," Dameon pressed. "We should have them both thrown out and that monster's head taken from its shoulders."

"Hush, human," Hassar muttered, lifting one hand to stop Dameon. "What is that sound he is making?"

Kuroda immediately stopped. Aris looked at him once more before looking back at the snipper.

"He was uncomfortable," she explained. "Nervous from everyone being upset."

"Nervous?" Hassar repeated. "And it is a he?"

"Yes, councilman."

Hassar eyed Kuroda, his dual-pupiled eyes scanning every inch. "Stand," he said, gesturing to Kuroda. Kuroda, after looking for guidance from Aris, did so. She knew Hassar would find nothing to indicate Kuroda's sex between the creature's legs, and as she predicted, Hassar's brows furrowed. "How can you tell?"

"I asked him," Aris replied. "He says he is both but likes 'he.'"

"Hm," Hassar huffed. "What does that mean, 'he is both?'"

"There are more pressing issues," Dameon cut in, scowling at his fellow council member. "This thing is a *Green*—"

"Human, you are on repeat," Hassar said. "Did you not hear your daughter?"

*Ah, there it is.*

Dameon's eyes flared wide before narrowing to dangerous slits upon his fellow council member's frame. The bristling hatred spilled off him and drowned the room in a suffocating tension.

"That *thing* is not my daughter," Dameon growled.

"Yes, yes, we all remember the situation with the window," Hassar said, shaking his head. "It is a shame such a legacy as yours couldn't be extended past one generation, hm? Why, I have three children of my own, and all their eyes are gold. And you had one, didn't you? Have you tried again, Dameon? Have you tried again and found any success?"

Dameon glared at the snipper. "Am I on trial, Hassar?"

"Not at the moment," Hassar purred. "I am just pointing out what a tragedy it is that your only offspring would become a Blue. And here we were all hoping the best for you." The human sneered and Hassar chuckled before looking back to Aris. "My point is," he chimed, "that this creature is not from our part of the galaxy. Cutting off its head may do nothing—it may not even be privy to our regulations and systems of eye color."

"Surely you don't mean that Vix's holy reach remains only within our small part of the galaxy?" Dameon said. "That just because it's an outsider that this *thing* isn't the tool of Ghawor?"

"Surely I mean that none of us here really believe that, do we?" Hassar replied, his cold gold eyes meeting Dameon's. "Unless, General Sell, I have offended you in some way?"

"No, councilman," Aris replied with a courteous smile.

"See?" Hassar hummed, looking over towards Kuroda. "Now, tell us, Sir Kuroda, what is it you're here for again?"

"Safe," Kuroda said after a moment of pause.

"You are quite safe here, yes," Hassar said, an amused smile in his voice. "We will allow no harm to come to you. What was it you were fleeing?"

"Monster," Kuroda replied, his voice echoing in the bare room. The small pair of hands on his chest motioned, searching for the right words as he fell silent. The trio of council members sat quietly, waiting for him to continue. "Monster," Kuroda said again. "Eat."

"Eat?" Hassar tilted his head. "What do you mean, eat?"

"He eat," Kuroda insisted. He tapped his chest. "Eat."

Hassar made a face, his pincers clicking together in thought. He looked to Silva, Dameon, then over to Aris.

"I am at a loss, General Sell," he said. "Explain."

"Of course," Aris replied. "From our conversations during our flight here, it appears that the person he fled from wished to *eat* him. I believe it's a metaphor. I asked if he was wounded, and he explained that he was forced to flee from his home. It seems this other person took over his rule."

"Curious," Hassar muttered.

"So does that mean someone will come for us? Come for him?" Silva inquired, a whine pitching her voice a few octaves higher.

"Stay," Kuroda said. With his smaller pair of hands, he pointed down towards his feet. "He stay."

"His attacker is happy to remain on his own planet," Aris interpreted. "That's what the attacker wanted—to take over."

"But this… this creature was a king?" Silva asked.

"Yes, councilwoman."

"You," Kuroda said, nodding to the woman. "Am you."

Aris watched as the woman's expression shifted from confused furrowed brows, to a pleasant, prideful smile. A king like her. Ruler over all the planet.

*Arrogant.*

"Where was it you said you found this… *man?*" Silva asked, looking to Aris.

"Councilwoman, that is something of a concerning matter." Aris exhaled and shook her head. "It is treason."

"Get on with it," Dameon snapped. "We aren't sitting here to listen to your feelings."

"Of course, councilman." Aris' words were smooth, like a knife between the ribs. She turned her eyes to Silva. "I had believed you all would've been alerted to this situation, but it seems General

11

Kasaar did not inform you he was holding Kuroda under duress on Sypher?"

Silva blinked. "What?"

"General Kasaar did this?" Hassar growled. He turned to Dameon on his right. "You should know about this."

*You are the head of the Opes, aren't you, father? My. What a scandal.*

"Lies spun by a worthless Blue child." Dameon waved his hand dismissively. "She has no proof of this claim."

"I do, actually, councilman," Aris said. "With all due respect, there are documents and files currently stored on the general's workplace computer, along with messages between him and a soldier under his guidance. They were attempting to conduct experiments."

"And you expect me to believe this?" Dameon's eyes narrowed upon her plump frame, searching for the weaknesses he used to stab at—her weight, her intelligence, the vitiligo hidden beneath her crimson uniform. But this time he would find nothing. She was stone. And with a small, confident smile, she answered him:

"After I returned home with Kuroda, I had my suspicions. I was able to remotely download the files, councilman."

"It is so easy to steal Opes files?" Hassar looked to Dameon, the threat clear in his voice.

*Oh goodness, father, are you failing at your job?*

"Impossible," Dameon insisted. "Security is tight enough."

"Apparently not," Hassar said, turning to Aris. "Do you have these files?"

"I do, councilman." Aris tapped her wrist holo—a small circular band cast in sleek metal with several buttons upon its side. She pressed one of them and a small holographic screen appeared above it. Displayed were the files, and with a quick swipe upwards, it was sent off to everyone in the room. The Golds looked at their own holos, pouring over the information with scrutinizing eyes and furrowed brows. Aris watched with mild satisfaction as her father bristled, his jaw locked.

"These all could have been forged," he said, dismissing the accusations with a flick of the wrist. "There is no way to guarantee she's not just making some petty power-play."

"That could be the case," Hassar remarked, "but I've never known a Blue to be so thorough. They are bred for violence, not espionage." He looked to Aris. "No offense, General Sell."

"None at all, councilman. If it so pleases you, council members, I would encourage seizing General Kasaar's folders for yourselves to verify these claims." She folded her hands behind her back and awaited their verdict.

"Surely we aren't considering—" Dameon started.

"I think there is no harm in searching the folders," Silva chimed, looking to her fellow Golds. "It'll be better to ensure our... *civilians* are safe from a treacherous Blue, no?"

"You do have a point," Hassar said, a smile pulling at his lips. He looked to Dameon. "Wouldn't you agree?"

13

Dameon, with a scowl dragging his features down, gave a stiff nod. On his holo, he initiated the order to his subordinates.

"As for you, Sir Kuroda," Hassar said. "We might be convinced to give you a place to stay should you provide us something in return."

"Make safe," Kuroda replied with a nod. "Hunger."

"We don't have a famine issue, sir," Hassar said. He rested his upper two elbows on the table and intertwined his fingers. "What else?"

Kuroda rested one large hand on Aris' shoulder and peered at her, his eyes searching. "Make…" he muttered.

"Fight?" Aris asked, arching a curious brow, as if this was news to her. As if they hadn't practiced this for hours. "Are you wanting to fight?"

"Fight. Make safe." Kuroda nodded and looked to the Golds, leaving his hand on Aris' shoulder. "Fight."

"You want to fight?" Dameon's voice was incredulous. "You want to… *what?*"

"I think he wants to make it safe here. As a thank you for letting him stay, council members." Aris looked at Kuroda. "Is that about right?"

"Yes," he said. "Yes. Fight make safe."

A cruel, malicious smile curled Dameon's lips upward. "Is that so?" he cooed. "You want to go fight on the front lines with General Sell here?"

"That does not change the fact that his eyes are green," Silva said. "Sending a Green to the front lines…"

"The Blues will not care," Dameon said with a grin. "They are soldiers. They will accept whatever help that is given to them."

"I believe if he wishes to prove his worth by helping secure Sobek for the Empire, that we should allow it," Hassar said.

"I agree," Dameon hummed. "And if he perishes during the fighting, then it can't be helped."

"Certainly," Hassar said. "And we will know then for sure that he was of no threat."

"If he survived the asteroid field, he should be able to survive a few little battles," Silva said with a nod. "Maybe he could show the Blues how to finally get things done."

"That would be quite beneficial," Dameon said.

"Then it is agreed," Silva said. "General Sell, you and this Kuroda will leave in the morning and return to Sobek."

*Tomorrow morning?* Aris stiffened. *No. I was supposed to have more time. A few days here, at least. Damn it.*

"There," Hassar added, "you are tasked with ensuring the Empire's victory by stopping the… ah, what is the silly name you Blues gave her?"

"Councilman?" Aris asked, brows furrowing, doing her best to calm her raging mind. *Everything has to change.*

"Some queen? Some…?"

Aris blinked. A cold finger ran down the length of her spine. There was no startled plan-making, no work-arounds being concocted in her skull. Everything was silent. She had stopped breathing.

"The Mad Queen?" she said.

"That's it! I heard she's quite the issue. Is that right, Dameon?"

"That's correct," Dameon purred. "She's been killing our useless Blues left and right. Perhaps these two can finally put an end to her."

Aris didn't look at him. She wouldn't let him win. Not now. Not when she had already sacrificed so much.

"Of course, council members," Aris replied, saluting, pressing her fists over her heart. "If it is what you wish."

Every fiber of her flesh grew frigid.

"Good. Take Kuroda with you, he can stay in your apartment for the night," Hassar said. "Keep that hood on. We don't need a panic over his eyes."

"Enough panic has happened from her having an apartment so high up," Dameon said.

Silva laughed. "Did you get letters about that, too? Well, we'll see what we can do about that if she gets back."

Dameon chuckled. Hassar waved his hands towards Kuroda and Aris.

"You are dismissed," he said. "Leave."

Kuroda pulled his hood up. Aris bowed. A forced, tight smile on her lips as the laughter rang in her ears. She turned on her heel and headed out the door. Her heart smashed against her ribs, quicker each second.

They wanted her dead. They wanted her blown apart by one of the Mad Queen's wretched bombs, legs caught in the limbs of trees.

But she would return. And when she did, she would pull them from their rotting thrones.

Chapter 2

Voshell Malkov spewed blood across the polished deck of her ship. Crimson splattered in thick globs, staining the fabricated wood, dribbling down onto her hand as she clutched her right shoulder. Her arm was cleanly severed from it. Her legs buckled and she collapsed to her knees, the impact jarring her bones and making her hips ache. Iron hung in the air and choked her lungs as she squeezed her human eye shut, her fingers digging into the oozing gore.

If only A'doxia hadn't interrupted. If only that lying bitch had remained loyal to her commander. *She fucked me. She fucked this whole thing.*

Now the Green still lived. Now there was a loose end. A possibility of that redheaded devil chasing Voshell to Sobek, chasing her to the war, demanding a rematch and taking more than Voshell's right arm. Voshell had barely survived the first fight. She was destined to lose a second.

The Plural's head began to spin. She opened her eyes to see the world double around her. Trying to steady herself, Voshell took a few deep breaths, the taste dry and shallow and filled with shards of broken glass. Did they have a medic on board? *Vix, we don't have medic, do we?*

"Our queen!" Shouts surrounded her in a panicked flurry, shapes darting through her dimming vision. She swayed and found herself in the care of several of hands, all keeping her upright. Someone knelt before her and spoke hurriedly, their faint pink lips parting. Voshell heard no words.

The queen blinked a few times, trying to push the blurry figure into one clear image as her true eye fogged over. Her mechanical pupil analyzed the world in crisp, vomit-inducing detail. Her gaze wandered over the person's face. The speaker was human with pale skin and white-blonde hair that held two small, golden feathers woven into her braids. Her striking red eyes held more care and compassion than Voshell had ever seen. Perhaps, just once, Thaddeous looked at her like that as a child.

An unworldly lightness made the new queen feel as if she were floating off the ground and churned her stomach full of burning bile. The woman before her was now two, now three. Voshell pulled her right hand from her shoulder and pressed her crimson coated palm against her mouth, attempting to keep the contents of her gut from spilling out upon the perfect beauties before her.

A wave of agonizing pain shot through her right arm, enough to make her fingers buzz and curl and tense, even though they no longer existed. Her breathing stopped altogether, her mind sharpened, and she spun to see a H-blade's edge pressed firmly to her pulsating mass of muscle and veins.

Voshell screamed.

"Keep her steady!" the blonde shouted, her voice breaking through the murk in Voshell's mind. It was strong and deep, rich with an accent Voshell couldn't place. The queen jerked back, but the hands held her in place, fighting to bring her to the searing blade.

"Don't stop!" the blonde ordered, pointing to the man with the blade. A greasy stench bubbled upwards in a white haze, sticking to the inside of Voshell's throat and cursing her tongue with the flavor of her own cooking veins. It twisted into her nostrils with hints of singed and acrid hair. Her free hand snatched the wrist of the soldier with the weapon. The blonde grabbed Voshell's face and forced the Plural to look at her.

"Just hold on, my queen," she said. "Hold on!"

Voshell's eye shut tight and her mechanical momentarily darkened as her teeth ground together, the pain in her jaw consumed completely by the cauterizing of her laceration. She felt a shadow come to her mind and threaten to overtake her, to pull her into the brink.

"My, what a morbid sight," an unfamiliar masculine voice purred. It sounded unnatural, though how, Voshell couldn't quite tell. She cracked an eye as the blade was pulled from her in surprise. Everyone peered at the human man standing a few feet away, diagonal from Voshell. His black hair fell upon his shoulders like curved daggers and his features looked as if they were cut out of stone. Vibrant fabrics of black, bright blues, and reds fell upon his athletic frame in the form of a coat with a train. His eyes, Voshell noticed, shone silver. She had never seen silver eyes before.

"Who the fuck are you?" she managed, her voice raspy and cut with gasps for air. The sound of her blood dripping on the floor drew the man's eyes.

"I'm surprised you don't recognize me," he cooed. "I am Malkov. The weapon's keeper." He swept his coat back and bowed deeply, his hair falling to frame his olive skin. His eyes did not leave Voshell's. Chills ran down her spine, but she forced herself to stay steady as she looked down at her breast pocket. From beneath the fabric, the circular device glowed blue.

"The distress message," she muttered, blinking hard. "That was you."

"It was," Malkov said. "There is nothing to fear from me. I am here to help." He straightened and folded his hands behind his back. He nodded towards her arm. "I can fix that and, at the same time, give you the power you want."

"The...?" Voshell whispered. The ship pitched beneath her and vomit boiled up in her throat.

"The weapon, yes. I suspect we have little time to discuss the details. Take that device and press it to your wound. In return for the blood, it will become the weapon you so desire."

The weapon. She needed that. For her people. For her family.

*No. That's not right...*

"My queen, we need to finish sealing that wound," the blonde said, turning back to Voshell. "You're losing too much blood."

Voshell peered at her quizzically. For someone so pretty, she wasn't that smart, was she? Didn't she know they needed a way out? Didn't she know that this was the only way to save themselves? The Blues would eradicate them within the year. That pretty face of hers would be lying on a battlefield attached to a corpse. But Voshell could stop that. She could stop the war for everyone. They would live in peace and finally, for once in their cursed lives, know what that was like.

Her shaking, bloody fingers fumbled with her pocket as she pulled out the disk, smearing red across the fabric. The blonde's brows furrowed but she said nothing. Malkov offered Voshell a slight smile as the portrait of him blurred with bloody fingerprints.

"Good," he said. "Now press it into your wound."

"My queen," muttered another soldier, "are you certain you should trust him?"

*Am I certain?* Voshell let out a soft, pitiful laugh, her chest heaving with the effort. *It's too late to ask that question. I nearly died getting this weapon off Soldar. I placed all my bets on this, not knowing how it worked in the slightest. I can't back out now.* She looked at the metal disk as a heaviness set upon her ribs. *If I won't, who will?*

There was a smile, the sound of a child laughing, the flash of raven hair and a little boy in a tuxedo.

Voshell gripped the weapon tight. *For you. For what you could not see.* She turned and jammed the item into the meat of her arm. A cry spilled from her burning throat as the disk broke through the thin cauterized layer, her nerves screaming along with her. Crimson bathed her down to the elbow. Her eye screwed shut against the wall of torment that seared each and every inch of her, ripping thoughts from her mind, slicing away regrets and guilts and justifications. Her stomach churned. Hot tears spilled down her cheeks.

"My queen!" She wasn't sure who spoke, but hands were on her again, holding her up, keeping her steady as something snaked around her collarbone, spread across her chest, dug into the freckled skin beneath her uniform. Her hand fell to her lap, the heat of her own blood making vomit drool out of her gaping mouth, covering her in yet another blanket of warmth.

Shouts filled her ears, hands grabbing and pulling, a buzzing sensation spreading across her nerves, numbing each one encountered. She tried to open her eye, to look at her side, to see what was happening to her. But neither it nor the prosthetic would not listen to her demands, both firmly locked in darkness as her body fell to lethargy. Panic began brimming behind her lungs. Her fingers would not move; her mouth, filled with the burning aftertaste of rancor, would not form words; and Vix above, she wasn't even sure she was breathing.

She couldn't be at the end so close to victory. She had to live. For all that she had sacrificed, all she had witnessed—she *had* to live.

"Sis?"

Voshell saw a figure before her, standing apart from the black that lingered in her skull. He was little taller than her hip, his hair a mess atop his head. He wore a tuxedo with a white bowtie around his neck.

"Vosh, are you okay?" Thaddeous asked.

Then there was nothing.

# Chapter 3

Voshell jerked upright in her cot, sweat on her brow, hair sticking to her face and neck. Her throat was filled with smoldering coals, making it impossible to swallow. She blinked and found her left eye ached from lack of use. Her right prosthetic buzzed and hummed as it reinitiated itself.

A canvas tent was erected around her, the grey fabric thin to allow airflow, but a tarp had been pulled over top as a trickle of rain danced upon it. Cots were set up in two rows inside the tent, four on each side. She discovered two other soldiers were sleeping across the way. One had a bandaged middle, while the other had gauze wrapped around his kodarian skull. As Voshell's breathing grew slower and her heart fell into a relaxed rhythm, she remembered where she was: Sobek. They were heading there before she passed out. Her soldiers must have carried her to a medic.

Voshell pressed her left hand to her forehead and exhaled, slumping forward. Her stomach was filled with bricks and hunger gnawed at the marrow of her bones.

That meant that all she remembered, all the hazy images in her mind, were real. Killing her father. A'doxia's betrayal. Her arm. Thaddeous.

She scratched at the scar across her face and took a slow, steady inhale to calm her nerves. Tentatively, she peered at her right side. Attached to her shoulder was a grey and blue arm, built from tightly woven tendrils of what appeared to be metal, a blue streak running down the center of each. She ran her fingertips across the chilled, smooth surface. The braids grew tighter for her fingers, which she flexed to find responsive. As her hand curled into a fist, a mild ache sparked in her shoulder. Voshell gritted her teeth and brushed sweat-soaked hair from her face. Investigating, she reached up and pulled the strap of her tank-top back to better see the seal. Her brows furrowed.

Instead of a connection of flesh to metal, the separation was swallowed up by more tentacles wrapping around the skin, reaching out to her collarbone and right breast, where the tips dug into her skin to act as anchors. There was a noticeably reddish hue around each entry point, but after prodding at them, she found she could feel nothing. They were completely numb.

"You're awake."

Voshell looked up to see Malkov standing at the foot of her cot. His hands were clasped behind him, his chin up, his eyes peering at her from over his nose.

"You've been unconscious for a week. I was beginning to wonder if making you that arm was a waste."

"A week?" Voshell hissed, a scowl pulling down her lips. "Shit."

He looked unamused. "Yes," he said. "Shit. You do plan on using that arm of yours, don't you?"

"This is the weapon?" she asked, turning her attention to her arm once more. She traced the blue lines with her forefinger. "What? Do I punch people with it?"

25

That rewarded her with a slight smile from the A.I. "You could," he hummed. "That would be rather enjoyable, I think. Perhaps it would help you with all those pent-up feelings you've got. I don't need you getting all choked up and forgetting your purpose here."

"Excuse me?" Voshell looked back at him, brows furrowed. "What are you trying to say?"

He eyed her before shrugging. "I can target—"

"I thought *you* were the guardian," she cut in. "Not the weapon itself."

His jaw tightened. "After being trapped alone for so long, I do not think there's much of a difference anymore, Voshell. All that you need to know is that this weapon can target anything identified in the blood. And you seem to dislike those little blue people, right?"

"The Empire soldiers," Voshell confirmed. "Yes." She cleared her throat, the rawness in it making it hard to speak. She looked around for a cup or a canteen.

"Mm. Well, that can be taken from their blood. I will need a sample. And I will then run tests. And *then* you will be able to use me to create a disease to run through your little bullies."

She stiffened and looked at him. *Bullies? What does he think? That this is some sort of childish game?*

"Yes," Malkov answered, much to Voshell's surprise. "I do. Nevertheless, it will make me glad to finally fulfill my purpose. And I believe you will be glad to make the galaxy safe for your people."

He waved one hand flippantly and looked away. "Then you can feel justified all you want with your family genocide."

"What did you say?" she growled, her fingers curling around her arm.

"Is that not what you did?" he replied. "Your beheading stunt? First your father, then your brother? You did what you had to do, Voshell. He would've gotten in your way. He would've tried to stop you. The only way forward is to kill those that are killing you, and you know that." His silver eyes met hers. "So don't feel guilty."

"I don't feel guilty," Voshell bit back. "If he lived, I never would've made it to Sobek, and the Reds would still be divided beneath the two of us. If he lived, he would've found some way to ruin this, and we all would've died. I can't exactly make the galaxy safe again if he's out there trying to undermine me."

Malkov smirked, a chuckle rumbling from his lips. "You're exactly right," he cooed. "All things have worked out for your destiny, Voshell. If he hadn't tried to stop you, if you hadn't killed him, that little redhead gal—Jade, if you remember right—wouldn't have been recklessly assaulting you. And you wouldn't have lost your arm, and we wouldn't be talking." He straightened the tie around his neck. "You're meant to bring your people the security they deserve. Everything is working out towards that, isn't it?"

Voshell's brows furrowed deep. "I… how did you know all that?"

"Queen General?" The voice drew her attention to her right, where the tent's entrance flap was pushed aside to allow the figure of a large woman inside. Basic armor covered the thick muscle and fat that wrapped around the six-foot tall human. Shaved blonde hair ran along the sides of her head, allowing for one ponytail and six tight braids—three on either side above her ears. Two golden feathers stuck out from the strip of hair at the top of her head.

"You're awake," she breathed, stepping closer with a smile on her lips. Voshell blinked. The god-like woman had been real, too? Malkov watched at the foot of the bed with dismay.

"Let's keep our thoughts clean, Voshell," he chided.

"Ah, good morning," Voshell offered. She itched the scar across her nose. "And… you are?"

"Private Sindri," the woman said. She came to Voshell's side and pulled a canteen off the belt around her hips. She unscrewed the top and offered it to her queen. "I thought you might be thirsty."

Voshell swallowed. Malkov's eyes narrowed.

"You are not the only one in that head of yours, Voshell. Do not subject me to your disgusting human habits."

"Can you hear him?" Voshell asked, taking the canteen.

Sindri's brows furrowed. "Hear who, Queen General?"

"It's just me then?" Voshell looked to Malkov.

The A.I. nodded. "Yes. You and I are linked by the arm. There is no need for me to speak or be seen by anyone else."

"Hm." Voshell took a sip of the water and cherished its soothing touch upon her sandy innards. After downing all of it, she handed the empty canister back. Sindri took it and hooked it to her belt.

"How are you feeling, Queen General?" Sindri asked, her crimson eyes flickering over Voshell's new arm. "Are you hungry? The pot has just been started—I can see if the chef has a bowl set aside for you."

"Yes," Voshell said, "yes, food would be quite nice, private."

The woman smiled, created an 'x' with her wrists, and pressed them against her right shoulder. "Right away, Queen General." She turned to leave.

"Wait," Voshell reached out to grab the woman's arm, thought better of it, and instead scraped her nails across her facial scar again.

Sindri turned, a curious brow raised. "Yes, Queen General?"

"What was that you just did? With your arms?"

"Oh. Right, you were… it's a new salute to honor you, my queen. You've sacrificed a lot for us." Her eyes settled on Voshell's metallic arm once more. "We wanted to show to you that we're grateful."

"Ah." Voshell found herself smiling. Her left hand brushed her right wrist, idly trailing over the curves. She was doing something worth praising. That was a first. Voshell cleared her throat. "Ah, give me a status report before you go, private."

"Yes, of course!" Sindri sucked in a breath and stood a bit straighter. "Over the last week we've held our ground in all but the

29

western front. There, we lost the river to the Blues, who have acquired a new general that has given us some trouble, Queen General. We suffered losses in that skirmish as several trees were cut down and crushed our troops before we were forced to retreat to a more defendable position."

"You were involved in this, private?"

"No, Queen General. I only overheard your lieutenants."

Voshell's lips curled into a smirk and a light laugh escaped her. "Nosey, then."

Sindri's eyes widened. "N-no, Queen General, I—"

"I'm joking, private. Relax. It's only us in here." *So long as no one walks in.*

Malkov cleared his throat. "There is more than just you two here," he growled, his silver eyes holding a glint of hostility. Voshell ignored him.

Sindri, meanwhile, offered a nervous laugh and her posture remained tense. "O-of course," she murmured. "Ah, should I go get your food? Or call for a medic?"

"She's eager to leave. You should let her," Malkov said.

"I lost a lot of blood," Voshell said, not sparing Malkov a glance. "Did we have a medic here, or did someone donate blood?"

"Both. I donated blood and the Healer was able to replenish what I gave you," Sindri replied. "The Helix didn't seem to have any effect on you. I hope that's not too upsetting, my queen."

Voshell shook her head. "Why would I be upset that you saved my life, private? Come. Help me stand."

Quietly, the private stepped closer and wrapped her arm around Voshell's middle. The queen placed her own around Sindri's shoulders and, with a quick intake of breath by both, they were able to stand. A lightheadedness made Voshell lean against the larger woman, forcing her to wonder just how much blood she had ended up losing. She blinked a few times.

"Queen General, are you all right?" Sindri asked, peering at the woman. Voshell nodded, keenly aware of how Sindri's muscular arm flexed a bit to keep her steady, how the woman stunk of sweat with hints of woodlands and wheat. The queen glanced up at the private, nearly half a foot between their heights, and noticed the woman's square jawline, the smell of her tea-stained breath. It had been so long since she had someone to call her own. A'doxia had, for a while, filled that need, but the woman was flighty and manipulative, always coming and going whenever she saw fit, leaving Voshell in cold sweats night after night. When they were together, the violent mess of limbs was exhilarating, but Voshell knew A'doxia wasn't hers. She was A'doxia's.

Still, a war-time fling was not anything she should logically get herself involved in. She had to focus. She had to finish off the Blues and bring her people into safety. Perhaps, however, if they both survived this mess, she could find Sindri during peacetime, ask if she'd like to get a drink.

"Focus," Malkov snapped, appearing suddenly in front of her. Voshell jerked back into Sindri's arm, which held her steady.

"Get lost," Voshell hissed, waving a hand at him. Malkov leaned back, avoiding it, his eyes narrowed.

"I did not give you this arm to do unsightly things with it," he snarled, an odd glitch appearing in his form, segmenting his left arm and displacing it off his body about a foot. A shard of pain dug into Voshell's mechanical eye and she pressed the heel of her left hand against it, scowling. It hadn't pained her since she had it installed after Jade—the wretched Green—had mutilated her original, organic one. The fact it was acting up now, in time with Malkov's fit of rage, was certainly concerning.

*Shit. Can he access it somehow?*

"Queen General?" Sindri gasped. "What's wrong?"

"You have a purpose," Malkov continued, his body severing more, pieces of him flipped and fractured all along his form. "Find Blue blood, give it to me, and use the weapon. You think pursuing some private will save your people? I doubt she'll even survive the first battle."

"Shut up!" More needles of pain jammed into her right socket and the eye began to warm to an unnatural temperature. "Fuck!"

"Forgive me for this, my queen," Sindri breathed. She bent down and smacked her arm against the back of Voshell's legs. With a start, the queen fell backwards, only to be caught and cradled in Sindri's arms, lifted from the ground, and rushed out of the tent.

"Medic!" Sindri cried. "Medic!"

"I was born for this," Malkov shouted, his form blurred now that her right eye was mostly covered. His mouth was where his left hand should be, his foot rotated ninety degrees, his ears both moved several inches to the side. Each piece of him flickered and jerked. "I will not allow you to destroy the hope of fulfilling my destiny. If you show signs of refusing your part in this, I will leave, Voshell. But I will kill you before I do."

Her prosthetic eye spiked in temperature and more daggers dug into her skull. She screamed and curled into herself, her left hand grabbing at her eye, gripping it around the sides, desperately attempting to yank it from her head. Her fingers slipped along its smooth sides as pain-filled tears welled in her left eye.

Her right arm spasmed, dropped to her side, and the agony slipped away like a nightmare during the waning moments of morning.

Malkov was silent now. She could not see him. She could not hear him. As her heart rate slowed, she found the murmur of commotion around her almost peaceful. She found the way Sindri held her warm and comforting. Voshell rested her head against the private's chest and wished for time to enjoy this. Time to enjoy life outside the ward, outside her father's demented accusations, outside the war. Her whole life she had been fighting. Her whole life she never had a chance to breathe.

But unease was already settling in on her bones. Malkov was out of his mind. Something was gravely wrong with the AI. She knew he had a way to hurt her. She knew, too, that he likely had a way to kill her.

# Chapter 4

After hours of hiking through the dense Sobek forests to the location of her platoons, Aris was underwhelmed at the sight of them. In the clearing, tents were bundled together in tight, disorganized gatherings, with no clear way to navigate between them all. Her roster indicated that out of the two hundred under her command consisted of at least fifty under the age of sixteen, with another one-hundred under the age of twenty-five. The younger recruits were scattered, but a majority resided in Platoon Four, or the platoon that was stationed closest to the Reds.

The general before her was a moron.

Nevertheless, he was regarded fondly, it seemed, before he was killed in battle. She would need to work hard to ensure her troops not only liked her, but Kuroda as well. He was crucial to ensuring her success. As the reinforcements of twenty additional soldiers found their own places to sleep for the night, Aris walked into camp, found an open location, and set up her tent.

Aris hardly slept. She spent the midnight hours illuminated by Sobek's constant dull blue glow spilling from the plant life. While Kuroda dozed on his back in front of the entrance, she sat on her cot, revising her message time and time again. Her holo screen was displayed above her wrist, and upon it was the Feed. An Empire-wide network for people to connect and talk no matter where they were located within the galaxy. While her identification key indicated she was a Blue and pushed her to a lower-ranking level of importance, she knew her message would reach others like her. And she had to get it right. It was the first step. The Blues would listen, if given time.

Besides, the Mad Queen hadn't been seen for months. There was no need to rush.

A hand rested on her shoulder and gently shook her awake. Aris blinked, opening her eyes, the light around her dim and her vision blurry. She made out Kuroda's form, who crouched beside her, his head tilted. She must've fallen asleep.

"Thank you," she croaked as she sat up. She rubbed the heels of her palms into her eyes, dots spinning around her sight.

"You stay late," Kuroda grumbled, watching her with curious green eyes. Sometimes it was hard to look at him and not remember Jade. "Do you well?"

"I hope so," Aris murmured, pulling up her holo again. She read over the message once more, then submitted it. The post was live within seconds. She clicked her holo off and got to her feet.

"Others believe. Follow. Good?" Kuroda asked.

"It doesn't happen that quickly," Aris said. She smoothed out her undersuit, the tight, black material being breathable and often what most soldiers wore to bed. She moved to where her armor and rye-mail were laid out on the ground.

"Golds bad. People we talk?"

"People we talk *to*," Aris rasped, her voice dripping with exhaustion as she knelt down to pick up her rye-mail tunic. She paused and grimaced a little. Aris couldn't afford to chastise him harshly, not even if she was tired. She looked over her shoulder and saw him on his knees, observing her.

35

"You're learning rather quickly, though, Kuroda," she added. "Yes, those people we talked to were Golds, and they were bad."

He tipped his head in a nod. She offered him a tired smile and tugged the small, layered scale shirt over her head, then stepped into the trousers. The mail was attached to a belt, and she cinched it around her waist before heading for the exit.

The morning light of Sobek speared through the forest in pinpricks, making the ferns and vines in the shadows of trees dim their glow. Kuroda stepped out behind her, his hot breath warming the back of his neck. He peered down at her for guidance, and she gestured him away. Understanding, he went off to make friends with whoever else might be awake. Aris, on the other hand, started through the canvas encampment, noting the thin fabric which allowed shapes and forms to be made out within. *The Golds really sent us to a planet known for rain with paper-thin tents to keep us safe.*

At least the Golds weren't helping their case. Aris would have an easier time convincing these soldiers of what they had to do after the war.

With sure steps, she weaved through the twisting walkways towards the heart of the site, grass crunching underfoot. As she approached, she could hear the rumble of boiling water. Aris cleared the final tent to see a circle set up with logs and trunks around a fire. Atop the flames was a large metal pot, which would be most certainly abandoned if they were ever attacked. For now, she wouldn't mention it.

The woman tending to the pot was human, with olive skin and dark, tightly curled ebony hair. A green bandana was tied around the front to keep any stray strands from getting in her eyes. With a defined jaw, a wide nose, and thick arms accented by the tight undersuit, Aris mused that the woman might be attractive. Unfortunately, the general had no time for such things, and kept her focus on the task at hand.

"Good morning," Aris said as she came closer.

The chef glanced up, blue eyes widening with surprise. "General Sell?" she breathed. "I didn't realize you arrived—I hope I didn't wake you."

"Not at all," Aris said. With further scrutiny, the woman was likely nearing her thirties. It was rare to encounter a Blue that lived as long as Aris had. Usually they didn't make it past twenty-five. Not with the shoddy armor and the dysfunctional weapons the Golds shipped them. "I came to help," Aris continued. "Would you allow me to?"

"To help?" The woman blinked. "General, surely you have more important…"

"What is more important than ensuring my troops are fed for the day?" Aris smiled. "I might be your general, but I'm a Blue just like you. I want us all to live through this."

"Very well," the chef conceded. She nodded to a row of wood boxes near one of the logs. "Open those first two. One has meat, the other has the instant bread."

"I can do that." Aris strode over to one and pried it open. Inside were packets of various labeled meats, all dried. She checked the expiration dates. All expired by *ten years*. Upon opening one, she discovered no rot or mold, but it didn't smell quite right. A bit like vinegar when there should only be pepper and salt.

She turned to the chef and offered it to her. "It smells a little odd," Aris said.

The woman took a sniff and shook her head. "It's old, but it's not bad. Not yet. Go ahead and throw it in. When it's bad, it'll smell like ass." She paused. "Erm, I mean—"

"I think I know what ass smells like," Aris said with a slight smile. "I'll check the others." She dumped the contents into the boiling water, chunks of various meats topping into the depths. She let her smile fall, let her voice dip into an aggravated whisper. "The fact the Golds think they can send us whatever they want while we're dying on the frontlines… it's like they don't want us to live." It was just loud enough for the chef to hear. Full of enough vitriol to make the chef's eyebrows lift and for her to stop stirring. Aris tugged surprise onto her face as she met the chef's gaze. "Ah, my apologies, I didn't mean for you to hear that."

"It's okay," the woman muttered. "Unfortunately there's not much we can do."

Aris went back to check the next few packets and put them in the water. "Perhaps that's true," Aris replied. The woman began to stir once more and reached into a nearby box of her own to toss salt into the mixture. "I didn't mean to come off as unprofessional."

The chef spat out a bitter laugh. "Unprofessional? General, everyone here hates Golds. They send us toys as if we're not actually fighting a real-life war with real-life people."

"Mm. Toys. That's fairly accurate. Sending us damaged armor or mangled weapons."

"What are we even supposed to do with any of that?"

"Count our blessings they send us anything at all?" Aris offered. More meat into the mix. The scent wafting off the water burned with spice-filled heat and mouthwatering salt.

"They act like they're gods," the chef growled, gesturing to the second box for Aris to open. "I've been part of this war for fifteen years. That's half of my life that I've been watching my friends die." Aris broke open the other box as the chef sighed. "It does things to you."

"Then they send you home for leave and you get to choke on fumes while you try to live on the third level of Nevar," Aris said, grasping one of the bags. Inside was a loaf of bread. It was likely to taste odd, considering it, too, was expired. But the kit couldn't be opened before cooking it, so she brought it to the watery stew and tossed them inside. The hot water would cook them.

"Level three if you're lucky," the chef scoffed. She reached into her box and tore open a bag with her teeth. She was missing a few, and considering the others looked white and healthy, Aris wondered if the woman lost them during a brawl. "Last year when I was home, someone complained that I was making them feel unsafe. Got kicked out of my apartment, so when I go home next year, I'll have to find somewhere new to live." She dumped the sauce packets into the stew. Thick globs turned the water dark red.

"Being a Blue is a crime, if you weren't aware," Aris said, watching the stirring motion of the woman's large, foldable metal spoon.

"Fuck," hissed a voice from behind. "Are we talking about our shitty lives?"

Aris and the chef turned to see a snipper approaching. The stout woman was covered with dark grey hairs and held two pupils in each of her eyes. She yawned and sat down by the pot.

"Once," the newcomer began, "someone said I broke into my own fucking apartment. Golds said even if it was my own place, my violent urges were clearly impairing my decision making, so they sent me back here." She rubbed her eyes. "I was home for one fucking day."

"Vix," the chef breathed. "Fuck the Golds."

Aris stifled a smile as she noted a few other Blues approaching. "Fuck the Golds."

# Chapter 5

The Thrax camp was made of a bundle of tents collected together in a clearing. Malkov had not returned and Voshell hoped that it would stay that way. Perhaps she could find a way to shut his systems down completely and use only the weapon. Considering it didn't seem like he knew where he began and the weapon ended, however, that could be difficult.

Voshell sat upon a fallen log, her bare feet pressed against the water-drenched ground oozing underfoot. Rain sprinkled down upon her matted, greasy hair, and she looked out towards the surrounding forest. The touches of the medic on her right arm did not distract her from following the twisting limbs of trees with her eyes, from admiring the cherry blossoms blooming larger than her face. Vines hung from gnarled bark, becoming easy targets for soldiers falsely claiming to see okehesa, large snakes that roamed the Sobek trees and underbrush. They came in all colors, the deadliest being those with scales of ivory, which hid in the morning fog that now clung to her ankles. This, however, was stained by the rising sun's orange hue.

The smell of the encroaching storm filled Voshell's nostrils with brisk, cool air, that breezed past in gusts against the otherwise humid morning. She saw a few of the glowing plants Sobek was known for within that darkness of the canopy: dimming blues and purples of flowers and vines, the twinkling lights of glowing bugs fading as the sun spilled onto the overgrown forest floor.

She looked towards the camp around her of bustling soldiers, who, upon catching sight of their queen, paused to salute with their wrists locked against their right shoulders. Voshell smiled at each, putting upon a front of assuredness that she did not feel. She refused to be held captive again—let alone by some machine. But her people were dying. If they did not win here, the Empire would slaughter and enslave them all. Voshell was running out of options.

"It seems to function like an actual arm," the medic said as he pulled away, the pincers on either side of his snipper lips clicking and squeaking to fill in the gaps between each of his words. "I cannot say how such a small device made all this, but it seems firmly planted against you shoulder. However, those points of entry where it digs into your skin by your collar and your breast are concerning." His brow furrowed and his dual-pupiled eyes looked to her. "They are still numb?"

"Yes," Voshell answered, her eyes drawn to Sindri as the blonde woman walked past. "Would you excuse me, medic?" She stood. The medic leapt up and grabbed her forearm as Voshell's legs began to fold.

"Queen General, please!" he yelped. Voshell scowled, leaning against his four arms to ensure she didn't fall. "You are not ready to walk on your own yet," he breathed, his face coming up to her shoulder. "Please take it easy, my queen, your body will be back to normal soon—but you lost a lot of blood. It'll take time."

"Is everything all right?"

Voshell looked up, Sindri standing before with lifted brows, leaning forward on her feet as if to grab Voshell should she collapse.

"It's all right," Voshell said to the medic. "Private Sindri here will tend to me. Private, would you please help me to the cooking pot?"

"Oh, of course, my queen," Sindri said. "Ah…" She reached for Voshell but hesitated before touching her.

The medic sighed. "Very well. Come to me should you have further concerns, my queen."

He loosened his grip on her, and Sindri quickly slid in to replace him, wrapping her arm around Voshell's middle and holding the woman steady. The queen knew she shouldn't enjoy this, the way a larger woman held her on the eve of approaching battle, but she found herself relaxing against Sindri, inhaling the woman's sweat-stained aroma, imagining what life might be after all this.

"The cooking pot, my queen?" Sindri confirmed.

Voshell nodded. "Please. Thank you, private."

"Of course, Queen General," Sindri murmured, walking slowly to allow Voshell an even and undaunting pace. "Are you feeling all right?"

"Better by the moment," Voshell breathed. No war. No death. Just walking with a beautiful woman.

"And your eye? It's okay?"

"Perfectly." A stroll through a clearing of trees, alone in a crowd, just the two of them.

"We were all worried about you, my queen," Sindri continued. "You were delirious the entire ship ride here. Do you… remember any of that?"

"No," Voshell answered. She rested her head against the woman's shoulder, the armor sleek and hard, but not entirely uncomfortable. "The morning is nice, isn't it?"

"Oh. Yes, it is, my queen." Sindri glanced over at Voshell and offered a small, beautiful smile. "You've been on Sobek a lot, haven't you? This is my first time here."

"It is?" Voshell arched a brow. "How long have you been part of the army, private?"

"A year," Sindri answered. "I've been in training until a few weeks ago."

*She's a recruit,* Voshell thought with growing anxiety. *Oh Vix, she's on the front lines. She'll never survive.*

"What made you…?" Voshell muttered, looking away to hide her swirling thoughts threatening to display themselves across her features.

"Ah, well," Sindri said with an uncomfortable laugh. "Just, ah, wanted to help the war effort." She swallowed and motioned ahead, towards a mass of soldiers waiting in line. The smell of boiling stew followed after, filled with salt, lentils, crushed herbs, and the fatty, thick aroma of meat. The bricks in Voshell's stomach grew heavier and her mouth began to water. Burning wood crackled in the background of joking soldiers. "We're here, my queen," Sindri said, her voice strained with the lie from before.

Voshell frowned. She opened her mouth to inquire when she saw someone pause to look at her a few feet away. She met the man's eyes, who stood taller than her, with black hair and…

Voshell's eyes widened. "Thaddeous?" she breathed. The man wore a black suit. He smiled, his crimson eyes alight from noticing his sister. He opened his mouth to say something, stepped forward with a reaching hand to touch her, when a thin, red line appeared across his neck. Blood began to trickle, then stream. He grabbed his throat, his eyes widening with panic. Voshell watched, rooted to the spot. Did she help? Did she stop this from happening? He had to die. She knew he had to die. But seeing him suffer like this…

Trails of gore dribbled out from his gaping mouth, down his chin, sloshing across the dirt. Tears filled his eyes as he staggered forward, one hand reaching for her yet again. But the momentum of movement was all it took, and his head tipped back with a sickening, wet tear, and it fell from his neck and splattered upon the ground. Voshell screamed as his body crumpled and she jumped, grabbing Sindri's arm. Nausea bubbled in the acid of her stomach.

"My queen?" Sindri grabbed Voshell quickly, using her own body as a shield against what she could not see. Thaddeous smiled at Voshell from where his head lay by his feet.

"Welcome home, Vosh," he garbled.

Voshell turned and retched. Sindri pulled the woman's hair back and held her steady as Voshell's knees weakened. Her body shook and a sweat coated her in a sickly sheen. Her hand gripped Sindri's belt, helping her stand, her breath uneven, shallow, chopped. A growing pain bloomed inside her chest.

"What was it?" Sindri asked softly. "My queen, what did you see?"

Voshell met the woman's worried gaze then looked past her, towards the corpse, towards the discarded carcass of her brother. But she found nothing. No splotches of red. No body. No smiling face. Voshell's head spun and she closed her eye, her prosthetic momentarily falling idle. Her lungs tightened and each breath was shallower than the last.

"My queen, breathe," Sindri urged. "It's okay. It's okay, breathe."

Why was she seeing him? Why was he showing himself in her waking moments? She did what she had to do. She did it for her people. There was no other choice.

"I'm sorry," Voshell gasped. "I'm sorry, private." She cracked an eye and peered at the woman. "I didn't mean…"

"Shh," Sindri whispered. "It's all right, my queen. You have gone through much. It can't be easy losing your brother."

Voshell's chest constricted and cracked. A grimace stole away her features, twisting them with the agony coursing through each chamber of her heart.

"I will endure," she muttered. "Please. I think I am over-hungry."

"Of course, my queen."

Sindri helped the woman towards the front of the line. Soldiers saluted as Voshell passed. A bowl of brown liquid was given to the new queen once she was sat down upon a wet, softened log. The meal held mystery meat floating alongside wilted leaves and blackened beans, some of which had been smashed during travel.

Voshell watched it before her eyes turned to Sindri, to the feathers in her hair as if she was some sort of bird-like goddess, with a frame as thick as any one of the trees on the edge of the clearing. As the private sat down beside her, a heavy weight rested upon Voshell's shoulders. Was she ever going to have that happy ending? Was she going to enjoy the peace she carved out of the galaxy's cruelty? Voshell stared into the private's crimson eyes, speckled with shades of red and gleaming rubies, as brilliant and beautiful as her youngest brother's. And she felt certain of the answer.

# Chapter 6

"Where are you from?" Voshell asked as she took her spoon and ladled up some broth. Each moment was stolen from time. Each moment she inched closer to her story's end. She would do all she could to make the most of it.

Sindri paused and cast a curious, but humored look back at her queen as she chewed on a piece of bread. A crooked smile sat upon her lips.

"Soldar, my queen," she answered after swallowing.

Heat touch Voshell's cheeks and a little laugh slipped past her lips, the throbbing dread inside her chest dulling. "Right," she said. "But, ah, what *part* of Soldar?"

Sindri snickered as Voshell brought the broth to her mouth and took a tedious sip. It was salty and thick with boiled fat. Hearty, and spiced with local herbs that made it earthy, but overall, nothing special. Not that anything special was expected on the frontlines of war.

"I'm from the west," Sindri answered after taking a mouthful of stew. "By the farms. My mother grows fruit trees."

"You grow fruit?" Voshell asked, her hunger renewed from the first taste of food.

"My mom does. I wanted to do more, I guess." She shrugged. "So here I am, doing more."

"Right, but...?" Voshell prodded as she chewed on the salty meat. Sindri focused intently on her food.

"I… wanted to do something good," Sindri offered.

"Private, I want to know who I'm living for. Who I'm fighting for," Voshell pressed. "It's okay. I just want to get to know you."

"Surely my life is of no concern of yours, my queen," Sindri said, poking at the herbs in her stew. "You're the ruler of everyone here. I'm just… a lowly soldier. I don't know why you'd… *care.*"

Voshell watched her. She got an odd feeling that Sindri wasn't just referring to the topic at hand. "Because you're who I sacrificed this arm for," she replied. Sindri blinked and looked to her with wide eyes. "You can trust me, private."

"Well, I…"

"Queen General!"

Voshell turned towards the newcomer's voice. Her lieutenant, a war-torn kodarian male with a scarred eye, stepped towards her. He pressed the new salute over his right shoulder, his blind right eye staring at her with a pale crimson iris. The man wore his armor per usual after waking, never again risking breakfast without it.

"I am glad to see you are awake. My apologies for not attending to you sooner, there were matters I was caught up in." He dipped his head, his curled grey horns catching the light and displaying the small carvings near the base of each: small figures battling with wicked-looking beasts.

"At ease, Ira," Voshell said, offering him a small smile. "I'm glad to see you're still alive."

"You gave me an order, my queen, I was not about to disobey it." He straightened, rye-mail peering through the joints in his mud-colored armor, all of it shifting upon him as he moved. Metal scraped against scales and joined the chorus of familiar sounds around them.

Voshell chuckled. "That I did. I'm sorry I've been away for so long. Things back home were not easy to handle."

"So we've heard, my queen. Many condolences. The Green appears not to be the angel we were led to believe."

Voshell smiled. *The Green killed him. Yes. If she never came to Soldar, Thaddeous would've never had that stupid idea in his head. Believing a myth like that, believing a single woman can end a war because of her eye color, when he claimed to be a man of science? It wasn't my fault. It was hers.*

"It could not be helped," Voshell replied. "But we can grieve after the war. I need only the blood of a Blue and the weapon can eradicate them."

"The blood of a Blue?" Ira blinked, his small eyes peering at Voshell's arm. "The whole race of them?"

"Yes," Voshell answered. "All of them. We'll be free of this blasted war forever."

"I would like that," Ira breathed. "Have you been updated on our position, Queen General?"

"Briefly," Voshell replied. "Private Sindri gave me some information."

Ira peered at the large blonde on Voshell's side, eyeing her before looking to Voshell. "Shall I update you in your tent, Queen General?"

"Certainly. Private Sindri, attend to me, would you?"

Sindri quickly nodded. "Y-yes, of course, Queen General." She set her bowl down. "I'll—"

"You may bring the food with you, private. I will not deprive you of a meal."

Ira watched. Voshell could see the disapproval in his eyes, the same narrowed glare her father so often greeted her with. The tight line his lips made, the way his nostrils flared, the crossed arms and straight spine.

But Voshell cleaved off her father's head. The stupid bastard was dead. And never again would he try to kill her.

In any case, Ira respected Voshell. While he disapproved, he would never say so in front of others, nor would he attempt to harm her. His loyalty ran deeper than the diagonal slash across his eye.

Sindri slurped up her meal quickly, downing it with such volume that Voshell felt a little warm between the legs. She somewhat expected Malkov to appear and hiss at her, but he did not.

Sindri helped Voshell up, held the queen's meal in her free hand, and followed Lieutenant Ira to the center of the camp. There, settled next to Ira's tent, was a place erected with hollow poles and covered with a breathable, light canvas. A tarp kept it dry as a slow, trickling rain began to spill from the gathering clouds above. When they ducked inside, Voshell found that it was exactly as she left it months before, though undoubtedly it had moved as the platoon travelled. A cot was set up in the corner, where she liked it, whereas a table was placed near the middle of the small space. A map was pulled out over it with several pins to indicate troop movements and strategies. Sindri brought Voshell inside, let the woman lean against the table, and pulled the cot over so Voshell could sit down. Sindri handed the Queen General her morning stew as Ira closed the tent flap. The morning fog, however, still lingered inside, and as Ira turned to her, it spun around his heels.

"The new Blue general has become a problem."

"Be less vague," Voshell said, taking a spoonful and relishing the warmth it brought to her bones, imagining it as strength she would once again have. She just needed to keep from vomiting again.

"She has used tactics to cut sections of our troops off from each other and massacre them while losing quite few of her own. I've been at my wit's end, general. I am not sure how much longer we could have lasted without your guidance."

"You are always needing me," she said, glancing at the man with a smile. Ira flashed one of his own back, the tusks protruding out from his bottom lip making the expression look a little grim. Unlike what Voshell had seen Blue kodarians do, Thrax kodarians did not file their tusks down. They allowed them to grow, and Ira's had become long and sharp, thick enough that even when his lips were pressed together, they still made his jaw jut out and some of his teeth visible.

"We are always lost without you, my queen."

"Are you aware of the Blue positions now?"

"We suspect where they are located, but we cannot confirm," Ira replied. "Their general is good at striking down scouts."

"How stands our current positions?"

"With some ground being lost to this new general, the Blues now occupy seventy-five percent of the planet."

"Air support?"

"Skirmishes with the Blue ships renders air support nearly impossible for any sort of barrage. Supplies have become sparse."

"How long will this food last?" Voshell asked, emptying her bowl and setting it on the table.

"Two weeks, Queen General." He paused. "A little more if we ration well."

Voshell frowned. She sat up a bit straighter and peered at the map. Created to be nearly waterproof, the map was on a lightweight material and showed the surrounding locale. Meant to be used to better strategize movements on something other than a small wrist holo, the map was full of small, pin-prick holes where the various colored pins were stuck and moved about its surface. Nothing to give away their plans proper.

Known topography was sketched upon its face, drawn in rushed, jagged lines created by a cartographer scout who weaved between battle lines to detail where her fellow troops would be fighting. But not everything was known, leaving parts of the map completely empty, the cream void holding the possibility of both safety and destruction. Voshell's mechanical eye clicked, the crimson light against the silver body turning dark for a second to clean its surface and readjust its alignment. When it turned back on, she could see the faint crimson glow upon the map lines.

The Thrax sat upon the southern side of a large river that divided the island. Mountains rose to the east, where the source of the river was suspected to come from. This was where the largest empty section lay, as the rocky terrain would take too long for troops to travel through, and thus was deemed unsafe and unnecessary to scout. The west led on through the forest, towards the other end of the island, where the river would spill off the side in a gushing waterfall to meet the ocean below. Due north, blue pins were used to indicate the Exuro Empire forces, scattered over the opposite bank as their true coordinates were not yet determined.

The Thrax themselves had three platoons, two situated to the west, the other to the east, both more north than her. Voshell's position was removed from the bank by a few inches, indicating a large amount of ground lost.

"With the new general, we don't have the bank anymore?" Voshell touched a single blue pin between her platoon and the river. Ira nodded.

"Yes. Our troops were disorganized and when the Empire struck, they launched trees on us." He shook his head. "They must have a good amount of Charge users to do such a thing without ripping their own arms off. As this distracted us, another unit came in from behind and slaughtered survivors."

"No trip mines?" Voshell asked, brows furrowed. "Surely there were some set up."

"There were many, Queen General, to all directions except the south."

"So the general predicted this, hm? Are the mines still present?"

"We've not heard any explosions, so I would assume so. Though there is no true way of telling." He peered at her, arms crossed, crimson eyes contemplating. "What are you considering?"

"We'll flank. Charge users in the trees to climb above the mines. I trust we still have the mine locations?"

"We have their coverage, not their exact positions."

"Acceptable." Voshell tapped the blue pin on her side of the river. "Troops in the trees armed with what snipers and long-ranged weapons we have. They'll come in from the sides and from the north to push them down south. Gunshots will rain down on them in the night, and when the Blues scramble, we—" she picked up the red pin with the number '3' penned onto its minimal surface—"will meet them in the dark." She placed the third platoon—the one she currently resided in—next to the blue one. "The snipers can take out those without armor and set off perimeter mines. Once we have this bank back, we'll plan our next move."

Ira ran his thumb across his left tusk, considering the board. "And the wildlife? Using their Helix to help them jump from tree to tree will drain them. They'll be vulnerable. Not only that, won't the armor they're wearing give away their positions?"

55

"I understand your concerns," Voshell replied. "But that is why they'll only be wearing their undersuits. No armor, no rye-mail. They will be light, allowing them to use less of their Charge, and they will be agile."

"There will be casualties."

Voshell looked at him. He knew there would be casualties. Why was he saying this? Why was he making a point of mentioning it? It did not matter how many numbers they lost. All that mattered was winning, was ending the war. Even if a handful survived, at least they would be free. At least they would no longer fear extinction.

Besides, they were soldiers. They decided to become pawns for this unending war. Their job was to die for others to live.

Ira's eyes flickered momentarily to Sindri, and Voshell understood.

"Gather a good striking force and bring them here for me to wish well," Voshell said. "I do not ask this of them lightly, Ira, but the Blues suspect our numbers are greater than theirs. I will not allow them to reconsider that idea."

"You think throwing bodies at the problem will really fix it?"

Voshell blinked and turned towards the voice speaking to her. A man stood nearby, directly on her right. His large form had a beard spilling over his wide chest, and his dark, crimson eyes narrowed upon her face.

"You are the monster I always thought you were," Daxgor hissed. "When your mother birthed you and I saw your eyes, I *knew*. You were destined to kill us all."

"You're dead," Voshell growled, every hair on her body standing on end. The room around them fell away. She sat in darkness, only her and her father.

"Is that what you think?" he boomed, before laughter spilled from his lips, the sound making her bones shudder, her ears ring. "You are so naïve, Voshell. Naïve and reckless, throwing away lives when we have so few. And that little thing on your arm, hm? What good is it now that it's silent? I was going to give you the benefit of the doubt after seeing that Green's violence, but here you are, proving me right yet again." Sprouts of feathers began to poke through his skin, tearing aside the flesh, splitting his cheeks. Each was stained red with the blood that began to pour from Daxgor's wounds. "I should've kept you in that ward," he growled, his jaw elongating, his face stretching before a blackened beak speared forward and peeled his flesh back. His clothes unraveled as the bloody feathers unfurled from him. Legs elongated, talons tore through his feet, tail feathers burst from his spine, and within several sickening seconds of transformation, Daxgor stood before her not of himself, but as a victer. One with a necklace made of bone and gripping, in his left hand, the intestines of Voshell's little brother, Lionel.

"You," he hissed, his voice coarse and filled with a familiar, otherworldly tone that she had only heard within her nightmares. Voshell scooted back, her spine hitting against something she could not see as the victer stepped forward. His beak dripped with blood.

"You're supposed to be in your room."

The victer lunged, reaching forward with his steel-cutting claws. Voshell swung immediately, her right hand smashing against his cheek, jarring his left eye from his skull as he was sent tumbling somewhere in the dark. Something grabbed her, shook her hard, spat upon her face. She went to swing again, wildly, heart pounding and head reeling when the darkness, in an instant, vanished.

Blinking in alarm, she saw Ira holding her shoulders, shouting in hopes of her hearing him. She was pressed against Private Sindri, who was gently rubbing the space between Voshell's shoulder with her thumb.

"Vix above, general, can you hear us?" Ira breathed. Voshell nodded numbly. What was happening? Why was she hallucinating?

"Thank Vix," Ira muttered. He fell on his knees beside the cot. "You were freaking out about something. Someone who's dead."

"Yeah." Voshell felt the bubble of sickness boiling in her gut. She saw, in the corner of her vision, the lingering form of the victer that gave her the scar across her face. It chewed on the intestinal remains of her brother. She blinked. And it was gone

"Perhaps you need some water, my queen?" Private Sindri asked.

"Please," Voshell rasped. "Water would be good. I apologize for... my outburst. Perhaps I am unwell."

"You lost a lot of blood, general," Ira said. He got to his feet and dipped his head. "I would be surprised if there *weren't* side effects."

"Tell no one of this," Voshell said, looking to him then to the private.

Sindri nodded, her eyes set as stone as she saluted over her right shoulder. "Not a soul, my queen."

"Not a soul," Ira repeated, bowing his head. He glanced between Sindri and Voshell. "Perhaps you ought to lay down again, my queen? Should I hold off bringing the soldiers here?"

"No, no," Voshell said. "I will wish them luck. They would think something was wrong if I didn't do it this one time." She offered the man a small smile. *And wishing them luck personally inspires them to throw their lives away with a certain determination.* "Please, fetch who you think is best. I will rest here a moment."

"Of course, my queen. Private Sindri, let us—"

"I would prefer for her to stay." Voshell glanced at the woman. "She needs to share water with me, in any case."

The woman nodded, grabbing a canteen from her hip and opening the lid. She handed the circular, green and brown case to Voshell with a sheepish smile.

"Here you are, my queen." Her voice was gentle, soft, as if she was worried any intensity would cause Voshell pain. Voshell took a sip from it, relishing in the refreshing—albeit warm—taste of the purifying liquid. Her eyes closed before she pulled it from her lips and handed it back to Sindri.

"Thank you, private."

"I shall return in a moment, my queen," Ira murmured, ducking out of the tent.

"I've frightened you, haven't I?" Voshell asked.

"Me?" Sindri shook her head as she screwed the lid back on. "I don't know why you say that, my queen."

"It's not a good look for the queen and general of the army to have a mental breakdown."

"You've lost a lot, my queen," Sindri said. She clipped her canteen to her belt and turned back to Voshell. Her brows pulled together and a concerned smile sat upon her lips. "It would be alarming if none of it was affecting you."

"Maybe so," Voshell replied, her eyes settling on her arm, her fingers tracing the woven metal and vibrant blue lines. There was silence between them, filled with Sindri's breathing and the chatter of soldiers outside. The private radiated heat in the already humid morning, and the patter of rain outside started to fall with greater heaviness.

If Voshell killed the Blues, would she live? Would she survive another morning, another two? Step around her fate? Did brother killers live long?

"My queen?"

Sindri's voice pulled her from her thoughts, relief washing over the queen with the warmth of a mother's hug. She peered at the woman at her side, a grateful smile crossing her lips. It was nice to hear the title. Hearing Sindri say 'queen' with such reverence after all Voshell had sacrificed to achieve such a position, after the years of being called mad, of suffering under her father's oppressive hand—it made her hope the woman would never call her anything else.

"I'm sorry, I was a bit lost in thought, private."

"Did… did you want me to leave you to your thoughts, Queen General?"

"No, I don't believe so. Tell me, what fruit trees did you grow on your farm?"

Sindri arched a brow, the laughter of a bear spilling from her mouth. Often fabled in human history, drawn by artists and speculated by scientists, the bear did not seem to exist here, in this galaxy. At least, not exactly like the ones from the human homeplanet, wherever that be. There were creatures like it, large, hulking beasts with sandy fur, long necks, and backs covered in moss and vines. But they existed on Daoth, A'doxia's home. And Sindri was nothing like those.

No, she was more akin to the beautiful, black-furred legend, smaller than those on Daoth, with stunning eyes and a stubby tail. Ones that were heralded for their protective natures. Sindri was something rare in this galaxy, bright and beautiful, a creature not at all supposed to be in this gruesome war. She was a soft, round beast, one that slept half the year away, only to stumble out and eat sugar and roar a breathy call that scared predators away. That was Sindri.

"I didn't know you were so interested in growing fruit, my queen," Sindri said, flashing a smile.

"I suppose you'll have to tend to me for a while longer, then," Voshell replied. "So you'll discover the things that interest me."

Sindri's smile remained, bright and humored. "I would be honored, my queen. Ah, well, my family lot isn't too big, but we manage to get by…"

Voshell listened as Sindri told her of the work her and her mother did, how they grafted trees together and grew several different fruits. Each morning they would wake to check their orchard, prune what was needed, water and speak to them. That was an important part—speaking to the trees. It was important to regale them with stories to help them grow. Sindri believed each had a spirit. It was important to nurture it.

Eventually Ira returned with a collection of fifteen troops, all with the Helix Charge. They were stripped of their armor, standing before her with belts tied around their undersuits, which were black and skintight, used to ensure rye-mail did not pinch. But now, it served as perfect camouflage in their stealthy maneuvers. Sindri helped Voshell stand before them, and the queen recalled each of their names to wish them luck. She promised to end the war within the month. She promised that soon, such sacrifices would no longer need to be made. Soon, they would be able to have drinks with bearish women, or finally rest as they rotted ten feet below ground.

# Chapter 7

"You can't use her to forget what you did." Malkov's voice spilled into her skull as Voshell woke the following dawn. She had slept in her tent after tending to other plans, and now, as the sky sat dark just before dawn, Malkov stood at the foot of her cot, watching her with cold, silver eyes. Voshell sat up, a layer of sweat sticking her clothes to her as heat and humidity hung in the air. The smell of cooking oatmeal hung with it; the chef was awake, it seemed.

"I thought you had broken," Voshell replied. "What happened to you?"

"Ah. Yes, I can see why you'd think such a thing." He eyed her before looking over the small room. "A mere malfunction. The issue has been isolated and deleted. There is no more cause for concern."

"Were you inactive this whole time?" Voshell asked, scooting to the side of her cot and rubbing her eyes. A yawn slipped from her lips as her fingers grabbed the bottom of her shirt and peeled it off. Movement still brought a rush to her head, but it was less so than before. She would be more than capable of leading the charge.

"I was resting, so not entirely. I spent my time learning more about you." He strode over to the map on the table. "You and I are connected, after all. I figured it was time well-spent. You plan on battle tonight?"

"I do."

"Good. I am eager to get to work." He turned on his heel as she pulled off her pants, her entire body slick and sticky. She set the clothes on the cot and moved to a blanket laid out on the ground, where all her armor had been set. She grabbed her undersuit, and with a breath, she bundled it up around the neck, and pushed her foot in.

"I trust it is as you planned: kill all the Blues?"

"Yes," Voshell replied, pulling the suit up to her hip before pushing her other foot in.

Malkov smiled. "Good. You will find you don't need your weapons in skirmishes. Your arm will protect you even when the hottest blade touches it. Collect that blood, and you shall have the holocaust you desire."

She pulled the undersuit up to her waist and peered quizzically at the man. He seemed well—and not only that, he did not appear angry with her. If he had only been sleeping, surely he had noticed her around Sindri.

*I'd better be clear than risk him freaking out and burning my eye again.*

"You expressed discomfort with my feelings towards the private," Voshell ventured, shimmying the suit up her stomach. "While I may wish for... *something* between us, we are at war. There is not much time for it now. I do hope to pursue her after this is all over, but I suspect you and I will have parted by then."

Malkov arched a brow. "Parted? And where would you have me go, Voshell?"

"I... don't know. I figured you didn't want to be attached to me forever."

"I suppose."

Voshell frowned and stuck one arm into her suit. "Unless you do? But you must understand, if we were together this whole time, I will act outside the war in a manner I see fit."

"We are connected, Voshell. There are two of us in this head of yours. And I will not be ignored in the matters of what we do with your body."

"It's my body, that's just it," she said as she pushed her other arm through. "It's not yours."

"And this arm of yours is mine, not yours."

"It would make more sense for you to go elsewhere. So neither of us are unhappy."

Malkov watched her. A slow smile crossed his lips.

"I do not like to be unhappy," he hummed. "From now on, do not attempt to remove your eye. Doing so may result in… unwanted consequences."

Voshell stopped what she was doing to look at him. Her heartrate threatened to escalate, but she took a breath to remain calm. "Is that a threat, Malkov?"

He chuckled. "It's a warning, Voshy. That little eye of yours helps you see me. Without it, me appearing in the world around you would take quite the toll on your mind. You might even start seeing things other than me." A smirk. "Well. More than you already do."

Tension pitched the queen's shoulders a fraction of an inch upwards. "I do not—"

"Please, don't lie to me." He glanced towards the tent entrance, where footsteps were approaching. "I hear your thoughts as loud as my own."

He vanished.

"Queen General, it's me, Ira," the man said outside her tent. "May I enter?"

Voshell's gaze lingered where Malkov had once been. Then she exhaled. *Just last a little longer, Voshell.* "You may, Ira. Come help me with my armor."

The man ducked inside, already dressed. He gave a quick salute before moving to help.

"The troops are waking. They will be ready to move soon, my queen."

"Good," she said, slipping into her rye-mail, the black scales dull and matte to keep from reflecting any light. The first section slipped over her head, while the second she stepped into, and hooked to her belt. She picked up the chest piece and pressed it to her body. Ira took the straps and brought one around her ribs, and the two others looped over her shoulders.

"We'll collect the blood necessary and start the process of ending this war."

Ira smiled. "I would enjoy seeing my brother again," he said.

"Does he still write to you?"

"He does, but I have not received any for the past few months. Nothing gets through the skirmish in the sky." Ira began strapping the other pieces of armor to her legs, many of which steadied themselves by attaching to her belt as well as wrapping around her leg. Voshell began on her arms, locking the pieces over the mail, and flexing her right arm beneath it all. Malkov had said the arm would be able to withstand a blade. But there was no harm in cladding it in armor, especially when the nigferra metal it was made of was lightweight and durable.

"Does it bother you?" Ira asked, following her gaze to her right arm.

Voshell flexed her fingers before shaking her head. "No, it… feels about normal. A little different. But it doesn't hurt."

"I'm glad, my queen. Will it withstand a fight?"

"I suspect we'll find out shortly." She turned to her lieutenant. "We leave after breakfast."


Her troops moved forward in a spearhead formation, their movements slow through the glowing woods. Night had long since fallen during the trek onward and all around them the forest had come alive. Vines dripped off thick branches, gleaming with spotted blues along their length, the tips of ferns shone with iridescent greens, flowers spread their petals to display their reds and pinks and oranges. They cast enough light to make the eyes struggle to adjust, everything beneath three feet cast in stark darkness. Voshell's mechanical eye managed to help her in this regard, able to adjust to see the shadowed ground where her human eye could not, keeping her feet from being snared by exposed roots and fallen ivy. She pushed her way through

67

the leaves that reached up to her ribs as trails of water rivered down her armor, the collecting storm clouds above spilling their contents upon the moving army. A haze of fog rose up in areas rain collected into pools, and when morning grew closer, Voshell knew those wispy white clouds would spread out across the entire island.

The rainfall caused a humid chorus around them, covering the snapping branches and shuffling leaves as her platoon marched. Sweat streamed down her forehead as she bore the weight of her protection, her undersuit doing what little it could to wick it all away. Her lungs heaved and her legs burned. After being unconscious for so long a time, she could feel the toll it took on her strength. Her ribs couldn't expand wide enough for her to breathe deep, her pulse thundered in each vein and artery, even her arm ached from the mere process of walking. She brought her left wrist up to peer at her wrist holo, which displayed a small map of them and their directive. There was no time for worrying. She would stay back while her soldiers fought and ensure it all went smoothly.

Sounds of gunshots popped out over the rain, met with shouts and screams, distant and nearly swallowed by the storm. Voshell stopped and quickly sent a message to all her soldiers from her holo:

*Spread out. Take no prisoners.*

Her people leapt into action, forming a rough 'u' shape to block the only safe passage out. An explosion lit up the sky and blinded them all for a split second, detonating somewhere through the trees to the northwest. For a moment, the forest fell dark, the lights snuffed out before, one by one, the plants began to glow once more.

Gunshots resumed. In a matter of minutes, Blues came sprinting at them.

Blood splattered across tree trunks and golden flowers. Thirteen-year-old soldiers, too small for their armor, some too frantic to have put any on in their flight, lost their heads in a spray of gore. The Blues knew no age limit. Voshell suspected that soon, ten-year-olds would be sent to die for their Empire. A society such as that did not deserve to rule. It did not deserve to outlast her.

From the corner of her eye, she spotted Sindri watching in horror as the first row of Blues were butchered. Voshell stared in the dim, blue light cast from a tangle of vines as Sindri's pale face grew green. As one hand clutched her stomach, the second wave of Blues came, but this time, they were armed.

A blade gleamed crimson as a Blue kodarian unsheathed his sword and lunged at the near-to-vomiting blonde-haired beauty. Voshell's feet moved without her consent. Her heart climbed into her throat and she found herself in front of the larger woman in a strange, reckless abandon for her life. Voshell reached up and snatched the downward arcing blade, adrenaline in her veins, her mind reeling, the breath in her lungs threatening to pop.

The edge of the weapon met her hand, the heat hot enough to melt the armor on her body if given the chance. But her prosthetic held. Her fingers wrapped around the metal.

And she snapped the blade in two.

The breaking of the H-blade was louder than anything in the forest, louder than the distant explosions, the gunshots, the storm and screams and war. In all her life, she hadn't seen one break like this before. The syphers crafted each weapon with the hardest metal in the Known Galaxy. And yet, without even trying, she had broken it. The kodarian's blue eyes widened, his mouth opened in slack surprise, displaying the sawed-down tusks within.

"Now!" Malkov cried, his voice ringing in her head, her mechanical eye warming. In a quick lunge, she smacked his dominate hand away and shoved him back. He rocked on his heels, tipping away from her. Voshell's prosthetic fingers sharpened to points. She slashed at the falling man's throat.

Thaddeous' head rolled from his shoulders, crimson showering the ferns, the flowers, the vines and the trees. His body vanished beneath them all, falling to the ground somewhere beneath the illuminated glow of plant life. His head splattered against a wide, fan-shaped leaf, rolled to a momentary stop, and smiled at her.

"It's okay, sis," he said. "I forgive you."

# Chapter 8

Voshell slew seven more Blues with her right hand, the metallic claws tearing through armor and ripping apart flesh. Blood stained the mechanical silver skin before the crimson was absorbed somewhere into her, given to an eager Malkov. He grinned at each strike and pointed out flaws in her opponents' armor. Voshell's entire body buzzed, her mind blank and empty. She struck and killed, each soldier Thaddeous, each death his.

When the battle was won and the surviving Thrax soldiers were counted, their forty-eight had dwindled to forty-two, two of which were injured. Camp was made as dawn broke, Blue bodies dragged away from the campsite and stripped of their armor and weapons. A pile was constructed of their remains, a bloody heap of meat and bone and flies, set aside until the rain stopped so they could burn them all. H-blades were salvaged, along with boots and gloves, but the rest was either damaged or too shoddily put together to be useful. Some of the Thrax took Blue dogtags as trophies, but everyone left the children alone. The thirteen-year-olds, the soft-faced, wide-eyed kids who didn't truly know why they were there. They were laid with their fellows, eyes closed, and solemnly acknowledged as the Reds worked to set up camp.

Voshell's tent was pitched first, the cook got a pot of tea going for the troops, and the others began to patrol the edges as more tents were erected. Voshell watched for a while before she found herself wandering north, stopping at the base of a tree and resting her shoulder against its moist bark. Vines sagged beneath the weight of the storm, spilling droplets atop her hair, which was tightly wound into a bun.

She peered through the ferns and twisting branches, past the flowers that closed their heads during the day, and into the darkness that swallowed everything up past a certain point. She knew the river was that direction, knew her enemy sat beyond that veil. Looking down at her clawed hand, Voshell exhaled slowly, watching as the talons softened and unwound to become rounded fingertips instead.

She looked over her shoulder at her people chatting in tired voices, of comrades laughing as they set up tents, of their single Healer tending to the injured. It was good the man was here, good he was able to take care of them. His Helix was rare, sprouting up in a handful of children every few generations. Often, they volunteered to work on the frontlines, to tend to the injured and keep them all fighting. Often, they ended up being the first butchered by the blades of those who sought to slaughter them all. Her eyes moved back to the trees.

"How long will it take, Malkov?" she murmured to herself.

"I'm so glad you asked," he hummed, flickering into view as her prosthetic eye warmed with the effort of materializing him. He stood before her in his long jacket, his metallic eyes gleaming in the low light of the forest. A small smile crossed his perfect lips as he held up a hand, a vial of blood appearing above it.

"You collected a good number of samples for me, and I should have no problem producing the virus for you, queeny." She scowled at this, which only brought more humor to his eyes. "It can be completed within two or three weeks, depending on how much you need that arm of yours."

Voshell arched a brow and peered down at her arm. "And that means?"

"That means, the more you move it, the less energy can go to producing this all-killing little virus of yours," he purred, his voice laced with annoyance, as if the answer should have been obvious. She frowned and let her arm drop to her side as she looked back at him.

"If I don't use it, it'll take two weeks?"

"Yes," he replied. "Oh, you are eager, aren't you?" He snickered. "Aren't those caves on Hallow deep enough to hide you? Can't you just take your little band of fighters and steal away deep into those mountains?"

Voshell's eyes narrowed, the hairs on her neck standing on end. "You've been snooping."

"We're connected," he hummed, clasping his hands behind his back with a smirk. "I have every right to prod around your head. When were you going to tell me that your floating metal home wasn't far away?"

"I wasn't."

"Exactly." He paced closer, his eyes half-lidded, his back straight, his chin pointed the smallest bit upward. "And how are we supposed to trust each other if we're not telling *everything*? Do they know?" He stopped at her side and nodded towards her troops. "Do they know how close you are to extinction? That you sent a small band of survivors to the tundra wastes to ensure your people live on?"

Voshell looked towards her people, to those who gathered around a small pot of cooking tea. She couldn't quite smell it from where she was, but as she watched, another few tents were set up and her view was obstructed.

"All that matters is we win here, Malkov," she said, the use of her own last name tasting weird upon her tongue. She looked at him. "I won't use the arm for two weeks. At which point...?"

"At which point, you point your finger at your victim and I take care of the rest," Malkov replied, meeting her gaze. "I will be busy with this process and unable to speak to you for the next two weeks. Do try to seem a little upset by my lack of company."

"Terribly tragic."

"Ah, you are a fun one, aren't you, Voshell? I'll leave you be. Do understand that allowing me to focus entirely on this job will mean your arm will not work until I am ready. Try not to die while I'm away."

His form flickered and vanished, her eye cooling and granting her a moment of relief. She sighed and rubbed it idly as she looked back towards the camp, only to be surprised to see Sindri walking towards her. Two metal cups were in her hands, and the larger woman flashed a smile as she approached. The smell of burnt tea filled the space between them.

"Hello, my queen!" Sindri called. "I thought you might need something to drink. Ah, I hope I wasn't..."

"You're not intruding, private," Voshell said, a smile coming to her lips. "Thank you." When Sindri was close, Voshrll took the cup in her hand. The contents were black, overboiled and oversteeped, but she couldn't complain. It would keep her awake, and it was something to do as the platoon rested from their battle. Still, the heat of the day was already beginning to climb as the rain began to slip into a gentler rhythm, and after a moment or two of having the steam billow up around her face, sweat began to form behind her ears and trickle down her neck.

"Were you, ah… speaking with the weapon?" Sindri asked, taking a sip of her boiling tea.

"I was. The war should be over soon, private. We just need to hold out a little longer." Voshell blew on the dark liquid, not too keen on burning her tongue.

"That's good," Sindri said, smiling.

*Vix above, that smile.* Voshell's heart climbed up her throat and she had to swallow to get it back to its rightful place. Voshell looked down at her cup. *Two weeks. That's all. Two weeks, and her and I can go get drinks.*

"My queen, if you don't mind, could I ask you a question?"

The queen looked up, her eyes settling on Sindri's troubled expression. Her thumb traced the rim of her cup.

Voshell tilted her head. "Something is troubling you, private?"

"In the battle, ah… you… you jumped in front of me when I froze," Sindri murmured. "I hate to chastise you, my queen—"

"Then do not."

"B-but you shouldn't have risked your life for me. You're the queen *and* our general. If we lost you, we would be doomed. No one would be able to lead us. *Please* don't do it again."

75

A frown dragged the corners of Voshell's lips downwards. She contemplated the woman's words, her request, and found herself looking back out through the forest. She hadn't really thought about what she was doing when she leapt in front of Sindri, hadn't considered how reckless that was, how illogical, how *foolish.* To risk her life for a private was idiotic. She was the queen, and without her, the Thrax would crumble and dissolve to nothing, eradicated by the heavy hand of the Blues massacring them one by one. Not even those beneath ice and snow would be able to bring them back from that.

Still, she didn't want Sindri to die. She didn't want to see her get sliced in half by a Blue's blade, didn't want to see the woman fumble to push her guts back inside her body, or slump to her knees after her throat had been slit. She wanted to sit down after all this, to perch atop a barstool, and share a drink with this beautiful blonde. That's what she wanted. Besides, neither of them had come to any harm from the protective instinct Voshell didn't realize she had. The two survived. Just like the queen wanted.

"I'll consider what you've asked," Voshell replied, looking back to Sindri. "But I would prefer you did not die."

Sindri laughed lightly. "I would prefer that too, my queen, but… this is a war. And even if it might end soon, it won't if you get killed. I understand this place might be where I die. That's okay. I—"

"It's not okay," Voshell cut in, her voice firm and her eyes hard as she peered at the woman. She took a sip of her burning tea and felt it scorch the tip of her tongue. Sindri glanced at her, silent and confused.

"I don't want you to die here," Voshell said, her teeth scraping against her seared taste buds. She grimaced and idly wondered if Healers ever had to deal with such domestic pains.

"My queen, surely you don't want anyone to die here, but—"

"No, I don't," Voshell said. It wasn't entirely a lie. "But specifically, I do not want *you* to die here."

Sindri stared at her queen, her body stiff. After a few seconds, she offered a single-note laugh, flashed a smile, and glanced away.

"You're teasing me," Sindri said. "That's cruel, my queen."

"When this is all over, perhaps we could get a drink," Voshell said, the words spilling from her lips before she could stop them. Sindri straightened and looked at the redhead, eyes wide, a blush beginning to color her pale cheeks.

"W-what?"

Voshell cleared her throat. "I'm sorry, forget that, I don't know what I'm saying," she breathed. A nervous laugh bubbled out of her chest. "Perhaps the nerves are finally getting to me, hm?"

"Right, ah…" Sindri smiled and looked down at her cup. "Should I leave you be, my queen?"

"No, you're welcome to stay, private." Voshell used the back of her hand to wipe sweat from her brow. "Perhaps you'd accompany me to my tent?"

Sindri nodded. "I would be honored."

# Chapter 9

At an easy six and a half feet, the kodarian before Aris stood with an air of superiority, her small, blue eyes glaring down at her higher-ranking officer. Aris met the woman's narrowed gaze, kept them firmly locked, did not spare a glance at the intricate carvings that ran long the woman's twisted horns. Aris kept her chest out and her arms neatly folded at the base of her spine. The dim morning light filtered in through the canvas that sagged beneath the weight of last night's rain. The shadow cast by Kuroda's frame just outside darkened a section of the wall.

"You lost the bank," Aris repeated, her face composed, voice even. "Explain yourself, lieutenant."

The woman before her scoffed and crossed her arms over the light armor she wore, which boasted thinner material and more gaps between the metal plates. Most of her rye-mail showed through, the deep purple scales covered with an incomplete matte finish, allowing a few select ones near her shoulders to catch the light and gleam. Even from the edges of her vision, Aris could see there wasn't a scratch across the polished surface.

"The Mad Queen was there," the woman said, her voice a collection a sore throats and raspy lungs. It almost pained Aris to hear it croak out of the kodarian's mouth.

"The Mad Queen? She's been gone for months."

"Yeah. She's back. There wasn't much we could do." The woman shrugged and looked away. Aris kept her eyes locked on the woman's despite this, not about to break contact. "Reds came in from all angles. They struck at night and pushed everyone to an ambush as to not set off the bombs.”

“And if there were mines in the woods, how did the Reds get through?”

“I… think they were in the trees?”

Aris’ eyes narrowed. “You *think?* Were you not there, lieutenant?”

“It was dark, general,” the woman growled, looking back at the shorter human. “It wasn’t easy to see.”

“How did you escape, exactly?”

The woman snarled, showing off a row of omnivorous teeth, her tusks ground down close enough to the gums that Aris almost didn’t realize they were there.

“I slipped through.”

“Ah. Did you? Unharmed?”

“You think I can’t do that? I’ve been on the front lines here longer than you—”

“Your armor is unscathed. With your mail catching the light like that, you would’ve been spotted.”

“I *escaped,*” the woman pressed. “What more do you want?”

Aris eyed her lieutenant. The way the kodarian’s shoulders were lifted, the sweat beneath her jawline, the flared nostrils. How she looked away before relaying what occurred at the battle.

"I want the truth," Aris replied. "You weren't there."

"You're fucking *accusing* me of abandoning my troops? This is ridiculous! I never would've suffered this under General Nyar!"

"There's no shame in not being at the battle, lieutenant," Aris said, lifting a hand to dismiss the hostility. "You cannot be present all the time. I don't expect that of you." She offered a cold smile. "Besides, other matters were likely important. Were you scouting our next move?"

The soldier paused, her stiff shoulders moving half an inch downwards, her eyes widening with confusion. After a few seconds of silence, she exhaled quietly and relaxed, eyes on Aris.

"I was scouting."

"Which area were you scouting?" Aris disengaged, turning to address a table at her left. There, a paper map with holes and stains was dragged across the surface. After the rain stopped, it had been pulled out of its protective tube and laid out to be easily seen once more. Aris touched the smudged map with her three middle fingers and looked back at her lieutenant. "Show me," she said, "on the map."

The kodarian reached out and tapped the shoddily sketched line labeled "river." She pressed her grey-skinned pointer upstream from the position she was given.

"I was looking for threats," she said.

"Ah." Aris nodded. "Thank you. You are hereby stripped of your rank. Join the privates and await your orders."

The woman blinked. "I'm *what?*"

"You're dismissed. Was that not clear?" Aris faced the larger woman, unimpressed. "And here I thought I spoke plainly."

"This is *shit!*" The woman shouted, her voice ringing like a memory of red-headed anger, of scowls, of reckless and stupid bravery that cost a friend her legs. "I have held this rank for *two years* with General Nyar before you even—"

"General Nyar is dead, isn't he?" Aris replied, her voice dry. "I'm beginning to think the incompetency of his advisors and underlings is what caused his demise. Get out of my tent."

The woman stepped closer, looming over Aris. Her hands bundled into fists and her body hunched forward the slightest bit, as if she might try to tackle Aris to the ground.

"Just because some stupid *Gold* said you were in charge, doesn't mean you can just act like you're the god of this forsaken planet."

"You're right, private. I'm your god because I *earned* my rank by keeping my fellow soldiers alive in my many years of service. I *earned* it by proving I'm loyal. I *earned* it by cutting down a demon. But I suppose if you hate being bossed around, private, you can leave the camp and enter the woods alone. Perhaps the local wildlife will let you live long enough to consider what a terrible life choice you've made."

The woman opened her mouth and leaned closer. A shot of hot breath hit Aris' nose, staining it with an acrid stench that she could nearly taste.

"A duel," the lieutenant hissed.

Aris smiled. "No. Kuroda? Please remove this woman from my tent."

The kodarian reeled back. "I—no? *No?* You cannot deny my right to a duel! I find your leadership unworthy and I demand we duel."

Kuroda ducked inside the tent, his swampy eyes settling on the woman as he did so. He had to hunch forward, the damp canvas brushing the top of his head. The kodarian glanced at him, scowled, and looked back at Aris.

"You're a piece of shit," she growled, "using him like that. I'll leave, but if you fuck this—"

"That's enough." Aris turned away, exposing her back, exposing a weakness to show she knew the woman could not strike at it. She peered at the tarnished map. "You have been dismissed."

A hiss of agitated air escaped the kodarian's nostrils before she spun on her heel and brushed past Kuroda to exit. Aris closed her eyes and rubbed them with her thumb and forefinger.

"Trouble," Kuroda said. "You are… troubled." He strode over to her, the wet tent dripping water down his shield-like face. His eyes sought hers as he came to the table, resting his larger hands against it as he leaned down to peer at her. Perhaps his rate of learning a new language indicated hyper-intelligence and was something to be concerned with, but as Aris pulled her hand from her face, she noticed how he looked at her like a scared animal. His eyes were wide, his slit pupils expanded, his tail brushing across the bare ground beneath their feet. He cared for her. And that was useful.

"I am," she replied.

He pressed his cheek against hers, his mandibles hard like bone against her skin. A questioning purr rumbled up from his throat which made her teeth chatter. She pulled away.

"Everyone holding a rank here is useless, Kuroda," she breathed, her voice dropping low. "We all lack training, but these— they're abandoning rank to save their own hides. No wonder the previous general died. No one here is trying to keep each other alive. I'm going to have to completely change everyone's ranks *and* make sure they know that it's for the best. And that they can't challenge me on it."

"Kill officers?" Kuroda suggested, tilting his head as he rested his elbows against the table.

Aris snorted out a breathy laugh. "We can't kill them, Kuroda."

"War. Missing. Animals." He gave a firm nod.

"I'm not hurting my own people, Kuroda. They're all Blues. They're like me. The only reason any of us are here is because of the Golds back home. I want my troops to trust me, not hate me."

"Trust?" he repeated, tasting the word as he spoke it. "What is?"

Aris considered this. "Well, trust is… if someone likes you. Likes you enough to be vulnerable around you, to share secrets, to…" *To tell you they have green eyes.* She scowled and shook her head. "I want them to like us both, Kuroda." She touched his arm. His mandibles flared the moment her skin brushed soft scales. "Please try to get along with them."

He straightened and placed his jaw atop her head, a purr returning.

"Will try," he said, his voice rumbling with the sound of his affection. "For friend."

Aris smirked. The air from the nostrils on his chest warmed her face, urged sweat from her pores, warmed an ever-cold part of her soul. It felt good to have him trust her. It felt good to have a pawn.

It felt good to have a friend.

# Chapter 10

Each of Voshell's platoons were ordered to remain positioned at different points along the river's bank. Mines were stationed along their flanks to keep the Blues from coming around the rear, and hopefully force them to cross the water. That would ensure the Thrax heard them coming and had some warning before an attack.

Voshell's current station was different, of course, considering it already had mines set up that kept the Thrax from being attacked from any side besides the rear. It would ensure the Blues had to get upon the mainland, and it would limit everyone's mobility. Not to mention, as seen before, it created one way in, and one way out. It was easily a deathtrap. The trick was ensuring it was the Blues caught in it.

After inquiring about who decided a ring of explosives should be placed in such a way, Lieutenant Ira shook his head.

"There was a corporal stationed here before we lost this position. She thought the Blues would set them off and they did—but they wised up, backed off, and went around." He sighed. "Would you like us to disarm them?"

"No, we'll make-do," Voshell said. "It'll be a fine position to hold for now." She considered their options in silence for a moment before nodding. "Tonight, I want two scouts sent from Platoon One, down to the west, to find a way to cross the river and see if they can locate where the Blues are stationed. I don't like not knowing where they are."

"Yes, general. I will relay the message."

"Good." She leaned back and sighed, rubbing her eyes with her left hand. "Get some lunch, Ira. I can't have you passing out on me, and you're looking a bit thin beneath that armor."

Ira glanced down at his lean frame. He chuckled and shook his head.

"I think you're just trying to fatten me up so I can't fit in this suit anymore."

"A case for that could be made," Voshell replied with a smirk. "Have the troops gather near the pot. I'll inform them about my arm."

"Of course, my queen." He paused. "Shall I call the private over to help you?"

Voshell glanced at him, noting the sheen of mischief in his eyes. "It's that obvious?" she asked.

"You're not the most subtle person I've met, my queen. But… she is a private."

"I know. I'll try not to get too attached."

A gentle smile pulled up the corner of his lips, his small eyes filled with sympathy. "But she is quite beautiful. I hope things go well."

"Thank you, lieutenant. Now go get fattened up."

He laughed, the voice booming and filling her with a certain warmth. He waved his hand and headed out, ducking through the tent's flap. His horns caught the fabric and dragged it along with him.

Voshell's smile fell, and her eyes returned to the map. She rested her palm across it, the callouses atop her skin scraping the surface. Waiting was a dangerous game that she hardly ever played, but there was little more for her to do. The weapon had to be prepared. And she couldn't fight nearly as well with her left hand. She would need to rely on those around her to keep her alive.

A heavy breath fell from her lips. It wasn't the first time she relied on people. As a child, she could not fend for herself. She trusted her father to keep her safe. She trusted that her father wouldn't have someone attempt to murder her. A victer with talons and beak, tearing and ripping at her brothers while she could do nothing—too small, too weak. She remembered gripping a wooden sword, swinging it as hard as she could against the man's black feathers, trying to batter him in some way. He looked down at her, beak dripping with gore.

Lionel had been the first to go. The oldest brother, second child, dedicated to keeping his family safe, dedicated to put his life on the line to protect all of them. He landed a blow on the victer's jaw, the beast's eyes narrowing and the feathers along its spine rising like ridges upon a growing mountain. His hand swept the toy sword away. Ebony talons seized hold of Lionel's arm. The victer lifted the boy off the ground. His beak spread wide. Adrian screamed. Voshell screamed. Lionel wept.

Droplets of water tore her back from her thoughts, brought her to the present to find tears dripping off her cheeks, dotting her knuckles and the map. With a sniff, she stepped back and shook her head, stilling her breathing as best she could. This was pathetic. She had bigger things to focus on now besides the past. She needed—

"My queen?" Sindri's voice was laden with concern, enough to give Voshell pause before she looked to the blonde in the entryway. The tent flap closed behind the woman, her crimson gaze full of worry. Sindri gasped.

"You're—you're—?" Sindri started.

"I'm fine, my eye was just bothering me." Voshell swept at her real eye, the only one producing tears. "It's nothing."

"You're hurting," Sindri said, stepping closer. "That's not nothing, my queen."

"It was dust."

Sindri flashed a small smile, one that made Voshell's chest tighten. "In this soaked forest?"

"Maybe it was mud."

Sindri blinked before a laugh spilled from her mouth, loud and commanding. Voshell's heart swelled and pounded hard as she stared at the woman.

And then Sindri's arms were around her, capturing her in a tight embrace before Voshell could protest.

Pressed against the private's armor, smelling thickly of sweat and mud, Voshell inhaled a distant trace of chalk. It had a heat to it, as if it had been left in the sun, allowed to bake. It was almost completely swallowed up by the other odors that clung to Sindri. As the woman's arms tightened around Voshell, pressing the queen closer to her chest, Voshell couldn't help but remember the victer, the blood, Thaddeous hiding under the bed. Sindri's thumb rubbed the back of Voshell's neck, working the tense muscles there as Voshell closed her eyes tight, trying to push out the memories, push out the screams.

"It's okay to cry," Sindri said. "I won't tell."

Voshell gritted her teeth. A general *and* queen crying in the arms of her subordinate? It was unsightly, unheard of. But her people respected her, changed the salute to honor *her*. And when was the last time someone held her? The last time someone pulled her close and rubbed her skin and smelled of chalk and sweat and mud? Emotion rose up in her throat, threatening to spill out into unbecoming sobs. She wrapped her arms around Sindri and pressed tighter, their suits keeping each other from fully touching. Humidity clung in the air around them, drawing heat from their pores, making the proximity sweltering and nearly unbearable. Yet Voshell clung still, wishing their armor was off, wishing they could touch, wishing to remember the last time someone hugged her.

# Chapter 11

On the third day since Malkov's silence, Lieutenant Ira delivered news that Platoon One was under attack. Voshell was sitting with Sindri, sharing a cup of warm tea in the dawn of a humid day. The queen had chosen to wear less armor in the morning, hoping, desperately, that Sindri would elect to hug her again. That desire was shattered upon Ira's arrival, his face grave. Voshell stood the moment he was finished speaking.

"Send scouts," she said, downing the rest of her burning drink. "I want to know the outcome of the battle."

A distant explosion spilled smoke into the sky. All heads turned towards the rising line against the citrus sunrise. Ira looked back to Voshell.

"General, our people."

"By the time we move around our own defenses, the battle will have been decided," Voshell said. "Hearing about the attack so late has crippled our ability to retaliate or help. Not only that, but if we leave this position, the Blues will likely claim it." She let her eyes be drawn to the spirals of black against the sky and considered what a fire would do in a forest such as this. Damp and wet, it would be difficult to start, and with unpredictable winds, she could see it backfiring and costing lives. She glanced towards Sindri. Lives she could not afford to risk. "Have our troops prepared," Voshell said, looking to her lieutenant. "The Blues ambushed First Platoon. They may seek to attack us here before long."

"Yes, general." Ira dipped his head, turned on his heel, and went to bark orders to the troops. Sindri set her cup down and stood.

"My queen, we're not going to help?" she asked, her voice soft as to not be overheard. Voshell studied the etched lines of worry upon the beautiful woman's brow, how her crimson eyes were wide and horrified. The queen could not help but wonder if she had somehow done something wrong.

"We cannot save them," Voshell said.

"Of course," Sindri whispered. She looked towards the smoke as another explosion startled distant birds into the clouds. Voshell frowned. Her eyes moved north, where her foe lay, somehow maneuvering Blue troops across the river and ambushing Thrax the moment daylight broke across the horizon. How? How had the opponent slipped past her like that? How had Voshell's troops been caught so soundly off-guard? She scratched at her scar, brows knitting together. She looked back at Sindri, watched how the woman pressed her shoulders up, how she hung her head, how she sighed as if the world had crashed around her. Why was she so sorrowful for those she had never met? Why did she care so much for lives that she may have never knew existed?

The queen looked away, and as she did, she spotted the pointed peak of the mountains to the east. It was then a new plan was unveiled.

"Lieutenant Ira!" she barked.

Ira, in the midst of telling soldiers to be armed and prepared, turned to face her. "Yes, my queen?"

91

"Have the Third Platoon head east, hug the mountainside, and cross the river. There, they are to hold position in a fortified area and await further instructions—and fend off any Blue attacks."

Ira grinned, his blunt teeth framing the tusks that jutted upwards from his lower jaw. "Yes, general! And us? What will we do, my queen?"

Voshell took a deep breath. It was a foolish task, one she understood little, but she hated to see Sindri pained in such a way. A pained Sindri might seek to remove herself from Voshell's company. That could not be allowed to happen.

And, if this was done properly, she and the other platoon would pinch both sides of the Blue front. It would be unexpected, a move Voshell—no, the Mad Queen—had never done before. Her enemy would not expect it, and even if Voshell saved no one from the ambushed platoon, it would increase Sindri's faith in her. And it could win them this wretched war.

"We will prepare to travel," Voshell declared. "Everyone, pack up! We're going to save who we can!"

# Chapter 12

Clouds choked the sun overhead, spilling rain upon the drenched Thrax soldiers as they marched beneath the dripping canopy of tangled branches and leaves overhead. Water made their metallic armor sing, sounding like chimes amidst the drowning ferns bowing beneath the storm's weight and the suction of clinging mud. Dim lights of glowing flowers protected insects seeking shelter, only for each bug to take a taste of poisonous nectar and, in turn, become sustenance for the unforgiving foliage. Even Voshell's mechanical eye had difficulty keeping her from tripping, the storm enough to make her steps uncertain, her path unclear. As she moved forward near the middle of her platoon, she spotted several soldiers slipping, disappearing beneath the overgrowth, only to return a moment later slick with mud. The night grew long and her legs began to burn. The platoon's speed slowed. Sweat dripped from brows and clung to necks. The hot, humid evening made each gasp for breath akin to swallowing a mouthful of water. But eventually they drew close to the sight of the First Platoon.

The company came to a welcome halt as a messenger rushed back to Voshell. "Queen General," he began, saluting, the snipper's top pair of hands against his right, uppermost shoulder, "we're approaching the camp." He took a breath and shook his head, trying to shake the water out of his hair, soaking beneath the light suit of armor across his body. "Shall we move into tactical arrangements?"

Voshell nodded. "All soldiers at the ready!" Her voice hardly carried over the storm, but with a click upon the wrist holo, a message was sent to all:

*Tree to tree. Don't let them know. Stay alert.*

Her troops scattered, moving through the crushing sound of the storm to hide their bodies behind moss covered trees, press their armored shoulders against vines that oozed upon touch. With her throat thick with saliva and the air's oceanic touch, Voshell swallowed several times just to keep from needing to spit. She found herself against a large, twisted tree, with moss-covered bark now blooming with flowers smaller than her pinkie. Their white petals were drooping from the storm.

For an instant, she wondered if Sindri liked flowers. She wondered if she might pluck a few of them, cradle them in her hands, walk them over and see if the blonde wanted to braid them into her hair. It would certainly only make her more beautiful. Voshell smiled. She reached up to the moss near her shoulder, grasped a flower by its stem, then remembered herself. Her fingers slipped away. She took a breath and blinked a few times as the world returned to her. She hadn't been distracted on the battlefield like this since she was first released. Since she first stepped foot on Sobek after the ward. Thoughts and pains and anger kept her from fully being in the moment then, but now… why was she here? Why had she brought her troops to this location? She shook her head and dashed to an open tree, her platoon zig-zagging through the foliage to keep their locations hard to pinpoint. Her right arm hung limply at her side.

Everyone knew they'd be too late. It was well into the dark of night. Hours had passed. Everyone was dead, and she had made them leave their secure position for what?

Her eye caught Sindri and both hatred and desire swelled inside her chest. This was the distraction, the person pulling her attention away from what was important. Sindri's compulsion to help, the expression on her face, the way Voshell's heart grew weighty beneath her ribs—all of it was making Voshell's decisions for her. In her years of leading her troops, this hadn't happened. She had never risk the lives of her people for one. All of it was Sindri's fault.

"Contact!"

A splatter of blood caught her attention as one of her soldiers sliced through a startled Blue. Voshell changed direction and her troops jumped into a clearing, swords at the ready. Around them was the sight Voshell expected.

The camp had been set up in a thick collection of trees with foliage cut down to a more manageable level. But to the west, lines of trees were toppled, black forms still glinting with stubborn embers. Bodies had been caught beneath them, Blue and Thrax alike, spines crushed, legs pinned, organs popping through their skin and splattering in a macabre display that spared no soldier. Decapitated corpses slumped against what trunks were still standing, some with heads beside their feet that did not match the body. Others had fallen with a blade in the chest, more still from losing a limb and bleeding out before a decisive blow had been struck. Rain drenched each of them, masking the scent of iron and sulfur. Voshell stepped further, her and her troops slowly scanning the area. Tents and hammocks were ripped open, hanging from broken branches and covering small warriors beneath the thin canvas. Food was scattered about, trampled with boot prints against the brown packaging, the contents long since washed away.

No other Blues could be found alive, and with a nod, Voshell let her soldiers return to the carnage and pull the dog tags from each carcass, searching for names and ranks and identifiable markers to indicate who was Thrax. With all eyes fading to a dull hazel upon death, those without tags were lost to the forest, left to be consumed by scavengers. Voshell sighed as she watched her Reds work. She knew they would be too late. They should not have come.

"Queen General," Ira said, approaching her with a dip of his head. Rain drizzled off his horns and tusks, spilling down onto his breastplate. The nostrils above his eyes had sealed during the storm to keep from inhaling water. "We found three of our own still alive. They're in rough shape, but we have a Healer. They should pull through."

Voshell arched a brow. "Survivors? Of this?" She frowned. "They need to be ready in ten. The Blues may be keen to send reinforcements here after this position was destroyed. We can't be here when they come—we need to be across the river and strike them when they're moving."

"General, the three we found will not be ready to move today," Ira said. "They're far too injured."

"I cannot stop the movement of my troops for the safety of three," Voshell said. She met his eyes. "We move in ten."

Ira nodded. "Of course, Queen General. Our troops will be ready as you command." He saluted over his shoulder.

She dipped her head in return. "Good. See to it the Healer does what he can."

The lieutenant turned and rushed away. Voshell ran her hand over her face with a sigh and glanced up towards the canopy above.

She could see a few breaks in the clouds overhead. Perhaps soon the rain would end and they could breathe oxygen again.

Retching caught her ear and she turned to see Sindri bent against a tree, one hand holding her hair back while the other clutched her stomach. Voshell pushed her way through the muck laden with gore she could not see and found herself nearing the private.

"Sindri?" Voshell called when she could be heard over the rain. The woman looked back, the contents of her stomach hanging from her lips in a string of saliva. She turned and spat before wiping her mouth on her forearm's armor. Whatever smeared across the metal was washed off by the storm.

"Queen General," Sindri said, her voice strained from the effort of speaking. She faced Voshell fully and saluted. "I have a weak stomach. Forgive me, and don't let me distract you."

"Did you eat something?"

Sindri spat out a sardonic laugh. "The bodies don't bother you?"

"I've seen it all before."

"We're down an entire platoon now."

"I'm aware."

"To see them…" Sindri's brows scrunched together and she looked at her feet. "To see them like this…"

Voshell frowned. "How many battles have you been in?"

"One earlier this week," she replied.

Voshell scratched the scar across her face as dread began to churn her intestines. "With me."

"With you." Sindri closed her eyes. "I won't slow us down, general. I'll be fine for whatever your next order is."

Voshell watched her, considering the woman's state, the way Sindri's body slumped a bit as she leaned against the tree for support. The way dark circles hollowed out the woman's eyes, how blood had fled her face and how she had just spilled her last meal against the ground. Should they get into a battle before their march was done, Sindri would be unfit to fight. Sindri could die.

"We will be making camp to rest," Voshell said. "We'll need to travel to a location a good distance from here, further downstream. I know everyone is tired from marching through the night."

Sindri looked at Voshell and offered a small, grateful smile. It made Voshell's chest warm.

"Really?" the private breathed. "Oh, that sounds great. Thank you, general."

"It's not just for you," Voshell lied. "But you're quite welcome. Perhaps we can find you some tea to settle your stomach when we make camp."

Sindri laughed sheepishly, a blush on her cheeks. "Ah, thank you. I'm sorry I'm taking up so much of your time, my queen."

"It is not time spent wasted, private," Voshell said. She smiled. "Shall you walk with me while we march?"

The blush grew brighter upon the blonde's cheeks. She nodded. "I would be honored, my queen."


The walk was grueling. As dawn splintered through the canopy, spilling a warm orange glow and eliciting a fog from the chilled mud underfoot, the Thrax were made keenly aware of how long it had been since they had last slept. The rain faded into a light patter of drops, allowing most the soldiers to begin to smell the humid stench of their own bodies. Leaves the size of Voshell's abdomen covered the forest floor, and upon stepping on them, the mud underneath attempted to swallow her whole. Each breath was sharper, more painful than the last, and her own weight became more pressing, more exhausting to carry around. She glanced to the woman at her side, at the blonde with a heart softer than the ground, the woman who should not be in such a war. Voshell watched the private's face, now filled with more color than before but cut with grave lines, hollow eyes, a taunt mouth.

Perhaps Sindri had noticed, then. Noticed that the children the Blues enlisted were not just in the battle from before, but in all their skirmishes, wielding swords, clad in armor too large for them, more suited for a life at home beneath their mother's protection. The war had a way of stealing everyone's innocence away. It stole hers the night her father decided to kill her, and again when he sent her away to Sypher, locked away in an institution until she could prove she was well. The day she was released, she had to find her own way home with no money and no belongings, and she showed up on Soldar nearly a week later to a father who did not acknowledge her.

But Thaddeous had. He had smiled when she returned. He had greeted her and hugged her and brought her to her room. He kept it clean for her. The sheets had been washed that morning. He would not hear her when she spoke of their father's treachery, but he told her he learned to cook. Told her he would make her something to eat. Returned with fresh gritberries atop roasted kennock breasts, laid over a bed of rice. She ate it and uttered nothing in the way of thanks. She had been so angry at him. So furious. He had grown up with Daxgor, how could he see their father was a villain? How could he hear that?

How could she kill him when all he did was not understand?

Her foot snagged on something and she stumbled forward only to brace herself on a nearby tree. She took a breath and shut her eyes, grimacing against a growing headache in her skull.

*I'm sorry I didn't believe you,* Thaddeous said. Her eyes shot up and she searched the misty trees. *I didn't know, Vosh. I didn't know.*

There was a tug on her belt and she looked down to see him: a young boy with raven hair and an ill-fitting tuxedo. He held a fuzzy brown blanket in his hands, its length trailing in the dirt. His wide, red eyes stared up at her.

*I'm sorry, sis.*

She reached down and touched his cheek, his skin soft and cold in the rising heat. Her brows furrowed and she kneeled, taking a few shaky breaths.

"Are you actually here?" she whispered. Her hands went through his smooth hair, across his face. Thaddeous giggled and swatted her hand away with a large smile.

*Of course I'm here!* he said. *Are we going to play soldiers? Lionel and Adrian are waiting for us! Come on!* He grabbed her hand and turned, running off. She quickly followed, nearly tripping over her own feet as her mind tried to comprehend. Her brother was here? All her brothers? Had they somehow survived the attack? Had they fled to Sobek to stay hidden?

Thaddeous brought her to a clearing. The trees sat back around a large, oval-shaped section of trodden grasses and flowers. Voshell looked around as Thaddeous came to a stop in the middle of it, and there, running towards them, was Lionel and Adrian. Her heart jumped into her mouth. She fell to her knees and spread her arms wide. All three of her brothers leapt into them, hugged her tight, giggled and squealed and teased her about being gone for too long. And she felt them. She felt each strand of hair on their head, pinched their clothes, smelled the flowery soaps used on their skin. They were here. They were alive.

*Look what you destroyed.*

Voshell lifted her head to see Daxgor standing a few paces away, dressed in dark dress pants and a white button-up that swelled around his stomach. His beard spilled down his chest and his dark crimson eyes peered at her. With a start, she noticed her brothers were no longer in her arms. They stood beside Daxgor, clinging to his pants with confused, worried looks between them.

*You ruined this,* Daxgor said, his eyes narrowing.

"*You* ruined this," she hissed. "Brothers, come back to me. It's not safe to be by him."

*Not safe?* Daxgor spat out a laugh. *I'm their father. Nothing is safer than by my side. But you? The texts talk about you, Voshell. They talk about your cruelty. They talk about the Plurals.*

"I don't believe in your shitty religion," she snapped. "Brothers, to me." She motioned for them. But they looked to their father for guidance. And there, stepping out of the trees, was the victer. A chill ran down the queen's spine and made swallowing impossible.

"Brothers," she insisted. "Come to me."

*I told them about you,* Daxgor said, his eyes watching Voshell with keen intent. The creases at the sides of his eyes deepened as he smiled. *Big sis had to go away because she was making up stories. Big sis said dad was a bad man.* He rested his hand on Lionel's shoulder. The boy looked to his father, turned, and sprinted to the victer.

"No! Lionel!" Voshell jumped to her feet and scurried after him. The distance closed. The victer slashed out with his talons. As Voshell's hand gripped her brother's soft, young fingers, the talons made their mark across Lionel's chest. It bloomed red.

"No! No!" She pulled Lionel to her, pressing him against her armor and retreating away from the victer with crimson-stained hands. "Medic!" she cried, looking around. "Medic!" Where were her troops? Where was her Healer?

*Don't you see? Everything you touch becomes ash,* Daxgor said. *Me. Your brothers.*

"My Queen!" Sindri grabbed her arm, appearing from thin air.

*Your little distraction.*

The world returned to her. The weight in her arms vanished while her soldiers appeared instead. Dotted about the clearing, setting up camp, chatting amongst themselves. Voshell blinked. She looked down at her arms, her good one wrapped around nothing while her right arm hung at her side.

"You were gone for a moment there," Ira said, standing at her left side. He flashed a small smile. "Are you all right, my queen?"

Voshell closed her eyes and exhaled. "Overtired, it seems," she said. "Is my tent prepared?"

"It is. Come, I'll—"

"Private Sindri is capable," Voshell murmured. She rubbed her forehead, wiped away the sweat gathering there. "See to it shifts are set up. We don't need the Blues discovering our position."

"Of course, Queen General," Ira said. He bowed his head. "I will ensure we remain on guard."

"Did the other troops see me?" Voshell inquired.

"No. I ensured their movements sent them away from you. Private Sindri and I followed you instead. Private Sindri, help our queen."

"Ah—yes! Yes, sir!" Sindri said, quickly straightening her spine. Voshell glanced at her, a fond smile crossing her lips.

"Tend to the queen's every need. And ensure she gets some water before she rests," Ira said.

"You're mothering me, Ira," Voshell said.

"If I don't, who will?" he replied. "Rest well, my queen." He turned and began barking orders to nearby troops. Sindri watched him go before turning her eyes to Voshell.

"Back to your tent, my queen?"

"Please, private," she said. "I am quite tired."


With Sindri's help, the two made it to the general's tent near the center of camp. The moment they were out of public eye, Voshell slumped her shoulders and let out another heavy sigh. She dragged her feet across the soaked, muddy mess of trampled grass and leaves and sat down on her cot, eyes heavy.

"Do you believe in Vix?" Voshell asked.

Sindri blinked. She scratched at her shoulder and shifted from one foot to the other. "What prompted this, my queen?"

"A bad dream," Voshell replied. "Sometimes there are those in the Thrax that believe a different sect of the Vix religion," she said. "Some believe that Plurals are the heralds of the apocalypse, and only their death can delay it."

Sindri frowned. She took a few steps closer to the queen, brows furrowing across those beautiful ruby eyes. "That's a terrible thing to believe," she murmured. "I don't believe that, my queen. I don't believe you're some sort of monster just because your eyes are two different colors."

*Neither did your brothers,* Daxgor said, his voice rattling in Voshell's skull. *They thought you were good and pure. Look what you did to them.*

Voshell shook her head, scowling. It was *Daxgor* that ordered that beast into their home. *Daxgor* that caused her brothers to die. It was not her fault.

The cot shifted and she turned to see Sindri sitting next to her. A lump formed in her throat—was she about to get another hug? When they were both in their armor? She wished desperately to not be so she could feel Sindri's warmth, feel the woman's strong arms around her.

*And me?* Daxgor cooed. *Surely you did not slay me in my sleep? Surely you did not enter my room and cut my throat in such a dishonorable way?*

Voshell gripped her head, her scowl deepening. Daxgor deserved to die. It was the only way to stop him from getting in the way of saving the Thrax people. If he had chosen the Green over her weapon, they would've all died.

*Is that so? And revenge had nothing to do with it?*

She would not deny that—she had hungered for his death after years of being trapped in that asylum atop the Sypher mountains. She wished to see him bleed. She wished for him to have his intestines eaten like that of her brothers.

"My queen?" Sindri touched Voshell's leg. "Are you unwell? Perhaps you need the medic?"

"No, I—" Voshell started.

105

*What of Thaddeous?* Daxgor whispered. *What of him? Your only living brother? The youngest of your siblings?*

Bricks pressed against her chest. "I had to," she breathed.

Sindri tilted her head. "My queen?"

*Did you? Or did you just tell yourself that and pretend it was justified? He fought to keep Jade from killing you. He fought to save your life. And you cut him down.*

Voshell's eyes clenched shut. "I had no choice—it was the only way."

*You always prided yourself in being a good liar, Voshell, but your lies don't fool me today. You cut him down. Have you even shed a tear for him? Have you even mourned him?*

"Shut up," she whimpered. "Shut up."

"Queen General?" Sindri's hands gripped Voshell's shoulders, curling around the spaulders there. "What's wrong? What are you hearing?"

*You've not even paid him proper homage, have you? He's not even gotten half the funeral some of your troops have. He's your brother, Voshell, and you killed him.*

"Stop!" the queen cried.

In an instant, Sindri's wrapped around Voshell and pulled the queen into the private's chest. Voshell froze. Her eyes opened and she stared, silently, at the scratched chest plate. The morning light grew more intense, spilling through the canvas tent and filling the embrace with almost unbearable heat. Sindri was holding her.

But Daxgor was not silenced.

*Did you take joy from it?* he asked. *Did you find yourself smiling when you killed him? Like you want to smile now? Does this woman fill you with less or more happiness than murdering your last surviving relative?*

The bricks sat upon her ribs, cracked them, filled her lungs with pain and blood and something she hadn't experienced before: a feeling of wrongness. A feeling that she might have taken misstep. She had never done that before. She had never made a mistake. Her stomach churned. Her mind reeled.

What was this odd sensation of regret doing in her soul?

She couldn't deal with it—she didn't *want* to deal with it. Daxgor laughed and she could hear the victer biting through bone and marrow and squashing intestines. Thaddeous was dying in her eyes again and again, and she found herself trying to stop it, trying to change the memory the more it played inside her head. The church meetings, the way her father's friends looked at her, the needles and the drugs within the asylum. The tormenting jailor, the way her lungs ached as she tasted fresh air during her single attempt to escape. How they never let her near another window again when she was caught.

All of it came upon her mind, crashing and tearing, ripping away any other thoughts, staining everything it touched within her cranium. The hug was not helping. The hug was not distracting her. She looked up at the private, at that face, at those lips. And Voshell sat up and kissed them.

# Chapter 13

Sindri tasted of dried beef, pepper, and bergamot. Her lips were soft. Voshell dived into them, gripping the woman's armor to brace herself as all thoughts began to fade from her mind. There was nothing else.

Just this.

After a moment, Sindri relaxed and responded to the affection. A desperate kiss turned passionate swiftly. Voshell's fingers wrapped around spaulders, Sindri's hands pressed against Voshell's spine. There was no war. There was no death, no massacre of families, no victers to tear her apart. It was just the queen and her knight. Nothing tasted better.

"Queen General!" Lieutenant Ira's voice cut through the tent as he burst in through the entrance. Immediately, Sindri pulled back, a flush on her cheeks and a string of saliva linking her to Voshell. Voshell exhaled slowly and wiped her mouth on the back of her hand before peering at the man in her tent. He had seen them—that was clear since his eyes were focused on the other corner of the tent as he pulled the opening flaps away from his horns and let them fall close behind him. He cleared his throat.

"I am sorry to interrupt, my queen," he said. "But we have just gotten word from the Third Platoon. It's a distress."

Voshell closed her eyes. She relished the lingering buzz of sensation from Sindri's passion, the flavors dancing upon her tongue. She took a deep breath. A momentary distraction. One that did not last nearly long enough.

"You may enter, Ira," she said, her voice low, holding exhaustion that dripped from each word.

"My queen," he said, dipping his head before approaching. He tapped the holo strapped around his wrist and a voice rang out, cut by static and rain and screams.

"Private Dalrium reporting in!" the feminine voice screamed, a screech from behind nearly swallowing her words. "While crossing the river, we were overtaken by rye-dragons! We're holding our ground now, but we've stumbled upon a nest! Requesting immediate support!"

Again, another screech, clearer than before, high-pitched and shrill like iron rods to an eardrum. Ira's crimson eyes shifted to Voshell.

"It would take a swift two days walk, my queen, but our troops have not rested. It could easily turn into a four-day hike."

Voshell's eyes narrowed with thought and she looked down at her limp, useless right hand. They would need to cross the decimated camp, a location the Blues would likely be investigating. They would need to trek around their abandoned previous post, one that could already be overrun. They would need to push through territory just to get to those troops. She gritted her teeth.

"Advise a retreat," she hissed, looking up to Ira.

"But with rye-dragons—" he began.

"Some of them will survive," she said. She stood up. "How many explosives do we have?"

"Four, Queen General," he said. "And two grenades."

"Tell the troops our break is over. We need to cross the river, scout the enemy out, and strike. We're losing too many. And we can't risk exposing ourselves so greatly to save a platoon that doesn't even have the wherewithal not to disturb a fucking rye-dragon—"

Wind whistled and canvas popped. Something hard impacted her shoulder, crushing into the metal there, pressing a dent no deeper than the tip of her finger. She stumbled to her feet and scowled, peering at it then glancing at the small, circular hole in her tent. Her eyes widened.

"Snipers!" she shouted. She turned and tackled Sindri off the bed and onto the ground, shielding the woman with her body. Voshell looked to Ira, who immediately ducked. "We need to scatter into the trees! Get out of the clearing, and into the brush! Everyone on their hands and knees, and stay beneath the ferns if they can't find a tree!"

Ira nodded. Another shot slammed into his horn, wedging itself deep into the bone and sending splinters across its length. He cursed and dived out the tent flap as panicked cries drenched the encampment. Voshell grabbed her H-Blade and cut a hole in the side of the tent. Soldiers were fleeing quickly, shouts of anguish rose up here and there, gunfire blindly returned into the branches of trees. They were using her own tactic against her. Voshell snarled and looked down at the wide-eyed Sindri.

"Up!" she snapped. "Move!"

Sindri nodded and scrambled out from under Voshell and through the gap, Voshell about to follow when she noted the map on the table. It displayed too much information to fall into Blue hands. She got to her feet, sprinted over, and clutched it in her hand. She shoved it into the front of her chest plate before diving after Sindri.

Voshell scrambled across the mud, smearing it against her hands, her neck, her armor. Another lead bullet impacted her back, ricocheting off and plunging itself into the ground. She got to her feet and bolted out of the clearing, side-stepping a few soldiers that were victim to a well-placed shot. Some bled and sobbed, trying to drag themselves to shelter. Others lay still. She spotted six dead.

They couldn't afford to lose that many. This entire rescue mission was killing them.

Voshell leapt behind a tree, her chest heaving as a few shots peppered trunks and spewed bark into the air. She closed her eyes. She wished she could be in that tent still kissing Sindri…

*Sindri!* Her eyes flew open and she looked around. She spared a look around the tree towards the camp, trying to see if the woman was one of the fallen, but a few sniper shots pushed her back into cover.

*Fuck. Fuck!* She grabbed at her right arm, her fingers digging against the metal.

*I told you, didn't I?* Daxgor hummed. *You destroy everything you—*

"Shut up!" she screamed, slamming her hand against her prosthetic. She pressed a button on her left wrist's holo against her useless right thumb, giving an order to all her troops:

111

*Units one and two in the trees, get behind the Blues; three and five get on their hands and knees and crawl beneath the ferns, get close without being spotted; and unit four is with me. Provide cover.* She paused. *Ira, on Sindri.*

She took a deep breath and grabbed her blade, her left hand gripping its hilt with less dexterity, but still enough to kill. All she had to do was survive. She inhaled.

*I won't die here.* She turned and shot across the clearing.

# Chapter 14

Dawn broke when Aris stopped behind a tent on the way to the boiling pot of oatmeal. The smell of early morning dew mixed with salted water and sweaty bodies filled the air alongside hushed whispers of treachery. Trees from the forest around them cast long shadows across the waking encampment, full of disorganized tents, cut foliage, and a fog that cloaked the ankles of those outside their bunks. On her way to her morning meal, Aris made it a point to take the long way around, skirting near the disgraced ex-lieutenant's tent. She suspected the woman would be bitter about her demotion. And here, Aris found herself correct.

She stood in the shadow of a tree and leaned against its trunk to listen in as Private Rasatha hissed to those gathered in her tent.

"They radioed in ten minutes ago to say most of their platoon was decimated," Rasatha began. "So our general just sent an entire *platoon* to die against the Reds. She's not even taking council from anyone but that *creature* that follows her around everywhere."

"Kuroda?" someone asked. "He's big, but he seems harmless. I saw him picking flowers last night."

"He's a beast. He can hardly even speak our language," Rasatha countered. "She uses him like a guard mutt, and he's too stupid to realize it."

"You sound like a Gold," someone else said.

"But it's *true.* Look, we need to gather our own and go support our platoon. They're going to die unless *we* do something."

"Who's to say they're not dead already?" said the second.

"We'd be going against our general," said a third. "She's hard when it comes to planning, but she cares about us. She's trying to keep us alive."

"She's only general because her asshole father is a Gold," Rasatha replied.

Aris chuckled and the tent fell silent. She stepped into the morning light and strode to the entrance as her shadow fell upon the tent. She ducked inside, a smile on her lips. Rasatha sat on a large fallen branch, while everyone else was squatting above the mud. In total, there was five of them, Rasatha being the sixth.

"G-General Sell!" a snipper stammered as she got to her feet. She quickly saluted. Aris dipped her head in a respectful nod and looked to Rasatha as the woman's shoulders rose with tension. She wasn't wearing armor yet, instead dressed in her black undersuit, which clung to every curve of her body in a matte finish. Slowly, the kodarian stood, eyes full of chilled daggers. She saluted.

"General Sell," she growled.

"My, Private Rasatha, it seems you're sowing dissent within my troops," Aris cooed. "That wouldn't be the case, would it?"

"Would it be?"

"It would. Do you think you'll be able to gather a little band of your friends to go play hero when you ran away from your own platoon in need?"

Rasatha's eyes narrowed. "I was scouting."

"Scouting an escape route, it seems. And now you're, what, going to cross the river yourself and find the platoon and somehow change the course of the skirmish?"

"You sent them all there to die."

"I did no such thing, private. I anticipated the bank would be littered with mines and other explosives, so I warned them to use their scouts and not to attack head-on. It seems all my lieutenants here are intent on ignoring my orders. Of being incompetent."

Rasatha scowled, flashing her sawed-down tusks, displaying them like an animal threatened. She stepped closer, fists clenched at her sides as her nostrils flared above her eyes. "Are you calling me incompetent?"

Aris kept her smile and peered up at the taller woman, unflinching. "I am. Because that is what you are. You will sit down now, private. Pushing your luck with me will prove fruitless. Private Bynerry?" She looked to the snipper, who still had her hands as a salute. She straightened and nodded.

"Y-yes, general?"

"Please disregard nonsense teachings your friend here has taught you. Any survivors will be safe enough where they are. The Mad Queen has never sought to rescue her own. The Blues there will act as spies and scout out the best possible routes for our platoon to strike against the Mad Queen herself."

"And they called *me* incompetent—" Rasatha started.

115

"Friend Aris!" Kuroda's voice rang with glee and, while Aris turned to lock eyes with her disgraced private once more, Kuroda could be heard entering the tent, his tail swishing across the moist ground beneath their feet. He came up to Aris without his cloak, his markings on full display. In his hand was a collection of blue and purple flowers, their petals small and stems thin. He held them in his massive hands, careful not to crush them. Kuroda rubbed his cheek against hers, and she disengaged her stare-down with Rasatha to acknowledge him.

"Hello, Kuroda," she said, offering him a more genuine smile. His mandibles flared with delight and displayed his rows of pointed teeth beneath, creating the image of a gruesome grin. He pushed the flowers into her chest.

"I collect for you," he said. Aris blinked and took them, her brows furrowing at his odd display. There were six in total. The tent watched in silence. "I saw others gather," he said with a nod. He looked to Rasatha and nodded a second time. "They smile. Gather for you, you smile." He nudged the blossoms with one of his fingers then looked to Aris. "Yes?"

"Well, thank you, Kuroda. I do smile."

Kuroda beamed, his tail swishing behind him and spraying a bit of mud on those crouching nearby. They stood and offered soft laughs. Aris took note of their expressions. Apparently, this affection made Kuroda more endearing. That was good. A happy purr rumbled from his chest.

"Gather more?" he asked.

"No, no, leave some for others, Kuroda," she said, touching his arm with her free hand, letting her fingers run across his scales. "These are just fine."

He leaned over and planted his jaw atop her head, his rumbling rattling her bones, making it almost difficult to breathe. He had been doing that more often now, an attachment clearly displayed for all to see. Peaceful and loveable, this monster from outside the Known Galaxy, this creature the Golds would surely hate and use for experiments should they be able to contain him. He was sweet to the Blues. And soon, he would protect them.

"Have breakfast together," he said, pulling away. He straightened, the point of his shield-shaped skull brushing the top of the tent. "Hungry. Need water."

A few chuckled and he blinked, casting quizzical looks at them which consisted of his mandibles slanting askew on his face.

"It's oatmeal," Bynerry offered with a squeak. Kuroda peered at her, the muscles above his eyes furrowing a bit.

"Oatkatamel," he said, then shook his head. "Oat…"

"Meal," Bynerry said.

"Mealeh," Kuroda said. He gave a nod. "Oatamealeh."

Aris chuckled. "Close. We'll work on it. Thank you, private."

Bynerry nodded, still smiling at Kuroda. Aris peered to Rasatha, who stood to near her full height to peer down at the shorter woman. Aris chuckled. She waved her hand.

"Well, you are all dismissed. Come, Kuroda. Let's get you some *oatmeal.*"

"*Uh*tmeal," he muttered, following as Aris stepped out of the tent.

During her meal, Aris received word that Rasatha and eleven other soldiers left their posts to travel across the river. Aris smiled. She called for her final platoon to join forces with hers. Their camp was packed shortly after. And with bolstered numbers, she followed after Rasatha.

If the suicidal private wanted so badly to be used as bait, Aris wouldn't complain.

# Chapter 15

Snipers fired upon Voshell and her troops as they dashed through the opening, changing their movements behind tarp-covered tents, keeping their heads down, lifting their free arms to cover their skulls in case a lucky shot rained down upon them. Five of her twenty were downed, either by injury or death. The survivors burst into the trees, weapons ready, slicing into the foliage as Blues quickly rose to meet them. Voshell's blade met with a teenager's, a snipper with wide, terrified eyes who kept her bottom two hands free. She grappled Voshell's right arm and pulled. Voshell cursed as she stumbled closer to the snipper and quickly slipped to the side so the woman's blade did not slice her in two. Voshell planted a kick on the woman's hip, shoving her back and forcing her to let go of the queen's arm. It dangled helplessly on her side. The snipper stared at it.

"You're injured," she breathed. Then, louder: "The Mad Queen is—!"

Voshell closed the distance between them and stabbed. The snipper yelped and jumped aside, narrowly avoiding being pierced through the opening in her armor just above her belt. Voshell sliced her blade to the left, forcing the Blue the parry, return with a stab of her own. A feint and a sidestep. A cut across the chest, blood drawn from the arm. The two stepped back, panting, the snipper's lower left hand bleeding, and Voshell standing tall, unharmed. Her mechanical eye analyzed the woman, and, having sparred long enough, formed predictive movements. The snipper jumped forward. The eye told Voshell where she would land. The queen leapt, meeting the lunge, and plunged her blade through the armpit, into the chest cavity, and held it there.

The snipper's eyes widened. Blood bubbled out from her mouth, staining the pincers, and drooling down her chin. She dropped her weapon and it clattered to the ground behind Voshell. Voshell pulled her blade out and let the Blue collapse backwards, choking and heaving. The queen turned away and watched as more of her soldiers appeared, meeting the Blues in trees, kicking them from the branches, the snipers breaking bones in the fall.

The Thrax that had crawled to their location turned the skirmish to the Red's favor, taking the enemy by surprise. The bloodbath was quick, effective, and over within minutes. There had only been twelve total Blues.

A kodarian with sawed tusks was pushed down to her knees before Voshell. The Blue grimaced as blood stained her armor, dripping from her lips in thick globs.

"Queen General," Ira said, dipping his head. "This was their leader."

"You?" Voshell said, eyeing the kodarian. "You're not what I expected. What is your name?"

The woman spat on the ground and scowled. "Fuck you, Mad Queen—"

In one swift movement, Lieutenant Ira sliced the woman's right horn off with his blade and allowed the bone to fall into the foliage, disappearing beneath the thick ferns. The woman's eyes widened, rage bubbled in her expression and her Helix began to bulge her muscles with Charge. Ira jerked woman's face towards him and smashed his knuckles beneath her eyes. The woman howled with pain. Her Helix died down and blood splattered into the air. The Blue's shoulders went slack.

"You disgrace," she wheezed.

"I'm not the hornless one," he replied.

"I'm going to kill you."

"I somehow doubt that, Blue."

"Who are you?" Voshell insisted. "I will not ask again."

Ira released the kodarian, and the Blue turned her bloodied face to Voshell. "Lieutenant Rasatha," she croaked. "And I was sent to kill you, you sadistic bitch."

Ira stepped behind Rasatha and grabbed her left horn, raising his blade to cleave it off. Voshell lifted her hand and he stopped mid-swing. Above, a crash of thunder indicated yet another Sobek storm. Rain began to pepper the canopy of leaves and branches, and drew streaks in the blood that stained Voshell's armor.

"That seems oddly foolish for General Sell," Voshell remarked, watching the woman's face. Animosity and hatred clouded the Blue's eyes.

"She's stupid all the time," Rasatha hissed.

Voshell frowned. Did this woman really believe she could take Voshell's platoon on with only twelve? Surely General Sell would never have—

A chill ran down Voshell's spine and a moment of horrific realization settled in her stomach.

"The rest of the Blues are coming," she breathed. She turned to Rasatha. "How many of you are there?"

"Hundreds. You'll never—"

"Kill her."

Rasatha blinked. "W-what? No! No, I—"

Ira reached around and slit the woman's throat before kicking her into the mud. Rasatha squirmed, her eyes flickering with terror as she felt her life slip from her second mouth.

Voshell's eyes lifted to Ira's. "We need to move. Where's Sindri?"

Ira nodded to the right, where the blonde was crouched behind a tree, keeping watch. "Safe, my queen."

"We need to move somewhere more protect—"

A body smashed into her from above, shoving her into the mud. The world spun and Voshell made out a raised blade only to see Ira's weapon spear through the man's eye. He pushed the body off her and helped the queen quickly to her feet.

"Our soldiers are exhausted," Ira hissed, eyes to the trees. "Your command?"

"Retreat," Voshell hissed. "Retreat to Platoon Three."

# Chapter 16

The blessing of rain had made Aris' soldiers inaudible to the unsuspecting Thrax. As Blues leapt out of trees and descended upon the Reds, she watched as blades made purchase with skin beneath armor, as blood stained the air, as a shout rose up among them.

*Retreat.*

Her smirk did not remain long; an explosion rattled the trees to her left, blasted a handful of her troops back. With a cry of agony, one had broken his leg while more still suffered burns across their faces. Aris' brows furrowed at the injuries, a memory clawing towards the surface: Salene with a smile, a joke upon the lips of an injured Jade.

"Friend Aris," Kuroda whined, stepping closer to her, his eyes peering around as his lower two mandibles fidgeted with worry. "Dangerous."

Aris looked at him, then towards the retreating Reds, barely glimpsed between the thick trees, now harried by the rain.

"Do you think you'd survive a bomb, Kuroda?" she asked, stepping forward as her Blues chased their prey.

"Unlikely," he replied. "Why approach?"

"We need to end this war, don't we?" She glanced back at him and offered a smile. "You'll help me so we can go home, won't you?"

Kuroda tilted his head. "Go home. Sounds nice. Yes." He stepped forward with her. "Help friend Aris."

He leaned down and nuzzled her cheek, affection she tolerated as her mind analyzed their next move. The Reds were quick to run. Did that demoted private truly do a number on them? Or was this a trap, some sort of lure to bring Aris' people into an explosive den and detonate after the last soldier crossed the line? It wouldn't be the first time the woman—

A flash of red hair drew her eye. Her heart clogged her throat, her expression filled with sudden, abrupt anticipation, excitement—joy, even. She wasn't dead. Of course she wasn't dead—but why was she still here? She should have hidden, ran, stolen away into the mountains. Being here now would ruin everything, being *alive* would ruin everything.

Two different colored eyes met Aris' gaze, one sunset orange, the other a crimson mechanical pupil. A large scar similar to the one Jade wore stole across the woman's nose. Her hair was pulled back into a bun, strands of red spilling out of it and soaked completely from the drenching rain. That wasn't Jade, Aris realized. That was the Mad Queen.

The queen turned and sprinted off. There was little time for logic. Trap or otherwise, Aris needed that woman's head to make any further progress on Nevar. Without it, Aris' pushing would lead nowhere and all of this would have been for nothing. Without it, Jade had no need to die.

She lunged forward, after the fleeing monstrosity. Her feet snagged on roots and vines and bodies. With a deep inhale, her legs swelled with Charge, bolstering her body's ability to launch her several feet through the air. She leapt after the Mad Queen, glimpsing that crimson hair once, twice—then a wall of fog rose up while she was mid-air. She landed within it and scowled, quickly retreating out as her soldiers rallied around her.

"General?" one asked.

"The Mad Queen is here," she said, looking back at the Blues in her command. She gripped her weapon and raised it high. "We end her and take back Sobek!"

Cries in agreement rose up and those with Atmo charged forward, using their own Helix to contest the Red's fog, pushing it away with gusts of unnatural wind, making a path for them to sprint through. Kuroda came to Aris' side, his chest heaving from sprinting after her. His green eyes met hers.

"Can track them," he murmured, his tongue slipping through his teeth and tasting the air. "Not sure which. But all together."

Aris smiled. She looked ahead as the fog began to dissipate. No matter how far that queen ran, she would take her head. She owed it to everyone here. She owed it to Salene.

In a small part, she even owed it to Jade.

# Chapter 17

Voshell had seventeen soldiers alive, not including herself, Sindri, and Ira. The strike had done more to them than she anticipated. Even their medic had been slain, his body loaded with supplies and trampled somewhere in the mud. The Blues trailed after them, never quite far enough for the Reds to take more than a few minutes to rest, to drink, and to jam their faces with what food they still had. Each snap of a twig sent everyone reaching for their weapons.

"Queen General," Ira breathed, coming to her side as they pushed forward through the blistering humidity of midday. "Are you certain we will make it?" His eyes met hers, both pairs ringed with dark circles of exhaustion. Sweat and rain alike dripped down his leathery skin. They were only moving now because to stop was to die. Each step brought with it a chance to trip, a chance to waste more energy to stand and breathe and sprint to catch up. Voshell looked at him and paused to glance at her soldiers.

Sindri was nearby—as ordered—but the rest of her soldiers were barely keeping up. Two of them had run out of water already. One held an injured arm, blood dotting leaves only to be washed away by the downpour. Four were covered in mud from falling due to leg wounds. One had a twisted ankle and dragged it along with a painful limp. Voshell looked to Ira. She touched her useless right arm.

"We need more time."

Ira looked to the mutilated six. He dipped his head in a nod and split off from her to tell them of their fates. Sindri frowned as she watched him go, her eyes shifting to Voshell's face.

"Where's he going?" she asked.

"To tell them their duty is done. Keep walking." She turned and moved onward.

"What? My queen, they have families—"

"And because mine are all dead now, *I* deserve to die?" Voshell bit back.

Sindri shook her head and hurried to catch up. "No, my queen, I—"

Voshell rose a hand and looked over her shoulder as Ira spoke to six troops lagging the furthest behind. Her human eye narrowed while her left focused on something in the trees. Movement.

"We must go," she hissed. She tapped her wrist holo, her movements sluggish and exhausted, fueled only by adrenaline. She grabbed Sindri's wrist and hurried ahead, tugging the larger woman along. Even as they gained distance, she swore she could hear shouting. She swore she could hear a young boy sobbing.

They risked sleeping that night. The Thrax climbed high into the trees and hoped not to wake from a Blue slitting their throat or a wild animal consuming their flesh. A watch was set up, each of them playing a part to ensure everyone got enough sleep.

Voshell woke last. She sat perched on the branch in a tree both Sindri and Ira were resting in, searching for signs of Empire soldiers. The rain had not stopped, but closer to the trunk she could almost get dry. She risked a moment to undo her bun and wring out her soggy

127

hair. A gunshot rang out and a bullet sliced the tip of her left hand's middle finger.

"Wake!" she shouted. "We're under attack!"

Her troops roused and she sought shelter on the other side of the tree, her heart pounding. Sindri jolted upright, eyes wide and full of panic.

Ira rose and situated himself next to Voshell with a grimace. "General?"

"We cannot be killed here, Ira," she hissed. She tapped her wrist holo.

*It has been an honor serving with you all. I ask one last sacrifice for the sake of your families—please, grant me more time. The weapon is nearly ready. The Blues will suffer for what they have done to us in a matter of days. Give me your names, and may we forever remember you as the final eleven that granted us victory.*

Their names were given, logged forever in everyone's holo. She knew they were willing to give their lives. Everyone always was.

A battle began as the three of them slipped away, Sindri pulled along with Voshell by order alone. Screams chased them on the wind.

And then there was nothing but the rain and the sound of their feet pounding against the sodden dirt beneath.

On the evening of the third day, mountains rose above the trees and its stone glistened in the waning light. The Third Platoon had come here, but besides the chittering of animals and calling of birds, it was silent. Voshell reached the edge of the forest, the trees giving way to a rocky ledge. She paused in the foliage, sweat-soaked and exhausted, grateful rain had held off for a few hours. As she peered up towards the mountain's tip, dark clouds moved towards her, indicating that relief would not last the night. No matter. She would get drenched before that regardless. With a deep breath, she looked to her final two companions, the last hope of the Reds. Ira stood at her right, at the side of her useless arm, his eyes dark and his face lined with guilt. His heart always hung heavy whenever they needed to sacrifice the grunts. She didn't understand it, but his misplaced compassion helped encourage the soldiers to throw their lives away whenever the moment called for it.

Then there was Sindri, at her left, panting heavily, having not spoken much since the first few injured were sent to die. She was beautiful, even when she hated Voshell's choices. The private would understand eventually. She would know that if those who stayed behind had travelled with them instead, all would've fallen to a grisly demise. Sindri was alive because of Voshell. Because Voshell knew she was worthy.

The queen looked ahead, dread building in her chest. A terrified, sinking feeling she hadn't felt before any battle before. Not since she was a child when that victer opened the door. Not since she watched her brother's stomach be ripped open. She reached over and gripped her shoulder. How long had it been? Had it been long enough? Would Malkov wake today, or would he wake sometime after? Would he ever wake at all?

*Did you think you'd found some sort of cure-all to this Blue disease?* Daxgor huffed. *You're nothing more than a child, Voshell. Nothing more than a Plural-eyed, useless child.*

Voshell gritted her teeth. It didn't matter now. None of it mattered now. All her pawns were dead. Her family was dead. Either she ended the Blues, or she died beneath their blade. She ran her hand across her face, up and through her tangled hair. The band that kept it in a bun had been lost, and now red strands hung around her face, stinking of mud.

She stepped out of the forest. A blade wasn't between her ribs yet. Until then, she'd do what she could to save the future of her kind from extinction.

Gnarled, twisting trees no larger than six feet broke out upon the rocky face of the mountain. To her left was the cliff, plummeting to a shore littered with discarded weapons and pieces of armor, some stained crimson. A waterfall spilled out of the mouth of the spire, gushing down to build a river that rushed along a crevice through the island. She came to the edge and peered down, the drop looking to be nearly fifty feet. A few ropes were tied to boulders nearby, proving that Platoon Three did descend if the metallic remains of their chest plates and boots hadn't given that away. Great beasts had certainly killed them. The question was: where were they?

Her eyes drifted back to the waterfall, where along the face of the mountain small, cylindrical holes were burrowed into it. As the sun began to dip below the horizon in the west, golden rays danced upon the river's face and made the spewing water look akin to jewels, revealing a collection of the holes bore visible claw marks. Her heart constricted. Each were dug deep, the larger the den the more likely for a mate. The males were often gone searching for food, but the females were aggressive, territorial, and extremely vicious when younglings were around. Indeed, seeing the dozens of holes across the mountainside, she understood why Platoon Three could not escape.

Strange, though, that no rye-dragon had spotted them yet, or heard them approaching. The creatures hunted during the day, their undersides stormy grey to hide themselves from prey on the surface. That left them all night to be back in their dens, and the creatures had an uncanny sense of smell. But if they hadn't noticed them yet, the mud the trio had traversed through must have somehow masked their scent. Nevertheless, they would proceed and hope to cross the river before the Blues caught up.

Voshell pressed a single finger to her lips and made eye contact with both her allies. She pointed to the only rope that hadn't been frayed then to Sindri, herself, and finally Ira. She pointed to the far side of the river. Their silence. Their order. Their destination.

Climbing down the rope without use of her right arm was challenging, and she constantly needed to use her knees and feet to brace herself as she dragged her good hand down the coarse material. It wasn't a fully straight drop, however, and where she could, she planted her feet and walked backwards, knowing Sindri's larger frame would catch her should she fall.

After a few minutes, the trio made it to the shore, careful as to where they stepped. A few chunks of gore were littered about. Voshell hadn't noticed them when she stood above, but they were speckled everywhere, making it impossible to not realize what happened to each and every Red who made it here. Her gaze fell on the caves and watched, for a moment, to ensure she saw nothing. Ira's hand touched her shoulder and pointed to the shore. Voshell nodded. Time to get moving.

To the water they walked, rocks shifting beneath their feet, gore squelching, discarded boots tumbling out of the way. Even their own armor shuddered across their bodies, the rye-mail scales beneath the metal plates singing with anxiety of being spotted by the dragons.

Voshell grimaced at each sound, shot a look to the waterfall, and found time and again that there was nothing. That was unnatural.

Something was wrong.

They entered the water, the chilled bite welcoming after a long hike over several days. A large boulder stood erect near the middle of the river, its sides polished and smooth from the constant harrying of the falls. Luckily the water did not rise more than Voshell's waist, and it was shallower for her taller human and kodarian companions. Each push forward was sluggish, draining more of Voshell's dwindling energy, until they at last reached that half-way mark, and her hand went out to touch it.

A shout of triumph and a bullet to the spine.

Voshell stumbled, her armor soaking up the attack. She spun to see Blues gathering at the cliff side near the ropes, crouching and looking down the sights of their guns in hopes of finding a weak spot and getting lucky. Voshell cursed and the three of them dived behind the rock. Sweat dripped down Voshell's face, her breath labored, her mind racing. The shore wasn't far, but it was open. They would risk being shot at. At this distance, it wasn't likely they would be killed, but there was always a chance. Her focus settled on Sindri. She couldn't take that chance.

Exaltations echoed through the ravine and gunshots rang out along the mountainside. Bullets punctured the water around them, chiseling holes out in the rock they hid behind. A curious, croaking chatter urged the three Thrax to look to the waterfall. And from it, eyes began to gleam in the darkness of the caves.

The muddy colors of the pups kept the creeping rye-dragons from being readily noticed by the attacking Blues. Stone-grey flesh stretched across their faces, the only section of their bodies without scales to allow for a larger range of expressions. Large, rice-shaped ears sat atop their flat, squarish skulls, tilted towards the sound of commotion and their piercing eyes of various colors flickered from one Blue to the next. Their long necks had hints of a mane growing out from beneath soft scales.

*No.* Her heart twisted. Her stomach surged. These children could be usable distractions, but she expected an adult. There should be more than one, considering how many burrows had been dug. There should be dozens. There should be enough to kill the soldiers pursuing her, enough for the bloodshed to mask her escape. Pups did not have hardened scales yet. Pups would not survive gunfire. Her heart pounded in her ears. She had lured these Blues here for nothing. She was going to die in a river. Her body would be eaten by Sobek animals. She would rot.

Where were the adults? Where were the mature ryes?

*You killed me for no reason?* Thaddeous asked, his voice jarring a headache into her skull. She gripped her temple, scowling. In the darkness of her mind, she saw him. He stood tall, a suit wrapped around his frame as perfect as ever, a constantly bleeding red line cut across his throat. It bubbled and spat, staining the top of his collar.

*You murdered the last of your family for nothing. Just to die hiding behind a rock like a coward. Some stupid Blue bested you.*

"Shut up," she hissed.

*No.* He stepped closer to her, clenched teeth shining like beacons in her mind. Perfect and white. Not a single one out of place, not a single crooked. Every little thing about him indicated he was nothing short of godly. Just like Daxgor wanted. Just how her parasite of a father nurtured her brother into maturity while she was sent to rot at the top of a mountain on Sypher, never intended to come home, never planned, never wanted.

*Father should have killed you. He should've shot you with our brothers. You're worthless.*

*Why couldn't it have been you?* Lionel asked, small, staring at her with hateful crimson eyes. *I would've made a great king. I wouldn't have brought us to this.*

*I would've learned how to improve our crops,* Adrian added, fidgeting with a book in his hands. *What have you done? You've sent us back. You've killed us. You're the reason we're dying.*

"Shut up!" Voshell lunged in her mind, in the river. She stumbled forward, out of the protection of the rock, eyes wide. She looked to her right, the galaxy around her slowing. The Blues were scrambling down the side of the cliff. Snipers on the ridge were taking aim at her. General Sell stood with a midnight monster at her side on the shore.

"My queen!" Sindri cried. Ira reached out for Voshell, trying to grab her hand and pull her back.

Her brothers were right. She should've died on that night.

An animal crashed into the river, stealing Voshell's feet from her and forcing her beneath the waves. An involuntary gasp brought water into her lungs. Her armor dragged her closer to the bottom where the current pushed her back towards the rock. Hands grasped and pulled, yanking her from the chilled depth as she coughed out what she had breathed, sputtering and grimacing through the burning in her chest.

A creature screamed.

The rye-dragon was ten feet tall, a full, ivory mane running down its neck and across its back. Scars cut across the flesh in its face, tore at spots in its wings and made sections of its throat bald. It was female, indicated by lack of external bone that would otherwise protect the rye's forehead and eyes. She opened her mouth and screeched again, displaying two incisors at the tip of her mouth, a fat, round tongue stabbing out as she cried. Her pointed nose flared as she sniffed the air and turned her nearly blind gaze to the Blues.

"Go," Voshell hissed to her two survivors. "We can cross the river. We can get the fuck out of here."

Ira's eyes were full of delight. "You knew this would happen?"

135

"Of course," Voshell replied. "Go." She grabbed Sindri's hand. "Stay behind the rock as much as we can for some sort of concealment. Heads down."

"Yes, general," Sindri breathed, her hands covered with sweat. The sun dipped beneath the horizon. The darkness would help. That would buy them time. And when the weapon was ready, all the Blues would die.

The boulder at their backs exploded.

In a rush of rock and gore, the rye-dragon tore through a body, shredded by claws at the knuckle of her wing. The boulder behind the segmented corpse had only been in the way.

Voshell, Ira, and Sindri threw themselves out of the dragon's path. The beast came to a stop over the remains of the rock, the wings she used as arms settling on the riverbed. Voshell splashed under the surface of the water and scrambled up to see the rye sniffing the air. The beast's eyes settled on Sindri. A hiss escaped her flat mouth, and the tail that swung at the base of her spine swept over the water. Voshell's eyes widened. She launched herself after the terrified Sindri, who turned and sprinted towards the shore. The rye's massive hind legs shot the creature forward. Voshell closed the distance. She shoved Sindri into the current.

And the rye sprinted between them, claws scraping across Sindri's back as the private fell into the water. Teeth caught Voshell's hand. Small fangs lining the creature's jaw dug into the queen's flesh, dragging Voshell along as blood squirted and spewed down her arm.

The jaws snapped shut. Voshell collapsed into the water. Crimson stained the fluids around her as she scrambled back to the surface. Sputtering and dizzy, she quickly looked down at her wound to assess the damage.

Bones jutted from the small portion of palm remaining and her thumb twitched, the only finger that survived on her left hand. Searing agony shot up her arm and dug into her eyes. She gripped her wrist with her right hand. A scream spilled out of her throat, echoing through the canyon, down the river. The rye-dragon turned. Bullets peppered her scales, nicked her face. She screeched, the metallic sound grating on Voshell's ears, and charged once more, splashing past the howling human. The rye fell upon the Blues, swinging the tail her species was named after: a wicked whip full of grain-like needles as large as a kodarian. Each could be flung, sent as a projectile to kill, or simply used to skewer those unfortunate enough to be caught in its arc.

But Voshell could not relish in her victory. Not while her hand spurted gore, while pain unlike anything else stole her breath away. Nausea rumbled in her intestines. Spots dotted her vision. Each thrum of her heart sent more of her life into the river. Each beat, and she could feel the talons of the victer cut open her face and eat her heart.

How was this worse than her arm? How did this pain linger more than losing an entire limb?

"Queen, your arm!" Ira cried, sprinting towards her. Voshell looked at him, then down at her hand, at the gleaming metal gripping her fleshy wrist. Her eyes widened. She could use her right arm again.

It was active.

She looked to the shore again. As the rye-dragon tore Blues apart, she spotted the general and her strange, ebony beast. Whatever it was, it stood taller than any sentient creature she had seen, and it locked eyes with her. Its eyes were green.

Jade was dead, then. Unless the galaxy made an exception to the rules dictating that only one Green could be alive at a time.

"This ends, Mad Queen!" the short, chubby general shouted over the noise of her soldiers being slaughtered. Voshell arched a brow and a laugh stole upon her lips. This woman looked at such a situation and somehow saw victory in it? The rye snapped its jaws over a Blue and tossed his body into the river before noticing the general and the creature at her side. She leapt towards them. And in a flash, so did the tattooed alien.

The dragon swept at the Green, yet her claws found nothing but air as the Green side-stepped. It opened its jaws and clamped down on the wing's inner arm, somehow finding purchase with its fangs and cracking the scales. The rye howled in torment, swiping at the Green with her other wing. Crimson blood sprayed as it yanked back, blood dripping down its mouth. A Green that could chew through a rye's thick hide? That was dangerous—

A blade's glint caught her eye and she kicked back before scrambling to her feet. General Sell stood opposite over her, forcing Voshell to ignore the warring beasts and focus. Her right fingers twitched.

"Sorry for the delay," Malkov cooed, the AI appearing in the air to her right. He stood just inches above the water and smiled. "What a sight. It looks perfect, queeny." He peered across the carnage. "Everything is ready for you."

"You're unarmed," General Sell hissed, her ice-blue eyes narrowing on Voshell's face. "Surrender and I'll take you in alive."

Ira was at Voshell's side in an instant, blade drawn, Sindri arriving a second after. The blonde Thrax looked pale and ready to vomit, but she held her weapon tight with unsteady hands. It was an effort, and Voshell appreciated the display.

"You're outnumbered," Voshell replied. She curled her fingers into a fist. Her left hand drooled red. "Ira, keep Sindri safe. Get to the shore."

Ira frowned. "My queen—"

"I'll follow you if I can." She looked at him. "Keep Sindri safe."

"I came to help," Sindri insisted.

"That's an order!" Voshell snapped.

Fog burst out across the water's surface, wrapping around General Sell's legs and barreling towards the three surviving Reds. Voshell cursed as Aris lunged, her blade smashing into Voshell's right arm. Vibrations made the Plural's teeth chatter and her ribs ache. But the heated edge wouldn't melt the prosthetic, something the Blue hadn't accounted for. With a scowl, the Blue's arms bulged with Charge, her strength multiplying as she stepped forward. Sell pressed harder against the queen's arm.

Voshell hissed another curse and stepped back, the rocks beneath her feet threatening to trip her. Her shoulder began to ache and the attachments of her artificial limb shifted against her skin. Metal scraped over her flesh. Sell drew back and assaulted the woman's middle. Voshell retreated.

Fighting a Charge wielder wasn't going to be easy. Most Helixes couldn't affect the queen, but that counted for Helixes that could touch her. Charge only influenced the user. And with the amount of blood her hand was gushing, Voshell knew there was still a growing chance she would be killed.

Sell stepped forward, the thick water slowing both women's movements. There would be no quick swipes from Voshell, but with Sell's Charge, the Blue might be able to move in a way Voshell could not. Sell jerked her blade down, the attack oddly clumsy and telegraphed for a general. Voshell narrowly evaded, grabbed the blade, and pulled. The Blue stumbled closer with wide, terrified eyes.

"Yes," Malkov breathed, a delighted grin cutting across his lips. "Yes!"

Voshell smashed her elbow into the woman's nose and it gushed blood. The crack of cartilage echoed through the queen's bones. With a yelp, Sell jerked back and swiped her blade blindly upwards, cutting a sizzling burn across Voshell's armor.

"Friend!" The voice held an accent Voshell couldn't place. It sounded deep, dignified, and tinged with ringing iron. She glanced towards the sound to find the gleaming green eyes of the ebony beast approaching through the fog.

"Shit." Voshell stepped a few paces back, raising her right arm to guard against his rye-crunching teeth. But with a screech and heavy footfalls, it was clear the rye-dragon was not yet finished.

From the fog's tight quarters, the dragon burst through, mouth open, blindly snapping at anyone it could. Voshell dived out of the way, her head falling beneath the waves. Garbled screams reached her waterlogged ears. When Voshell pushed herself back up to the surface to take a deep breath of air, stabs of icicle daggers filling her airways, she saw the rye shaking her head. A figure flailed in the clutches of her teeth.

The Blue general. General Aris Sell.

General Sell cursed and spat, smashing at the creature's teeth, breaking a fragment of them off before changing tactics and reaching up to push against the beast's gums. But the rye bit down anyway, and a broken tooth with two jagged edges punctured the woman's side. Armor crushed the woman's ribs before two other teeth stabbed into the woman's calves. Blood oozed, spilling down the creature's throat. The dragon shook her head and the Green wailed, throwing itself on the rye's wing and biting down once more. Voshell watched as the beast yanked off another chunk of meat and muscle and scales, forcing the rye to yelp. She dropped the general before turning her attention to her assailant.

The Blue smashed into the rocky riverbed hard. She struggled to push her head above the water, eyelids flickering. She wasn't too far away, still visible despite the fog.

"Now's the time," Malkov urged. "Go! Use me!"

Voshell nodded. Her arm buzzed with activity, vibrating as it warmed, blue lights glowing upon the neon lines. They pulsed once, twice, before her pointer finger held all the light at its point. The queen lifted her hand. She pointed at the general.

From the tip of her pointer came a radiant cerulean beam. It struck General Sell in the chest, shunting her back, her head forced beneath the water. It lasted a few seconds before the Blue climbed back towards oxygen, the fog making her nothing more than a shadowy shape to Voshell.

Then came the screaming.

Chapter 18

Raw and violent, the noise burned Voshell's throat just from hearing it. At the sound of their general's howls, the fog fell, dispersing in what seemed like a strong wind, revealing Sindri and Ira engaged in skirmishes of their own. The Blues looked to General Sell. And so did the rye.

In a flash, the Green sprinted between the dragon and the general. It opened its mouth, flared the four mandibles on the side of its face, and sprayed a sickly green liquid upon the rye's cheek. She screeched and reeled back, thrashing her head around. The smell of rotting, searing flesh spilling into the air in moist white smoke, sizzling and popping in splatters that fell into the water. They drained downstream in long, acrid trails. Voshell's eyes widened.

"Reds, to me!" she shouted.

The rye shrieked and flared her wings, beating them against the air. The river surged around her, splashing up against Voshell's armor and making her stumble. Sindri turned and bolted towards her, as did Ira after making a quick slice across the Blue's neck that he was engaged with. The Blue gasped and grabbed the bleeding wound, staggering back before the pressure of the wind toppled him into the water. The rye leapt into the sky, howling in agony, thick sections of flesh falling from her face, dripping into the river as it flew off downstream.

The Green looked to Voshell, eyes narrowed, viridian liquid drooling down its chin. Voshell stepped back. It turned its focus on the nearest Red, someone closer than the queen that it could kill. And sprinting towards her general in a desperate attempt to live, Sindri fought against the river's waves to travel the thirty-five feet to Voshell.

And about thirty feet from the Green.

"Sindri!" Voshell jerked forward. Sindri turned and saw the Green dash closer, a sac beneath its jaws swelling, its mouth clamped shut in preparation. With a swell of its chest, it spat. Voshell's foot caught on a rock and she tripped.

Ira shouldered Sindri into the water. The arching substance spilled over his face, his neck, his upper chest. Sindri came up for air just in time for her and Voshell to witness Lieutenant Ira's flesh falling from his body in clumps, revealing pulsing, throbbing muscle beneath. His lips were chewed through, displaying his teeth, which blackened and fell from his jaws as the gums were consumed. Terrified, pained eyes turned to Voshell, tears spilling down the acid burns that tore holes in his cheeks. With shaking hands, he saluted her one last time, his fists pressed against his right arm. The Green swatted the man out of the way and Ira's body fell into the water.

"Will it work, Malkov?" Voshell breathed as Sindri scrambled to her feet and dashed for her queen. The Green lunged after her, narrowly missing grabbing her armor. It steadied its footing and sprinted after the Red.

"Will what work?" Malkov hummed. His eyes watched the carnage. Watched the Blues hauling their general to shore, listened to the woman's hoarse, agony-filled screams. "The illness?" His eyes turned towards the Green, where it clamped its jaws closed, preparing for another spray of whatever acid it produced. Malkov chuckled. "Of course it will."

"Can you survive acid?"

Malkov looked at her, a scowl on his lips. "Excuse me?"

Sindri was about to reach her. Voshell jumped forward, pushed Sindri towards the shore, and threw a wild punch at the creature's jaw. Her knuckles cracked against it, the uppercut forcing a thin mist of his acid to fall upon both of them. The droplets descended upon Voshell's skull, into her hair, dotting her face. Despite the sensation of her nerves being lit aflame, no flesh slewed off her. So long as she could keep it from throwing a full blast of that shit, she might be able to do this.

The beast closed its eyes and its flesh shimmered, each scale becoming perfectly outlined in a hardened gleam. Ivory stained the plates where acid touched.

"Voshell!" Sindri cried.

The Green opened its eyes and swiftly kneed her in a stomach, the impact cracking her armor, jamming broken shards against her gut. Splinters of torment twisted her nerves. Before she had a chance to jump out of range, his right fist cracked against her temple. She staggered several feet to the side, blinking as her vision blurred. Her head swam with jumbled thoughts and horrific agony lacerated her mind. Voshell's mechanical eye focused first, and she swirled it upon him to see the pouch beneath his jaw still swollen with acid.

It opened its mouth.

Sindri brought her Charge-filled arm to bear against its ribs. The scales gleamed just before impact, and when the Thrax's fist made contact, her arm popped, shattered, and jutted a jagged, blood-smeared

145

bone out of the middle of her forearm. The Green backhanded her out of the way.

The queen's breathing grew shallow. She gripped the wrist of her right arm, felt the cold steel oiled with her blood, watched as the beast focused his eyes on her. Acid oozed from its throat, spilled across its green-soaked tongue. Should she run? Without her, the Thrax had no one to lead them. Without her, everyone still stationed on Sobek would die.

But the sickness was planted. The war was won. Every Blue would die. She swallowed hard and glanced to Sindri, who tried to shove the bone back into her arm, eyes burning, curses falling from her lips in droves as she spared a glance to Voshell. To her queen. They had shared a kiss. They had shared breakfast.

Perhaps, after what she had done, after Thaddeous, after Lionel and Adrian, that was all Voshell could hope for.

She took a breath. Maybe she deserved death. But she wanted those drinks with Sindri. Voshell wanted another kiss. She wanted her happiness.

"What are you doing?" Malkov hissed. Voshell brought her fists up. "I do *not* intend to die here!"

The Green spat. Voshell jerked her right arm up, blocking a large section of acid, though a few streaks stained her ears. The tips burned. She had no time to worry about what that meant, however, as she closed the distance and smashed the same right arm against the Green's jaw.

Malkov screamed, grabbing at his face as his form flickered and glitched, stained with red. As Voshell grinded her knuckles against the beast, she caught a glimpse of the damage done to the metal.

Sections of it were being eaten through, gouges in the silver, liquid settling in the bottom of the bowl-shaped wounds. Her fist cracked against the beast's face, and the arm bent slightly, screwing the slightest inch upwards along the forearm. She jerked back to retreat. The Green grabbed her arm. As she yanked, it snatched her left wrist. Blood soaked its fingers. It inhaled, a garbled sound of swallowing air and liquid rising out of his throat.

"You fucking *idiot!*" Malkov cried. "It's *eating* me!"

Voshell squirmed and tried to kick out of the beast's grasp. But she saw its fangs, she saw its jaws part, and she saw the green acid rushing out to meet her.

A force smashed into her, tearing her arms from her sockets as she was freed from the Green's hold. Her head cleaved into rocks beneath the water.

Her eyes rotted first.

Her mechanical eye flickered, the vision corrupting as blackness pooled in, static cracking before it fell silent. Her right eye boiled beneath the waves, popping after a second or two of horrific pain. As blackness enveloped her, as terror filled her throat, she screamed and clawed at her face, trying to pull the acid off her, feeling her thumb begin to rot. Her voice did not travel beneath the waves— that, or perhaps she had gone deaf from the acid chewing on her eardrums. She reached for them. Her right arm, however, did not heed her call. She felt tendrils snap out of her, pulling away from the entry points in her chest, her collar, her breast. And then she could not feel it at all.

Nerves across her whole frame began to convulse and her lungs seized up. She couldn't breathe. She couldn't stop screaming.

"Shh, sister," Thaddeous whispered. She felt his hand against her pocketed cheek, felt his perfect skin brush over hers. His lips pressed against her liquifying forehead.

"It's okay," he murmured. "I'm here with you. I'm here."

Her throat tightened as she inhaled water, felt it spill into her bones, weigh her down, tumble her over the riverbed. She reached out and felt her burning hand brush against his arm, up to his shoulder, to his face. She felt him smile.

"I'm here."

# Chapter 19

The world came to Aris in flashes, brief moments of consciousness filled with blurry eyes and sandpaper lungs. She coughed hard, spitting water from her airways as hands grabbed her, pulled her from the water. Screeches of baby rye-dragons stained the air, cutting across the bustle of activity, the indistinguishable words exchanged between people. A warmth spread across her chest, oozed out of her legs. It was like she was home, swaddled in a blanket by the chef, carried into her bed and laid there with a secret cookie that Aris would hide from her parents. As her eyelids cracked open, the world was almost peaceful, despite the coughing. The noise that filled her skull reminded her of Nanza City, of her home on Nevar. Maybe she was there. Maybe she was curled up by the lazy river outside, high above poverty, napping the day away. Unconcerned with being woken by someone else's nightmares, by a friend in a terrified state that she refused to explain, by the haunted look that followed her even into waking. No, maybe she was sleeping alone in her home city, no longer worried about someone else.

A slap to her cheek made her eyes flutter, the stinging sensation spilling through her face. She blinked and opened her bleary eyes, colors bleeding together as she attempted to make out the shape above her. The form was humanoid, two arms. Their voice was full of urgency, but she could not understand the garbled language that flooded her ears. Aris' eyes drooped close once more as warmth crawled up her throat, draining her of energy. A series of coughs forced chunks from her throat, sprayed saliva into the air, only for it all to come back and splatter across her skin. The voices grew more urgent. Rocks shifted beneath her, scraped against her armor. Hands grabbed at her. She was whipped partially off the ground only to fall back to the shoreline.

Terror forced her eyes open fully, both unruly as they attempted to roll back into her skull. She forced her vision down and saw her armor torn off, the leather straps that held them in place ripped and useless. The rye-mail beneath glistened with blood, and the ebony undersuit under it held a massive hole where the rye-dragon's tooth had punctured through.

The wound garbled, spilling more crimson out of its mouth with each pound of her steadily increasing heartbeat. It was much deeper than it should be. It was much deeper than what she could survive. Aris coughed once more, the rough, liquid sound spewing blood into the air. Something inside her had been punctured. An organ.

She was going to die.

A gentle hand touched Aris' stomach, and she followed the arm to see Kuroda. He spoke something to her, something she couldn't understand. Was it in his language, or was death already that close? Tears burned in her eyes.

*No, I can't die. I can't die! Not after what I've sacrificed, not after all I've given up for this!* She shut her eyes as a wave of pain accompanied by that ungodly warmth rolled up her body, sizzling and burning each nerve until her mind itself was ablaze. Frost gripped her muscles in its wake.

*I'm here dying just like my father wanted me to.*

A final snap of pain, one that crunched her bones, one that spread beneath her skin like a maggot ever consuming. Lava melted her hip away. This was it. This was what dying felt like.

# Part Two

Chapter 20

The news of the Green Demon's death circulated the Exuro Empire's public Feed for a week. Salene watched the first reports, where Golds congratulated a Blue soldier for the monster's death. Where they praised her before the entire Empire for her loyalty. Where they rewarded her with an apartment in the upper levels of Nanza City. The woman's name was plastered all over the headlines for a week.

*Can Blues truly be trusted?*

*Are Blues capable of holding back the Green Demon threat?*

*Can General Aris Sell be considered the exception to the bloodthirsty Blue rule?*

Each time she saw the name, the poised smile, those blue eyes staring back at her, Salene felt a bitter fire began to spill into her throat. Jade trusted Aris. Jade *loved* Aris. And that Blue bastard killed her.

Salene bit her lip and rolled onto her back in bed, letting her arm fall to her side and the screen displayed over her wrist holo to flicker and die out. She remembered what the Hazel support Feed had to say about anger: take deep breaths, and let go. She inhaled. She counted to ten. And she bottled the hatred up.

There had to be some sort of reason Aris had done all this publicity. Aris was smart and cunning. Maybe she and Jade came up with a plan once Jade's eye color became a real threat. Maybe this was all a grand, fake demonstration to fool the galaxy into believing the redhead had died. Aris had never been religious, anyway. Why would she suddenly buy the idea of Jade being the Demon?

Again, Salene took the rage and stuffed it deep inside her chest, smothering it as best she could as she sat up in her dimly lit room. Violence and rage were discouraged in the support feeds. It made the rest of the Empire hate them more.

Salene's parents had allowed her to move back in after everything had happened. The Empire provided no support for veterans, wounded, disabled, or otherwise. Once her final pay came in from her service in the Empire's army over four years ago, she had no means of income. And thus, she saw little point in spending what she had on changing her childhood room—besides taking down a few photos of the men and women she had crushed on when she was growing up. Now the walls sat bare, the cream color surrounding her and dotting a few spots on the wood floor. She didn't have any personal belongings after she was discharged, so nothing sat on her dresser, her nightstand, her windowsill. The only mementos she had were those saved on her holo. The messages Aris sent every few months, and the singular recording from Jade after Salene had been let go.

Salene clicked the band around her wrist, brought up a menu, and played the recording.

Jade was younger then, evident by the softened jawline, the shorter hair, the goggles strapped over her eyes. In this, grease stained her cheeks, and her hair was pulled back into a messy ponytail. She flashed a wide, pained smile.

"Hey, 'Lene," Jade breathed. Salene smiled a little at the nickname. "I'm so sorry for what happened. I'm so sorry for... for

153

leaving you on that beach." She exhaled, and the camera shuddered. She was recording from her own wrist holo, and that was evident as she kept dipping out of frame. "I know, in some way, that this is all my fault. But I'm going to make it right." The camera rectified itself and the holo's blue light reflected in Jade's goggles. "I'm going to make this right, 'Lene. We've had each other's backs for years. And I'm going to have yours. It's the right thing to do." Jade paused then, for about five seconds. Salene knew the pause by heart, had scrutinized Jade's slight lip movement, the way her jaw tightened and went slack again. The redhead had been considering saying something. Was this the moment, Salene wondered? Was this the moment Jade had intended to tell her, to take off her goggles, to reveal the viridian hue beneath?

Whatever Jade had thought about saying, she let it fall away. The message cut out and Salene was left staring at the menu once more, asking if she'd like to repeat the video for the two-thousandth time. Salene let her hands fall into her lap as her chest constricted in on itself. She had kept herself awake at night wondering for years what Jade wanted to say in that moment, but Jade never sent another message. She never said anything else. A deep, vile part of Salene loathed her for it.

Scowling, Salene pushed the feeling away and swept the blankets off her legs. She grabbed the remote on her nightstand and activated the hover chair resting on the floor nearby. After the aging machinery coughed and spewed smoke, it shuddered upward to match the height of her bed. Dexterously, Salene transferred herself into it and looked down at her legs.

She wore shorts, the blue fabric hanging loosely just under her knees. While her legs had thinned a little over the years, she had done all she could to exercise them, to build their strength and ensure her bones remained as strong as she could manage. If she sat down in a diner, someone might think she was able-bodied.

It would never last, though. Not here, not in the Empire. Not where scars were scrutinized for any evidence that they were received in the shameful war all Blues were sent to stop with their dying breaths. If she entered a business here—those that even allowed a Blue or Hazel inside—there would be stares, whispers about the scar on her face. The burn that wrapped around the back of her skull and consumed most of the flesh there. Being a Hazel was bad enough, but being one with noticeable wounds or disabilities made things worse. Street-side preachers often proclaimed that their god, Vix, punished the wicked soldiers so they might never forget their place in the galaxy. As tools to be used.

Salene took a breath and ran her hands down her legs, checking for any bumps or bruises she might've missed during last night's check. Thinking about it all made her stomach churn. It was better to smile and let it roll off her shoulders, because making a fuss only made things worse for the rest of the Hazels. Besides, it wasn't as if the other citizens realized what they were doing. They were all just part of a system. Should she really be mad at them, when they didn't know any better?

When she was satisfied with her check, she hovered over to her dresser and glanced in the mirror as she got her top changed. She had kept up with her upper body routines to keep her mind off what bothered her about the Empire, and she had to admit that she was rather pleased with the outcome. A smile slipped onto her lips. Jade would be jealous of her progress.

With a brush of her fingers, she pulled the dark curls over her scar, partially covering it. The little hair she had left wasn't exactly enough to hide it all, but just a small amount allowed for her to pass down the street without immediately drawing attention. A woman using a hoverchair, while not common, wouldn't draw the same attention as a woman with a chair and visible scars. Assumptions were made then. Assumptions about her eye color, which were almost always true.

She looked back to her bed and fetched a thin blanket from the mattress, snatching her small H-dagger from her dresser and tucking it between her legs. She covered it with the sheet and looked out the window on her right. The street was beginning to glow with morning light, sun drifting in through the drapes. She could already hear people passing by, chatting, laughing, rushing off to their jobs.

With a deep breath, Salene steeled herself. She would be one of those people. By the end of today, she would have a job. Try number one thousand, four-hundred and sixty would be her lucky number.


Breakfast with her parents was nice, as it always was. Brief, perhaps, with her mother needing to rush out for work and her father only popping in to quickly swallow his hash browns and fruit slice, before returning to his work on his next novel. She knew they had to work a lot harder now that she was living with them again.

Salene finished her breakfast and set the dishes in the kitchen before she moved to the front door. Today was the day. She could feel it in her bones.

Sypher's afternoon suns bore down on her. As one of the galaxy's largest planets, it had dragged small stars into its orbit to help heat the massive planet more evenly. Two smaller ones were in the sky today, residing nearly directly overhead as she pushed her chair haltingly forward. In the distance, past the city of Freightmore's thousand-mile borders, were the rising peaks of Sypher's grand snow-tipped mountains. On Nevar, a city like would be thousands of feet tall, but here the sypher people had restrictions on such things. Only the ports were allowed to be skyscrapers, and they were gathered in designated areas. Everyone else was settled into two story buildings at most, and despite the massive size of Freightmore, the population of the planet hadn't even managed to use up one-fourth of the planet's surface. And, unlike Nevar, Salene could actually see the sky.

It was beautiful here.

A train whizzed past somewhere nearby, rumbling through rows of trees and making Salene's chest thrum with thunder for a few seconds before it was gone. Because cars were outlawed, all the citizens of Freightmore got around by walking, biking, or taking a train. While there were a few select bikes that would work for someone in need of mobility aids, they were expensive. Just like the train. She needed that money for food, which, given the state of her aching stomach and wheezing hover chair, was about time to find.

As she looked around at the rows of buildings to her left and right, she noticed a few people gathering in front of various stores. Cautiously, she turned herself towards one nearby, the smell of fatty noodle bowls drawing her closer before a customer was shoved out of the crowd. The snipper man stumbled and fell, a massive laceration scar across his right eye highlighting his hazel gaze. The other citizen, a kodarian with chocolate brown eyes, spat on the dust.

"Didn't you fucking read the sign, turncoat?" the Brown snapped. "Get lost."

The Hazel, grimacing, pushed himself to his feet. He was missing three of his four arms. Quietly, he slipped away, and Salene pulled back from the crowd. She peered at the windows of all the nearby restaurants she could see, and sure enough, surrounded by the choking fumes of candies and cinnamon and roasting kennock, she saw them. The plastered displays stuck to the inside windows on scraps of paper or written on the glass with broad, painted strokes:

*No Blues! No Hazels!*

*Only Loyals!*

*Blues and Hazels Are Not Welcome!*

Salene sighed. Well, if she couldn't buy food here, she could at least rest her chittering chair in the shade before it decided to completely give out on her. She used the joystick to guide it to a nearby alleyway, shaded from the sun, and weaved past two dumpsters before coming to a stop. Salene grimaced as her chair settled on the ground with a wheeze, but at least it would get some rest, and that would hopefully keep it going until she was able to pay for repairs.

*Or a whole new chair. Vix, what a thought.*

Salene leaned back and closed her eyes as the stench of garbage and acrid vinegar stained the air around her. It was almost enough to ruin her appetite, but her mind was distracted by noise to the window on her right. She cracked an eye and spotted the unshuttered opening, which she hadn't taken notice of before. From inside, she caught a man's voice ringing out:

"… and so the Blues were created out of the heart of a volcano, crafted from the burning excess and gifted with Vix's teeth. For they were born to have a hunger for destruction and fangs to fuel their bloodlust. Vix has placed them under our guidance and given them primal brains so that we may point them to our enemies and allow them to drive wrong-doers out."

Salene's lips tugged into a frown. *Church.*

"This is why the Blues are devoid of a moral compass. If their feelings of right and wrong got in the way of war, they would not make for good weapons against our enemies. This was clear when the Blue soldier killed the Green Demon only a short time ago. She had been a friend to the Demon, and had that marred her morality, that monster would have run rampant through our cities already."

*She lived twenty-seven years of her life without running rampant,* Salene thought bitterly. Coals sparked and sprang to life in her chest. She rubbed her legs, hoping to calm down. She just needed to give her chair some time to rest in the shade. After a little while, she could leave. *Just calm down.*

"But no, that Blue stood strong in the face of a monster that tried to manipulate the Blue with friendship! It was foolish. Perhaps such a tactic would've worked on you, on me. Blues, however—they're something else. These ties they create are not as strong as yours or mine. They are capable of being cut with a single moment, and the Blue will not suffer for it."

*He's acting like we're all fucking animals. That we're incapable of any sort of relationships.* Salene dug the heels of her palms into her legs. *Like we're less than animals. Like we're less than insects.* She gritted her teeth. *Stop it. Stop it. Deep breaths. Just like the forum said. Deep breaths.*

"This, my fellow Followers of Vix, is why we cannot allow the Blues to gain the right of inner-city housing."

Salene's eyes widened. An inferno spilled into her mind.

"They are incapable of understanding what friendships mean, and their first reaction to problems comes with violence. They are dangerous around us, around our children."

"Around your children," Salene muttered under her breath, vitriol seeping into each syllable.

"The young Blues may seem like children, but they are scientifically more likely to cause harm than any other eye color! The Hazels, even though they are traitorous to their own identities, at least are less likely to harm others."

"Because half of us starve to death," Salene hissed. Her hands bundled into fists against her legs.

"The Blues, on the other hand, have been the root cause of violence in many sectors around the Known Galaxy. On Nevar, their crime rates are higher than any other!"

"Because we all live in the fucking slums." Salene's voice grew in volume.

"Consider what that means for your children, when they are young and impressionable. Not only are they at risk of being victim to a Blue's violence, but their eye colors, their *loyalties,* are still quite impressionable! And there is nothing more a Blue loves than converting a child to their ways!"

"We're not after your *fucking* kids!" Salene screamed.

A dreadful, deadly silence spread across the alleyway and through the congregation in the building beside her. Salene's hair stood on end. She clasped her hands over her mouth. Her heart thundered in her ears.

*Please, Vix, tell me they're going to ignore that.*

"Who said that?" the preacher cried. "What demon dares defile this sanctuary?"

Footsteps started towards the window. Salene slammed her hand against the button on her chair and it coughed out a thick, gassy fog into the surrounding area.

"What the—?" the preacher gasped.

Salene's eyes burned and her throat closed up. Starting her chair now was a bad idea. It wouldn't last long under this abuse, but she couldn't sit around to see what a mob of Vixens would do to her when they discovered she was a Hazel. A turncoat. A Blue who betrayed their identity.

The chair lifted about a foot off the ground before she pushed the joystick forward. A door slammed open behind her somewhere, her chair's footrests scraped across the gravel ground, and Salene shot out of the cloud, trailing black tendrils behind her and forever staining her clothes and hair with the stench of burning metal. She veered through the street, to the other side, and wound through back alleys and lesser-used footpaths. People leapt out of her way as she slipped through the maze of buildings.

At last, she broke free of the houses and businesses and into a small recreational area. An upraised train track cut through the grass and trees, and there was an underground walkway beneath. She could see it was shadowed and dimly lit. Without hesitation, Salene steered herself there, reached the darkness, and shoved her hoverchair against the wall before abruptly deactivating it again. It skittered across the gravel before jolting to a stop. Her chest heaved and she spat black saliva onto the dirt, iron and oil coating the inside of her mouth.

Salene looked over her shoulder towards the light of the afternoon, waiting. She hadn't been the victim of anti-Hazel or anti-Blue brutality before, but she knew all too well what it looked like. She had seen the stories on the Feed. She had seen the pictures. She clenched her eyes shut and listened.

Nothing.

With a sigh of relief, she leaned back into her seat. Sweat drooled down to her lips and mixed with the flavor on her tongue. She spat once more. That's when she noticed she wasn't alone.

On the other side of the path were a pair of blue eyes watching her. Tension returned to her chest, restricting her airways. Blues weren't violent by nature, and she knew that from being one herself. But that didn't mean they didn't hate Hazels just as much as the rest of the galaxy. That didn't mean they didn't consume the same indoctrinated bullshit as everyone else.

"It's just me," the man said, his voice like a wheezing ox. "I don't hate Hazels."

Salene relaxed. "I don't hate Blues."

He chuckled. "Then we're in good company. What made you fly in like that?"

"My mouth got away from me."

"I can relate," he rasped. His shadowed form shifted, and she could see from his outline that he was a muscular man.

From all around, the ground began to shake as a train approached, speeding through on electric rails faster than she could fathom. Her ribs shuddered as it whipped by overhead and, for a brief moment, she shut her eyes and heard gunshots.

The train passed.

"Reminds you of the war, huh?" the man asked, looking upwards. "It reminds all of us of the war. The shaking. The bombs. The gunfire." He shook his head and ran a hand over his face. "At least we didn't have to search dumpsters for a meal when we were on the frontlines, though."

Salene peered over at him. Though his eyes caught the light, she couldn't quite see what species he was. "Do you have no family?"

"No. Mom died in the war a few years ago, and dad followed shortly after during his deployment on Taotar."

A flash of Jade's face ran through Salene's mind. The way shadows lingered under her eyes. The way she woke up screaming at night after going missing for several days on Taotar. She had told the Reds nothing. But she had come back with wounds that laced her back and mind.

"I'm so sorry," Salene breathed. "I know how hard it is to live as a Blue. I'm with my parents right now, and we don't have much, but maybe you could—"

He held his hand up, and she caught a glimpse of the pale grey, leathery skin dragged over amputated fingers. "I appreciate your kindness," he said. "But I could not impose myself upon a Hazel."

She peered at him as he lowered his hand. He had to be kodarian. But why didn't she see horns? "I know most Blues avoid people like me."

"I know what it's like to be ostracized from the few groups that might still accept you," he said.

Salene's eyes widened. Sorrow swallowed her lungs. "Your horns."

"They broke them on my first day home about a year ago. They take years to grow." He scoffed and shook his head. "Not sure if a human knows that. Our tusks grow faster than we can manage, but our horns? Break those, and we bear that shame for a decade." He gestured vaguely at her legs. "Did they—?"

"No, no," Salene said quickly. "No one at home did this. This is what caused my eyes to turn."

"Ah."

She rubbed her thighs idly. He lifted his wrist and pressed a button on his holo, the dull blue screen illuminating his face. Small eyes were pressed into his skull and lacerations mangled his face, scars mixing with recent scabs. His temples were naked, and the ivory growths that should be sprouting from his cranium were jagged stumps, barely an inch in length. Salene watched him as he tapped the screen then stood, walking over to her.

"Living like this is torture," he said, looking down at his full height of six feet. "But there's a Feed to vent frustration. And a Feed to change things."

"Oh, ah…" She brought up her holo and received a notification indicating someone wanted to share a post with her. Salene accepted it. A chill crept through her intestines.

*How Would You Change The Galaxy?*

The author was General Aris Sell. Below it were hundreds of posts, one after the other, each growing in ferocity about wrongdoings inflicted upon them. Each stating they wished something changed. There was only one comment by the author, highlighted in the chain of responses.

*Then let's make a plan.*

"I must be off," the kodarian said. Salene nodded numbly. He turned and headed towards the way she had come. It wasn't until she read the news headlines that she realized he had been carrying a gun.

# Chapter 21

Out of the fog, Aris dragged herself to consciousness. Her throat was heavy with salt, each swallow bringing tears to her eyes. As she blinked, her eyelids tried to stick together, and only with great effort did she manage to rouse herself once more, peering into the piercing, blurry light.

As she took in her first ragged inhales, something akin to roast meat flooded her senses, the sound of chatter and drips upon a popping fire following shortly after. With a grimace, she tried to focus her eyes, squinting into the light in hopes of making sense of the white and yellow shapes that meshed together in her vision. Slowly, the colors separated, and she saw she was resting in a tent with the sun above her flooding through the canvas.

Trees cast shadows on different beds around, filled with injured soldiers. Most of them didn't look like they were breathing. As she turned her attention towards the smell of meat, she noticed the tent entrance to her right, the flaps closed loosely, allowing her to see shapes moving just outside. A crack of thunder far. A memory of a redhead curled in a corner, muttering that she wouldn't say, she wouldn't tell.

Aris shook the thought out of her head and tried to push herself up, only for a stab of pain to force her back, a hiss of agony slipping through her clenched teeth. She reached down to her side to assess the damage, only for her fingertips to meet cold, metal tendrils. She peered down, brows knit together.

While her breasts were still covered with her sports bra and her crotch clad in boxers, the rest of her was exposed. The discoloration of her flesh shone with near-white vitiligo spots across her stomach, chest, legs, and inner arms. With her left hand, she covered one as best she could and spared a moment to look for a blanket. She saw none nearby.

Her legs were wrapped, each soaked with red. She tried to flex her right foot and a surge of agony ran up into her hip. She managed to point it downward, but when she attempted to lift her toes up, she was unable to. She tried her left. With great difficulty, she was able to move it, but barely, and the moment she stopped trying, it dropped, hanging limply. It, too, came with burning bones and sizzling nerves.

Then was the item attached to her side, where a deep, deadly wound should have been. Silver, streaked with bright blue lines along each reaching tendril, like a beast with several legs, dotted with rust-colored holes. One limb reached out across her rounded gut, another up towards her ribs, two down towards her leg, one towards her spine. Such a machine was foreign to her. She did not bring it to the front lines, nor had she heard of any sort of device before she left. Unless the Golds somehow graced them with a good thing—which she doubted—this item was unknown. And thus unwanted.

She reached towards it, gripping the small, flat surface of it, trying to hold on tight enough to pull it up. Her fingers slipped, however, and she found herself quite unable.

"You're awake," came a voice she did not recognize. A rumbling headache boiled up in the back of her skull and a moment later, a man was there, at her side, smiling. She jerked away and met his eyes, frowning when she saw they were silver. She had met too many people recently with eyes she didn't recognize—first the pirates, now this. Even Kuroda's eyes weren't clear.

The man was tall and angular, with long raven hair falling in messy waves down his shoulders. A jacket rested around his torso and it fell into a tail behind his feet, stained deep blue and vibrant yellow accents. He flashed a small smile and each of his perfectly white teeth were set without flaw into his gums. Nausea churned Aris' gut. She grimaced and looked away, placing her hand over her mouth as she shoved the contents of her stomach down.

"Ah. I'm guessing you'll get used to that," he said with a hum. "As I assume you'll get used to the eyes. I'm sure they're quite strange for you all to see." He chuckled. "Though, I'll be honest, it's much stranger for me to see you all share the same color. Well, except you. Yours are a little icy, aren't they?"

Aris narrowed her eyes at him as she laid back against her pillow. "Who are you?" Her voice was coarse.

He tapped his lower lip as he watched her. "You're a general, aren't you?" he asked. "General Sell?"

"You didn't answer—" The nausea came again, and this time she could not keep it down. She turned, her injuries aching, and vomited stomach acid onto the muddy floor beside her bed.

"I'll take that as a yes," the man said. "Well, General Sell, I have some wonderful news for you."

She gasped for breath at the side of her cot, closing her eyes as sweat gathered on her brow and the aching headache grew louder.

169

She wiped her mouth along her forearm, saliva and bile smearing across skin. Her eyes caught on the white spot on her arm.

He could see her vitiligo.

"Get out," she hissed.

He grinned. "Don't you want to know who I am, General Sell?" he purred. "Why I'm here and my voice has not brought any of your soldiers in?"

Her brows furrowed. She looked towards the entrance then back at him. Her troops were still chatting outside. She could hear a few of them cheering.

"Yes, you're curious," he said. "Quite curious. Curious about me, about that little device in your side. Well, I'm here to help you, General Sell. I'm here to make your life easier. I poked around your head while you were asleep. I know what you're trying to do." He leaned towards her. "My name is Malkov, superweapon of legend, capable of destroying anything you desire." He bowed. "Currently, I am packing your wound."

An AI. Her eyes jerked to the metal in her side. "That's… *you?*"

"Aren't I stunning?" he hummed, straightening and running his hands over his dress shirt and jacket. "Compact, concealable, all you could want. Truly, my creator knew what he was doing." He looked at her. "Once connected to the flesh, I am able to properly respond to my master's will."

*The weapon. Jade mentioned a weapon. She said Voshell had it...* She frowned, eyes on the blue streaks across the metal.

"That light that hit me in the chest." She looked to him. "That was you."

"Ah, unfortunate." Malkov sighed and shook his head. "But not to worry, I have properly paid for such an act. That little... *friend* of yours managed to burn some of me." He smiled again, blood drooling from his lips. "It was quite unpleasant."

Aris blinked. He was back to normal. Her frown deepened.

"What was it you shot me with?" she pressed.

"Oh, that?" He laughed. "A virus, of course! That redheaded *monster* wanted to kill all of you." He shook his head. "Truly unwelcome, truly barbaric, if you ask me. But not to worry, Miss Sell. So long as I am with you, that virus will not kill you, and neither will your wounds."

"I'm infected."

"In a way." Malkov nodded.

"And I own you?"

Malkov's smile dropped. "In a way."

"Create an inoculation and cure to the virus constructed to kill us," Aris ordered. "I want it to be contagious so we are immune to whatever this illness is and was. It needs to spread to each and every Blue easily so no one can get sick from what you put in my body."

"You think she gave you something like that?"

"I'm not a fool," Aris hissed. "I'm well-aware of how my enemy thinks—*thought.* She would not have just wanted to kill me. She wanted to kill my entire race so the war would end."

A slow, creeping smile curled his lips upwards. He chuckled. "You are intelligent. No wonder that Voshell wanted you dead. Yes, you've shed to your fellow soldiers celebrating out there. The symptoms won't appear for another week or so, but I'll make that inoculation in approximately five days. None will die from it."

"Explain how you function to me."

Malkov clicked his tongue, amused. "How badly do you want that cure?" he asked. Aris grimaced and gripped her head, a hammer smashing away at the inside of her skull. "Should I waste time explaining everything to you now, or just get to work?"

She scowled. He was hiding something. But for now, she needed the cure more than she needed answers.

"Very well. Get to work."

"I look forward to our work together, Miss Sell." He bowed, and with a blink, he was gone. The headache faded as well. And soon, her stomach settled.

She disliked having an AI attached to her in such a way—an AI that was working for the enemy days before. She rested her hand against the metal and brushed her thumb across its pocketed surface. He was cunning. And she hadn't been naïve to the fact that his presence came with a series of side effects. Still, this was what Jade feared—this machine that Voshell had gotten her hands on. Jade had failed to stop the Mad Queen. Aris did not.

A smile crossed her lips.

# Chapter 22

The damage to her legs made it so Aris couldn't walk. Her left tibia suffered a full break with a partial break on the right. The medic, a snipper with grey hairs and vibrant tri-pupiled blue eyes, suggested there was likely further damage to the muscles and perhaps the nerves, but until Aris healed or returned home, there was no telling for sure.

Upon her request, Aris was given clothes donated by her soldiers, which covered the spots on her skin. Getting the pants on was agonizing, but it had to be done. She had earned their respect. She couldn't lose that the moment they saw how ugly she was.

Her arms were sore given her overuse of Charge during the previous battle: both to attack the Mad Queen and break the tooth of the rye-dragon. The knuckles of her right hand were bruised and caked in layers of dried, reddish-brown blood. Like this, she was a liability to her troops. But she was alive. That was more than could be said for the majority of her platoon.

Aris relied upon her medic and Kuroda to inform her of the well-being of her troops. She had Kuroda carry her out during the evenings to chat with her survivors, twenty in total, who were glad to speak with her, and glad, too, for Kuroda's company.

The camp had been moved away from the rye-den, brought back into the trees upon the cliff, where it was too dense for the deadliest—and oldest—rye-dragons to go. The troops took time to recoup, to rest, to mourn and be merry. Not a single Red had been spotted nearby. The bodies of the Mad Queen, of her advisors, had all been dragged downstream. They had won. And the Blues deserved to go home to their families.

On the fifth evening, Kuroda entered the medical tent with a bowl of soup. Aris was the last one on a cot, the others either recovering from their injuries to rejoin the others, or succumbing, and being tossed over the cliff and into the river below. Keeping carcasses too near would bring the attention of larger predators willing to risk entering a group of Opes for a meal. The mangled platoon didn't need to fend off the wildlife in their state.

Aris gingerly pushed herself upright. Her legs ached, but her side had long since gone numb. In fact, all the places the tendrils of Malkov's body touched were a blind spot for her nerves.

"You are looking better," Kuroda said, his words punctuated and slow. He nodded, his mandibles flaring out in an expression of delight. "Practice. Friends show."

He knelt beside her cot and handed her the thin metal bowl, warm from the steaming broth. Flower buds and chunks of mystery meat floated within the thick liquid, topped with various leaves and herbs. The chef must have harvested nearby plants. She hoped they were actually safe to eat.

"Thank you, Kuroda," Aris said. She set the bowl on her lap and curled over it. She spooned up the muddy-colored food and brought it to her lips. The heat was almost too much for her to bear, but as she chewed the mystery meat and herbs, the buds popped in her mouth, spilling bitterness across her tongue and mixing with the salty vegetables she thought were protein, and the bland dried rations that were mixed in. It was hearty, but she couldn't help how her nose scrunched. Kuroda watched this reaction curiously, tilting his head as she attempted another bite.

"Almost out of food," Kuroda said after a few minutes of silence. Aris frowned and peered at him.

"Are we?" She sighed and shook her head. "I've been delaying us too long. We should get moving. Head back to base." She looked towards her legs as a particularly strong flower broke in her mouth. Her lips pursed and she swallowed hard. If she could walk even a little, that would be beneficial. As it was, she would need to be carried.

"Are you able to hunt?" Aris asked slowly. She looked to him. "When you fought that rye-dragon, you were able to do so unarmed and without getting hurt. And you're the one that tracked the Reds. The others would really appreciate you if you were able to bring more food."

He huffed. "Bring food for friend. Help get stronger."

"They're all you friends, Kuroda."

"You most friend."

Aris allowed a smile. "Thank you, Kuroda. That means a lot. Have you already eaten?"

"Will eat after you finish." His tail dragged across the ground, pushing dirt and pebbles along with it. "Stay with friend."

She chuckled. "All right, Kuroda. Thank you for your company." After another bite, her face screwed up once more, and with his small right hand, he pointed at her.

"Strange faces," he said.

She peered at him as she got her expressions under control. "Strange…?"

"You do not make faces like that," he elaborated. "Your point—it gets wavy."

"My nose, you mean?" Aris idly rubbed the bridge of her nose. "It's because of the bitter food."

"Bitter?"

"Yes. Ah. Have you not had bitter food before?" She investigated her bowl and scooped up one of the pods, draining the broth against the side of the bowl to see it better. Leaves were tightly woven together and came to a point, making the round shape nearly oval. The broth left brown stains across it, but she could see the green and yellow colors bleeding through underneath.

She offered it to him. "Why don't you try it? Then you'll know what bitter means."

He leaned forward, his mandibles spreading as far as they could go and his jaw dropping to allow his viridian tongue to roll out. As he closed his teeth around the spoon, she could see his tongue pull the bud into his mouth. He then leaned back, scrapping fangs against the spoon, and rested on his knees once more. Due to the gap between Kuroda's mandibles, some of his pointed teeth were still visible, and behind those, she could see glimpses of him rolling the pod around in his mouth. She snickered and rested her spoon in her broth.

"You have to bite it for it to be bitter," she said.

177

His eyes met hers and an expression crossed his face that she had never seen before: his upper mandibles curled, making an angular 'J' shape, before he looked away. There was an audible pop as he adjusted his jaw to break the flower. His brows scrunched together.

"Bitter," he said before swallowing.

"Yes, that's what it tastes like. It's generally a little intense."

"Many like this at home." He turned and rested his head against her cot.

"What's your homeplanet called, Kuroda?" Aris asked as she returned to her food.

"We call it *Keklakak*," he replied, slipping into a language that wasn't Os. "It same word for home."

"I'm sorry you had to leave. You must miss it." She scraped up the last of the chunks into her mouth before bringing the bowl to her lips and drinking the broth.

"Do. Would like to return. Not for long time."

"You learned our language really fast," she replied. "Have you always been good at learning?"

"Language easy," Kuroda replied, sitting up and taking her empty bowl from her hands. "*Keklakak* has many. Was king. Learned all."

"You learned *all* the languages on your planet?" Aris' brows lifted. "How many were there?"

"Twenty-seven. Three most spoke."

"That's amazing, Kuroda."

Kuroda chuckled, the sound like a rumbling engine deep in his chest. "Friend praise. Is good."

"Yes, well… why don't you help me up? I'd like to see my troops."

"Why wear thick?" He tugged at the long sleeves that covered her arms, soaked with sweat. "Hot."

"It is," Aris admitted, "but it's necessary. I have to be decent. Having clothes on makes sure that I'm appropriate to be seen by others."

Kuroda tilted his head then looked down at his own body. "Descent."

"*Decent.* You don't need clothes, Kuroda, you, ah… well, there's nothing for you to cover."

"Like marks. Good to show them." He nodded and after making sure the bowl was out of the way, he stood and put one arm behind her back, and gingerly slipped the other beneath her knees. His smaller hands grasped her clothes, tugging her closer as he lifted her up. Pain shot through Aris' hip and into her jaw as her injured legs moved. She inhaled sharply and shut her eyes against the pain. Kuroda paused to peer at her when she was settled next to his chest.

"Am sorry," he murmured. "Did not mean to hurt."

"It's okay," she breathed, exhaling the aches away. "It's fine, thank you." She looked at him and smiled. "They're just sensitive, is all."

179

"Mm." As carefully as he could, he walked her out of the tent, backing out of it in hopes of her legs not catching on the fabric. He turned around and she saw the familiar sight of the new camp: tents set up in a tight circle around a fire pit, where the chef had his pot of stew, dishing it out to those who still needed to eat. Aris could hear the man's ladle scraping the bottom. Trees surrounded them and the distant sound of the waterfall could still be heard. Though screeches and cries came from the mountain, no ryes ventured towards them. It seemed the mother was not interested in revenge.

Sixteen soldiers were before Aris, one of which was the chef, sitting on logs and chatting while she spotted two other soldiers patrolling and keeping an eye out for Reds and predators. They were a large enough party that most wild animals shouldn't bother them, but there was always a chance.

The chef spotted her first, an aging kodarian man with deep ebony skin and horns that greyed closer to his skull. He was clad in a tank top and shorts. Sweat dripped off his brow and splattered into the meager contents of his pot. He flashed a smile when he saw her and quickly saluted.

"General Sell," he said.

The others heard his reverence and turned to see Aris in Kuroda's arms. They all stopped what they were doing to salute her. To give her respect. To acknowledge her. It was hard not to notice how warm her chest grew, how pride made her fingers buzz with electricity.

"Thank you," she said, dipping her head to them all. "But the true honored ones should be you all. The battle with the Reds was not easy, but I'm glad you're all here."

The chef chuckled and returned to ladling out his stew to waiting soldiers. "You say so each time, General Sell. Just because we salute you doesn't mean we don't respect our own efforts in this."

"You say that, private, but have you eaten some of your own stew yet?"

He smiled. "You've got me, general."

"Kuroda, if you would, set me down on that log there, please. I should be fine being able to sit up on my own."

Kuroda dipped his head and set her down on an overturned log, moss and grasses growing across its slowing rotting length. However, it still seemed firm enough not to collapse beneath her. Her legs ached, but Aris managed to endure it and look at all those around her.

"We've battled hard over the past month, troops—longer, for many of you. You've had two generals in recent memory, and both of us were nearly claimed by this war. You've lost many friends and comrades, but the Mad Queen is dead. And the Reds will be scrambling to find a way to recover for some time." She took a breath, legs burning, her toes curling from the pain. All eyes were on her, so she kept any indication of such agony away from her face. "I thank you all for fighting alongside me, for being the force that brought that monster down. Because of you, many more will live. And it's because of that, I do not think we can wait for me to recover any longer. We must move on." She looked at the faces turned to her. She smiled. "We must go home."

"Home?" The soldier nearest to her, dressed in her undersuit and rye-mail, stared at Aris with wide eyes. The human looked to the woman at her left, before both looked back at Aris. "You mean…?"

"Yes," Aris said. "After how hard you've fought, how much you've suffered, you all deserve to go home and be with your families."

Smiles and cheers rose up, and a few sprinted off to tell those keeping watch the good news.

"Pack up!" Aris continued. "We move in ten!"


The main Blue encampment was a few weeks away. Chasing the Mad Queen through Sobek forests had drawn Aris further and further away from that semi-reliable safety, and during the battle with the rye-dragon, their long-distance communicator had broken. While they still had local maps and an idea of where to go, there would be no way to tell her higher-ups that she was coming, nor any way to have them send out a party with food and water should Aris and her limping platoon run out. With twenty total mouths to feed, their limited supplies would expire soon. Still, as exhaustion hung onto them and dragged their feet, and sweat dripped down their noses, Kuroda managed to keep everyone's mind occupied with conversation, his curiosity never ending.

"What is your home?" Kuroda asked the snipper on his left as they walked. Aris was cradled in his arms, and as Kuroda walked, he did his best not to bother her aching legs.

"My home?" Private Katlego repeated. His upper shoulders shrugged while his lower pair of arms swung by his hips as he walked. "I was born on Nevar. My parents are there, too, so I'll go back to live with them after all this."

"Family good," Kuroda said with a nod. "Good to stay with family."

"Yeah," Katlego replied, a sigh on his lips. "Sometimes I wish I could live alone, though. Have my own place to call home."

"Why not get?"

"Well, if I left now, I'd only have enough kniri to buy a place down on the first level of Nevar. And if I'm down there, I'm bound to get a disease from the factories, or get shanked before I'm thirty." He chuckled. "I'd rather not bleed out because my apartment got broken into one night."

"My old apartment is up for rent," Aris offered. "The Golds ransacked it since the Green lived there, and ah, because of that, it's fairly cheap. It's on the third level, so not much better, but it has a taxi pad outside and we've never had any break-ins."

"Home alone is… better?" Kuroda asked. "Live alone?"

"It's nice for some people," Aris explained. "You get more privacy when you're alone."

"And my parents' place is pretty small," Katlego said. "It's impossible to watch any shows or read or even take a nap because everyone's always talking." Katlego snickered. "Hopefully they kept everything I recorded. I've been away for nearly two years now."

Aris let out a breath as an ache bloomed across her lungs, her trachea, slipping down into her lobes like oil, forever doomed to coat everything in a layer of blight that kept her from breathing. With each inhale, she could feel it spread further, spill down her throat and slosh into her intestines.

The last time she saw her mother was after the victer assassin was killed. When she and Jade stood over the body like criminals, lit by the neon signs that illuminated Nanza City's night with blues and bleeding oranges. Her mother had looked at her then, blood trailing from her lip where the victer had cut her. The woman's fair skin was perfect, even in the odd light, her blonde hair flowing over her shoulders in gentle waves. Her golden eyes gleamed like beacons of royalty.

"I see you've gotten fatter," she said then. "Get off my property."

They travelled until the sun dipped out of sight and night forced them to halt. Camp was made, a place for a fire was cleared in the overgrown forest, and dinner was cooked up for the exhausted party. Stories were shared about who was returning where, and what awaited them. Most were returning to their families, to their parents, because they didn't have money to live on their own. One Blue, clad in light, oversized armor, was hardly sixteen. She had a roommate and had moved out with someone to the lower levels of Nanza city. But that roommate had been killed in the previous battle. Rent was due upon her return.

Conversation spiraled into discussions of politics, expertly led by Aris' subtle hand. There was distaste of how things were going, how the Golds, shrouded in their cloaks to hide from their political adversaries, directed the war.

"I met with them," Aris said as ferns glowed blue around her, as orange bugs danced in the dark. "I met with the Gold council. I saw their faces."

Her soldiers turned to her, eyes wide. "You *saw* them?"

"Yes," Aris replied with a nod. A distant growl echoed from within the trees. "There is practically one of each of the main races. I knew their faces when I was a child, though. My parents are Golds." She chuckled and shook her head. "They disowned me when my eyes turned blue."

Katlego scoffed and shook his head. "Just like Golds."

"How old were you?" another asked.

Aris knew there was no way for them to check if she told the truth here or not. Unless one of them made it to the rank of general, or higher, it was unlikely they'd have access to records like that. And if they did, it would be far too late to cause an uproar about her lie. Still, she thought she'd better opt for the truth, as that was much more powerful.

"I was pretty young. Ten? Eleven? Maybe younger?" She shrugged. "I was at a party. A masquerade. We went to a lot of those. My eyes were still malleable. We didn't realize that, but they were. I dreamed of being a powerful and noble soldier, while my parents wanted me to lose weight and be a politician."

The Blues chuckled at this. Aris smiled and adjusted how she sat, her back against a tree, her legs spread out. As she shifted, water oozed up from the moist dirt beneath her and insects skittered away.

"We all see how that turned out," Aris offered. That was enough to bring a few laughs from her soldiers, distracting them from the eyes in the forest, the watching reflective pupils of animals that blinked in and out of existence somewhere in the shadows. They had scouts, of course, keeping an eye out for Reds, but most had turned their attention to Aris' story. Kuroda, standing beside her, would likely deter any attacker as it was.

"We went to the party, and my mother turned around and said to me: 'Don't you talk to anyone about Blues, Aris. Do you hear me?' And, of course, I said yes, I heard her. We got to this massive building, high up on the city levels, and arrived to see this ballroom with chandeliers and hardwood floors, and wine for all the guests. Except me, of course. I was the only child there, dragged along to be shown off, nothing more. So here I am, and eventually I see some people talking poorly about my father. Well, that can't do, so I go to listen but I spot this girl being pulled along by this older guy. She looks drunk. I had seen people drunk before, and she looked completely out of it. And he seemed entirely sober.

"I have a bad feeling so I follow them," Aris continued, her voice growing grave. She looked down. "I followed them and saw them in this room together. She was telling him to stop. To get off her. He was covering her mouth."

"Oh my Vix," breathed a young private. "You were *how old?*"

"Young, but I knew this wasn't right. I knew it was vile and she was telling him to stop. So I sprint in with ideas of being a hero, and with my Helix, I grab him. And there was this massive window in that room, like all fancy Gold houses. Huge window that took up the entire wall. Well, I yank him away from her, and he's startled and confused and telling me to let go, right? He's saying he's important, and who is my mother, and all this. The girl on the bed is crying. And I'm so angry, I just... Throw him." She took a breath, the air hot and heavy. "Everyone heard the window break. His body made it down to level ninety-nine before it hit a walkway." She shook her head. "When the trial came about, the woman who was hurt wouldn't speak out. She was scared of the Golds and what they might do to her if she slandered one of their own. She said nothing was happening. They were just talking. They were going to sentence me to jail when they saw my eyes had changed. So they sent me off to basic training instead." She took a moment to look up at her soldiers. "Golds are shit."

The camp burst into laughter. Their voices echoed in the camp before Katlego cut through it with a question:

"Your parents didn't support you when you told them what happened?"

"I killed a political leader," Aris replied. "As a Blue. And since the woman didn't speak the truth, they didn't believe me. I fell

187

into the stereotype of violent, reckless Blue. To save face, they publicly disowned me during the trial, and I was sent to training with nothing but the clothes on my back." She shrugged. "But can you expect anything else from a Gold? They do this constantly. They belittle us and send us out to die. They don't care what happens in the war, they don't care that they're sending out thirteen year-old kids to die. All they care about is that they stay in power, and they keep their hands from getting dirty." Aris pushed a frown onto her lips, readied herself for the final sell. "I apologize, my friends, I should not be speaking this way to you all. It isn't befitting a general in my position to complain about the way things are back home."

"But it's true," said the chef. "They don't care. They'd rather we all died out in the war, I think."

"They don't even think we're sentient," said another.

"Why else would they send children to fight?"

"Look at the armor they give us! The Thrax have it better. Why do we have to scavenge the battlefield just to have a chance to survive?"

"Or buy it ourselves? We can't even make a living back home with the wages we're given. How do they expect us to purchase armor?"

"They don't," Aris cut in. "Because we are nothing but tools for them. Tools to send out to fight and die and delay the Thrax longer and longer. They profit off this war, my friends, don't think anything else is going on here. We make them money with our dying bodies."

There was silence then, cut only by the buzzing and chittering of bugs, the fire between the group flickering and spitting out sparks that fell upon glowing vines and glimmering flowers. Aris watched her troops as they looked at one another, faces grave. And she waited. She waited for the single question she needed to start it all.

"What are we supposed to do?" Katlego asked, looking to her for guidance.

Aris smiled at him. "I'm so glad you asked."

# Chapter 23

By the time the sun broke across the horizon and spilled crimson hues across the morning mist, the Opes soldiers were already breaking down camp. Breakfast was the same as dinner from the previous night, and though the bitter flavors elicited complaints from the troops, everyone ate all they could. Rations would be spread thin from this day forward, and hot meals like this wouldn't be frequent.

Aris sat on a log and watched curling strands of white fog obscure four feet above the ground. As was every morning on Sobek, the air was heavy with enough water to drown, which stuck to foreheads and dripped down arms as each Blue pulled their armor on for the morning trek. Their general turned her attention to the medic by her feet, which rested upon the length of the log. She leaned against her hands to keep herself upright. The bark oozed moisture and threatened to make her slip. One soldier stood nearby, using their Atmo Helix to keep the fog clear as the medic looked over Aris' wounds.

"Tell me if you can feel anything," the medic said softly, touching her left foot and rotating it. A sharp spike of pain snapped Aris' jaw shut and breath speared out of her lungs.

"I can feel that," she hissed. "The fracture hurts."

"But you have feeling. That's good." He nodded. He moved to her right. He took her boot in his hands and turned it. It took a few seconds for pain to come, the sensation delayed.

"Minimal," she reported. "Minimal feeling."

"Ah." He nodded and stood. "We'll check it again in a few days, General Sell. For now, you will need to continue to be carried by Kuroda. Otherwise your condition will worsen."

Aris exhaled. "That—"

Her skull rang with agony as a headache began to pound behind her eyes. She grimaced and touched her forehead as a bit of nausea rolled into her mouth. She swallowed hard.

"It's a good thing I'm here," Malkov hummed, appearing on her left, hovering just above the wavy surface of the mist. "Otherwise you might never heal."

"General?" the medic breathed. "What is it?"

"Nothing," Aris replied, motioning him away. "Leave me for a moment. Join the others in packing up. Ask Kuroda to come to me if you see him."

The medic frowned but nevertheless saluted and slipped away, bringing the private with him and leaving her to Malkov in the midst of camp, surrounded by noise and motion. Aris looked to the hologram that made her skull feel as if it were being split in two.

"What did you say?" she asked.

"I will be able to heal you," he replied, a smile resting on his perfect lips upon his eerily symmetrical face. "You surely have noticed how that wound in your side hasn't killed you yet?"

Despite her desire to, she did not touch her side. "And I suspect that is somehow your doing?"

191

"It is," he said. "Of course, if I am removed, I cannot promise your injuries will not kill you within a few hours." He shrugged.

"Ah." *A power play.*

"Indeed," Malkov hummed, "a power play. Let us speak plainly, General Sell. You are nothing without me." He leaned in. "So you'd better cooperate."

"If you're trying to threaten me, you're wasting your time," she said, her voice even and cold. "If you need me as a host, then we simply need to work together." She wiped her hand off on her breastplate idly. "What is it you want?"

"You didn't like my little scare tactic?" Malkov mused. "You are an interesting sort, aren't you? Yes, well, I would only like to uphold my primary function. I would like to be used. I would like to kill."

*A homicidal robot. Interesting.*

"Not just a robot," Malkov interjected. "An Artificial Intelligence. More than simple gears. I have a *soul.*"

Aris arched a brow. There seemed to be little point not to speak her mind with him, so she replied: "You're a bunch of gears who believes it has a soul?"

"*He,* to be precise. Though I suppose 'she' would work fine as well, or 'they.'" He waved his hand dismissively. "But not 'it.' And who is to say I don't have a soul?" He smiled at her. "You?"

Each of his teeth were perfect. His canines pointed, each one glistening white.

"It's a surprise, is all. Most religions believe that if you have a soul, it's immoral to kill," Aris replied.

Malkov laughed. "Then I suppose we all go to hell?"

Aris watched him. She said nothing and kept her thoughts as focused on emptiness as possible. He smirked.

"And what is you want, Miss Aris Sell?" he purred. "I've had a look, of course. I have an idea." He pointed to her side. "I can target down to the smallest strands of DNA. I can target two people only."

"Why would I want to kill two people?"

"You know why."

A flash of surgical tables, of tears, of blood and vomit spilled upon the floor. The cold golden gaze of her parents. Aris grimaced and shut her eyes against the burning headache, grabbing the bridge of her nose with a hiss.

"Did you do that?" she snarled.

"Did I?" Malkov shrugged when she looked up at him. "Who is to say."

"Is your damn vaccine ready for my troops?"

"It is." He smoothed out his dress shirt. "Prepared and safe for use. As I've not… *requested* access to your arm, the process shall be a bit tricky. I will need your troops to stand within range of your hip, where I am located, and allow themselves to be shot."

"Excuse me?"

"It will be quite harmless. Not blood or vomit or whatever you spat up into the river," he said. "They shall be perfectly able to live their little lives." He grinned. "But I do hope things on Nevar will be more exciting."

Aris turned and looked at her troops as the last tent was packed away. "I suspect it will be."


Her troops were inoculated, one by one. The blast sent each of them staggering back a few steps, but none bled, not gagged, all seemed well enough after the fact. Aris didn't enjoy putting blind faith in a robotic creature who seemed keen on murdering, but there was little choice.

That, and she had an odd feeling that he was telling the truth. That her troops had been infected and that these shots were the only things that saved their lives. Usually she could read someone's face to glean if they were lying, but now she simply *knew* he wasn't. Perhaps their connection allowed her such insight.

They began their hike towards the main Opes camp once more, trudging through the fog, their feet snagging on roots and causing many to stumble. Kuroda seemed to have little trouble pushing through the forest, holding Aris close to his chest as gently yet as protectively as he could. Over her shoulder, she could see her soldiers trudging along in misery. Several fell beneath the mist and rose again a moment later, covered in mud and leaves. She wished she was with them. It would be better for a general to be seen struggling along her troops.

Four days passed. Their food reserves were in dire need of replenishing. They reached a pass across the river where the water was slower and allowed large boulders for steppingstones. They rested before crossing, allowing Aris' troops a moment to catch their breath, but soon a storm approached, and they were forced onward. Those with Charge helped those without it. Everyone made it to the other bank. And further they travelled.

There were six days left of marching by the next dawn. Their progress had been impressive, but their food was down to scraps and by the evening, there would be no more. They began their trudge through the trees at dawn. Thunder crashed and rain punctured small holes in the fog around them. The smell of soaked flowers and drenched leaves hung in the air next to the damp scent of drowned mud beneath their feet. The morning sun spilled orange and red across the landscape, highlighting the dark circles beneath eyes, silhouetting the slumped figures of exhausted soldiers. They were close. They just needed to keep moving. Aris turned to look over Kuroda's shoulder and opened her mouth to urge continued perseverance.

That's when Cadoc, a human male perhaps twenty-two of age, screamed. He stopped near the middle of the pack, yanked against something unseen beneath the fog, and was pulled beneath, vanishing from sight. Aris' breath caught in her lungs. Her heart stopped.

"Kuroda," she whispered.

Kuroda quickly spun around to face the Opes soldiers. Cadoc dragged himself up, his head just visible above the wispy, ivory grasp of the air around him. Another private lunged to help him. A massive serpentine head rose.

It was a diamond-shaped skull, larger than that of any sentient creature Aris had met before. Flattened, as if stepped on, with eyes gleaming gold on either side of its face. Spines rose out to form something akin to eyebrows with three nostrils running on either side up to its unblinking gaze. The pale beast practically was the fog, melting into it with ivory scales that did not shine. It opened its jaws and two fangs unfolded from the roof of its mouth.

"Private, get back!" Aris shouted.

Her words were swallowed by the sound of the beast snapping at Cadoc's arm. Its teeth smashed against the man's armor as Cadoc's companions leapt to his defense. Katlego swung his blade, slicing a line into the creature's neck, spraying blood onto his lips. The beast turned and dove beneath the fog. Kuroda pressed Aris tighter to his chest as a growl rumbled from his throat. He licked the air before angrily snorting out a huff of air against her face.

"Can smell you," he grumbled.

Aris cursed. "Everyone, stay close! We need to get out of—"

Screeches rose. Dozens of voices joined the horrifying chorus. It was a nest. A nest of okehesa.

The sound of the storm seemed to fade, rain stalled during its fall. Dozens of heads rose from the fog.

All of them lunged.

She had no time to bark orders or to think. Within moments, Aris was assaulted by three okehesa. Fangs dug into the gaps, pressing against the rye-mail but unable to cut it. She groped for the weapon on her hip as her other hand clung to Kuroda's neck. He jerked them back as jaws snapped down around his shoulders, as snakes wound around his legs. Aris' fingers grasped her weapon.

The okehesa clamped down around her arm and yanked.

She fell beneath the fog hard, her legs aching with horrific pain that made her teeth ache and her head throb. She squinted through the white field of nothingness, the chilled air blinding. Two beasts started to wrap around her legs.

Her bones snapped and crunched, and her own screams rose to meld with those of her soldiers. Aris dug her fingers into the soft earth and tried to pull herself away, but the beasts were determined. She could feel them wrap over each other and pause above her knees. They jerked, lunging at one another, yanking her left and right and bringing tears to her eyes. She grabbed for her weapon again, blindly feeling in the void. Two pairs of yellow eyes appeared at her left. An okehesa rose up, materializing from the fog. Its jaws opened and its fangs extended from the top of its mouth. Aris clutched her H-blade. The beast lunged.

In a terrified, wild swing, Aris activated her weapon and extended its blade. It found purchase, digging into the scales and the meat of the okehesa's neck and tearing through the other side. The head landed next to her face, barely visible except for the gleaming yellow pupils and the crimson blood oozing from its throat. Her legs popped as the snakes below her waist warred over who should eat her. With a shaky breath, her mind bleary with agony, she swung once more. The pressure around her legs slackened and she quickly sat up, shoving the thick, hot forms from her. Sticky blood coated her hand.

197

She looked around, shouts and yells and cries of horror still staining the air with fear. She curled her toes and felt something snap in each of her legs, a searing iron pressing to her nerves. Her people needed her. Her troops *needed* her. She could not remain beneath the fog. She had to stand.

She pushed her Charge to her legs, the Helix thick and warm as her bones shifted beneath the bulging muscle. Then, with a sharp inhale, she pulled her legs to her.

The pain was unlike anything else. It forced her hair to stand on end, her stomach to churn, her head to reel. The world spun around her and she felt as if she might lose consciousness. But she couldn't stop. She had to help. Aris situated her feet beneath her.

And she stood to the chorus of her own bones cracking.

Chapter 24

Above the choking fog was a bloodbath, crimson staining the air and drooling down the lips of Aris' soldiers—those that still lived. A small band was huddled back by Kuroda, following him as he fumbled through the mist, searching for her. Katlego caught Aris' eye.

"Our general lives!" he cried.

The two other soldiers couldn't spare glances. They sliced another okehesa and shouted to one of their comrades to run. Aris gripped her blade until the leather handle dug seams into her palm. She stepped forward, her Helix cushioning her bones enough that, hopefully, they would not break further.

Another okehesa struck at her. Teeth cracked against her armor as it tried to take a bite out of her stomach. Aris staggered and quickly sliced the throat of her attacker. The snake screamed, its voice ear-piercing. Gore spewed while it whipped back. Fatty, acrid blood splattered into Aris' mouth, staining her tongue with its flavor. The beast fell beneath the fog. Two ebony hands grabbed her shoulders.

"Friend," Kuroda breathed. Aris jolted at the touch, but had enough sense not to strike him. She blinked a few times and offered a nod. He picked her up and cradled her in his arms again while Aris clung to her blade, ready to strike at anything that came close.

But nothing did. Red dripped off tree branches and the fog that was once whipped into a frenzy now calmed, relaxing into a slow, rolling motion. Aris looked at the soldiers she had left. Three. Only three had survived the nest.

That would have to do.

"Are they done?" Katlego whispered, the blood of his enemies staining the hairs across his face, dripping from the pincers on either side of his mouth.

"They're not hungry anymore," said the second, Private Qiu, a kodarian female with oxen horns. "They've eaten enough."

"We need to go," Aris said. "Do any of you have Atmo?"

"I do, general," said the third, a sickly looking human. The man's face was dotted with stubble and dark circles hung under his eyes. His skin had an odd green hue to it. Aris frowned. But now was not the time to ask.

"Can you clear some ground beneath us so we don't step on another okehesa?"

"I can't do a big space since the fog is so thick, but I could do it for myself so long as everyone follows me." He coughed into his hand. His fingers were already bloody, but Aris could've sworn she saw him spit out more.

"Do it," Aris said.

And so they went. Step after step, the group left the scene of the massacre. There was hardly any water left, no food, and now with such small numbers, animals were sure to take notice of weak looking prey.


They lost the human before they made it ten feet out of the okehesa den. He started to cough and would not stop. He fell to his knees and vanished beneath the mist. The two soldiers looked to Aris for guidance.

"We have to keep moving," she rasped. Thunder from above. Rain soon.

They kept moving.


Kuroda protected the small band the best he could. The wildlife of Sobek was relentless, creatures stalking in during the night and beasts charging them through the day. Aris wondered how the Mad Queen hadn't been killed off by such aggressive monsters, only to remember that her full platoon was stalking the woman and likely scared off any would-be attackers.

They had brought down a creature with fingered feet and tusks, a beast with viridian fur and yellow eyes. Aris had no name for it, but Qiu knew how to gut and skin animals from her time on Daoth. A planet of plains and deep ravines, a planet that a redhead with green eyes hailed from. A storm rolled in while Qiu worked, and they could not find dry wood to start a fire.

Kuroda was able to consume some raw steaks without issue, saliva and blood dripping down from his jaws and splattering on Aris' spaulders. He used the fur of the beast to wrap the meat, then tied it around his tail. He held the carcass off the ground and, with only one mouth fed, the platoon headed out once more.

The rains didn't stop for another few days, but at least they had water. Aris checked her map. Three days until they arrived. Despite the good news, no one was particularly happy about it.

When the rain broke, everything was damp and unusable. Qiu had Blue Lightning as her Helix, and she tried several times for a spark to light the driest bundle of branches they could find. It was no use. And with the meat bringing unwanted attention from the eyes of predators, they abandoned it after Kuroda took another chunk for himself.

A day away from camp, Katlego couldn't stand. Starvation made his body weak, his hands shake. As the fog settled in around them, Aris reminded him of home. Of his family, of how he wanted to watch shows with them. He couldn't die here. Qiu helped him to his feet and slung his upper right arm over her shoulders. Travel was slow. Perhaps the animals of Sobek could smell death on them, as beasts stalked just out of sight, in the trees, between trunks. Kuroda growled, his eyes watching a form somewhere in the waking forest. An okehesa slithered along a tree branch above. Aris eyed it as they all passed below, its yellow gaze on her, ivory tongue tasting the air. It continued on its way without another glance.

Another storm could be smelled in the air as clouds gathered above. The sun reached its peak then began its decline. The troop drank the water they had gathered during short breaks. When the sun had dipped beneath the tops of the trees and spread long shadows over the forest floor, bringing the heat down to a more bearable level, the sounds of chattering voices began to rise in the muffled distance. At first Aris wasn't sure what she was hearing: perhaps chittering birds or scampering beasts? But then she could make out the distinct sound of Os, the garbled mess of people talking over one another, the distant sound of laughter. The forest broke open into a clearing, where stumps and uprooted ferns still littered the massive space. As an operations location for all Opes on this island, the encampment could house at least three or four platoons easily, with room to grow. Between her and the first tents was about thirty feet of open ground, and the moment Kuroda stepped forward with her in his arms, the guards spotted them immediately. An alarm was sounded as the last of the sun's rays died upon her armor.

To her left, Katlego collapsed.

# Chapter 25

Katlego was rushed to the medical tent, Qiu, Aris, and Kuroda following close behind. The man was hardly breathing, chest rising a fraction before falling once more. His legs dragged across the ground as several soldiers hauled him towards the tent, Qiu ducking in after him. Before Kuroda could follow, they were stopped.

"General Sell," snapped the harsh voice. Aris placed a hand on Kuroda's chest, below the man's nostrils, and Kuroda turned to face the one speaking to her.

Standing there was General Kasaar, with gleaming blue eyes and a set of armor clasped around his body. His horns were adorned with black jewels, and his tusks were perfectly blunted.

"Why are you being carried by that… *thing?*" he asked.

Kuroda's eyes. A growl tinged his voice as he spoke: "Not thing. Kuroda."

Kasaar regarded the larger beast, glanced around at the Blues watching, and smiled back at Kuroda. "It can talk."

"This is Kuroda, General Kasaar," Aris replied, her voice even. "Because of him, we made it back alive."

"Ah. Then I shall report the mission as a failure." He turned to leave.

"Did I dismiss you, general?" Aris asked. She watched tension line his shoulders and he looked back at her, eyes narrowed.

"Excuse—"

"I don't believe I did. Not only that, I never said I failed in my mission," Aris continued. "The Mad Queen is dead, and so is her army. The rye-dragons at the mountain's base tore her apart."

Kasaar blinked. He turned fully to her. "You…?"

"I did what no one else could, yes," Aris said. "I suffered severe damage to my legs and the Mad Queen massacred my platoons in the process, but she was slain. The rest of the Thrax forces will be in disarray."

His mouth fell agape. "*You* slew the Mad Queen?"

"Repeating myself is unnecessary. My troops and I did what no one else could." She inhaled sharply. "They deserve leave, as do I. I am requesting a transport off this planet back home."

Kasaar regained himself as a scowl curled his lips downward. "That isn't something you can—"

"Unless you are admitting to your own incompetence," Aris replied, her voice smooth. "Unless you're saying you need me and the last of my troops to finish off the disorganized Thrax stragglers across the planet. Is that what you're saying, general?"

General Kasaar glared daggers at her, silent. His blue eyes flared with hatred. His jaw tensed. He was hardly breathing in the sickly wet air.

"We have managed just fine without you," he said at last.

"Is that so?" Aris said, a smile curling her lips. "I seem to remember quite the opposite, general. But perhaps you've forgotten what that was, hm? Perhaps you've forgotten your shitty decisions while you hid behind lies and secret messages." She leaned forward, a smirk on her lips. "Perhaps you've forgotten who is in charge here."

"If you think you can intimidate me—"

"I *know* I can, general. I know because I've already done it. You will call for a ship. You will take me and my soldiers home. And you will take care of the rest of these Thrax before I return."

"You do not outrank me," he growled. "I have half a mind to warn the Golds of what you're planning."

"And what would that be, Kasaar?" she chimed, leaning back into Kuroda. "Have you figured it out, then? Or are you spouting half-truths and rumors? My plan was to kill the Mad Queen. And as you can see, I've already done that." She smirked. "Oh, forgive my manners. Have you met Kuroda, general? *Properly?*" She patted Kuroda's shoulder. "I'm sure you've been dying to meet him."

Kuroda's eyes were on Kasaar. The slits that served as his pupils were in a tight, hostile line, hardly visible in his murky green irises. Kasaar gritted his teeth, his eyes shifting to the tall beast.

"You *just* introduced us," he said. "Whatever game you're playing, it is not amusing."

Kuroda snorted out a breath, the hot air pushing strands of Aris' locks into her face. He stepped closer, and Aris could see the slight twitch of Kasaar's muscles, the way his eyes flickered from toe to head on Kuroda, how he looked ready to step back before deciding to hold his ground. Was that sweat, or just moisture from the air that collected on his forehead? Was that momentary frown a sign of fear?

"You send men," Kuroda growled. "Many men. None worthy. Little to eat." Kasaar held Kuroda's gaze. Kuroda flared his mandibles. "Perhaps you worthy," he said. "Perhaps fight. Perhaps no scream."

"What is he talking about?" Kasaar said, rooted to the spot.

"You want blood," Kuroda said. "I give blood. Give your blood."

"That's enough," Kasaar hissed.

"Oh, I don't think he's done," Aris said with a smile. "Or perhaps he should vent his frustrations to the council?"

Aris watched his fingers bundled into fists. So the Golds had not told him that he was under investigation for treason. Or perhaps the message hadn't reached his ears yet. Interesting.

"We're on the same side, general," he said.

"Are we?" Aris asked, the warmth in her voice replaced with a menacing chill. "I seem to remember differently. I seem to remember you praising the demon for all that it did for you while it was useful, and telling no one of your discovery regarding its eyes. I seem to remember you placing me under planet-arrest. I seem to remember your shitty tactical moves getting us killed." Her eyes narrowed. "I told you what you were doing was foolish, but you only listened when the Green spoke. And now look, general: I've done what you couldn't do. I've surpassed you."

There was silence. No one spoke for a long while. Kasaar held her gaze unending until, at last, he took a breath and dipped his head.

"I will request a ship, general."

Aris smiled once more. "Good man."

# Chapter 26

"*You're* Salene Vyrr?"

The Blue soldier stood on the dock of Sobek's pier, clad in a light suit of armor consisting of little more than a chest plate and rye-mail. With the mail exposed, the small, individual scales could be made out in the dim light of Sobek's dawn. Her hair was pulled back into a tight black bun, her dark brown human skin akin Salene's. The soldier rubbed her eyes.

"I thought you were a Blue," she muttered. Salene flashed an uncertain smile, situated on her hover chair as it rattled and clanged above the deck of the privateer. A blanket lay over her legs, and her hands clutched the armrests on either side as the Blue regarded her once more.

"Ah, I was," Salene offered. "I fought here—"

"Whatever, Hazel," the woman hissed. "Get off the ship."

"Oh, right." Salene pushed the joystick forward on her left armrest, and her chair, after a moment of sputtering, hovered over the plank and down onto the harbor. The dock rocked a little beneath her, this particular port being situated on the water of Sobek's surface. It extended over to the base of the floating island, where a series of walkways shifted and swayed, leading all the way up to the land above. By far, it was the most unpleasant of harbors in all the planets she had visited. But laying anchor in the water allowed for the ships to be hidden by scanners due to the highly magnetized force of the islands themselves. It kept them safe, sure, but Salene still remembered her first time disembarking and having to climb miles just to get to the island proper.

"No one said you were a cripple," the soldier said, flicking through her wrist holo, eyes scanning over the messages she had received. Salene idly combed her hair over the right side of her face, her fingers brushing the burnt skin beneath. The Blue looked up and stared. Just like everyone did back home. Salene cleared her throat and looked away.

*Why are my scars worse than yours?*

"Getting through the forest is going to be impossible with you on that. Can you walk?" the Blue asked.

"No, I can't," Salene replied.

"What, do you expect me to carry you?"

*Do you think I'm incapable just because my body is different than yours? Do you think I'm an infant that needs to be carried? Do you somehow think I'm fucking lesser?*

"I should make it through just fine behind you," Salene said, trying to temper her inner voice. Getting angry wouldn't help anything. It never did. She just had to stay calm. "Last time I was here, there were some paths that—"

"Vix, do you ever stop talking?" The woman turned on her heel. "Come along, turncoat."

Salene winced at the word, but she followed nonetheless in silence. The harbor met the walkway, which was attached by ropes and logs, held up by itself and by the occasional connection to the island. The Blue stumbled a few times as a wind picked up, but luckily Salene's chair remained mostly steady. As steady as it could be, at least, considering it was a few generations old and parts were missing.

The Blue's brow was slick with sweat thirty minutes into their walk, and as the sun continued to rise, more sprouted from her forehead, dripping off her chin and nose as her breathing grew labored.

"Should we rest?" Salene asked, her voice almost a whisper. "You look like you could—"

"I don't need you to tell me what I look like," the woman snapped back. "Just shut up, Hazel."

Salene sighed. She couldn't blame the woman. It wasn't her fault Salene's eye color changed, and the woman didn't know any better. Still, the bubbling rage that rolled to a boil in her throat ensured she kept her mouth shut. As she watched the sun continue to climb, she considered how things might be different if she was able-bodied like the rest of them. But she had never met a Hazel that wasn't disabled in some way. Age, physical limitations, chronic illness—not once had she met someone who proclaimed they were like the rest of the Blue army. It was as if the moment they became useless in the eyes of the Empire, their own eyes reflected that.

With a scowl, she pushed her attention to the view. Whatever the Empire said about her, whatever her eyes proclaimed, she was whole. She was a full person. There wasn't anything wrong with her.

At least the view over the water was something to calm her mind. The way the orange and red hues danced across the twisting waves, how she could see dozens of islands spread out towards the horizon, ranging from miniature lands that could only house a few homes—or farm animals—to those that expanded past her visibility, filled to the brim with trees and mountains. Waterfalls spilled from their sides, sparkling in the aging light.

Salene, of course, was on the largest of the islands. That was where Aris needed her. Salene looked to her guide, whose pace had slowed, and considered asking the woman if she knew anything about why Aris—no, *General* Aris—had called Salene here. Why, after abandoning her on Sypher, Aris wanted to talk now. Then Salene recalled the color of her eyes and decided against it.

Perhaps it was about Jade. Perhaps it was about how their best friend turned out to be a Green, someone to be feared, a monster that haunted children in their sleep. Or perhaps they were going to talk about how Aris killed her.

After two hours had passed and a few hundred feet scaled, the two arrived at the encampment above. Salene's chair spilled a steady stream of smoke, and the seat beneath her had begun to grow searing hot. The Blue pulled out a flask and took several long draws from it while Salene looked around, partially for a place to land, partially to see what had changed.

It was different than what she remembered: tents were placed here and there, but a few structures had been built as well. More trees had been cleared around the encampment to allow for better defenses. The entrance to the harbor partially hidden with ferns and vines, however, a few dozen trees left standing in case there ever happened to be an attack. There hadn't been one for nearly ten years. The Reds never managed to get close enough.

Her guide wiped her brow and, without even a glance in Salene's direction, moved ahead, stepping around ferns and ducking under branches. Salene tapped a few of her controls and changed the hovering height to get under and over obstacles in her way. A few branches snagged against the metal, and several vines attempted to tangle themselves around her legs, or around the gears beneath her seat. It was good the plants were all damp from a recent rain. A fire would not help the war efforts.

After a few minutes, they were in the encampment proper, the voices of chatting soldiers accompanied by the smell of a cooking meal. Those that saw her arrive went from jovial conversation to frowning gawkers, each scrutinizing her eyes, whispers spreading from one on-looker to another. Gazes lingered on her burnt cheek, on her legs. She leaned into her right palm, trying to cover the scars as best she could.

*I don't need to do this. I don't. Put your hand down, Salene. Lower it.*

But she couldn't. When she saw the hatred in their eyes, she desperately wished her body was different.

"The general is waiting for you in her tent," the woman said. She lifted her hand to wave at the other Blues and headed over to join them.

"Wait, where's her tent?" Salene inquired, only for the woman to ignore her and enter a conversation where the word "Hazel" appeared up plenty. Salene took a breath and did her best to steel herself. This wasn't any different than looking for a job on Sypher.

She just had to find Aris' tent. Surely, someone would have pity and point her in the right direction.

"Um, excuse me," Salene began, hovering over towards a kodarian man carving intricate swirls into another's horns. "My name's Salene, and I'm looking for General Sell's tent. She called me here and I need to meet with her."

"General Sell?" the carver asked. He scoffed. "You hear that, Paavo? This Hazel thinks she can just walk up and meet with the general."

"Walk up?" Paavo said with a snort. "You mean hover up. Where'd you get the money for a chair like that, turncoat?"

Salene rubbed her right leg idly with the heel of her palm. "From the savings I had as an Opes," she answered. "Please, she called me here and I don't want to be—"

"You weren't an Opes," the carver snapped. He lowered his chisel and scowled at her. "Your eyes prove that, Hazel. You weren't ever an Opes, you were just a pretender. Get lost. You ain't seeing the general."

*Do you think I'd be here if Aris didn't want me?*

"Well, you see, Aris called—"

"*Aris?* Are you fucking kidding me?" Paavo stood, shrugging off a hand from his friend. He sneered at Salene. "You think you can just call our general by her name? Do you have an *ounce* of respect for her, Hazel? You piece of shit—you came here because you got some Gold money, didn't you? Some Gold thought it would be funny sending a turncoat here. Well, Hazel." He stepped closer. They were eye-to-eye. "I ain't laughing."

"What's going on here?" Aris' voice cut through like holy water. The Blues blinked and immediately turned to their general, saluting. Salene looked over to see the blonde woman standing with a crutch under one arm, leaning against it to take the weight off her left leg. She was only in her undersuit, the sleek black material hugging every curve of her body up to the top of her neck. Salene felt her lips curl upwards upon seeing the woman, though confliction rose in her chest cavity.

*She killed Jade. But she also… did the right thing, didn't she? On the Feed she seems to want to change things. It's… got to be some elaborate scheme.*

"General Sell!" Paavo said. "The Golds sent a stupid prank again. This time it was a turncoat." He snorted in Salene's direction.

Aris' cold gaze narrowed. "And did someone tell you Salene was a prank sent by the golds?"

The carver blinked at the use of Salene's name.

Paavo cleared his throat. "You actually requested this Hazel here, general?"

"I need to discuss matters of importance with her, yes," Aris replied. "The Golds would never go through so much trouble to arrange travel for a Hazel, anyway. Sending us rotten fruit is more their style." She looked to Salene. She did not smile. "Follow me, Hazel."

215

Salene pushed her chair to trail after the limping Aris. Salene suffered glares as she went, up until she entered the woman's tent near the center of the camp. There, Aris dropped herself down on her coat and exhaled slowly.

"Vix, it's good to see you again, Salene," she said, lighting up the space with a smile. "Sorry about out there—I had to, you understand. There are things that… must be discreet."

A weight lifted from Salene's chest. She smiled and hovered her chair closer.

"I understand," she said softly. "I'm so glad to see you, too, Aris. And you're a general now! How exciting."

*When did you find out? How did you know? Why did you kill her?*

Aris chuckled. "It's a lot of work. But I did do something two weeks ago that I think you'll be happy to hear." She beamed up at Salene. "The Mad Queen's army is gone."

"The…?" Salene's eyes widened. Water splashed over her head, suffocated her lungs. A sharp pain stabbed into her spine and then nothing below ever again. Jade had been the one to find her, to pull her out of the water, to carry her back to base.

*Aris killed her.*

"You did it?" Salene asked, grinning. "Oh my Vix, you did it?"

"I did." Aris stretched her leg out and grimaced at the pain. "It was tricky, but I got her cornered against the rye-dragon den up by the mountains. And her entire group was killed." Her smile faltered. "That's actually why I called you here, Salene." Her voice dropped to a whisper. She looked around, searching for any shadows on the tent walls that would indicate anyone was listening. She leaned forward. "The Golds have denied me and my surviving troops passage home until I can prove the Mad Queen's death. But the river swept her body away, and I was gravely injured from the battle. I need you to track her, to find where her body ended up, and if there's anything left of her armor or person and bring it back."

Salene blinked. "What? Me? Aris, I appreciate this, but... hover chairs aren't made for forests. Mine can hardly keep up in the city. I can't just go out searching for a dead body."

*Why are we talking about the Mad Queen? Why haven't you mentioned Jade? Did you do the right thing? If she's a demon because of her eyes, do you believe I'm a turncoat because of mine?*

"Everything is arranged for you, Salene. The ship you came in on also brought technology to give you your legs back." She smiled and continued speaking, but the words were nothing more than garbled noise in Salene's ears. All thoughts faded. Her mind stalled.

*Give me my legs back? My legs?* Her hands ran down to her knees. *They're not... they're not gone. They're still here, they're just... different. I've been using this chair for so long. I've gotten used to it. She just expects me to... what? Get rid of it? Cut off my legs and have them replaced with metal? I want to help, but...* Jade *would help, but...*

"Salene?" Aris waved her hand in front of Salene's face. "I'm sorry, I shocked you with all that, didn't I?" She offered a small, apologetic smile. "Where did I lose you?"

217

"Why did you kill Jade?" Salene blurted. She gasped and covered her mouth, eyes wide. "Oh, no, I—I'm sorry, I didn't…"

Aris sighed and looked down. "Right," she said. "I figured you would be wondering." With a deep breath, she looked at Salene. She pressed a salute over her heart, where her left fist sat above her right. It was incorrect.

"Salene, Jade is dead. She was a demon and I did what I had to do. You must push past the memories you once had of that creature and forget it as the person you thought you knew. It was nothing more than a monster." She held Salene's gaze a moment longer. She clenched her saluted fists, then she let them drop. A slow realization dawned on Salene.

*She didn't kill her*, Salene thought. *Jade is alive. Oh my Vix, Jade is alive!* Tears burned in the corners of her eyes. *I knew Aris couldn't do something so terrible to her best friend. I knew there had to be a reason. The galaxy realized what Jade was, and Aris did what she had to do to fake Jade's death! Vix, where is she? Where is she hiding? Does Aris know? Can I get a message to her? Tell her to stay safe? Or would that compromise her location? Oh my Vix, she's okay.*

Salene swallowed hard and nodded. "R-right," she muttered. "Right, you're right, general, I'm sorry for bringing it up."

Aris smiled, her eyes cold. "It's quite all right, Salene. I understand this is hard for all of us."

"I-it is. Um." Salene wiped her eyes. "You mentioned prosthetics?"

"Prosthetics? No, Salene. I said I'd give your legs back."

The memory slipped across her mind like evening frost. *The hours of trying, the days of agony. She could swear her feet were being sawed off by blunt rocks, but there they were, intact, unharmed. The Healers shook their heads, sweat rolling over their lips. It was no use. She was not worth the effort.*

*Besides, her eyes had already turned.*

"The Healers couldn't do anything," Salene pressed, frowning. "You remember, don't you?"

"I have something better." Aris smiled. "I'll show you to the medical tent, Salene. And the doctor will tell you everything."

# Chapter 27

Salene hovered over to a cot, glancing around the medical tent to see several Blues wrapped in bandages and resting in the choking humidity. Since they were nestled closer to the middle of the camp, no trees protected them from the sun's gaze, and the thin fabric above them might as well not have been there.

Aris stood near the front of the tent, leaning against her crutches and waved someone over.

"Salene, correct?" chimed a snipper man, dressed in an undersuit and rye-mail. He approached from an adjacent cot, a smile on his face. Sweat dripped off the small hairs that covered his arachnid body and he reeked of a pungent, acrid odor, like everyone else in the camp.

"Ah, yes," Salene replied, looking to him. "Are you the doctor?"

"I am. Is there any way we could get you down on the cot, Salene? We'll need you to take off your pants as well."

*Sure. I'll expose myself to you first and ask questions later. That makes total sense, you complete shit.*

"Before that could, uh, could I ask exactly what's going on? General Sell didn't fill me in."

The doctor crossed his arms and chuckled. "Ah, then that would make all this a little confusing. I understand." He nodded and shrugged his upper shoulders. "Well, let me go fetch them real fast, and I'll show you what they are." He turned and headed over to a small shipment of various medical supplies on the ground by the tent entrance. There were a few boxes that had clearly been there a little longer, as their wooden bottoms had grown soaked from the ground and had since been stacked upon one another in an effort to keep the containers dry. He returned with a small device, no longer than the top knuckle of his thumb. It was mushroom-topped, with a long needle extending from its base, and a single light upon the uppermost section. He glanced from it, to her.

"Here it is," he said. "This will make you walk again."

Salene peered at it, brows furrowed. It certainly didn't look like much.

"How will one little… *thing* make me walk?" she asked.

"One little…?" He laughed and waved her off with his lower pair of hands. "No, no! There will be a series of these placed along your legs. They will start at your hips and spine, and run down all four sides of your legs and feet. They will be able to stimulate the muscles and reactivate nerves for their affected areas. That's why you'll need so many," he said. "They only spread out for a small space. We'll be placing them even distances apart, so you'll hopefully have no blind areas in feeling or motion." He smiled. "They are powered by Ultraviolet rays, but we've let them soak for a while before bringing them here. They should have plenty of charge for a few days, but you'll want to make sure to take some rests where the sun is bright whenever you find feeling numb and your legs slowing down. You'll need to make sure each one gets some sunlight, and you'll want to avoid extreme heat and cold and… well. You get the picture." He

221

snickered. "Quite incredible, no? On planets like Doath, this technology hardly ever slows down!"

*How did Aris afford this? Did faking Jade's death really give her a large amount of kniri as a reward? Why is she giving me this so readily? Last time I saw her was on Sypher, and now she calls me here and gives me this?*

"You're confused," Aris said, interrupting her thoughts.

*Shit, I forgot she was good at reading expressions.* Salene looked over at Aris, who hobbled a little closer. Aris offered a smile.

"It wasn't my money that got all this for you, Salene. It was… a friend's. They were saving up to get you something for a few years. Since they passed away, they wanted their money to go to you. I just added the little amount of kniri that was left to make the purchase."

Salene blinked. *Jade got this for me? These are… these are from Jade?* She looked at the device once more. *She wanted me to walk again. She spent years not talking to me, but want to give me this?* Her chest constricted and her fingers curled around her chair. *How am I supposed to say no to Jade? I have to help. I have to help end this war and make sure everyone can go home. That's the right thing to do. It doesn't matter what I feel. It doesn't matter what I think. Aris deserves to go home and she deserves to try and change things for everyone.*

With a breath, she hovered her chair closer to the free cot and lowered it down so she could push the armrests up and slide onto the bed. Her blanket slipped off her legs as she did so, which bundled up on the floor, and revealed a small H-dagger that she had brought with her just in case. The doctor stepped back as Salene fumbled to cover it with her hands. Aris laughed.

"No one searches a Hazel," she said with a smile. "You can keep it, Salene. You entered a warzone, it only makes sense that you can defend yourself."

Salene relaxed a little. "Thanks, Aris. Erm, *General Sell.*"

Aris beamed. "It does have a nice ring to it, doesn't it?"

"You've earned it, my friend," Salene said, her voice soft. "You really have."

Aris reached over and took Salene's hand. She squeezed. "It means a lot for you to say that, Salene. Will you accept our friend's gift?"

*Do I really have a choice?*

"Of course I will," she replied. "I'm sure you have other things to attend to. And even if I get my movement back, they'll be a little sore. It'll take time for me to be able to walk properly."

"I'll come back tomorrow," Aris said. "Doctor, make sure she eats during mealtimes, all right? And keep her hydrated. She is important, and I don't need her dying of thirst."

"As you say, General Sell." The man dipped his head respectfully. Aris looked back at Salene one last time, squeezed the woman's hand, and limped out of the tent. The doctor turned to Salene with a grin.

"Shall we begin?"

He started with her back, installing the main node for conveying information to the parts of her spine still active. With her shirt pulled up and her pants folded onto her hovering chair nearby, she could feel the sun burning her skin with unrelenting intensity. Sweat dripped off her and soaked the cot she rested on. The doctor's fingers danced over her flesh as he ran them along her back. He paused and pressed his thumb down.

"This will hurt, Salene," he said. "In three, two…"

An icy cold needle sliced through her nerves and forced itself into her vertebrae. Salene gritted her teeth and gripped the pillow beneath her stomach.

*Jade wouldn't cry. Jade wouldn't cry.*

She kept her tears of pain at bay and bit her tongue to strangle her whimper. Salene's eyes clenched shut. A few shaky breaths escaped her lungs.

"Very good," the doctor said. "I will activate that one once the others are in place. You won't feel any of the others, considering your disability." He nodded and folded his hands behind his back. "But to be precise, this will take some time. I ask for complete silence while I work. Is that acceptable?"

Salene sighed as the pain began to dull. She nodded.

*Nothing but sweat and thoughts while a doctor pokes needles into my numb body,* she thought sarcastically. *Vix, Jade, what a gift.*

Still, as the doctor continued his work, she couldn't help but smile at the thought of her friend. Even after all this time, Jade hadn't forgotten. Despite the redhead sending no messages, no letters, she still remembered Salene, and had been saving up for a gift until they saw each other again. It was kind.

And yet everyone called her a demon.

Salene opened her eyes with another tired sigh. She looked over her shoulder to see the doctor's hands carefully measuring distance between each node, then pressing it into her skin. Pinpricks of blood bubbled up, some nodes bleeding enough to spill over the side and create a small, crimson streak across her skin. She tried to curl her toes—in case she somehow could. But they were unresponsive.

Salene rested her chin against the cot once more and stared at the tent wall in front of her. Shapes moved and conversations filled the air in garbled, overlapping sentences. A spider crawled along the surface, no larger than the tip of her finger, searching for something unknown to her. Maybe it had been called here by Aris to search for the body of the Mad Queen, too. Maybe the spider was confused about circumstances just as much as her. But if Salene could get her legs back and search the woods for the Thrax's body, well, perhaps she could look for other things, too.

Perhaps she could search for Jade.

Chapter 28

The procedure lasted over an hour, at which point Salene had drifted asleep. Her mind still pondered the possibility of discovering her friend in the woods, replaying an imaginary scenario over and over where she followed footprints in the soft earth to a cabin. There, she discovered Jade, who greeted her with a smile and brought her inside for a cup of tea.

An itch pulled her from her dreams, drew her to the waking world of sweat and humidity, where she heard distant thunder under the rumble of chatter outside. Salene rubbed her eyes and yawned before she rolled over onto her back and leaned down to satisfy the itch. Her fingers raked across her knee.

And she felt the nails against her flesh.

She sat up, heart in her throat, tired eyes wide. Across her legs, over her hips and pressing against her buttock and spine, were the small, rounded devices that sat seamlessly against her skin, gleaming with a dim, blue light. There were perhaps thirty in total, all jacked into her skin with an expert hand—or four, in the doctor's case. She ran her fingers down her hips, over her knees, to the tip of her toes. Her eyes closed. The pressure of softened fingers across flesh, the buzz of warmth, the way sweat tickled her nerves as it rolled across her skin. She curled her toes and felt the muscles flex, strained from lack of use. She stretched, her body elongating, her lower half groaning with stiffness. Though she had made sure to work her legs, the travel here made many of her excises unusable—or at least, brought glares and sneers from other passengers she wanted to avoid.

Her ankles rotated and her knees pulled up to press against her chest. Tears spilled down her cheeks despite her attempts to stop them. *Jade wouldn't cry like this. Jade never cried.* But she could do nothing against the wave of emotion. How was she supposed to feel? Elated, excited? She had grown used to her body over the last four years. And now, here she was, with an aid that made her interaction with the galaxy once again different. Jade had given them to her, and she was thankful for the chance to be able to walk, but at what cost?

Sobs shook her shoulders and constricted her chest. Would her eyes turn blue again now that she was useful? Would everyone start to treat her differently once more? Or would she be met with further hatred, with people not knowing about her aids, and being hated for being assumed able-bodied *and* a traitor?

Salene dragged her fingers across her smooth legs, gleaming with over two dozen blue lights. *This is the right thing to do. Nothing else matters. If I can walk, I'll be more useful. I'll help Aris change the Empire. I might even find Jade.*

With a shaky, tear-soaked breath, she moved to the side of her cot, and tried to stand.

# Chapter 29

In the middle of the night, Aris was woken by whispers. She lay upon her back on a cot, her legs aching with each beat of her heart. As she blinked, her bleary vision cleared to show a dim tent, the distant light of a fire at the center of camp flickering somewhere past her feet and through rows of other tents. To her right, two people passed by, their voices low.

"…saw her," said one. "She had red hair. It's the Mad Queen, I know it."

"The Mad Queen's dead," replied the second, voice equally as quiet as they moved along the length of Aris' tent. "You heard the report. She was killed by the rye-dragon."

"But what if she survived somehow? You insisted that he saw her…"

Their voices trailed off. Aris ran her hands over her face. The Mad Queen was dead. There was no coming back from that. Whatever they saw was an illusion.

"How many times have voices woken you talking of phantom redheads in the woods?" Malkov asked, his voice bringing with it a pounding headache.

Aris covered her eyes and groaned. "What is it you want, Malkov?"

"Oh, nothing," he purred. "Just to offer some advice. From my count, this is sighting number five since you've arrived here. They're increasing."

"She's *dead.*"

Malkov laughed. "I know that, general! Don't act like I'm unaware of what a human can survive. A demon, however…"

Aris paused. She lowered her hands and squinted at him in the darkness, where the shadows did not seem to affect him. He sat in the air, cross-legged above her legs, as bright as any other time she'd seen him during the day. He smiled at her.

"What do you mean?" Aris asked.

"You know what I mean," he cooed. "One of your supposed kills wasn't all human."

"She was fully human," Aris said. "It's some stupid superstition that people make her out to seem demonic. She couldn't survive that fall."

"But she didn't fall, did she?" Malkov's smile grew cruel. He leaned forward. "Someone rescued her in a ship. You shot it down, you searched the wreckage, and you found nothing."

His fingers were inside her skull, groping and grabbing at every piece of information, yanking it from the tissue of her brain, eliciting a wince each time he found something else he wanted. She gripped her temples as the headache burned with more vigor.

"Stop doing that," she hissed. "Stop prodding around my head."

The fingers retreated. A momentary relief.

"Ah, that's painful, is it?" Malkov clicked his tongue. "Good to know."

229

"Two people cannot survive on Sobek alone," she said. "The wildlife would've killed them if they didn't get caught in a skirmish. She would've been badly injured, anyway."

"You did cut off her arm," Malkov mused. "I can't imagine that's easy to recover from. You don't feel guilty—?"

"No. Is there a reason for your pestering, Malkov? Or might I go back to sleep?"

Malkov sighed. "You're always so impatient with me, Aris. Yes, there is a reason for my pestering: who's to say someone else isn't helping her survive in the woods? She is, after all, a Green. And who knows what people believe about things they do not know." He straightened his jacket and appeared at her left, standing now. "All I'm saying, general, is if you tried to kill me, I wouldn't be too happy about it." His metallic eyes settled on hers. "I'd want revenge. How many times have you bested Jade in a fight?"

"She's dead," Aris hissed, shutting her eyes.

"Well. I look forward to seeing how she reacts to your claims."

He didn't speak further, and the headache began to dull. Aris sat in the darkness, eyes closed, and listened to the snoring of her troops, the patrols pacing through the tents. Five times she had awoken to the claims of redheaded beasts in the woods. Five times was too many to be fluke.

Unease settled upon her bones. Jade was dead. It didn't matter that a ship appeared out of nowhere and caught her on its deck. It didn't matter that it sprinted for the sky, and Aris managed to have it shot down before it could get far. It didn't matter that the wreckage was without bodies, that a nearby search gave them nothing, that without a carcass, she couldn't be sure. None of that mattered. Jade was dead. She had to be dead.

231

# Chapter 30

Aris poured over the message the Golds sent when dawn broke. She hadn't slept. She was occupied with wondering, with considering the possibilities, worried that perhaps she had indeed missed something. The redhead had never been vengeful. She wouldn't come for Aris if she lived. There was no way.

But it wouldn't hurt to be safe.

*Attn: Opes General Aris Sell*

*Directive: Until evidence of the Mad Queen's death is presented, do not leave Sobek.*

*Mission: Incomplete*

*Signed: Gold Council*

She assumed her father had sent it. She could practically see the smile on his lips as he typed her death warrant. Trying to find evidence of someone's corpse on a planet so hostile as this wouldn't be easy. She flicked her wrist and swiped her wrist-holo's display to a map of the nearby area, updated with more recent information after linking back up with the rest of the Opes. The river was marked where the Mad Queen had last been seen being pulled away by the current. She trailed her finger down and stopped, noticing another user-placed marker further down the bank. Her brows furrowed.

*Crash Site*, it read. The Green's ship had crashed not far from the island's edge, tearing a massive hole through the forest. Only the empty boat had been found. Those sent into the nearby woods hadn't returned, killed by wild beasts the forest was well-known for.

Or by whoever had been piloting the ship. But surely they would be injured from the crash, not strong enough to hold off several Opes troops. It hadn't made sense then, and it didn't now. Still, there was that slim possibility that whoever was allied with the demon was powerful enough to protect her while she was weak. Yet even the redhead wouldn't be foolish enough to stay on the planet for longer than necessary. She could've chartered a ship, or had her companion bully their way onto one headed away from the war. The demon's finances had been seized, so even if she couldn't pay, surely she would consider a different way to escape.

A chilled, jabbing pain spread through the back of Aris' skull as a new consideration slipped into her thoughts: unless the demon stayed on purpose. Unless the demon remained for her.

"General Sell?"

Aris shook her head free of the thoughts and shut her holo off before turning to the doctor standing in her tent. The snipper smiled.

"Your patient is doing well," he said. "She wants to see you."

"Of course," Aris replied. "Tell her I'll be there shortly. Have you seen Kuroda?"

"Yes, he's getting breakfast for the both of you."

"Thank you, doctor. That will be all."

The man smiled once more, dipped his head respectfully, and slipped out of the tent. Aris rubbed her brows and let her gaze fall to the ground. The demon—*Jade*—had to see what Aris was trying to

233

do, right? She wouldn't come back. She couldn't. She probably died in the woods. She likely bled out without medical attention.

Unless her companion had a healing Helix, or could stitch wounds closed, or they found someone to help them survive the forest floor that had shelter and food and medicine—

Aris gritted her teeth. *Stop. Stop. This is illogical. Jade is gone. The Mad Queen is dead. Just get Salene to find anything I can use to prove the Mad Queen is dead, and go home. Finish what I started.* She took a few steadying breaths. *Everything is going to work out.*

Aris grabbed her crutches nearby and hoisted herself up, her left leg burning with agony, while her right buzzed with an odd numbness. She peered down at it curiously and resolved to speak with the doctor after she visited Salene. She limped outside her tent and paused as she took a breath of the thick air around her. People milled about, weaving through the tangle of tents and structures, some holding their morning breakfast of grits. Others sparred down the way on her right, with bystanders cheering and placing bets. Thin morning fog struggled to survive in the center of camp, small wisps of ivory not even tall enough to spill across her foot. Her eyes lingered on the waves, watching the fog tumble over changes in the mud, pool into holes made by footprints. It slithered along like a snake. Her skin crawled and she pulled her eyes away.

*Breathe. Focus on Salene.*

Aris swung her leg along as she moved through the stream of soldiers and reached the tent a few minutes later. It was larger than any of the others, allowing for more occupants than a single person.

With the thin fabric the way that it was—cheap and useless and one of the many gifts from the Golds—she could see Salene's figure on the cot nearest the front entrance, perched on its side, stretching her legs and testing their strength against the ground. She was eager. Eager to walk. Eager to help. Aris smiled. She had chosen well.

Upon entering, Salene looked up, her hazel eyes gleaming in the light. Sweat spilled down her face, curling over the burns and collecting in the woman's collarbone. Salene reached up and combed her tightly wound curly hair, covering what parts of her injury that she could.

"I take it they're working?" Aris asked, offering a smile as she approached.

"Working?" Salene smiled. Her eyes held a hint of pain. "Vix, Aris, they're amazing! The medic has been helping me through it all so I can get them working well. So I can help."

Aris chuckled. "I'm so glad. Our friend would be happy to hear that, too." She sat next to Salene, body aching. Salene peered at her at the mention of Jade.

"She'd be proud of you, you know," Aris whispered, looking down at Salene's legs. The woman was only in her boxers, leaving almost her entire lower half exposed. "For coming here despite how everyone acts around Hazels. For helping me with this. I want to prove to people Hazels aren't traitors, Salene." She looked at the woman, pushing a saddened hope into her expression, holding it for a moment, then looking down after three counted seconds. "Perhaps if you can help me with this, I can work on showing that eye colors don't dictate how a person acts. I could... help our friend."

235

Salene's eyes widened, surprise painting her expression with a clear and obvious brush. "What? You think you could bring her back to…?"

"I'm not sure," Aris muttered. "But it's worth a try. If we start with Hazels, we could get them recognized, maybe change society. I'm already working on it for Blues." She reached over and touched Salene's hand, both of theirs dripping with sweat. "Proving the Mad Queen is gone is nonsense from the Golds, but if we can find *anything* that shows she's dead, we can start to change things on Nevar." With a glance, Aris easily read the expression on Salene's open face. She wanted to help. She wanted part of this noble cause. Salene had suffered beneath Gold rule just as much as Blues.

That was why Salene was here.

"I have the location," Aris continued. "Of where the Mad Queen last was. You can…" She paused as she turned to her wrist holo. A moment of hesitance, a moment of considering another option. Just in case. What was the harm? All it would prove was everything she already knew. Perhaps then she would stop waking at night to hear rumors of people who no longer existed.

"Sorry," she breathed, flicking her wrist holo and bringing up a map. She pointed to the crash site near the end of the river. "You can start here. The Mad Queen has one mechanical eye, and the other is orange. Red hair and a scar across her nose." Her voice lowered. "Our friend visited this spot. Keep an eye out while you search."

Salene face flashed with a quick, sharp smile. "Our…? Yes, yes, of course Aris. I will begin there and work upstream? See if I can find anything of interest and report back? I'm going to need some time to get used to my legs. How many are coming with me?"

"I can't spare people," Aris breathed. "But I can spare weapons and armor. I know it's dangerous, Salene, but if you were to find *anything* on our friend being okay…"

"Right," Salene muttered, looking down at her hands, a frown tugging at her lips. "No, that makes sense. But the woods are deadly."

"If she survived it, Salene, so can you."

Salene blinked. Determination glinted in her eyes. "Right," she said. "So can I."

Chapter 31

*The sounds of battle filled Salene's ears, ringing full of gunshots and slashing blades and breaking armor. Sparks of electricity from Red and Blue Lightning Helixes made the air tingle with energy. She took a few steadying breaths as a bombardment of lead dug holes into the boulder she hid behind, clutching a sniper rifle to her body. A sting of pain brought a hiss to Salene's lips and she spared a look down at the light armor she wore, covered in cuts and soaked with mud from Sobek's forest floor. Along her left leg was a drizzle of blood, spilling out of a gash in her rye-mail, right where the armor stopped to allow her knee to bend. She curled her toes and inhaled sharply as the cold fingers of agony wrapped around her throat. She wasn't supposed to be so close to the front line, not on this mission. But here she was.*

*Her eyes caught a glimpse of a massive form covered in heavy armor that, instead of having the metal plates attached via leather straps, had hand-woven links that were sewn into the rye-mail itself. The process for such armor was painstaking, and the cost was enough to drain a soldier's entire three-year savings. It made them untouchable in the war, however, but the Golds didn't care to give the Opes any helping hands.*

*The form rushed to Salene's side and pressed a shoulder to the rock. Pulled over its head was an ebony helmet.*

*"Where's Aris?" the woman asked, Jade's voice coming out of the external speakers. It was heavy with concern. Tinged with an immense amount of worry. Salene fought away the tangle of jealousy*

*that threatened to garble her words into something bitter and repulsive. She wiped the sweat from her brow and licked her lips.*

*"She's trying to convince the Lieutenant to call for a retreat," Salene shouted over the death cries of their comrades. Jade cursed.*

*"We're getting torn apart and they're over there* bickering?" *Her visor pointed downward, and she gestured to Salene's wound. "You're bleeding."*

*"I'm fine," Salene replied. She took the chance to peer around the rock. Opes troops fired behind the cover of trees, blindly hoping their lead ammunition would manage to crack open someone's skull. Otherwise, there was little hope for guns to kill armored foes. A few Blues sprinted past, wielding their H-blades, the superheated metal gleaming a violent red against the green and brown foliage around them. Another wave of pain reminded Salene of her leg and she grimaced, turning back to Jade.*

*"What's the plan?" Salene asked. Jade always had one, and though she and Aris might claim that Aris was the brain behind all the operations, Salene knew the truth. Jade's quick-thinking and reflexes were the only reason any of the strategies worked.*

*Jade chuckled. "This little plot of land is surrounded by water. If we can get you behind the enemy lines, maybe you can snipe them in the back of the head?"*

*That was the worst idea Salene had ever heard. Getting behind enemy lines would be suicidal. Doing so would separate them from their troop, from security in numbers. The moment they were discovered, they would be slaughtered.*

239

*Jade put her hand on Salene's shoulder. "It'll be tricky, but you're the best sniper in this army, and I know you can fuck them up."*

*A swell of pride warmed Salene's chest, filling it to overflowing. A smile rose up on her face. She gripped her sniper and nodded. "Let's do it," she said.*

*"A retreat has been called!" Aris shouted, sprinting up to them, face dripping with sweat. "We're pulling back! Jade, stay by Salene. Salene, can you use Sight while moving?"*

*Salene blinked. She peered at the blonde, clad in light armor with plenty of space between each piece. It hadn't been fit for someone her size—none of the issued sets had been. Her fierce blue eyes gleamed like oceans.*

*"Did you hear me?" Aris snapped. "Salene!"*

*Salene jolted. "No! No, I'd have to be carried!"*

*"Jade, carry her. Salene, use your Helix and see what we're backing into." She looked between them and exhaled softly. "I've got your guys' backs."*

*Jade nodded. "Got it. Salene?"*

*Salene held her sniper tight and with one quick movement, Jade swept the woman into her arms. She turned and sprinted through the overgrown forest, ducking under branches and crushing foliage beneath her boots. Aris was behind, Helix bolstering her legs to help her keep up. Salene's gaze rested on Jade's emotionless helmet. They could play hero another time.*

*With a deep breath, she centered herself, closed her eyes, and reached out to her Helix in the depths of her soul. As always, it felt like catching a fistful of fire in both hands, hot and overwhelming as the flames engulfed her. She was pulled from her body, left as a silent, wordless specter hovering over herself. She looked down, saw the way her hair was pulled back, how her scar gleamed in the afternoon light. Her soft nose, her fluttering eyelids. A surreal experience, one she had slowly grown accustomed to. She turned her attention to the path ahead of them.*

*She pushed forward, floating as nothing but a sense of sight, winding around trees and slipping beneath leaves. She passed her fellow soldiers, all sprinting for safety that retreat was supposed to bring. She spotted her general, Kasaar, shouting orders along the bank of the river. She paused above the crashing waves and peered ahead, at the forest before them. She attempted to move forward once more, but a wall of some sort prevented her from seeing any further. A headache blossomed in her skull, threatening to yank her back to her body. She managed to keep her grip on her Helix, trying to peer into the trees as a low, ivory fog rolled in.*

*It was a trap.*

*A chill shot down her spine and the sensation jerked her back to her physical body. A slow mind greeted her with even slower hands and lips. The world was a series of blotches splattered over a canvas before her eyes, shifting and melting together. She remembered how to breathe after a few seconds and took a large lungful, filling herself with the humid taste of Sobek air. She blinked a few times. Sounds came to her next. Shouts from familiar voices. Then feeling as she was set upon her feet. Her vision cleared and she saw Jade motioning, pointing ahead, towards the fog, towards the trap. Then she turned and sprinted back towards whence they had came, weapon bared.*

*At last, smell. The smell of fire. The smell of ash.*

*"It's a trap!" she screamed as her daze lifted. "It's a trap!"*

*The world exploded and with one final inhale, she found herself underwater.*


Salene gasped, jerking upright. A shirt tied around her waist kept her from falling out of the tree. The branch groaned beneath her as she exhaled, leaning her back against the backpack between her and the trunk, sweat already drooling down her lips. She could hear a distant river trickling further off between the sounds of chirping birds and croaking insects. Sleeping near the banks was evidently a poor idea. Too many memories.

She stretched her legs out on the branch before her, watching her legs move, clad in an undersuit with rye-mail resting atop. They ached, buzzing with sore muscles. Yesterday's travel had been eventless, as being close to a large camp meant most animals kept their distance. But today's journey would be more difficult. Today she'd be away from that safety net and into the forest proper. There was no telling what animals might take interest in a lone wanderer with weak legs. She'd need to make it to the river and undress so she might recharge her systems before the drained. Aris had sent her with a way to manage how many hours she had left via her wrist holo, and currently, she had six hours.

Still, she couldn't help but smile. She leaned over and ran her hands down her knees, relishing in the sensation of touch. She rolled her feet, stretched her calves out. It was different than what she had been used to over her last few years of retirement, but she had to admit, being on the battlefield, venturing out on her own two legs, it filled her with delighted nostalgia. As if everything was as it were before, as if she was still a Blue, as if her eyes had never changed and her life had never fallen apart.

Salene had waited a few more days before leaving the Opes encampment to practice walking, but Aris sent her with crutches just in case they began to ache to terribly. She used them as often as she could to take pressure off in case she needed to run, but now they were in her lap, balanced carefully as she pulled the thin sweatshirt over her head, swung her legs to one side of the branch, and strapped on her pack. The weight of several days' worth of water, food, a flare, and a single tarp dug against her shoulders. She peered down past her feet, down to the foggy floor below. It could be dangerous if something was lurking beneath, so she situated herself to lean against the tree, closed her eyes, and reached out for her Helix.

With a surge of flame, she was ejected from her body, left hovering a few inches away. She peered back at herself to ensure the activation hadn't jolted her away from her safe spot. When she found she was still perfectly situated where she was, she dived below, into the fog, and looked around the immediate area. Her Sight dipped beneath the surface of the mist, enveloping herself in the twirling ivory, and moved through slowly, noticing the bugs crawling over leaves, fighting over food, chittering and humming for a companion. She spent several minutes checking the area, and a few paces down the path she planned on taking, and found nothing but insects. Her Sight closed off, and with a breath, she pulled her vision back to herself and she opened her eyes in her body. So long as she took the time to properly return, she wouldn't be dazed for several minutes after. Salene blinked a few times and pressed her hand against the moist bark of the tree.

"All right," she murmured, "let's get going."

She pushed the crutches down and watched them plummet to the base of the tree. With a press of her wrist holo, she brought up a map to see that Jade's ship had crashed just on the other side of the river. It would take the day to reach it, even in her weakened state. She just had to be sure not to be attacked by wild animals.

And hope Jade hadn't been attacked, either. Admittedly, it was uncomfortable Aris hadn't had contact with the redhead after she shot down Jade's ship, but perhaps she was playing things safe. Letting Jade escape and having Salene check in on her so Aris wasn't directly connected. It was smart.

"…them."

Salene blinked. Was that a voice? Was someone approaching? That couldn't be possible, she just checked with her Sight. Branches snapped and leaves shifted. Someone was coming.

"…no condition to… up there just… them."

*Is it a Blue scout? I could talk to them, I—fuck, my eyes. I could tell them Aris sent me—no, shit, would they believe that? Fuck!*

She pressed herself against the tree and took another breath. Her Sight yanked her vision from her body and she lowered herself down to where she heard the sounds. A headache bloomed, and she could see the blurry, unfocused form of a human. Her eyes were red.

Salene pulled herself back quickly before the pain did so for her. She rubbed her temples with a grimace.

*Why is a Red so close to the Opes camp? Is it a saboteur?*

"Don't die on me," the Red muttered, grunting as if the feminine-sounding person was hauling a heavy object. "We'll get you patched up. Just stay with me."

Brush was pushed aside and a few snapping branches indicated that the Red was directly below. Salene peered past her dangling legs to see a redhead being propped up at the bottom of the trunk, right arm missing, armor in tatters. Salene's heart climbed into her throat and pounded hard and fast. Sweat made her palms slick as she stared down at the shape. Another person kneeled in front of the injured figure and, with pale human hands, touched the person's spaulder and lifted a canteen to their lips.

That couldn't be Jade, could it? Salene was close to the crash site and that shape had no right arm. Why was she with a Red? Salene's mind spun back to the official report, broadcasted several times on all Exuro Empire channels:

*This generation's Green has been discovered and disposed. The Opes soldier known as Jade Wren Cavvar has been cut down by General Sell after returning from captivity by the Thrax. The beast's right arm was captured for further study.*

245

Did that mean a Red took to Jade and was helping her survive this war-torn planet?

"I'm going to need to clean your cuts again," the woman murmured, drawing Salene's gaze downwards once more, peering past the tangle of branches and leaves to see glimpses of the Red moving. "I know it hurts, but they need to be cleaned. If you get sick, where will I be?"

There was the sound of gurgling water as it was poured out, spilling through the fog and onto the foliage hiding beneath. Salene inhaled sharply. Jade would leap down, demand to know who everyone was, best the caretaker in combat if she was denied. She had a habit of using her strength to bully her way through any situation. But Salene's legs still ached with yesterday's hike and she knew it would be an ordeal simply to climb down to meet the newcomers.

She grimaced as she tried to think through another way to descend, her mind momentarily walking back to the war, to using her Sight and seeing Jade through her Helix.

Salene's heart twisted. It was someone else, then. Just two Reds walking towards the Blue encampment, walking towards their deaths. It didn't matter what happened to them. It didn't matter if they died. Salene gripped her chest, her fingers curling against the rye-mail.

"Hello?" she called, her voice as strong as she could made it. There was sudden movement below and the shifting of leaves. "Please, I'm not your enemy," Salene continued. "I climbed this tree to stay off the ground while I slept. But I would like to come down now, if that's okay with you."

"No!" the Red called. "No, you stay in that tree!"

"I heard you mention your friend needs their wounds cleaned," Salene pressed, glancing around and preparing herself to move towards the ground as soon as she was cleared to do so. "I used to be a field medic. I might be able to help."

*It's not exactly accurate, but it's close enough.*

"A field medic for who? Which side are you on?"

Salene paused. "No one's," she answered. "My eyes are Hazel."

"Hazel?" The woman was silent for a while. "I've never seen hazel eyes on anyone but the dead."

"If I come down, you can see them yourself."

"Are you a Healer?"

"No, but I can keep someone from dying."

"All right," the Red called. "Slowly."

Luckily for Salene, slowly was the fastest she could go, each shift down from a branch giving her legs a chance to keep her balanced while her arms held most her body's weight. Scratches laced Salene's palms as the bark broke off against her, and when she reached the foggy forest floor, her legs nearly caved beneath the effort of standing. She threw her hands out and steadied herself against the trunk, letting her knees bend as sweat rivered down her forehead.

While using the chair, she had kept up with upper body strength and did what exercises she could for her legs. Still, as she

247

settled onto them, it was as if each muscle had been overworked. Crushing agony filled her bloodstream and coursed to her chest, constricting her breathing. She blinked a few times to try and wash herself free of it. Salene looked to the Red, who met her eyes.

She was a blonde woman, built tall and wide, with a square jaw and soft crimson eyes. Feathers sprouted from her hair, and across her right cheek were sections of burnt flesh, modeled as if something splashed against her and oozed down her skin before being washed off. Salene kept herself from reaching up to touch her own scarred face. She pulled her eyes away to look at the injured party. A sharp gasp forced her back, eyes wide at the horror of what she was witnessing.

It looked as if the woman's entire face had been melted off. Her nose was gone, replaced by a sickly hole with flesh stretched over it. Her lips no longer existed, parts of her cheeks were eaten away to reveal the teeth behind—many of which were blackened and rotten, holes speckled across them. There were spots where her hair did not grow, as if whatever had melted her face had splattered and burned behind her hairline.

But worst of all were her eyes. Her right was a blackened hole of flesh and gore with bits of metal seared into the meat, while her left was covered with what must have been her eyelid, stretched across swollen remains of an eyeball. A scratching cough spilled from the injured one's mouth, and with the additional light flooding in from the breaks in her skin, Salene could see that the woman's tongue was partially burned away.

"Easy," the Red said, kneeling by the woman. The Red's right arm was wrapped with leaves and vines, pressed against her chest, while the other lifted the canteen to her lips, allowing her to bite it off and offer it to the woman. The person drank, her lipless mouth pursing and twisting the seared skin, water visible from the pockets in her cheeks. Salene grimaced. She had seen cases like this during her time at war before. Survivors of the Mad Queen often limped back to camp looking similarly.

The Red pulled the canteen away and the burned woman slumped against the tree, her breathing hoarse. "Can you help her?" the Red asked, looking to Salene. "I don't know what I'm doing. Please, I… I don't want to lose her."

Salene's chest filled with daggers. She couldn't help the enemy, could she? She couldn't aid them in surviving just for them to turn around and kill more Blues, could she?

"You're headed for a Blue camp," Salene said. "Do you know that?" Rocks laden her legs and turned her bones to dust. Nothing in the world sounded more relieving than sitting down, but she could not, not with a Red nearby. She held onto the tree's bark a little tighter.

"A Blue—? Gods! *Shit!*" The woman grabbed at her hair, scowling, her armor shifting across her rye-mail as she did so. "Are you kidding? How far away is it?"

"A day," Salene answered, watching as panic and despair crossed the Red's face. Tears swarmed the woman's crimson gaze.

"A *day?* We have to go. We can't…" She looked at Salene. "I… please. I don't know if we can trust you, but I'm supposed to meet a Healer at a crashed ship. I was supposed to follow the river and then I couldn't remember if I went North or South, and… and she was going to help us off-planet. She helped the Green—"

"Sindri," the injured woman hissed, her voice strained and slurred.

*Off planet? They're not staying? They're trying to leave?*

Salene looked to the melted form of a woman, and it seemed as if the bloated eye might have been trying to open, the skin sealing it shut starting to stretch, holes Salene had not noticed before beginning to spread wide. Beneath was a glimpse of corroded eye, and its juices began to drool from the gouges now widened.

"Stop, stop," Sindri muttered, turning her attention to her companion. "I'm here, I'm here."

Fog wrapped around them, a welcome chill before the day's unrelenting humidity. The injured woman didn't say anymore, her inhales taken between rasping coughs and desperate swallows of water. They were trying to escape this cycle of death, this war. They were trying to flee. Neither of them stood a chance if Blues found them. Sindri didn't even move to check Salene for weapons. She was fresh. She couldn't be more than a month-old recruit.

Whatever did this to them was likely the Mad Queen. She never cared for how many of her people she hurt. She never cared if she lost half as much as the Blues. All that mattered to her was wounding the Empire.

Salene couldn't just let them die.

"You said this Healer helped the Green get off planet?" she asked.

Sindri looked up, brows scrunched together. She was silent, her eyes searching Salene's. "Do Hazels hate Greens?"

"I don't," Salene answered. She shook out her legs, the sore, stinging feeling rolling into the arcs of her feet.

The only place Jade could run to was somewhere the Empire wouldn't look for her. She couldn't flee to Red planets, she couldn't go home to Daoth. Sypher was a possibility, but she was more likely to be found on a planet populated by both sides of the war effort. No, there was only one planet she could retreat to.

"I know where the ship you're trying to reach is," Salene said, looking to them once more. "You went the wrong way. When we reach the river, we'll need to wash those wounds better, they're getting infected." She walked over and knelt by the injured woman. "What's your name?"

"Shelly," the woman breathed. "My name is Shelly."

"Shelly," Salene repeated with a nod. "Okay. I'm Salene." She offered a small smile and turned to Sindri. "I can't offer to carry her, and I can't walk too fast myself. These are… prosthetics, sort of." She gestured to her legs. Did she tell them the Mad Queen hurt her, too? Admitting that would mean admitting she was in the war, and her efforts to help would be stunted. She pushed the information away and stood.

"Travelling together will keep us better protected from animals," she continued. "I've got the location marked on my map. We just need to head this way and we should reach it by nightfall."

A few tears ran down Sindri's cheeks and she nodded hurriedly. She wrapped her good arm around Shelly and lifted her to her feet, allowing the woman to lean against the blonde's side.

"Thank you," Sindri breathed. "Thank you so much."

"No one deserves to die like this," Salene said. *Not even you.*

# Chapter 32

Ferges. Salene had reported in, sending a single message in text format. Ferges. The demon had escaped. The demon had fled to an entirely different planet. Aris knew she should send an extraction team to ensure Salene returned safely since she had recovered vital information, but as she stood to limp towards the exit of her personal tent, her head filled with fire.

"Why would you do that?" Malkov cooed. "She knows where the Green went. And we both know who she would side with if it returned."

Aris grimaced. "It's not coming back. It *ran*."

"Ran to Ferges," Malkov purred. He steepled his fingers as he appeared before her, dressed in vibrant blue and gold. "The planet full of deadly victers. You remember how they nearly sliced you two in half in Nanza City."

"And they'll slice *it* in half."

"Will they?" Malkov chuckled and shook his head. "Or will your little demon go there to make friends? To hire enemies? To find forces to slay you?"

"If it wanted to kill me it would've stayed here!" Aris snapped.

Malkov arched one perfect brow. He shook his head. "You think it escaped according to your plan, don't you?" he asked. "But you're not thinking clearly, Aris. You know it's strong. You know it's not about to go to a planet it thinks it'll die on. You know this beast.

It's stubborn." He leaned forward. "And it's going to come back for you. You tried to kill it. You wanted it dead."

"I didn't—"

"Don't lie to me!" he shouted, his body fragmenting, stained crimson as static consumed part of his body before he reformed, calm, normal once more. Aris recoiled and stumbled a few weak steps back, gripping her crutch.

"There was an instant," he said, his voice a hiss. "An instant that you wanted the beast dead. It might be stubborn, but it's not stupid. You cut that line through the demon's stomach. You stabbed it. You took off its arm—its *dominant* arm." He smirked. "You think it won't be angry with you, Aris? Perhaps you're more naïve than I thought."

She scowled. "The victers have stayed out of the war. They shoot down any ship that comes within range of their planet. The demon won't live."

"Aw, won't it?" He laughed. "What have you been telling me all this time? Telling everyone else? That it was dead. That there was no way it could still be alive. And yet? It lives, Aris. And if it lives through its entry to this little Ferges planet, what then? If it makes a friend or two there, if it proves to be a strong warrior to those tribal folk? What then, Aris?"

"It's not coming back," she insisted. With a locked jaw, she pushed out of the tent, into daylight.

"So you say. If the demon escaped this planet, Aris, wouldn't someone know about it? Wouldn't someone have aided it?" He appeared at her side, a smile on his lips. "Wouldn't one of your soldiers have betrayed you?"

Aris stopped. She looked at him, frowning. Soldiers around in the morning rush of activity acknowledged her with a smile and a salute before rushing to their duties.

"Explain," she whispered.

"I don't need to," he answered. "One of your people sold you out. One of your people *knows* you to be a liar. And if that catches hold? If that gets spread? Your little plan will fall apart."

She looked around, at the tents, at the morning fog beginning to fade, and the faces of Blues who strode past. Kuroda could be seen chatting with someone a few tents down, his ebony scales catching the light and making them shine violet.

"Perhaps it went to a Healer," Malkov offered. "That would be logical, no?"

"Healers hurt it," she muttered. "But that would make sense. it would need someone to patch it up, even a little bit. But it might've gone to someone else—a different base. A different camp."

"Oh?" He smirked. "You don't believe that, do you?"

Aris frowned. "Mine are loyal."

"The two that survived the snakes? Perhaps. But Kasaar's?"

Aris' frown deepened. "Kuroda?" she called, looking in his direction. He met her eyes, nodded, and approached. Aris retreated into her tent, and Kuroda pushed his way through, his mandibles shifting to show his teeth in something akin to a smile.

255

"Friend Aris," he grumbled. "You look… worry."

"Worried," Aris breathed. "Yes, I am." She sat down on her cot, exhaling with relief, her legs given a chance to rest. He tilted his head and approached, kneeling in the dirt in front of her. He placed on hand on her knee.

"What is wrong, friend Aris?"

"Do you think you could track someone?" Aris asked. "Someone who might've passed through here a long time ago?"

"Maybe. This is important to you?"

"Very," she replied. Malkov chuckled from his spot on the table. "I had a friend once, Kuroda. A bad friend. It—*she* never thought I was good enough. She pretended all my ideas were hers. She got all the awards I deserved." Aris shook her head. "A bad friend, Kuroda."

"She make you cry?"

"Yes," Aris said. "Many times."

Kuroda growled. "I am sorry."

"It's okay, Kuroda. You're my friend now." She smiled. "But I thought she died, you see? I thought she died, but she might still be alive, and that's not good."

"She might come hurt again." He shook his head. "Bad."

"Bad, yes, you're right. I have something, maybe you can see if it still smells like her? Find out if she came through here?"

"Yes, friend Aris. Yes, I will help you." He scrutinized her face. "When will go back to Nevar?"

"Soon." Aris shifted to the bottom of her cot and grabbed a small box. She opened it and inside was a small robotic spider. It looked up at her, its back legs crushed.

"This was hers," Aris said, grabbing Spidey and dropping it on the cot. "It should still smell like her."

Kuroda peered at the thing. He grasped it and held it up by one of its broken legs. Spidey squirmed, but could not escape. It looked to Aris once more.

"If the smell leads to anyone in particular," Aris said, looking to Kuroda, "I want to talk."

# Part Three

The burning wreckage of the clinker ship snapped at A'doxia's arms as she pulled the near-dead body from its jaws. Her flesh was covered in bruises, cuts, and burns. Her gloved fingers gripped the woman's blood-stained shirt and pulled, muscles straining, sweat dripping into her eyes.

The trade vessel was on its side in the heart of Ferges, and A'doxia tugged the larger woman out a hole in the ship's belly as a section of itcaved in, spilling metal and wood and carcasses into the hull. A'doxia gritted her teeth and yanked again, and the body came free. She stumbled a few steps in the moist ground as the redhead collapsed beside the ship, unmoving. Her right arm was bandaged. Her stomach was bandaged. Everything about her was gauze and bruises and dehydration. The ship shuddered and A'doxia scrambled forward, gripped Jade beneath the armpits, and pulled, her boots digging into the moss-covered forest floor. Strips of the sails fell like snow around her, as did ash and sparks. Cargo crackled and spat, water sizzled. The engine within exploded.

Shards of metal and wood sprayed out, burning fragments slicing A'doxia's skirt, her bare arms, her stomach. The hiss of cooking flesh joined the chorus of chaos around them as pain made her shudder. The intoxicating agony brought her attention to her loins.

A piece cut Jade's leg, blood gurgling from the wound. With a bitter curse, A'doxia pushed aside thoughts of self-gratification and threw herself over Jade, protecting the woman from shredding rain. A'doxia peered around them, the flames behind her making it difficult to see into the thick darkness of the trees. But it would be better than staying here with a beacon alerting stars-knew-what to their location.

"Just a little further, love," she rasped, her chapped lips splitting open. She let her gaze fall to Jade beneath her. The scabbed wound across her face, much like Voshell's. The tangled crimson hair, the sweat and dirt and mud. And those eyes. Those damn eyes, never opening, hardly waking to greet the day. A'doxia put her fingers to Jade's throat and waited for a few seconds. A pulse pressed against her skin and she let out a breath she didn't realize she was holding.

Jade was still alive.

# Chapter 34

The moment Jade awoke, her nose was bombarded with scents: burning wood crackled somewhere to her left, and each sizzling drip spilled sweet maple into the air; cinnamon stained the scent of bubbling milk, audible somewhere over the fire; flowers spewed a strong aroma that choked out the smoke; and the acrid stench of sweat. She grimaced as she tried to open her eyes, her head throbbing. A sliver of light stabbed through the gap in her eyelids and she jerked against the pain.

Screaming agony flared up in Jade's torso, chewing away at her stomach and ribs. Her muscles grew rigid as she gasped, her toes curling, her hands reaching for her gut. Her eyes snapped open and dots blurred her vision. She blinked and tried to look down, see what was tearing her in two. Searing lights drew tears to her. Her stomach growled, demanding food. Her throat burned, her mouth was dry. Strands of her hair stuck to the bridge of her nose.

Why did everything ache? Was she hurt on the battlefield? Did someone see the color of her eyes? Jade rested her hands on the mat beneath her, the soft fabric folding against her fingers. She tried to sit up.

Before she could get halfway, her right arm gave out and she collapsed, face smashing against the mattress. A jarring, stomach-churning dagger shot hotly through her shoulder. She inhaled through her clenched teeth and looked to her side. Why had her arm given way? Was it hurt, too?

Jade's face drained of blood and ice crystalized her veins. Her entire body shook. Where was her arm? She grabbed at her side, feeling for it, for another hand, fingers, a forearm, *anything*. But all that sat attached to her shoulder was a few inches of her bicep, wrapped in thick bandages.

Her arm was gone. Someone cut it off.

She looked around the room, her eyes brimming with tears of panic and fear. She was in a small cottage, with wooden floors and walls, all of which were tied together with vines and held cracks between each plank. Small crystals hung from the ceiling by ropes, along with several potted plants and jars full of odd liquids. A fire was set up in the middle of the room, atop a flat stone. Above, the smoke filtered out of a small hole in the roof. Jade was on the floor on a mattress, but other than that, there was a single chair in the room and no other furniture. Movement, and Jade's eyes focused on the door across from her, past the fire, as it opened.

And there stood a victer, one of the most deadly creatures in the galaxy.

"Fuck," Jade rasped, her voice hoarse and filled with shards of glass. She searched for a weapon, something to defend herself with. That's when she saw the woman kneeling next to her, the woman that had said nothing. A human with bobbed hazel hair, with a perfectly pointed face, with almond eyes and a scar across her crimson lips.

A'doxia smiled. "Good morn—"

Jade grabbed the blanket that lay over her and threw it at the Red, hoping that would disguise her next move as she turned and rolled off the bed and onto the cold, wooden floor. Every internal organ protested, screeching within their prisons, wishing to spill out of her and onto the wood beneath. Claws tore from inside each of them, enough to constrict Jade's breathing and fog her mind.

A'doxia kidnapped her. A'doxia kidnapped her and cut off her arm? Why would she bring Jade somewhere with victers? Why were they in a victer's home? Jade groaned as the flesh on her torso tore beneath her shirt. At least she still had clothes. But that didn't explain—

"What is she doing?" the victer squawked. "Jade, stop!"

The victer knew her name. Why did they know her name? Jade grabbed the floor and dragged herself forward—to where, she didn't know. The hut wasn't large, and in the nearest corner all there was were a few jars stacked on a small cabinet.

"Jade, stop!" A'doxia yelped, tossing the blanket aside. Jade looked over her shoulder to see the Red stand. "You're *hurt.*"

"You hurt me!" Jade spat. She rolled onto her back and kicked herself away. "Stay the fuck away from me!"

The victer looked to A'doxia. Their expression was impossible to read since they held no human-like facial muscles—no lips, no brows. When it turned those orange eyes back to Jade, the redhead's skin crawled. She gritted her teeth.

"Stay the fuck away," she hissed. "Don't fucking touch me."

"We're not going to touch you," the victer replied, their mouth opening once as their vocal cords did all the work their lipless beak could not. They snapped their mouth close when they were finished and set a jug of water down on the kitchen counter, diagonal from Jade.

"She's going to hurt herself," A'doxia growled. She stepped over the bed, closer to Jade. "Stay still."

Jade pressed herself up against the cabinet at her back and reached over it, grasping a glass container. She shattered it on the floor and held the broken jar towards A'doxia.

"Try me," she snapped.

"Leave her be, A'doxia," the victer said. They held one clawed hand out to the Red, resembling the feet of an avian beast. The victer looked to Jade, their ivory beak streaked with orange and red from the blaze of the fire. "I promise we will not come near you unless you want us to, Jade. You are safe here. No one will hurt you."

Jade scowled. "My arm's gone already, so it seems that didn't apply to whatever the fuck A'doxia did to me."

"The wound happened before I met you," the victer replied. "As did the one on your stomach and face. I stitched you up the best I could, but you should be careful not to tear them out."

Jade cast a look at A'doxia then quickly grabbed the bottom of her shirt and lifted it a few inches. Her eyes widened. She lifted the cloth higher.

From her left hip up to her lowermost right rib, a massive gouge grew deeper the closer it grew to her missing arm. Stitches wove through burned skin and formed a blanket across the wound.

Between the gaps, the injury looked as if it had reached bone. She let her shirt fall. She looked to A'doxia.

"I didn't do that to you, love," A'doxia murmured. She sat down on the bed and showed her hands in a manner to appear less threatening. She wasn't wearing her gloves. Scars crisscrossed across her flesh and on her right hand, the top digits of her innermost three fingers were severed.

Jade frowned. "The victer…?" she muttered, looking to the beast that waited by the kitchen. Their feathers flattened against their head and they spat out a coarse laugh.

"My name is Dagmey, and I did not hurt you, Jade. As I just said, I only met you after your injuries." They motioned to the fire, where a pot of the boiling milk was spilling over. "I'm moving closer just to tend to this, since A'doxia doesn't seem keen on doing what I ask."

A'doxia frowned. "I was tending to Jade."

A shiver ran down Jade's spine. "Don't tend to me."

The Red's eyes narrowed on Jade's face. The Green gripped her broken bottle tighter and held it out towards her once more.

"Leave it, A'doxia. Stop looking at her like that." Dagmey paused and turned to Jade. "Feminine pronouns are accurate for you, yes? That is what A'doxia said, but it's better to ask you personally."

"Yes," Jade replied. She eyed the victer. Orange and brown feathers covered their frame, with black ones sprouting around their face, down the front of their neck, and across their chest and stomach.

Purple sprouts framed the ebony around their face but showed up nowhere else.

This was the first victer Jade had spoken to that wasn't trying to kill her. The first one that seemed compassionate. Perhaps that was something else the Exuro Empire was wrong about—perhaps victers weren't barbarians after all.

"And you?" Jade asked.

Dagmey's facial feathers fluffed up. "Feminine as well, thank you." She tilted her head at Jade. "I appreciate you asking."

"Where did you find me?"

"A'doxia pulled you out of a burning wreckage. I came to investigate since I lived nearby. I spotted you in the roots of some trees, and when I got closer to see what you were, A'doxia attacked me." Dagmey shrugged and knelt by the fire to pull the pot off. She waved her hand over it, trying to cool it off. "When I saw you were both in rough shape, I brought you back here. You've been unconscious the last few days. I was beginning to think you might not wake up."

Jade set the bottle down and touched her stump, where her right arm should be. "And this was…?"

"Already gone."

Jade closed her eyes. There was a flash of cold, blue eyes. The gleam of a blade. Falling. Jade pushed the memory away, refused to see more.

"Was my helmet with me?" Jade croaked, opening her eyes again. "She gets lonely."

"She's been quiet," A'doxia said, her voice unnaturally soft. "But I brought her. I knew you'd want her here."

"Where is she?"

A'doxia moved to the other side of the bed and grabbed something Jade couldn't see. When she turned back around, Chloe was in her hands, a long crack running down her visor. A'doxia moved closer and set Chloe down next to Jade's feet before backing up and resting atop the mattress once more.

"Chloe?" Jade coughed, her throat feeling as if it was full of sand. Chloe didn't answer. Jade grimaced and pushed herself forward, gripping her gut and dragging Chloe near. "Chloe, can you hear me?" Jade asked, leaning back against the cabinet as she set Chloe in her lap. "Are you all right?"

No response. Jade ran her thumb across the fracture, feeling how uneven the glass was.

"Chloe?" Jade's throat closed up. The glint of a blade. Blood. Falling. Blue eyes.

"Chloe, please don't ignore me," Jade whimpered. Tears spilled down her cheeks. "Chloe, *please.*"

The sharp pain of her arm, the buzzing nerves. The crack of her spine against the hard deck. Coughing blood.

"Something terrible happened," Jade murmured. "Something really bad, Chloe. Please be okay."

Blue eyes.

"Chloe, *please.*"

Anger in those blue eyes.

"Don't be dead," Jade cried. "Please, Chloe, don't be dead."

"Why did she do it?" The voice came through, accompanied by static. Chloe's voice. "Why did she do it, Jade?" Her voice was in clear Os, audible to everyone in the room. "Why did Madame Aris try to kill us?"

Chapter 35

Kuroda found the traitor.

A female kodarian with a cracked horn and the Healer Helix. She stood in Aris' tent, spine straight, as the general scrolled through ship logs under the woman's name.

"Corporal Ukaleq Maaike, is that right?" Aris asked. The kodarian nodded stiffly, hands resting at her side. She was dressed in her undersuit and nothing else. Kuroda paced behind her, blocking her exit.

"Is something wrong, general?" she asked. Her voice sounded like rocks against Aris' skull.

The general rubbed her temple. "It says here you authorized a shipment of supplies back to Nevar about a week ago. Is this true?"

"Yes, general."

"And was there anything unusual in that package, corporal?" Aris looked up from her wrist holo. "It doesn't say on the manifest."

"Just the normal, general: broken swords and armor for repair. Dog tags."

"Mhmm."

"Are you going to let her lie to you?" Malkov asked, standing at Aris' left. Aris sighed, running a hand over her face.

"There was something else, wasn't there, corporal?"

"I'm sorry, general, I don't know what you mean," Ukaleq replied. "It was all normal."

"Mm. If that's the case, why hasn't the ship been logged as having arrived back in Nanza City?"

"I'm… not sure." She glanced away.

Aris' eyes narrowed. "I think you have a suspicion."

"Perhaps pirates, general?"

"They're all lying to you," Malkov murmured. "Look at her. She's brazen."

"I don't appreciate your lies, corporal," Aris said. "Tell me the truth."

"I am, general." The woman looked at Aris, meeting the woman's cold gaze. Her own eyes narrowed. "I sent broken weapons and—"

"Liar!" Aris snapped. Without anything needing to be said, Kuroda seized Ukaleq's arms and held the woman tight. The corporal's eyes widened and she struggled against the man's hold.

"General, what is this?" Ukaleq breathed.

Aris grabbed her crutches and stood, limping closer. "You sent the Green off-planet," Aris whispered.

Ukaleq's eyes widened a fraction of an inch. She quickly looked away, scowling, nostrils above her eyes flaring. "I don't know what you're talking about."

269

"You know exactly what I'm talking about. Where did she say she was going? What part of Ferges?"

"I don't know—"

Aris slapped her. The sound rang in the small tent. Kuroda growled, pulling the woman against his chest to keep her from retaliating. Ukaleq's blue eyes filled with hatred. She looked at Aris.

"She was your best friend," Ukaleq hissed. "And you tried to kill her. She's not a monster—you are!" She spat, the glob of saliva hitting right under Aris' left eye. Kuroda roared in fury and threw Ukaleq to the ground. He pressed his foot against her back and kept her from standing.

"No!" he shouted. "No!"

"You don't understand anything, corporal," Aris muttered, wiping her face against her undersuit's sleeve. "I never tried to kill the Green."

"Liar," Malkov whispered. Aris shot him a bitter look. He smiled.

"You cut off her arm," the corporal grumbled against the mud, struggling to lift her mouth off the ground. "You threw her off the side of an island! All she wants is to go somewhere far away from you!"

Aris paused. "Far away from me?"

"Can you be so sure?" Malkov purred. "She got a way off this planet, she can get a way back on. And if this soldier corporal believes you tried to kill her, who would she have heard that from but the Green itself?"

"I didn't do anything wrong," Ukaleq growled. "She was injured. She would've died!"

"Good!" Aris spat, the words ringing in her ears, sending adrenaline through her heart. "You should have let it! It is *dangerous*, corporal! And now you've let it—" She took a breath and lowered her voice. "Who else knows?"

"What?"

"Who else knows you sent her off-planet?"

"Just you," Ukaleq said. "I didn't tell anyone else, general."

"Good. Kuroda, let her up."

Kuroda huffed and stepped away. The woman got to her feet, scowling, and wiped the mud off her face.

"You are on scouting duty today," Aris said, waving dismissively. "Begin now. Report back whatever you find."

Ukaleq narrowed her eyes at Aris, but she saluted, dipped her head respectfully, and walked out. Kuroda watched the woman go before looking back to Aris.

"She disrespect," Kuroda grumbled, walking closer to lend a supportive hand. Aris took it and leaned against him a little. "She bad for friendship with others. She bad."

"There's little I can do," Aris sighed. "It's not like…"

"Forest is danger," Kuroda said. "Anything happen."

Aris looked up at him. She stepped away. "Anything could happen. Kuroda, do you fancy a hunt?"

271

Kuroda flashed his teeth, his mandibles flaring in a gruesome grin. "Will return when done."

# Chapter 36

Jade couldn't sleep. She laid awake as night fell, as the fire reduced itself to hot coals. Rain danced upon the roof, pairing with the sound of snapping twigs within the crimson flames. She laid on her back and stared at the ceiling, where rope tied the beams together, and thick, heavy leaves were woven to create a roof. The trickle of sweet-smelling smoke filtered out through the hole in its peak, but even through that, she could not see the stars. She let her hand rest idly on the stitches across her gut, her warm fingers curling beneath the tattered fabric of her shirt. It ached at a constant degree and skin was peeling. Jade closed her eyes. Aris stared back at her in the darkness of her mind.

With a heavy sigh, she looked to her right, where Chloe was situated on a pillow only a foot away. Jade let her fingers trail over the A.I.'s shattered visor.

"Want to get some air?" she murmured.

"Is it safe for you to move?" Chloe asked, her voice soft and gentle.

"Safe enough." Jade pushed herself up into a sitting position, her arm straining with exhaustion, a drip of sweat falling from her nose. Her wounds burned. The laceration across her face itched. Jade looked past the foot of her bed, at the ring of blankets and pillows that circled the fire pit. There, the victer, Dagmey, was curled up, legs pulled to her chest, hands beneath her head. A'doxia was opposite of her, sleeping on her stomach with one arm stretched above her head.

It was her right, the injured one from their battle with Voshell. From their battle with Thaddeous.

Jade grimaced and gripped her stump, a searing, biting pain drilling its way into her bones. The bandages creased beneath her grip as she held her breath, waiting for it all to pass.

"Perhaps we should stay in," Chloe said in Os. "It might be better."

"No," Jade rasped. She took a few deep inhales and pressed the pain away. She released her arm and gripped her shirt instead, clenching her jaw. "I'll be better in—" another sharp inhale— "in a moment."

Chloe fell silent as Jade waited. She swore her fingers curled on her right hand, swore she could feel her forearm throb with agony. Was this a dream? Maybe she still had her arm, if only she could wake. Maybe Aris hadn't tried to kill her. Maybe she wasn't without a home, on a planet with a woman who wished to torture her.

"Do you think she really meant it?" Chloe asked after a few minutes. Jade started to loosen her grip on her shirt as the pain dulled to a low throb. She grabbed Chloe and pulled the helmet to her as she got to her feet. Her toes flared as she stumbled onto the wood floor, legs shaking from the effort of supporting her weight. The room spun as her head grew light.

"Jade?" Chloe said. "Jade, to your right—there's a shelf, use that to lean on."

Jade did as Chloe said, blindly reaching out with her right hand only for her ribs to smash against the shelf. She cursed bitterly and set Chloe on the mantle, grabbed her shoulder, and cursed again. She kept forgetting. All day she kept forgetting. A swell of emotion bubbled up in her throat. Was this what her life was going to be now? Stabs of pain from her wounds, the phantom memory of an arm she no longer had? Why did Aris hate her? Why did Aris try to kill her?

"It's okay," Chloe murmured, "I'm here, Jade. You and me. We made it through all right."

"And look where we are," Jade whimpered. The light from the fire flickered across Chloe's visor and Jade's reflection shone within it. She saw a woman with ratted red hair, with a scab from her jaw to the bridge of her nose. A woman with brows pulled upwards together, with green eyes, with tears shining in them. The large fracture split the image in two. It was unfamiliar. It wasn't her.

She grabbed Chloe again and stumbled towards the door of the small shack, clumsily making her way past Dagmey, nearly stepping on her feathers a few times. At last, she arrived, and she pushed the door open with ease.

A deck encompassed the home, made of similar craftsmanship as the house: planks of wood tied together, with knots and holes frequent. The railing consisted of scavenged branches, some of which boasted leaves. Vines and moss hung wherever it could get a foothold. As Jade's heels pressed into the soaking overgrowth, water oozed out of it and stained them green. She padded over to a clearer spot and sat down. She set Chloe beside her as she stared at her surroundings.

No one had ever returned from Ferges. The only information on the planet was what had been relayed before whatever forcefield that shot ships down was put in place. They knew it was home to a planet-wide forest. They knew the trees were tall. But no one had realized how tall.

Jade sat perched in one such tree with no way of telling how high up off the ground she was. The trees around her extended into darkness, massive branches full of leaves spreading out in every direction, pelted by raindrops as they splattered across viridian fans. When she looked up, she saw a similar sight: trees curving into the black above, not even a speck of stars peering through the thick canopy. She took a deep inhale, felt a fresh, bitter cold that swallowed up her lungs, chilled every vessel in her body. The shower continued around them, filling the air with a sweet scent unlike any other. It almost smelled of strawberries—a rare human fruit salvaged from wherever they came from before arriving in the Known Galaxy.

Jade scooted to the edge of the deck and let her legs dangle over the side. A sinking feeling rose up in her gut as her body recognized the risk. But falling through a forest like this could hardly be considered a horrible outcome to her wretched life. Her lungs bursting with fruit as her body flew free? How could she hate such a thing as death when it could come to a candied conclusion?

"Jade?" Chloe asked. Jade blinked and looked away from the abyss, over at the helmet. A few misty drops rolled across her visor and collected in the crack. "What did we do wrong?" she asked. "Why does Aris hate us?"

Whatever joy the drizzle had brought her, whatever joy that filled Jade's mouth with dessert in the form of fresh, clean air unlike the polluted planet of Nevar—it all left her that instant. Instead, she tasted ash and a weight fell upon her shoulders that she couldn't shake.

Jade closed her eyes. She placed her hand on her right arm, felt her fingers press through the air where it should be, and remembered once more that it was gone.

"I don't know," Jade murmured.

"Why don't you know?" Chloe asked. "Why don't you know why she hates us?"

"I don't know, Chloe," Jade said again. "We were gone for a while. I… I guess anything could've happened." She looked down at the shadows of the trees. Pondered for a moment what dying would feel like. "But she tried to kill me. She…" Jade gripped her shirt, choking on her words. "I don't know why, Chloe."

"Did we do something?"

"I don't know," Jade said.

"Could we just apologize?"

"Chloe, I don't *know!*" She turned to the helmet, rage and sorrow straining her sandpaper voice. "I don't know what we did! After so long, I just… I just wanted to make sure she was safe." Tears trailed down her cheeks. A few drops of rain fell atop her head. "Maybe we just…" She trailed off and looked down at her hand, at the callouses and scrapes. She lifted it up and watched as water dotted her palm, filled in the ridges and seams, spilled off the side and between her fingers. Emptiness made a nest in her ribs. It situated itself there with heaviness and remorse. Jade closed her eyes.

"I thought she was our friend," Chloe said. "Jade, I…" A strange sound emanated from Chloe's speakers, pulling the redhead away from her grief to peer at the helmet quizzically. Something akin to static and sobs spilled out of the A.I.

"I am feeling so much," Chloe continued. "I do not know what to do. What am I feeling, Jade? Did I damage something?"

Jade's shoulders slumped, her brows pressing together. She pulled her legs off the edge and curled them up against herself and brought Chloe into her lap.

"*You* were hurt," Jade breathed. "Not something physical, but who you are, Chloe." She took a shaky breath, her wounds burning. "You're *feeling*. Emotions. Like me."

"Like… you?" Chloe fell silent a moment. "Am I alive?"

"You're alive, Chloe," Jade said. "I'm sorry you've been gifted emotions now of all times." She closed her eyes. "I know it hurts."

"We can hurt together," Chloe whispered. "You and me. As we've always been."

Jade offered a slight, small smile. Tears clogged her throat.

"Okay," she managed. "You and me, Chloe."

# Chapter 37

Aris limped towards the top of the port, where the walkway met with the island. Salene did not return after four days of radio silence. It would be a waste of resources to search for her. More so— discovery of Salene's task would place Aris in a bad light. She would need to find evidence of the queen's demise in a different way. She would need a different path forward. Perhaps if she was called back for a different reason? Perhaps if there was a threat on Nevar itself?

"General Sell?"

Aris looked up to see a snipper standing nearby, holding a log of items received in the recent shipment from the Exuro Empire. Around him, boxes were stacked at the edge of camp, each container held together by stripped screws and thin, cracking metal. Aris held her hand out for the log, and the snipper offered it over.

"It's half of what we asked for," he reported as she scanned over the manifest. A meager amount of armor, a few dozen H-blades, extra-small undersuits unusable for most platoons. Enough rations for a few months, but there was a note on the holopad, which she clicked on to bring up an alert:

*20% of rations damaged in transport.*

A scowl crossed Aris face and she handed the holo back. "How are the rations damaged?"

"A few of the boxes cracked," the man said. "As the rations spilled out, a few of them cut themselves on the sharp box edges and opened up. We've no idea when this happened."

She rubbed her eyes. "Of course." *They want us to die.* "Was anything else damaged?"

"We've not finished looking through the armor and weapons they sent," he said. "But I'll let you know if we find anything else, general."

"Thank you, private." She offered him a small smile. "I would like to ask that you and anyone else pause that work for now, however. Please, come to the breakfast area. I want to speak with the troops."

He blinked. "Oh, of course, general. All the troops?"

"Yes, all of you. Gather who you can. I'll be there soon."

"Yes, general, of course." He saluted before running off towards the harbor.

Nerves buzzed beneath Aris' skin for what she was about to do, paired with the excited jitters that made her toes warm. She turned and used the crutches to limp her way to the chef's pot, a smile on her lips. To soldiers she passed, she informed the request to see them at the pot shortly. And as she neared it, Kuroda found her, flashing his rendition of a smile on his lipless face. He had a section of bone dripping with blood. Leathery, grey skin stretched across the meat. Kuroda took a bite of it, crimson oozing from his mouth and dripping off his chin.

"Friend Aris," he said around his mouthful. "You smile? Happy?"

"I am, Kuroda," she said, her mind focused on the task at hand. Sweat collected on the nape of her neck as Sobek's thick, hot air bore down on her. "How many friends have you made here?"

"You."

"Other than me, Kuroda. It's important."

Kuroda hummed with thought. "Four."

"Four?" Aris clicked her tongue. Less than ideal. But four was better than none. She would make do.

With a nod to a passing soldier, she invited them to the pot. Kuroda continued to chew on his food. He must have found it in the woods, but there was no time to ask. Aris would test the waters here, make her point to her soldiers.

Perhaps she didn't need the Mad Queen's head to go home with. Perhaps she just needed an army.

# Chapter 38

Jade often found herself fantasizing about her own death. As she lay in bed, Chloe resting on the pillow beside her, she wondered again what it would be like to step off the deck outside, to fall through the leaves. The pressure would likely render her unconscious. She wouldn't even feel the impact. But then Chloe noticed she was awake and said, in a voice that seemed to hold a smile:

"Good morning, Jade."

Jade smiled. "Good morning, Chloe."

The dawn broke with a pattering of rain and the sounds of an overfilled pot spilling onto the fire. Nutmeg and cinnamon paired with the aroma of boiled apples and honey.

"Shit," Dagmey breathed. Her talons scraped across the floor as she rushed to the fire's edge. Jade lifted her head and peered over at the victer as she quickly pulled the pot from the fire, gripping the handle as if it didn't burn. She lifted it up and muttered clicks and caws in a distinct, repeated series. Jade hadn't thought of it before, but she supposed the victers had their own unique language. And if that was the case, how did she know Os?

"Did you sleep well?" A'doxia's voice startled Jade, a shock of remembrance of where she was, who was there with her. She looked to the chair perched in the corner, where A'doxia sat. Bandages around her severed fingers were partially unwrapped, as if she had been tending to them when she realized the redhead had awoken. She also appeared as if she had bathed, her hair wet and dripping onto an oversized shirt, with lettering plastered across its green fabric that Jade couldn't read. It hung low enough to show the hints of a scar across the woman's chest from their struggle in the apartment. A'doxia smiled at Jade. Jade looked away.

"*Are you all right?*" Chloe asked, her voice masked now in their specific coded dialect.

"I'm all right," Jade murmured, the lie burning her tongue. She glanced at the helmet, a pang of guilt spreading through her mouth. "As all right as I can be," she added.

"Your helmet has been speaking plainly for a while," A'doxia remarked. "Is that normal? I thought it always spoke to you in its own little code."

Jade didn't answer. She laid on her back and stared at the ceiling. What good was answering, anyway? What did it matter what A'doxia wanted to know? Jade wanted to go home. And she wasn't going to get to. Why should A'doxia get anything if Jade didn't?

"Breakfast is ready," Dagmey chimed, her feathers fluffed around her face. "A Ferges specialty, so I've been told. And I'm fairly certain all this is edible by humans." She glanced into her pot, still clasped over the fire. She tilted her head. "Fairly certain."

"*Should we stay here?*" Chloe asked, her voice much like a whisper. "*Is it safe?*"

Safe? Did it matter if they were safe? They had lost everything, hadn't they? Their home, their friend, their purpose? What were they but just an image to hate, a scapegoat, a demon? What did it matter if they were safe? Aris should've killed her. Aris should've driven the blade into Jade's heart.

With a grimace, she placed her hand on Chloe's visor, focusing on the smooth glass, how it met with the metal, the seam that connected them both together. Jade let her thumb cross over the crack once more, let the edges bite at her skin, let it hurt. Chloe was becoming more alive. Jade didn't understand how, or why, but the A.I. wasn't calling her 'mistress' anymore. She wasn't being formal. She was mourning, confused, afraid. Jade had to stay.

At least until she knew Chloe would be safe. And if either of them were near A'doxia, they weren't safe.

"For now," Jade replied. She took a deep breath and pushed herself into a sitting position. Dagmey looked over, chirped, and quickly brought her pot into the kitchen. There, she set it down on the wood counter and ladled out the contents into two bowls and one mug. Steam spilled towards the smoke and spiraled up into the outside air above. Jade leaned against the wall behind her pillow, relieving her aching muscles, and felt the wind slip through the gaps in the wood and chill the collecting sweat on her spine.

Dagmey walked over and offered the bronze soup to Jade. "Here you are," she murmured, her voice gentle. There was no expression on her face besides her purple feathers fanning out behind the black. Jade reached forward to touch the cup held out to her, brushing her fingers across the thick wood, and was surprised to find it cool to the touch. She gripped the handle.

"Thank you," she rasped, looking to the victer's orange eyes. Jade's brows furrowed. Did orange eyes mean something? She recalled no mention of them in the Followers of Vix's sacred texts. Yet the texts told the galaxy that Greens were demons, so could such beliefs hold any merit? Perhaps Oranges were the same as Greens—a simple color in the eye, one that had no deeper meaning.

"The twigs in there are protein," Dagmey said, using a claw to point towards Jade's soup. "I would eat all of them to help keep your energy up. You need all you can get to heal that wound of yours."

Jade investigated her soup, saw pieces of softened apples bobbing at the top along with leaves and small twigs. She inhaled the smell and it warmed her lungs, reminding her of apple cider on Daoth with her parents. Sitting outside as snow fell across the fields around them, enjoying a warm drink before they geared up to train once more. Were her parents alive? After the galaxy declared Jade was a demon, would the two of them be hunted down? She suspected her mother would have brought her father far away from Daoth, perhaps fleeing to Sypher and finding a home far in the mountains, away from any prying eyes.

Jade noticed Dagmey was watching her, and quickly nodded. "I will," she breathed. "I'll eat it all. Thank you, Dagmey."

Dagmey's feathers fanned out in full. "You are quite welcome, Jade. We'll look at your stomach after you've eaten and replace the bandages, hm?" She paused. "You went outside the other night. Would you like to sit out there after breakfast?"

Jade blinked. Dagmey had heard her leave? She supposed that shouldn't be overly surprising, considering how clumsy Jade was on her feet. She started to nod.

"Outside?" A'doxia said, arching a brow. "You let her leave unwatched?"

"She was well enough," Dagmey said. "It's good to get fresh air when healing." She stood and walked over to A'doxia, handing her the other bowl.

"She could've hurt herself," A'doxia hissed. "I need a spoon."

"You drink it, and she didn't."

"With all that moss out there, that thousand-foot fall? Are you insane?"

"I have been told I am many times," Dagmey said, voice dripping with icicles. "And yet, not insane enough to underestimate one such as your friend."

A'doxia sneered. "Look at her. She can't hardly sit up without pain. If she were to fall, she wouldn't be able to grab onto anything long enough for us to get to her. Do not suggest things that will get her killed."

Jade closed her eyes. The two argued for a time, their voices snipped and garbled in her head, rattling about like bolts in the hilts of broken H-blades. She set her cup down on the wood floor while the two bickered about what she could and could not do. She looked down at her shirt, the white fabric worn with stains of mud and blood. Near the edge of the shirt there was a beginning of a tear, and she pressed her fingers into it, expanding it, the thread biting and digging red lines into her flesh. When it was about as wide as the tip of her thumb, she reached over and dragged Chloe closer, took the clip on the back of her helm, and linked it through the hole. And as her mind muted words spewed about her abilities, her life, her survival, Jade picked up her cup, struggled to her feet, and limped out of the house.

The air was fresher on the deck. Jade's bare feet sank into the moss, soaked themselves in the green water that oozed from the surface. She leaned her left shoulder against the house's exterior wall to keep her balance as her intestines ached with protest and her stitches itched. She paced to the opposite side of the house before settling down on the floor, vines dripping the morning condensation onto her back. She went to scratch her stomach, forgetting her right arm was gone with a disgruntled huff.

"It is nicer out here," Chloe said. "Thank you for bringing me with you."

Jade looked out over the forest, peering through the trickling light that speared through the canopy above to illuminate some of the upper branches. Still, when she cast her gaze upwards, she could not see the tops of the trees, now blinded by the sun instead of by darkness. Birds chirped and sang around her, along with chittering bugs and a chorus of sounds she had no names for. To her left, a tree stood tall with bark stripping off its form, curling in long streaks and revealing beneath each a different color. Blues and crimsons painted it, along with yellows and vibrant greens, and sometimes an occasional purple.

"I'm glad you're here," Jade said, her voice a whisper as she looked around at the world surrounding her. "I've always liked forests."

"I know you have, Jade," Chloe replied. "It is a good place to be. A good place to recover."

"Is that what I should do? Recover?" She looked down at her cup, swirled it a little, inhaled the smell of wet grass with the soup's spiced apple aroma.

"I think it's all you can do. It is good to heal, isn't it?"

"Can I heal from this?"

"I hope so, Jade."

A small, sad smile crossed the Green's lips. She lifted the cup and took a sip of its contents. It tasted near identical to spiced cider, something she had on several occasions back on Daoth, where trees were planted in groves and the humans guarded these relics of a planet they could not remember. She and her mother had walked to the nearby market, goggles placed firmly over Jade's emerald eyes, and picked up boxes of apples Jade would have to carry back as part of her training. Her father, the creator of all things, would be the one to spice and boil them, bring out their juices and spill them into cups for all three of them to enjoy on cold nights while they watched the stars. More than once, he climbed onto the roof where Jade would lay as a child, ask her which stars she wanted to visit, what she would like to see. Her father was always good to her. She hoped he wasn't dead.

Jade bit down on one of the twigs and a burst of cinnamon and vanilla spread across her tongue. As it plunged into her stomach, it filled her as if it were meat. She smiled and closed her eyes.

"Jade, look!" Chloe whispered a few minutes later. Jade opened her eyes and saw a bird perched upon a branch not far away. Covered in bright blue feathers with an orange underbelly, the white-beaked creature chirped as it peered at its surroundings. It looked no larger than Jade's fist and was perhaps twenty feet from the edge of the deck, flicking its tail and singing its song. Another series of twittering responded to it, and the bird looked around, trying to find the source. It hopped a few steps up the branch. A snake struck its neck.

The ivory creature, about the size of Jade's forearm, clamped down on the bird's neck and flung its body around the bird, wrapping it up tight to prevent its prey from flying away. Jade watched, eyes wide. When the bird collapsed, the snake unhinged its jaw and swallowed the animal whole. How had something so bright evaded notice before? How had it snuck up on a bird with such vibrant scales?

"Oh, thank the stars." A'doxia's voice pulled Jade's attention from the small beast and to her right, where A'doxia rushed across the surface of the deck to kneel and throw her arms around Jade's neck. Shivers ran down her spine before they faded into a distant buzz of anticipated danger.

"I was so worried," A'doxia breathed. "Don't you dare do that again."

Jade frowned and looked back towards the snake. After its prey had been consumed, it lifted its head and peered at her, its black eyes meeting hers. An ebony tongue flickered from its mouth before, surprisingly, it chirped.

"You could have *fell*," A'doxia said, pulling away to look at Jade. Jade lifted her cup and sipped its contents, the chill that rushed down her vertebrae solidifying, stiffening her back. A'doxia's brows furrowed in the corner of her vision.

289

"Are you listening to me, love?" the woman murmured.

Jade met her crimson gaze. "Stop touching me."

A'doxia blinked. She pulled back and rested her hands in her lap. It was strange, perhaps, for Jade to be so calm in A'doxia's presence. Strange, perhaps, that Jade did not feel the music of fear drumming in her veins. Yet there was little A'doxia could do that Jade had not already endured. There was little to fear from a woman who reveled in such an emotion.

Jade looked back towards the snake as it lowered itself along the branch. It slithered along, towards the trunk of the tree, where it curled into a shadowed crook.

"Does the outside air help?" Dagmey asked, coming up alongside A'doxia, the woman's talons gripping the moss and tearing holes in it whenever her feet lifted. "I know it calms me when I'm troubled."

"It helps," Jade replied. "Your soup is good."

Dagmey's facial feathers fanned out. She dipped her head with a soft chuckle.

"Thank you, Jade," she said. "Would you like more time out here alone?"

Jade nodded towards Chloe. "I'm not alone, but yes. It would be nice for Chloe and me to be here by ourselves."

"Very well. If you need anything, just holler." Dagmey looked to A'doxia. "Shall we?"

A'doxia was still watching Jade, her expression clouded with confusion. She pushed herself to her feet, the torn skirt she was wearing stained green along her knees. She followed Dagmey out of view.

"You handled that well," Chloe said.

"Thanks, Chloe."

"Perhaps you're healing after all."

Jade finished off her soup and set it by her side. The uneven surface caused it to topple over as she touched her right stump.

"Maybe," she murmured, closing her eyes again. "Why don't you call me 'mistress' anymore, Chloe?"

"Would you like me to?"

"No, but I could never deactivate the programming in you before to make you stop. What changed?"

Chloe was silent for a few thoughtful moments. "We're friends now, aren't we?"

"We have always been friends." Jade moved her hand away from her shoulder and placed it atop Chloe. "Even when you called me fat."

"You needed to lose weight, Jade."

Jade laughed, her voice echoing through the trees, blooming warmth in her chest like the breakfast she had just finished. She gripped her stomach as she found herself unable to stop, each breath shallower than the last. Joy twisted into mourning, into pain. She

291

gritted her teeth as tears sprang to her eyes, as she leaned against the hut, as her fingers crimped the fabric beneath their grasp.

"Jade? Jade, please! It wasn't that funny!"

Jade couldn't help but smile at that, yet the emotions came still, flooding her with agony and hatred and remorse. Everything was so wrong now, so perverted. Her best friend was gone, her home was gone. Her arm had been taken, her body maimed, and years before that, her mind had been contorted by the blade A'doxia held. Jade slumped and let her back slide down until she was splayed out, her ankles over the edge of the deck, her face up towards the leaves far above. Tears spilled down the side of her face, dripped into her ears, made it difficult to hear as Chloe whispered two words:

"Fuck her."

*Which her?* Jade wondered. *Which woman is deemed worthy of your first profanity?* Between sobs, Jade laughed. *Fuck them both. Fuck them all. Fuck A'doxia, fuck Aris, fuck Voshell. Fuck all of them.*

Jade's grip on her stomach lessened. "Yeah. Fuck them."

Chapter 39

Whispering within tents overflowed to rants around the fire. Aris' name sat on the lips of soldiers, fractions of her plan passed from one to another, cheered over at dinner. The Healers worked overtime on her legs, doing their best to get them into better shape before the trip. Aris kept a small smile on her lips, pleased with her work, pleased that it was turning out the way she desired. Perhaps her plot had to change from time to time, but the end result was going to be the same. She would return to Nevar, return to Nanza City, and she would do so as a revolutionary.

Her soldiers only needed to know half of it.

"What is the meaning of this?" Kasaar stepped into the medical tent, his face twisted into a scowl. Aris placed a hand on the woman tending to her legs, and the snipper smiled and stepped away to give them space. Granted, the medical tent had a few other soldiers in there, including Katlego—who was receiving his last bout of healing—and Qiu. The two surviving members of Aris' platoon watching from a nearby cot.

"General Kasaar," Aris said, stretching her legs out across the bed, feeling the bones better fused together beneath her flesh. She ran her hands across them, exhaling. They no longer throbbed upon contact, though there was a buzzing reminder not to push her luck with what they could do.

"The troops are talking about… about *revolt?* They are saying you're going to help them earn respect? What on Nevar does any of that mean?"

"Oh, I would've included you, Kasaar, but we both know you're a Gold lapdog." Aris smiled at him.

His eyes widened. "How *dare* you speak—"

"I do dare, general, because I understand that I will outrank you very soon. And I understand that my abilities far outweigh your own. I will take a galleon and fill it full of soldiers to join me in returning home and making the push to become equal citizens. I will entrust the rest of the war here to—well, not you, general, but our third general companion here, General Retez. I think she'll do just fine finishing the Reds. Recent reports say they've retreated to some fortified location, am I right? I say that's proof the Mad Queen is dead." She pulled her legs off the side of the cot. "Unless you'd rather us Blues not have any basic rights? Perhaps stay here and die forever? What happens when the war is over, general? Do we go home and suffer as third-class citizens for the rest of the Empire's life?"

Kasaar's eyes narrowed and he stepped closer. "You're going to doom us, Aris. You're going to make a move that no one will back. You think you can just fly home and convince, what? The Golds that you deserve respect?"

Malkov chuckled as he sat on the edge of the bed. "He doesn't know even a breath of the plan, does he?"

Aris shook her head. "Not to worry, Kasaar. I won't mention your little secrecy issue to the Golds while I'm fighting for our liberation."

"You think the Golds would care about a few messages when you're bringing such a foolish proposition to their doorstep?"

"You seem to think the Golds would appreciate your own little treachery." Aris grabbed one of her crutches and started to stand. "I think—"

Kasaar shoved her back onto the cot, and she blinked as she hit the canvas. He glowered down at her, kicking her crutches away.

"If you think I'm going to let you leave and ruin Blue chances of surviving past the war, you're more stupid than I thought."

"Get away from her." Qiu stood by Katlego's cot, teeth bared. "You have no right to lay hands on her."

"I have every right. General Aris Sell, with these two as witnesses, I challenge you. A duel, now, outside. Loser steps down from their position."

"She's *injured*," Katlego hollered, sitting up in his cot. "You piece of shit—"

Kasaar waved him off, eyes on Aris. "Do not refuse, Aris."

"I name Kuroda as my champion," Aris said.

Silent as a leaf settling on the forest floor, Kuroda entered the tent, his shadow falling upon Kasaar.

Kasaar quickly spun. "No champions!" he shouted. "Just—!"

Kuroda smashed his open palm against the man's jaw, throwing him into the muddy floor, muck splattering across his horns and into his mouth.

A growl rumbled from Kuroda's throat and he looked to Aris. "He touch you?" he asked.

Aris pushed herself upright and nodded. "He doesn't want us to leave, Kuroda."

"He try to hurt friend." He looked down as Kasaar got to his feet. "Take care of."

"Just knock him out," Aris said. "The Golds would want us to kill each other. We shouldn't be like them." She spoke a little louder so Katlego, Qiu, and the other soldiers in the tent could hear her. There were a few murmurs of approval. A few whispers of praise. As Kuroda grabbed Kasaar by the horns and broke them from his temples, Aris couldn't help her smile.

# Chapter 40

Dagmey insisted Jade rest inside until dinner to help herself heal, and reluctantly, Jade complied. For the final meal of the day, she was given thick broth. Light faded from above, and the small gems hanging from the ceiling emanated gentle, colored glows. Most of them were blue, but one near the door was orange, and the one over Jade's bed was silver. As she peered into her wooden cup, the orange broth took on a more metallic gleam, heavy with the smell of herbs and toasted nuts. Jade took a sip. The smooth flavors of almonds, onions, celery, and a fatty, meaty liquid spilled past her tongue.

"Is it good, Jade?" Chloe asked.

"Very. Thank you, Dagmey."

Dagmey dipped her head as she handed a cup to A'doxia. The Red had taken up residence on the chair and hadn't said a word since she left Jade outside on the deck. Her eyes were distant as if she was contemplating something that took her full attention. Still, she grasped the cup and sipped it thankfully.

"I was wondering if I might join you on the deck tonight," Dagmey said, looking to Jade. "The forest is truly beautiful in the evening."

"Sure," Jade said. She didn't mind the victer's company, but she didn't desire A'doxia's. Dagmey walked over and took Jade's cup for her as the woman clipped Chloe to her shirt. Jade stumbled to her feet and Dagmey returned her dinner.

"I saw you were watching one of our resident snakes this morning," Dagmey said, pushing the door open and allowing Jade out first. "If you're lucky, they'll come back tonight and you'll see them hunt again."

"Does it hunt birds in the evening?" Jade asked, exiting the hut and walking along the deck to her previous spot on the opposite side.

Dagmey shook her head and followed a short ways behind. "They hunt bugs at night, but they have a rather special way of doing it. If they don't show up, I'll tell you, but it's much more interesting to see."

"Do all victers know so much about their world?" Chloe asked from Jade's hip.

"Oh! Ah, well, I'm not entirely sure. I've been outside normal society for a long time, truthfully. Since I realized what I was, honestly." Dagmey shrugged. "I think if you live on your own a few days away from the nearest city, you tend to get familiar with your surroundings."

"What do you mean, what you are?" Jade asked, reaching her spot from the morning and lowering herself down. Her shoulder buzzed with phantom pain and Jade pressed her warm cup to the bandages, hoping that might help.

"I forget that you aren't familiar with victers," Dagmey said, sitting down next to her. "I wasn't born as a woman, you see. I have different parts. Most can tell because of the purple feathers around my face." Dagmey gestured to the edge of her black facial plumage, where dusty violent fringe poked out. "Usually people like me dye their feathers to pass better, but I like them."

Jade nodded as she pulled her cup from her bandages, the pain fading into an infuriating itch. She took a sip of her dinner. "I'm sorry they didn't accept you, Dagmey."

"That's sweet of you to say. Thank you, Jade." Dagmey dipped her head to the woman at her right before tossing some of the broth into her beak and swallowing. Around them, the Ferges night was underway, with small lightning bugs flying through the air, settling on branches, a shadowy shape with wings swooping down and eating them up. Further below, Jade could make out faint glowing spires with colors like those in Dagmey's hut.

"You haven't spoken much about how this happened to you," Dagmey said after a few beats of silence. "Do you remember?"

"I remember," Jade replied. She exhaled slowly. "I wish I didn't, though."

"It's good to remember," Chloe offered. "That way she can't do it again."

"You're right, Chloe," Jade said. "And I have you with me, anyway. Who needs anyone else?"

"Is your companion not a friend?" Dagmey asked. "I had assumed… the way she was protecting you and looking after you… perhaps something other than a friend?"

"With that wretched bitch?" Chloe hissed.

Jade chuckled at Chloe's response and shook her head. "I share no love for A'doxia," she said, eyes gazing at the trees. In a nearby branch, perhaps twenty feet off the side of the deck, there were a series of lights that flickered on and off, one by one, along the backdrop of a faint, white glow. Jade watched it with a furrowed brow.

"Oh, forgive me," Dagmey muttered. "I just…"

"I have heard worse," Jade said, looking to Dagmey and offering a small smile. "You're not upsetting me, Dagmey. I have no doubt she said things to you while I was unconscious to indicate she was… *with* me, somehow."

"And you're not."

"No," Jade answered. "I'm not and have never been. Not with her, not with anyone. I don't feel that way towards people."

Dagmey watched her before she tossed back the last of her broth and set her cup down. "Did she do this to you?"

"No, she didn't." Jade looked to the branch, watched the strange lights. "Not these recent wounds, anyway."

"But she hurt you at one point?"

Jade closed her eyes and sighed.

"Oh, I'm so sorry," Dagmey sputtered quickly. "I'm not trying to upset you. You don't have to talk about it."

Jade rested her head against the wall at her back, listened to croaking and buzzing insects.

"A'doxia is a cruel woman," Chloe whispered.

"I see."

A certain sound came from Jade's right, akin to some sort of string instrument on a small scale, paired with a more woody, earthy sound.

"Ah, Jade," Dagmey breathed. "Look, your friend is back."

Jade open her eyes to see Dagmey pointing to the branch with the strange lights. Her brows furrowed and she was about to ask where, when she spotted an insect land on one of the lights only for a snake head to whip around and gobble it up. Jade blinked, unable to help a small laugh, joy and delight fizzing up in her throat.

"Amazing, isn't it? They've got these little spots all along the sides of their bodies to help them produce light. They use it to lure in bugs at night, but have to be careful not to get confused by the flying predators who also hunt little glowing bugs," Dagmey explained. The snake's lights faded as it lowered its head back onto the branch and slithered somewhere darker where the bright scales would not get it caught. Jade smiled.

"Are they just called snakes, or…?" she asked.

"We call them *krekatakc,* but it's likely easier for you to call them glimmering snakes. That one's a bit different, though. Albino. Usually they're green and brown. Poor thing must have had a hard life to make it this far."

Jade nodded, watching the branch in case the snake returned. She knew what it was like to have the odds stacked against her, for creatures to attack on sight. She knew how hard it was to constantly be in hiding.

"I was never the linguist," Jade said. "That was always Aris." The name tasted bitter. She frowned and looked down at the contents of her mug. "She's the one that cut off my arm. I… we lived together. We were friends." She closed her eyes. "I don't know what happened."

"I'm so sorry, Jade," Dagmey murmured. "I can't imagine how horrible that must feel."

"Aris said I made up everything. How I woke up at night, the nightmares. If… if only A'doxia didn't find me on Taotar, if she didn't… none of this would've happened." She gestured wildly to the hut, but as she spoke the words, she found no truth in them. As much as she wished she could blame A'doxia, this wasn't the woman's fault. She wasn't the one who made Aris hate her. She wasn't the one who cut off Jade's arm.

Dagmey tilted her head. "I…" she began, before looking down at her hands.

"No, I wish I could say that." Jade took a sip of her meal before resting it in her lap. "But A'doxia's not at fault. Aris did this to me."

"But A'doxia still hurt you," Chloe murmured. "She still scarred you."

Jade closed her eyes, remembered the lips against her skin, the tongue in her bleeding wounds. How the knife split her open along the lines electricity made upon her flesh.

"Do you want to talk about it?" Dagmey asked, her voice gentle. "You don't have to."

"There's not much to say," Jade said. "She tortured me."

Dagmey blinked, every feather on her body fluffing up before she quickly used her hands to smooth them all down. "She *tortured* you?"

"We were on opposite sides of the war," Jade explained, looking out towards the trees. "Her troops captured me, and she tortured me until sunrise."

"She did more than that," Chloe said. "It wasn't just torture."

"It was torture." Jade placed her hand on her stomach. Hands along her sides, running over her arms. Weakness sapping strength from her bones. A'doxia kept her exploring fingers above the waist, kept Jade on her stomach and couldn't access her breasts, but the way she moved her hips against Jade's, the way she moaned in Jade's ear, what she offered to do if Jade begged to lay on her back.

That wretched, echoing lullaby.

Jade gripped her shirt and, with it, the skin beneath. Agony stabbed through her stomach.

"Jade, careful," Dagmey urged. "You shouldn't touch your stitches like that."

The giggling, the laughter, the way she sighed when Jade couldn't scream anymore.

"Jade, let go!"

Numb skin, sand rubbed into every wound.

"Jade!"

Hauled by the armpits to the outskirts of the base. Further, into the desert. A'doxia waving goodbye. A'doxia kissing her cheek.

"Jade!" A rough hand grabbed Jade's wrist and yanked her hand away from her stomach. Jade blinked, surprised to find her eyes bleary as she looked at Dagmey's expressionless face, then peered down at her gut.

She had torn some of the stitches free and blood oozed from the reopened wound.

"I'm sorry," Chloe said, "I'm sorry, Jade, I didn't mean to make you hurt yourself!"

"It's not your fault, Chloe," Dagmey assured her. With her free hand, Dagmey touched Jade's cheek. Tears dripped off Jade's chin. Her lower lip quivered.

"What did she do to you?" Dagmey asked. "What did A'doxia do to you?"

The galleon was stocked. One-hundred and twenty-two soldiers chosen, among which were Qiu and Katlego, both healed enough for duty. Aris needed officers, after all. With her hands on the steel of the ship's railing, Aris looked out over the waters of Sobek where it had landed. Her legs weren't perfect. There was still something quite wrong with them, but she didn't spar much herself, anyway. Generals didn't need to prove their worth that way. She had Kuroda for that.

He stood beside her, inhaling the sweet, salty breeze off the waters with a purr rumbling in his throat. Aris watched him, a smile playing at her lips. None of this would have worked without Kuroda. She didn't realize it when she discovered him on Sypher, but Kuroda had been the key to all of this. The key to her rise.

Her blue eyes flickered over the seas once more. Clouds were gathering in the distance. There would be a storm, and a great one at that. There would be thunder, lightning. If she had a demon with her, that demon would fear such a storm, would grow anxious. Aris would have to calm it, tell it everything was fine. Aris' fingers gripped the railing tighter. But that demon was gone. That liability had fled. Just as she intended. Just as she planned.

*Except she might come back.* Aris grimaced and shook her head, turning and limping her way to the helmsman. Her right foot had gained much of its mobility back, but her left dragged across the deck and her right struggled to lift its toes up. Scaling the stairs proved difficult, but manageable.

*Now you can't run when she comes for you.* Aris gripped her temple as she reached the helm, grimacing as a flickering headache spread behind her eyes. *If you wait for her to find you, she'll be stronger. She'll be ready.*

*No,* Aris countered, taking a breath and gripping the wheel of the ship, looking out over the deck. *No, I'll have an army to protect me. I'll be safe in Nanza City.*

*Have you ever known the demon to be sensible? Have you ever known it to look at the odds and not strike out despite having fewer numbers in its favor?*

Dread climbed up her spine. Sweat beaded her brow. Kuroda looked over his shoulder at her and tilted his head.

*She'll come for you.*

*She won't. She won't come for me.*

*She'll come.*

"You're shaking," Kuroda breathed. Aris looked at him, eyes wide. She investigated her hands, watched as they shuddered out of her control.

*She's coming now.*

Her eyes flickered towards the sky, the growing storm.

*She's going to gather a victer army and kill you.*

Shallow breaths, a pounding heart.

"General Sell?" Qiu peered at her, brows furrowed. She stood on the steps, peering up at Kuroda and her both, dressed in a regal crimson uniform, ready for their voyage. She frowned. "Are you all right?"

"What is it you want?" Aris grasped her hands and pushed them down, trying to restrict her growing panic.

*She's going to take your arm.*

"The ship is ready to set sail. Can you confirm our destination?"

*She's going to take your heart.*

"Our destination?" Aris repeated, the words a whisper on her lips. A spark of lightning could be seen in the furious clouds, the dark horizon crawling closer.

*She's going to make you fall.*

"Set course for Ferges."

Chapter 42

Dagmey pressed a moist cloth to Jade's stomach, soaking up the blood that oozed from her wound. Jade squirmed on her bed, scowling against the building, grinding pain. The cloth lifted from Jade's skin and, quickly, Dagmey produced a needle and thread. She looked at Jade.

"I have to re-stitch it."

Jade blinked, her face swollen from tears. A'doxia stood in the corner, hands over her mouth, eyes wide. She lurched forward a few times, as if she wished to draw nearer, but she didn't. Jade looked back at Dagmey and nodded after a thick swallow.

"Okay," she breathed. "Okay."

As Jade watched, Dagmey used her talons to snap the string that held Jade's gut together. The far left corner had begun to heal, and didn't flare open when it was freed from the cord, but as Dagmey travelled up to Jade's right, closer and closer to her missing arm, her flesh flayed outward, revealing how deep the laceration was. Before the deep cut could fully expose itself to the galaxy, Dagmey snatched her thread and needle and dipped it in a cup of clear liquid. She balanced her tools between her talons and started at Jade's ribs. The peeling burn provided fresh, pink flesh that screamed at the insertion. Jade sucked in a breath between clenched teeth. Her fingers grasped the mattress beneath her.

"You're hurting her," A'doxia breathed. "Alcohol. Dagmey, do you have any alcohol?"

Dagmey glanced at Jade. She clicked her tongue and focused on her work, piercing the other side of Jade's skin. The Green shut her eyes, but spots appeared in the darkness of her vision.

"Under the sink," Dagmey said, "the red liquid."

There was clattering, the sound of rushing footsteps. Someone kneeled next to Jade and touched her cheek. Jade opened her eyes to see A'doxia with a wooden cup full of a thin, fizzing liquid.

"It'll help," Dagmey said. Jade took it. She tossed it back and swallowed laying down, some of it getting caught in her throat, forcing her to clear it, try again. It buzzed in her mouth, sizzled going down her throat, and splashed a warm, nurturing blanket through her body as it settled in her stomach. Jade had forgotten how sweet alcohol was, how much she craved its taste, its welcome arms. She exhaled slowly. A dull, distant throb radiated from her lower half, but she paid it no heed. She stared at the jars hanging from the ceiling as they shone from the crystals' illuminating glow. She smiled gently.

"How much did you pour her?" Dagmey was saying.

"A full cup."

"A *full*—shit, no wonder she's…" The voices trailed off. Jade did, too.

# Chapter 43

Chloe had never experienced such fear before. As she watched, Jade's eyes fluttered close and blood began to seep from her stomach. Her body went limp and the victer—designated as Dagmey—continued to weave a thread through Jade's flesh. The bitch—titled A'doxia—was sitting nearby, watching. She was too close to Jade. Too close.

"Get away from her," Chloe said, her voice fierce. A new emotion spread across her circuits, warmed every connection within her systems. It burned, sizzled, made an internal sensor alert that she was overheating. A'doxia blinked and looked down at her. She frowned but scooted back.

"Does she need blood?" A'doxia asked, as if anyone told her she could speak. "We have the same blood type."

"She'll be fine," Dagmey replied, voice short. "Do as the helmet requests—keep your distance."

"I heard what she told you."

"Am I supposed to be surprised?" Dagmey replied. Chloe let out a sound, mimicking the one Jade made when she smiled—a laugh, sentients called it. Chloe laughed. The feathers around Dagmey's face fanned out, and she laughed, too, her eyes flickering up to look at Chloe's broken visor.

"Are you going to throw me out?" A'doxia ignored their humor. Her brows furrowed and her lips made a tight line, as if this information was inconvenient, upsetting. How could it be? Why would she remain here when she was unwanted? Chloe wished

Dagmey would slice the woman in two. Maybe Jade would feel better afterwards. Maybe she'd laugh more.

"That depends on what Jade wants," Dagmey reached the end of her sewing job, tied it off with dexterous claws, before snipping the excess off. She looked to A'doxia. "Do you regret what you did?"

"On Taotar?"

"On every planet."

A'doxia was silent for approximately four seconds. From her spot by Jade's hip, Chloe could see all that the visor faced, which luckily included a wide range of vision. From the leftmost corner, she watched as A'doxia inhaled.

"Yes," she said.

"Don't lie to me," Dagmey snapped. Chloe couldn't help but be impressed. Perhaps staying with her was a good move. Perhaps this is where they would be safe, by the side of a deadly, sentient avian.

"If I say no, I suspect you'll do your best to get me to leave," A'doxia said.

Dagmey shook her head and stood, fetching bandages for Jade's injury in a kitchen cabinet. She returned a moment later and knelt, beginning to gently wrap the unconscious Jade. Chloe analyzed the process, scrutinized where Dagmey's eyes fell. As the woman used the back of her hand to lift Jade up ever so slightly, her citrus eyes flickered to the scars that coated Jade's back. And now, Dagmey knew why they were there, who had given them to Jade.

"She's safer with me here," A'doxia said. Chloe wished she had hands to slap her with.

"Mhmm." Dagmey made the first loop. A'doxia moved towards the bandages, likely to find pleasure in Jade's blood, to smear it across her face, to taste it.

With the same overheating warnings popping into her circuitry, Chloe shouted: "Don't touch her!"

A'doxia jerked her hand back and scowled at the helmet. "I'm trying to help, you shitty piece of junk."

More overheating warnings. More fire. Chloe quickly calculated seventeen different ways A'doxia could die in this room.

"I am made of better material than you," Chloe said. "From my stored memories, those scars on your hands are self-inflicted due to your lack of immunity to your own Helix. When I run mathematical equations, it does not harm me, yet when you do the one thing you are capable of, it inflicts pain upon you. To many, that would be a defect."

A'doxia's eyes narrowed. "I have half a mind to—"

"Having half a mind would explain your inability to understand simple logic. You tortured Jade to the point of harming her mentality and her sleep cycle. You should not be around her. You should be removed from all situations involving her. She is *not* safer with you around."

Dagmey laughed. "You're a spicy little thing, aren't you?"

"It's why Jade likes me."

"A friend like you will keep her on her toes," Dagmey remarked, pulling the bandages taunt at the end to ensure the wound would not open. She regarded A'doxia, who sat less than a foot away, seething. Seething was an accurate word, Chloe figured, considering the woman's red eyes seemed to be burning into her visor. Chloe wished she could smile back. Humans hated it when people smiled at them when they were seething.

"I am in need of visiting the local city for my bi-monthly supplies," Dagmey said. "We will all travel there, and you will find somewhere to stay, A'doxia. But it will not be with me."

A'doxia gripped the fabric of her skirt. If she were an animal, she would bristle, her fur would stand on end, but as it were, she simply locked her jaw and focused her full attention on the victer who could—and should—throw her off the deck.

"I'm the one that saved her," she hissed.

"Jade has a way of surviving everything," Chloe remarked.

"You think she would've survived without my blood? You think if I hadn't hauled her out of the winter wastes on Hallow, she would've lived?"

"Uncertain. But likely." Chloe, in truth, had no stored memory of the events. Jade had ordered her to sleep during that time, and she didn't wake again until she was being held by A'doxia.

She hated being held by A'doxia.

"Then you're delusional," A'doxia sneered. "I pulled her from that ship, *I* got her here. Without me, she'd be dead."

313

"That doesn't give you some right to her life," Dagmey said. "You may have saved her, but you abused her, and you hurt her. If you heard what she said, you heard her crying."

Jade would hate to know that A'doxia heard she was crying. Chloe stored the memory away and locked it deep within her databanks.

"And?" A'doxia said.

"And you don't care?" Dagmey tilted her head. "It's settled then. We'll walk to the city, and you'll be on your way."

"She can't *walk!* Look at her! She can hardly sit up properly!" A'doxia gestured wildly at Jade and her fingertips brushed against Chloe's visor. It was only appropriate Chloe discharge surplus energy into a high voltage shock out of her physical form. A'doxia gasped and snatched her hand away. She snarled at Chloe. Like an animal.

"I will help her along the way. I could fasten some crutches for her from nearby branches. She will be fine," Dagmey said.

"I'm not about to let her go with you unprotected. I don't trust you," A'doxia hissed.

"She has her helmet," Dagmey cooed, looking to Chloe. "I think she'll be protected well enough."

Chloe's wires warmed pleasantly. "I promise to keep her protected," she said. "Especially from A'doxia."

A'doxia scowled. She looked between the two before she retreated onto her chair, furious but silent. Dagmey turned to Chloe.

"You are a good friend, little helmet. Jade is lucky to have you. Let me know when she wakes, hm?" She dipped her head and turned to tend to the fire.

Chloe sat by Jade, listening to the woman breathe, tuning into her heartbeat and monitoring its progress. It was good A'doxia would be leaving. It was good Jade would have a chance to heal. She had seen how Jade stared into the shadows beneath the deck, how her body leaned forward as her eyes grew distant. Without access to a planetary feed of information, Chloe couldn't determine the exact reason why her friend continued to do this. But she didn't believe it to be a positive one. Maybe, if A'doxia was forced to leave, Jade might smile and laugh and hold Chloe to her chest. She would like to be held.

# Chapter 44

Jade sat outside in her favorite spot on the deck, a cup of tea in her hand. Chloe was on her hip, and across the way, she saw the glittering snake slithering across a branch. Jade had woken fifteen minutes after the alcohol knocked her out, and while Dagmey was surprised, she informed her that in three days, they would set out for the city. Jade exhaled.

"What do you think it'll be like?" Jade asked, lifting the herbal drink to her lips and taking a sip. It was strong with a spicy heat, but without being bitter. She let out a content hum as the snake lifted her head and began to chirp. The white scales made her noticeable, but she slithered beneath the branch to hide whenever small birds responded to the song.

"The city?" Chloe asked. "Likely big. Probably not as polluted as Nanza City."

"As all of Nevar, you mean," Jade teased with a smile. She took another sip. A bird answered the glittering snake's call somewhere in the distance.

"I do not understand why sentients live there, Jade."

"Ferges *is* a lot easier to breathe on," Jade murmured. A small bird landed on the snake's branch. Its green feathers and red plumage around its throat made it look rather festive. "How are you doing? With not being able to connect to the feed or anything?"

"It's… uncomfortable," Chloe murmured. "I do not like being so disconnected."

"I'm sure."

The bird chirped curiously and looked around. It lowered its head to peck at the wood.

"Are you… well?" Chloe asked.

The snake struck, throwing herself up from the opposite side of the branch and snatching the bird from behind. A large shadow flew over.

"The walls aren't thick," Jade murmured. The bird panicked and managed to leap into the air, flapping its wings to keep afloat. "I know she heard me."

"Jade—"

Massive talons, black as pitch, wrapped around the struggling bird. The beast yanked the bird and snake alike off the branch, tipped its wing, and swept back around in a lazy curve towards the hut. Jade leapt to her feet. The snake, dangling from her prey, threw her tail around the larger predator's leg. In one quick lunge, she threw herself up to ebony hawk's body and clamped her teeth into feathers.

"It's attacking the bigger bird?" Chloe gasped.

"She doesn't have a choice!" Jade gripped her stomach, eyes locked on the creatures as they flew overhead. The hawk screeched in agony and dropped the dead bird. It fell past the railing, down into the depths below. Jade followed it for a moment before quickly focusing on the snake. The hawk dived towards the hut and Jade ducked as it swooped past overhead. It landed on the slanted roof, turned, and yanked the snake off with its beak. Jade's eyes widened.

"No! No, you can't!" She looked around for something, anything. She bent over, her stomach screaming against the movement, but she ignored it.

"Jade, what are you doing? It's just a snake—it's okay!" Chloe said.

"No, it's not!" Jade grasped a bundle of thick moss in her hands and tore it from the deck. She rushed to a better angle as the hawk shook the bleeding snake back and forth. The snake struck at the bird's beak, trying to find something else to bite. Trying to get free.

"Let go, you asshole!" Jade shouted, throwing her moss at the bird. With a startled flurry of feathers, the hawk leapt into the air. The snake fell from its jaws and into the moss a few feet away.

"Yeah, fuck off!" Jade howled, rushing to the snake, standing over it as the hawk screeched at her and circled overhead.

"Jade?" Dagmey appeared around the corner, head tilted. She looked towards the predator circling overhead, then to Jade. "What on Ferges are you doing?"

Jade knelt, pressing her knees into the soft foliage, and peered down at the snake. The creature lifted her head and hissed, but she was bleeding badly. A deep cut dug into her side. She oozed crimson across the viridian deck and let out another weak hiss. Jade looked at Dagmey.

"I couldn't let her die," she breathed, looking back at the snake. "She was just trying to get away."

"Jade," Chloe muttered. "It's just a snake."

*Just a snake.* Jade peered into the black eyes as the snake lowered her head, hissing once more, weaker than the prior. *What was I supposed to do? Just sit there and let her die? Sit there and let that hawk eat her? She's struggled to live this long. The whole world is trying to kill her with bright scales like those. It's not her fault she was born like this. It's not her fault.*

"Shh," Jade whispered. "Shh, it's okay. It's okay. I'm going to help, all right?" The snake's head dipped. Jade slipped her fingers under and gently lifted her from the ground. "We can help her, right, Dagmey?" Jade looked over to the victer, who tilted her head as she watched the scenario continue.

After a moment, Dagmey sighed. "The little gal is pretty hurt. Come along, let's see what we can do."

There was a creak of wood and Jade looked behind her. There, A'doxia stood, though she ducked around the corner when Jade turned. Jade looked down at the ivory serpent in her hand, then followed Dagmey back into the house.


The little creature was badly injured, but Dagmey cleaned and wrapped her wound, placed her on soft moss, and set her in a container with a fabric lid full of holes. That way she could recover, and she wouldn't bite anyone while she did so. Jade had the snake placed by her bed and unclipped Chloe from her shirt to set the helm next to their new companion.

"Why are you so concerned about the snake?" Chloe asked after Jade was settled on the mattress again, laying on her back so Dagmey could check her stitches.

"I couldn't let her die," Jade murmured. Dagmey began unwrapping her. "I don't think anything tore, Dagmey."

"I have the be certain," she replied.

"But it's just a snake," Chloe said. "It's the circle of life."

Jade frowned and peered at the ceiling. "I know."

"It's because she glows, isn't it?" Dagmey asked, her voice holding a smile. "She made you happy."

"I would've saved her anyway," Jade said.

Dagmey chuckled. She pulled the last of the bandages off and peered at the wounds.

"The lights *were* pretty," Chloe said.

"They were," Jade replied.

"You're clean," Dagmey said with a nod, wrapping Jade up again. "But if we're keeping the snake, you're going to need to take care of her." She looked at Jade. "*You'll* need to make her food."

Jade frowned. "Make her food? She… eats bugs? And birds?"

"She'll eat meat. You can cook her up something over the fire now and then."

"Dagmey, I have one arm."

"And you saved her well enough with one," Dagmey said, pulling the bandages tight. "So you'll have to continue saving her with one."

Jade looked to the snake, wrapped up around the middle just like her. She wouldn't be able to hunt. She wouldn't be able to take care of herself. If Jade didn't want to kill her, she'd have to provide for their hissing friend. Jade's right arm itched and she fought the urge to scratch empty air. With one arm, it would be near impossible to cook and tend to a whole other life, but she made the choice to help, and she had to try.

Her eyes fell on Dagmey. "Can you show me?"

# Chapter 45

Jade's right arm ached more and more as the days went on. As she stood near the counter, knife in hand to cut meat into chunks the snake could eat, her left struggled to hold the blade properly, struggled to stop shaking, struggled to keep the lump still. Time and time again she tried, furiously grabbing her hair with fingers covered in raw meat before Dagmey shouted at her, insisted she would be taking a bath later that night.

In desperation, Jade grabbed the slab of muscle and tore pieces off with her teeth. Dagmey made her wash her mouth before she was forced to drink several cups of bitter herbal tea.

Chloe suggested that Jade find a way to sharpen the knife so it cut easier. While Dagmey brought out a bucket of warm water and washed Jade's hair on the porch, Jade stabbed the knife into the wood and used a whetstone to sharpen its edge. Cutting the meat was easier the next time, and Jade and Chloe laughed about how simple the solution had been.

From the corner of the room, A'doxia watched, but she said nothing.

Next came making a special drink for the snake to have. Jade had to smash several leaves together, mix them with water and boil them over the fire. She managed to crush the herbs, used her teeth to pull on a mitt to keep her hand protected from the flames, and held the pot until her arm ached and the liquid boiled.

The trio didn't leave on the third day. Or the fourth. While A'doxia sulked in silence, Jade struggled with the tasks given to her, raged countless times, before Chloe calmed her and offered another solution. Slowly, Jade started to understand how to do things different, how to cook, how to clean. Her stomach pain waned, and while she still tried to reach for items with her right hand, and often found her right palm itching or singing in agony, she felt the pain of its loss less and less. And as Jade recovered, so did her snake companion.

At first, the snake hardly woke, and when she did, the serpent hissed at anyone passing her jar. When Jade wrapped her legs around the container to hold it steady and twisted the top off, she had to be wary of the creature striking up at her. The little beast could not reach Jade's hand in her condition, but attempting to do so it would hinder her recovery.

But as the days passed, as mornings turned into two, three, five, and seven, the snake began to realize Jade was helping her. Each time Jade sat down, the reptile lifted her head, flicked her tongue into the air, and happily let Jade place miniature pieces of meat and a small container of herbal liquid inside. After nine days, the snake's bandages came off, and the first thing she did was slither up Jade's arm and perch upon her shoulder. Jade, Chloe, and Dagmey all laughed. A'doxia watched.

It was decided that with the snake healed, and with Jade feeling more capable, they would gather themselves for the journey to the city. It would be a two day walk to keep their pace slow for Jade, and they would leave in the morning. Jade's bandages were changed, her wounds washed, and Chloe offered to host their new friend inside her helm. As Jade settled in, she set Chloe upside down, picked the snake up and felt the creature's soft scales, then placed her inside the overturned helmet. Chloe heated the pads inside a little, and with one large yawn, the snake curled up and fell asleep.

Before dawn, Jade was woken by the sound of sobs. She thought, for a fleeting moment, that she was in her apartment, that Aris had returned from a date that went poorly. With a grimace, Jade sat up and looked for the blonde, only to see the dimly lit room from dangling crystals with Dagmey on cushions beside the fire, curled up and sleeping peacefully. The pyre was reduced to a small flicker above coals, but the hut remained warm enough to keep any nightly chill at bay. Still, Jade heard the soft, faint sound of crying. Whimpers muffled, as if trying to be hidden.

"Jade?" Chloe whispered, doing her best not to wake their new friend and Dagmey.

"I'll be right back," Jade said, hissing through her teeth as she stood. "Watch the snake for me."

"I should go with you."

"I don't want to wake her up." Jade gripped her stomach and carefully headed for the door. Chloe didn't call after her, knowing that would be too loud. With more deft feet than the first time Jade snuck out, she slipped between the pillows, and padded to the door. As she pushed her hand against the polished wood, she suddenly realized who was crying. And as she stepped outside, she saw A'doxia curled up on the deck, face in her hands.

The woman's shoulders shook and sad, choked wails of anguish escaped her lips. Jade let the door close behind her, frozen.

A'doxia looked up, her eyes bloodshot, her face puffy and swollen. The first rays of dawn shot through the trees and made the woman's skin glisten with tears. Did Jade care? She searched herself for an ounce of sympathy. Did it matter if her abuser was crying?

"Jade?" A'doxia breathed. "Did I wake you?"

"Yes."

A'doxia flashed a smile and looked away, wiping her face on her scar-riddled hands. "I suppose you hate me, don't you?"

Jade eyed the door on her right, considered going back inside, considered making sure she was safe. She had to watch out for the little snake without a name and had to keep Chloe company. Her hand gripped the shirt around her stomach. And she wanted to see the city. She didn't want to die. Not yet, anyway.

"Why are you crying?" Jade asked.

"Do you care?"

Silence again. Residents of the forest woke and began singing to the rising sun. Jade looked at the trees and saw the glimmering lightning bugs who stayed out too late begin to dim their lights. A'doxia chuckled.

"You remind me so much of her," she said.

Jade watched as the woman swung her legs over the side of the deck. "Who?"

A'doxia ran her thumb along the scar on her lips. Jade stood there until her feet grew cold.

"I don't want you to leave me in the city," A'doxia said, at last turning her crimson gaze to Jade. "I want to stay with you."

"I don't care." The words came without Jade having to think. They spilled from her mouth and sat in the space between them. Jade watched as A'doxia's eyes narrowed.

Then the woman closed them, took a deep breath, and calmed herself before speaking again. "I want to be friends."

"No."

"Companions. Nothing sexual."

"No."

A'doxia's jaw tensed. "We would look out for each other. I could protect you."

"No."

"Would you stop saying no?" A'doxia snapped. Jade frowned. "See? It's not that hard. Listen, Jade. If I wanted to hurt you, I could have all those times we were alone. You were unconscious, and even when you were awake, you couldn't fight me off, hm? I could've hurt you, but I didn't. I saved you."

"I don't care." A shot of pain in her right arm. Jade grimaced and gripped her stump.

"See? You're still hurting, love." A'doxia got to her feet. "I could help you. I could help you heal. I could teach you to fight again."

"Fuck off," Jade snarled, her pain burning through her patience. "I don't need your help. I don't need your healing. I want you out of my life."

"You don't mean that," A'doxia purred, closed the distance between them. "You're just upset. It's okay, love. I'll tell Dagmey that you want me to stay. And we can be friends."

"We can't be friends," Jade said. "You molested me."

"That's a strong word."

"You tortured me for hours and licked the blood off my back." Jade pulled her hand from her shoulder and reached for the door. "I'd say it's accurate."

A'doxia grabbed her wrist. "You'll tell Dagmey that I'm staying," she whispered, voice holding daggers. Her grip tightened. "You'll tell her I'm staying, and we'll be friends, Jade."

"Let go, A'doxia."

"I told you to call me Dox."

Jade kicked the latchless door open. It slammed against the wall, shuddering the jars, shaking the crystals. Dagmey shot up in her bed.

"Jade!" Chloe cried. There was a surprised chirp.

"I'd rather call you a bitch. Let go of me."

"A'doxia!" Dagmey got to her feet, throat feathers bristling. "Let go of her."

A'doxia scowled. She released Jade and the Green held her gaze, then walked inside. A'doxia sat down on the deck.

"Are you all right?" Dagmey asked as the door swung closed and Jade settled back on the bed.

"She didn't do anything," Jade said, placing her hand at the edge of the helmet and extending her fingers. "She said she wanted to be friends."

"Friends?" Chloe repeated. The nameless snake wrapped around Jade's pointer finger before winding her way up Jade's arm. Jade set Chloe upright.

"She thinks she can just ask you to be friends and you'll forget about how she hurt you?" Chloe asked.

"Apparently." The snake poked her nose against Jade's cheek. Jade smiled and reached up, doing her best to scratch beneath the snake's chin with her thumb.

"She'll be gone in two days," Dagmey said, shaking her head and yawning. "I'll get breakfast going. We'll leave right after."

"Dagmey, what are the eye colors here?" She looked away from her snake and over to the victer. Dagmey tilted her head curiously.

"The eye... oh, yes. I forget sometimes. You have a system around your eye colors. We don't here."

Jade blinked. "What?"

"It seems to us to be nonsense. Besides, naturally, victers only have orange or yellow eyes. We don't often have blues or reds or greens. Sometimes some hazel colors? But even then, it's more often when we breed with those that came from outside Ferges." She shrugged as she found some fruit in the fridge and set them on the counter, chopping them with her talons.

"You don't… do you have lore around Greens?" Jade asked. A'doxia's sobbing fell away in her mind, forgotten momentarily as she fixated on this. Surely, somewhere in this perfect scenario, there was a catch and it would all fall apart.

"Us victers? No, not at all," Dagmey cooed. "Some of your kind tend to bring their stories here, but I've never heard anything about Greens. Why? Is there a concern?"

"I…" Jade scratched at her stump. "Back home, Greens are considered demons. We're rumored to destroy things when we're born. Apparently only one is ever alive in the galaxy at a time."

Dagmey looked over at her. "What would they have done if they found out?"

"They would've killed me," Jade whispered.

Dagmey closed her eyes. "I can see your concern. No, there will be no one killing you, Jade. The chief's guards will be patrolling, and they break up fights. You'll be safe there." She gave a firm nod. "No one's going to hurt you."

Jade offered a weak smile. Part of her hoped Dagmey was right, that no fights would break out, that no one would throw a dagger into her throat.

Another part of her hoped exactly that would occur.

329

To set out towards the city meant standing on the deck as Dagmey climbed onto the railing. It creaked beneath her weight as she pointed to a distant tree with one pointed claw.

"I'll glide to the platform over there, fetch the rope bridge, and glide back. Shouldn't take more than a few minutes." She looked to Jade, then to A'doxia, who hovered not far away. "Behave."

Dagmey spread her arms, flaring out the membrane that ran from wrist to ankle, then leapt out into the open air. She stretched her legs out and as the thin material became taunt, she was caught by unseen currents of the wind, and pushed towards the darkness of the trees further away. The snake chirped from her spot around Jade's arm.

*"She's watching us,"* Chloe muttered, her voice coded. Jade sighed, eyes resting on the place she saw Dagmey last. Of course A'doxia was watching them. She wanted to say something. One last thing while Dagmey was gone. That much was clear.

"I killed for you," A'doxia said.

*There it is.* Jade rubbed her eyes with her thumb and forefinger then dragged them down, running them across the scar on her face. Jade didn't turn around, didn't answer.

"You want me gone, but *I've* been the one here for you. The one fighting for *you.* Who else will do that? You think Dagmey will do that?"

"You tortured me for hours," Jade replied. "I don't care what Dagmey does in comparison."

"She doesn't love you, Jade."

A sick churning began in her stomach, her muscles tensing, her bile boiling. Jade gripped it, a grimace pulling her lips into a tight, downward line.

"Not like me," A'doxia whispered, coming to the railing beside her. "Not like I do."

"Stop it," Chloe snapped. "Leave us alone."

"You remind me so much of her," A'doxia murmured, reaching her hand out to touch Jade's cheek. "I love you, Jade."

Jade slapped the hand away and, angrily, her snake companion started to screech like a gathering of furious birds. Jade stepped back, swallowing the contents of her stomach several times before she could speak.

"No," Jade growled. "You don't get to say that to me."

"It's true, Jade," A'doxia said, letting her hand fall, her eyes full and wide with emotion. "I love you."

"Stop saying that!" Chloe barked.

"I don't care." Jade clutched her stomach. "I don't care if you love me, A'doxia, because you don't get to. You get to go to some city and remain there, forever away from me, so I can get some *fucking* rest."

"You can't stop what I feel for you." A'doxia reached out for her again. "We can be friends, Jade. Please. We can take things slow. I won't hurt you."

"Your words don't mean anything."

"I *swear* I will not hurt you again, love. Don't send me away."

Jade remained out of reach. "No."

Dagmey landed on the railing between them, startling A'doxia back a step. The wood creaked beneath the victer's talons, foliage snapped, sections of bark fell to the floor. In both hands she held the four ends of a rope bridge. She tilted her head to peer at A'doxia, orange eyes flaring with an unspoken anger.

"I told you to behave," she said. Her voice was even and cold, but her grip on the rope was tight enough for Jade's teeth to ache.

"I didn't touch her," A'doxia hissed.

"Leave Jade alone, A'doxia." Dagmey watched the Red, then hopped off the railing before tying the ends of the bridge off on the supports. After all four were secured, she nodded, and looked to Jade.

"Victers are rather light," Dagmey said. "We don't often require more than just rope. I'll travel behind you and if you slip, I'll catch you."

Jade turned her attention to the pass. The ropes extended past the deck and seemed to vanish somewhere between where Jade stood and the tree further off. While the cords seemed sturdy enough to walk over, it was clearly designed for talons, for feet that could wrap around the lines. Jade had no idea if they would hold her. She had lost weight over the past several weeks of being unconscious and injured, and while she had gained a little back, she knew that if she fell, her left arm may not be able to pull her back up.

With a breath, she unclipped Chloe from her shirt and awkwardly pulled the helmet over her head. It wasn't easy with only one working hand, but she managed. This way, Chloe wouldn't be at risk of falling. Not unless Jade did, at least.

"The bridge shouldn't tip," Dagmey said. "Take it slow, this is the only one like this on our journey."

"Someone else should go first," A'doxia said. "To make sure it's safe."

"Are you suggesting yourself, A'doxia?" Dagmey cooed, looking back at the woman.

A'doxia frowned, but nevertheless nodded. "I can go. I can make sure the bridge holds steady on the other side."

"If you fall, my priority is Jade."

"As it should be." A'doxia slipped under the deck's railing, grabbed the sides of the bridge, and took the first step onto it. It sank an inch or two beneath her weight and, after a pause to ensure it wasn't going to break, the Red began to travel across. While the connection shuddered in a light breeze, A'doxia didn't look like she was ever in fear of plummeting. But she had two hands to hold onto both sides of the bridge. Jade had one and a tendency to forget she did not have the other.

"What did she say to you?" Dagmey muttered when A'doxia was far enough away.

"That she loved me," Jade replied. She rubbed her right shoulder, frowned at the buzzing pain within it.

"There is something wrong with her," Dagmey said, picking up a backpack outside the door. She held it in her hand, unable to put it on because it would restrict the movement of her flight membrane. She nodded to the bridge. "I'm sorry she insists on antagonizing you."

"In two days I'll never have to see her again," Jade said. Vocalizing it made her notice how sweet the air smelled as it was pumped inside the helm. A smile crossed her lips. "Vix, doesn't that sound amazing?"

"I'm sure it does," Dagmey said, her voice holding a smile as her feathers spread out along her head. "I know I was excited when I first moved out here. The people who had hurt me… none of them could reach me when I was so far away."

Jade climbed over the railing, holding tight to the vine-covered surface as her feet rested on the other side. Her snake companion chirped.

"I'm sorry you had to move so far away to feel safe," Jade said. She took the rope in her hand. It was coarse and dry.

"Don't be. It's nice to be out here, isn't it? It's a good place to heal."

"It is." One foot forward, onto the single rope link that served as the foothold. It dug into her bare feet as she put more of her weight on it.

*"You can do this,"* Chloe whispered.

"Thank you for, ah, letting me stay with you," Jade said. She grimaced as the twine ground against her arch before she stepped onto the next strand. She slid her hand across the railing and moved forward. Her stomach ached already. Sweat beaded her brow. Below, darkness swallowed the bottoms of trees.

"You're welcome," Dagmey said. "I know… I know what it's like, Jade. To be abused by someone like you have. Not the exact same way—I've never been to war—but similar. I know how hard it is to heal. I want to help, if you let me."

Another step. "I'm fine."

"You're not." Dagmey's voice dipped into something soothing, a light coo. Jade gritted her teeth. "You're hurting, and that's okay, Jade. It's okay to hurt. You told me what she did to you, to your body, but what she did to your mind is worse." She was silent. Jade stepped forward, her palm growing slick. "When I was with someone romantically, they took advantage of me. I told them no, I told them to stop, but they did it anyway. I thought… I thought maybe I had done something to deserve it. That we were together, so they had a right to me. A right to my body."

Jade stopped. Her brows furrowed.

"They made me believe that it was my fault," Dagmey said, coming to a stop behind her. Jade looked over her shoulder at the victer as the woman spoke. "They manipulated my mind and I still suffer because of it. I don't feel like I can trust myself, I don't feel like I can make the right decisions. All of it… it's hard for me."

Jade looked at her toes, curled above the black expanse below her. She looked down the length of the bridge, towards a dimly lit platform in the distance. A'doxia's form could be seen making her way towards it.

"I can't make everything better," Dagmey said, "but I can try. I didn't have anyone to help me while I went through my situation. But… I want to be here for you, Jade. I want to help. I think you being able to tell her no is a huge and amazing step. You should feel proud of yourself."

A smile crossed Jade's lips. *Proud. For saying no.* She looked to her hand, the only one she had. *For some reason, it feels nice to be proud of myself for that.*

"You did great," Chloe said, inside and outside the helm. "You told her to leave you alone."

"If she attacked me, Dagmey would stop her," Jade said. "It's not really my own strength I'm relying on."

"It's okay to rely on me," Dagmey said. "I would protect you, Jade."

Jade closed her eyes, felt the air rush against her clothes, play with the strands of messy red hair that stuck out of the helmet by her neck. A chill washed over her stump, followed by a buzz of pain. The last time she relied on someone, her arm was severed. But that had taken years to come to its bloody conclusion. Maybe by that time, Chloe would be safe, and Jade could welcome the end.

"Thank you," Jade said. She opened her eyes and started forward again. "I would like that."

## Chapter 46

Dagmey was correct—the only rope bridge of that nature was from her hut to the main pathway through the trees. After which, rope and wood were put together to make it easier to cross gaps between trunks, made stiffer and straighter by weaving branches into the railing strands.

Platforms circled around the trunks and strange crystals illuminated the paths as they grew out of nearly every surface. They were primarily orange, though as group walked through the treetops, purples and yellows were seen as well. While the terraces nearest to Dagmey's abode had growth on them—consisting of small tree sprouts no larger than Jade's hand, to flowers and moss and large-leafed vines—as their day wore on, the connecting passages were better cleaned. More avenues arched out from each scaffold, bridges leading to other distant destinations. Dagmey guided them by gesturing Jade onto a bridge first and always staying between her and A'doxia.

Dagmey and Jade spoke, Chloe chipping in whenever she felt it necessary. They broke often, allowing Jade to rest her aching stomach and scratch the chin of her chirping snake. She still hadn't thought of an appropriate name. When Dagmey inquired about it, Jade had no answer.

The first night found them sleeping on one of the decks, with Dagmey between her and A'doxia. A'doxia, however, kept her distance. She hadn't said anything to Jade or their guide since their journey began, and Jade caught the woman often looking towards distant trees, humming to herself. At least she was leaving Jade alone. That was a relief.

Sleep was riddled with waking spurts of ripping nerves and tearing flesh, Jade's right arm constantly replaying its end as she tried to rest. What little she got clung to her eyes in dark rings the following morning. Her bandages were checked, her snake watered, and Chloe donned. Jade asked Dagmey about the trees with stripping bark that had colors beneath. For a long while, they talked about the beauty of forests. And for a long while, Jade couldn't stop smiling.

As the sun began to fade, they reached the outskirts of the city. A single rope bridge was the only obstacle between Jade and the groups of people walking around in the dim light. Crystals were tied to posts, along railings, dangling from branches overhead, casting blues and purples and reds across the people passing through. Jade gripped her side, her fingers digging into her bandages as she peered out, her eyes wide as she took it all in. Climbing up the branches were homes, crafted near the trunk of the trees, perched on outer branches, all linked by a maze of overpasses, stairs, and winding pathways. Jade stumbled onto the bridge and this time the entirety of it was secured by thick branches on either side, keeping the whole thing from twisting, and ensuring it hardly shifted underfoot. The coarse rope beneath her hand was dripping with small crystals, tied up in string, illuminating the path underfoot.

She had never seen such a city before—it was like Nevar, but without toxic clouds, without billboards flashing lights, without vehicles and drunks and fake trees. These were real. Her pace quickened, nearly tripping over her own feet as she hurried closer.

These were real trees, these were real lights, this was all from the land, from this planet, without a single thing wasted.

This was beautiful.

The air in Jade's lungs, the freshness of the breath, the crisp, after-rain smell lingering in the air. Sobek was bloodied with war, Taotar held violent sands and deadly suns, Nevar was choking its own planet to death—Soldar wasn't even *real.* Hallow tried to drown her, and she had never even been to Sypher. But this place? She could see birds roosting atop pointed roofs, each slanted to allow rain to drip off the sides. She could see bugs buzzing through the air, some with glowing bodies, some bumping into the crystals as if they were in a violent battle. She had seen the trees from Dagmey's hut, seen the bugs and the animals, but here? A whole city built upon nature, built upon each other, without a single thing in sight that was made of steel, or crafted from nigferra? Maybe it was the lack of sleep that made her heart thunder in her throat, maybe it was the smile that somehow seeped into her chest and warmed her muscles to run.

Ahead, there was a large platform held up by the branches of three different trees all reaching out to the space between them, allowing for the circular arena to serve as a sort of entrance, a place to stand and gawk and as soon as her foot hit it, as soon as she climbed upon it, stumbling into the middle, she did just that. She stood, and she stared. She spotted a few victers leaping from one platform, spreading their arms, and gliding down to another. There were snippers, outside a building forty feet above and about a hundred feet away, identifiable by their four arms as they chatted and drank something in wood mugs. A kodarian approached from the left, across a wood walkway wide enough to accommodate four people and then some standing side-by-side.

Jade looked at him, her heart in her throat. Part of her feared for her safety, urged her to look away, to keep her eyes from being seen, but she wanted this. She wanted to walk without the lingering knowledge that she'd be dead if it weren't for Chloe over her eyes. She wanted to stand as who she was. For once.

Jade reached up and slipped Chloe off her head.

"Jade?" Chloe breathed. "Jade, what are you doing? We can't be sure…" she trailed off.

The kodarian's horns were full and stabbing forward towards the direction he was looking, and his tusks curled a few centimeters away from his lips. He wore a silk shirt that reflected the glowing lights around them and similar trousers. He came upon her, heading for a walkway on her right, and smiled. His eyes were hazel. And he kept walking.

Joy threatened to erupt from her throat in a scream of victory, her heart soaring in her chest as she spun towards Dagmey, the victer just now reaching her.

"He hardly even noticed me," Jade breathed. "My eyes—"

"Stop," Dagmey said. She looked from one of Jade's eyes to the next. "Why are your eyes blue?"

Jade's heart plummeted to her stomach. She couldn't even let herself relax to show this man who she really was, to see if the people here would be just as eager to push her from this height as those back home would be. She had no idea. She closed her eyes and scratched her right shoulder.

Dagmey's hand smacked Jade's away and the redhead jerked back, looking at the woman with alarm. Dagmey pointed one clawed finger at Jade's nose, all the feathers on the woman's throat flaring out.

"Stop that," she said, her beak snapping shut to emphasize her order. "If you keep scratching at it, it'll never heal. Care to explain why your eyes are…" She tilted her head. "Green again?"

"It happens when she's afraid," A'doxia said, coming up beside Dagmey. "After living a life of being targeted for her eye color, it's understandable she'd be concerned about the opinion of one."

Dagmey snorted and placed a hand on Jade's. "Leave your friend by your hip," she said. "You'll see. People are good here. I'm sure they'll accept you for who you are. For now, Jade—" she gestured her hand widely to the entire scene around them— "welcome to Mahong, the capital city of Kettpo. Home of a single chieftain, who somehow keeps this whole thing in line." She chuckled. "Let's go find ourselves a room, hm?" She turned to the left walkway and headed down it. Jade glanced back towards the lights, towards the city sprawling out before her. Somewhere, she thought she heard a river.

"Jade," A'doxia said, pulling Jade's attention to the Red. A'doxia nodded towards Dagmey. "We should keep going."

Jade peered at A'doxia. How the crimson light rested upon her cheek, lighting up half her face. How her eyes held dark circles beneath them, how the inch-long scar across her cheek and lip had sealed to stiffen the flesh around it. She looked horribly sad. And she wouldn't meet Jade's eyes.

"Who was she?" Jade found herself asking. "The person I remind you of?"

A'doxia's brows raised and her eyes flickered to Jade's for an instant before falling back to the floor. She exhaled slowly, prolonging a silence between them.

"She was my everything," A'doxia murmured. "Everything I lived for. Everything I fought for. She was all the family I had and… and when I lost her…"

"You joined the Reds."

"Voshell came to me when she'd seen what I'd done. After they hurt my sister, after I hunted those bastards down and—" She cut herself off, grimaced, and glanced to her left, towards Dagmey. The victer had noticed them and shifted her keen eyes to Jade. Jade lifted a hand to tell her to wait. A'doxia frowned. "Voshell came to me before the authorities could. She asked me to accompany her, and I did. And over time, my eyes turned red. Just like everyone else's. I became her top general, and she became my bed companion."

"How old was your sister?"

"Twelve. My sister had just turned twelve. It was her birthday."

Jade was silent. She looked down at her hand, wondered how her life would be if she had a sibling and lost her. Lost her family. She thought of Aris, of the thorns in her chest whenever she pictured the

343

woman's smiling face, remembered the times her friend would calm her down after the terrors of the night startled Jade awake. It didn't make up for what A'doxia did. Of the torment Jade endured for years, day after day, because of the dagger A'doxia put to her skin.

"We should get going," Jade said, hesitating where she stood, before turning and heading after Dagmey. She heard A'doxia's footsteps behind her and knew it would be the last time.

A small inn was stationed down the walkway Dagmey lead them across, situated close to the trunk and wrapping around it in a semi-circle. They stepped inside the reception area, decorated sparsely with jewels inlaid into the wood, with the far wall boasting the bark of the tree they were up against. Dagmey purchased three rooms, fishing tokens with seeds pressed into the middle out of her bag and setting them on the counter. The victer behind the smooth, polished surface was smaller in size than Dagmey, with a flattened, hooked beak dipped in ebony; a tan coat with black, white, and brown spots lined across their feathers; and no thick plumage. They handed the group silver keys and did not glance up once to check the color of their eyes.

"Breakfast is in the morning," they said. They scratched their talons down the shelf they rested their arms against. "Served in the dining hall, but it can be brought back to your rooms, too."

"Thank you," Dagmey replied. She turned and everyone was given their respective lodging, with Dagmey once more separating A'doxia and Jade. "I'll wake you when it's time to eat," Dagmey said, nodding to Jade. "Try to get some rest. And don't scratch at any of your bandages. I'll check them in the morning."

Jade offered a small smile. "Thanks, Dagmey. Could I have a few snacks for my snake?"

"You need to come up with a name," Dagmey said, sighing and shaking her head. She reached into the front pocket of the backpack and handed Jade a few pieces of meat.

"I will," Jade said, clipping Chloe to her torn shirt and grabbing the handful. Her snake friend chirped at the sight of them. "I just… I'm not sure yet."

"Well, don't go too long without naming her," Dagmey said. "We may not have beliefs around eyes, but we do have beliefs around names. If you go too long without giving something a name, something *else* with a name will possess it. It's never pretty."

Jade arched a curious brow. "I'd really like to hear about what you believe sometime, Dagmey."

"Luckily we have all the time in the galaxy to chat religion." Dagmey unlocked the door to her room and opened it. The wood creaked upon its hinges, which appeared to be made of timber as well. "Get some rest. I'm right here if you need me."

"Thank you." Jade opened her room and stepped inside, closing it behind her. It was simple, with a bathroom to her right and a bed straight before her. A dim crystal glowed by the door, illuminating a small space, but as she headed to the mattress, it was comfortably dark. She sat down, her stomach grateful for the relief, and placed Chloe on the pillow before handing the snake a few bites of the food.

"You'll sleep with Chloe again tonight, okay?" Jade said, scratching the tip of the snake's head, who chirped and licked the air. Jade smiled. "You like Chloe, don't you? She keeps you warm." She set Chloe upside down and placed her hand inside. Understanding, the snake slithered down Jade's arm and curled up on the cushions within the helm.

"Thanks for letting her sleep with you," Jade said.

"She is rather cute," Chloe murmured. "I think I understand why you saved her."

Jade slipped beneath the blankets and placed the final pieces of meat for the snake's breakfast beneath her pillow. She tugged the sheet up to her chin and closed her eyes.

"You are… all right, aren't you?" Chloe asked.

"I think so," Jade answered. "I think… maybe we should stay here, Chloe. Forever. Maybe we could be happy here."

Chloe chuckled. "I would like that, Jade. It would be nice to stay here. You, me, and our little snake."

Jade closed her eyes.

# Chapter 47

Nightmares were blissfully absent from Jade's rest, and when she woke, it was to the sound of gentle knocking at her door. She rubbed her eyes as birds began to chirp—no, a single bird, one perched on her chest. Jade blinked and peered at her little snake, curled up on her shirt, singing a gentle morning song. Jade smiled.

"Good morning, girl," she said. She stroked the snake's head with the tip of her finger and glanced at the creature's scar. While the scales looked less vibrant where damage had been done, she otherwise appeared well. Jade turned to Chloe. "Good morning, Chloe."

"Good morning, my friend," Chloe said. "You didn't wake last night. You slept well?"

"I did." Jade stretched her arm over her head. "Did you rest? It's good to pause your systems now and then."

"I rested once I was sure you were asleep," she answered. "Then our little friend wanted to be with you, so I condensed some air and used it to tip myself over. She happily slumbered atop you since."

"That's cute," Jade murmured. "Well, shall we have breakfast?" She reached beneath her pillow and produced the last thin slice of meat. The snake happily snatched it up and swallowed it whole. Jade chuckled.

"Be careful, girl, you'll choke. C'mon, I've got to eat now." She lifted the reptile up and placed her on her shoulder, where the snake then wrapped herself through a small hole in Jade's shirt. Jade sat up with a stiff stomach and grabbed Chloe, linking the helmet to her, which tore an even larger gouge in the fabric. In fact, on her left hip, the curling tendril of her scarring showed, upraised from A'doxia's torment with a knife. The corner of the wound from Aris bled through as well, both barely visible, both glaringly there.

Jade sighed and looked towards the door. It didn't matter now. She wouldn't see Aris again. She wouldn't see A'doxia again. After today, she would start her new life, and she would heal, and she would live with Dagmey. A life without war, without bloodshed. A life where the color of her eyes no longer mattered. She stood and walked towards the knocking.


Dagmey led Jade outside the inn, her facial feathers puffed up in happy anticipation. "I know they're serving food in there," Dagmey chirped, "but the market is much more interesting. You're going to love it. *And* we're going to get you some proper clothes." She looked back at Jade and let out a croaking laugh. "Come on, I'll show you something good to eat!"

People bustled about everywhere, carrying boxes, snacking on fruit, offering each other items to trade and drinks to try. Victers sailed in from higher perches, landing soundly on railings or empty sections of walkways. Shouting traders offered their goods to passerby, and someone brushed up against Jade's arm.

Jade stepped back and retreated towards the inn's entrance, where more space granted her to breathe. Her heart was racing, eyes wide, and she scanned everyone for a weapon, for a narrowed gaze, for ill intent.

"Jade?" Dagmey turned to peer back at her.

"Breathe," Chloe said. "Breathe, Jade, breathe. It's okay. We're not on Nevar. We're not even in the Empire. It's okay. No one is going to hurt you."

"That's right," Dagmey said, returning to Jade's side. "No one will hurt you, Jade. Is it the crowd? Does it make you uncomfortable?"

"I—someone could stab me," Jade murmured. *I knew there would be crowds. Stop it, Jade. I knew this would happen, I just have to breathe. Fucking—I thought we were over this.* She grabbed at her tangled hair. "I'm sorry, it's just… there's people *everywhere*."

"There are, but have you noticed?" Dagmey gestured to the folks passing by. "No one is looking to see what color your eyes are. No one cares, Jade. No one cares. You've got me, Chloe, and your little snake friend to protect you, anyway." She nodded. "There's nothing to fear."

"I'll make sure no one sneaks up on us," Chloe chimed. The snake pressed nose against Jade's jawline.

Jade swallowed and screwed her eyes shut. *No one cares about my eyes. No one cares. You're not special here, Jade. You're just you. Just you.* She focused on her breathing, in and out. Slowly, her heart returned to a normal drum. She opened her eyes.

"Okay," she said. "Okay." She reached up and scratched the snake's smooth scales.

"You're going to be fine," Dagmey assured her. "Come on." She offered her hand, and Jade took it. The victer turned and pulled Jade through the crowd, deftly avoiding the thickest parts of it before, at last, they broke out onto the largest bridge Jade had ever seen.

The entire structure was built between two branches of neighboring trees. Boards were placed horizontally, with five-foot tall railings made of smaller branches. Stalls of varying sizes and designs were packed into separate rows, with each stand serving at least one customer.

Jade blinked as she peered over the marketplace, activity as far as she could see. Snippers haggled with halos, victers and kodarians chatted with humans. The only species she didn't see were syphers, but as they were smaller than most other sentient life, it was possible Jade was overlooking them. As she took a deep breath, scents she had never before inhaled filled her senses. Spices with heat and chocolate, something smooth and milky, another with sweetness that made her mouth water. She had no names for the things she was breathing in, but she wanted to try them all.

"Well?" Dagmey chimed. "Which row shall we try first?"

Dagmey purchased a stuffed roll for Jade. The crisp bread crunched as she bit into it, but beneath it was moist and buttery, and a black substance filled the middle. It was ripped to shreds and coated in a thick, flavorful broth. The vendor claimed it was mantis bark seasoned with flowers of a chomphgie tree, but the words made little sense to Jade. She did note, however, how the bark was meaty, holding a sweetly spicy heat that burned the back of her throat and was touched with a saltiness that made her thirsty. She scarfed the roll down to the last bite, then offered a piece to her snake friend, who happily gobbled it up before flicking her tongue against Jade's jawline. Jade smiled and followed as Dagmey led her to another vendor. This stand, like many of the others, was made up of a wooden lean-to, with large, thick leaves acting as a canopy held up by wooden posts. The snipper with blue eyes smiled as the two approached.

"Hello, dear customers!" she chimed. Her eyes settled on Jade's and, for a moment, anxiety boiled in her chest. "Your eyes… you know, I've never seen them that color before! Back on Nevar, I heard it's said that Green means something like change, or whatever nonsense." She waved her hand dismissively. "But what do they know? What can I get for you two?"

Unable to help herself, Jade beamed. A slight comment, a wave, and back to business. She looked to Dagmey and the victer nodded.

*"We found it, Jade,"* Chloe said, her voice coded. *"We found the perfect place for us."*

"Four, please," Dagmey said, placing more tokens on the counter. The snipper smiled and turned, quickly getting to work. As Jade watched, the woman set forth four cups. Inside the wooden goblets were eggs with the top half of the shell broken. The contents had been drained of some of its liquid and warmed, perhaps cooked for a brief time, before being heavily spiced with leaves, flowers, and perhaps more of that blackened mantis bark. The snipper grasped a small, squarish container, shook it, and opened its lid to pour a blue liquid into each of the eggs, filling them all up to the brim of the clean-broken shell. The smell wafted over Jade, the savory cooking egg mixed with an odd sweetness, like berries that had been steamed for a pie. Dagmey picked one up, nodded to Jade, and tossed everything but

351

the shell into her mouth. She clamped her beak shut and swallowed. Jade blinked.

"It's good," Dagmey hummed. "Go ahead, two of those are yours."

Tentatively, Jade took up one of the eggs and brought it to her lips.

"All at once," Dagmey said. "That's how drinks are had here. The flavors are better with one swallow."

With a breath, Jade dumped the liquid down her throat, the complexity of the flavor swirling over her tongue. Savory and thick, but mixed with berries, cinnamon, and sugar. It was like some sort of dessert and, after she swallowed, she was firmly convinced she liked it.

"Fuck that's good!" Jade cried.

The snipper laughed. "I'm so glad you like it!"

"Have the other," Dagmey said, her facial feathers spreading. She and Jade both grabbed the two remaining eggs and swallowed them, setting the empty egg shells back into the cups they were provided in.

"Thanks!" the vendor hummed. "Please come again!"

"We will," Jade said. "Thank you." She walked with Dagmey down the aisle and chuckled. "That was a delight."

"You sound like you're feeling better," Dagmey hummed. "You still hungry?"

"So long as you're paying," Jade teased.

"Only because you don't have any money." Dagmey snickered. "There's one last thing you've got to try. We've got this fish that lives in the river east of here. It has these tentacles all across its body, and we harvest those and throw them on sticks and cook them up in broth."

"Sounds good!"

"You'll try just about anything, won't you?"

"Today I will," Jade said, smiling. "Today's a good day to try new things."

"Jade?" Chloe murmured. "Something's wrong. I can access the Galaxy Feed again."

A dark rumble grew like a beast growling at a rival predator, the familiar sound of an Opes ship approaching growing louder and louder until Jade's chest constricted with dread. Thunder roared in the barrel of fired cannons. Wood splinted above. Jade looked up.

And then the sky rained fire.

# Chapter 48

Canon fire. Branches snapped above as explosions rocked Jade off her feet, throwing her to the ground. Dagmey dug her claws into the bridge's floor to stay upright. Above, the canopy flashed red and yellow. Leaves rained down upon them, all aflame. Smoke choked the scents of boiling lemons, vinegar, and the thick, fatty smell of roasting human corpses.

Jade checked her shoulder and saw her snake, then her hip and saw Chloe. She unhooked the helmet and pulled it on.

"We have to get to safety," Dagmey shouted, her voice barely breaking through the sounds of screaming and panicked cries. "Back towards the inn!"

"I thought you weren't part of the war!" Jade cried, climbing to her feet. "What's going on?"

"Something's wrong! Nothing should be able to get through that shield above!" She grabbed Jade's hand and pulled the woman towards that side of the bridge. Another explosion and a branch splintered free, spiraling past the bridge and crashing into the ground far below.

Jade's eyes widened. "Keep moving!"

Guards rushed past as the duo stumbled forward wielding spears with the glowing crystals as jagged weapon tips. Jade did her best to keep an eye on them and watched as they headed for a spiral staircase that reached upper levels.

Children screamed. Another branch came down and crushed a different bridge to Jade's left, throwing the wood, rope, and people into the depths below.

*What is going on? Why is Ferges being attacked?* Her jaw locked and a blossom of fury curled her hand into a fist. *Why can't I have one fucking day?*

"Jade, above us!" Chloe cried. Jade jerked her head up, to where a third branch crumpled beneath the weight of canon fire and tore itself free from the trunk, plummeting down towards them.

"Wait, Dagmey!" Jade yanked the victer back. "The branch above us!"

Dagmey followed Jade's gaze just as it hit. Large enough to span over the entire bridge's girth and thick enough to crack the supports, its impact crushed a handful of civilians and rattled the rest. Jade gripped onto Dagmey to keep from falling. They were already almost halfway across, nearly to safety, but the branch was massive and—

A series of splinters cut through the terrified cries. They travelled up, through the supporting branches, snapping and tearing and dropping Jade's stomach.

"We have to go. We have to go!" Dagmey cried, spinning them around and charging the other direction, dragging Jade along with her. "Don't stop running, Jade, don't stop!"

Ash coated the air and Jade was glad Chloe was filtering it out before it could cake her lungs. She checked her shoulder to find the little snake holding on tightly, pressed against Jade's shirt.

"Hang on," Jade breathed. "We'll get out of this. Hang on."

They sprinted through the market as others ran with them. Halos dropped to all fours, rushing ahead in hopes of making it before the bridge snapped. The other tree rose up towards the sky, growing closer with each step.

With a startling crack, the ground beneath their feet pitched downwards, and the bridge began to fall.

Dagmey dug her sharp talons into Jade's forearm and threw herself against the ground, sinking her free hand and feet into the wood. The bridge swung downwards and smashed into the trunk of the tree, jostling Jade's skull and startling a chirp from her snake. She seized hold of Dagmey's arm.

They both looked up at the steep, ninety-degree angle climb as vendor stalls and bodies fell past them of snippers that could hold onto nothing, of halos as their claws gave way, of humans and of kodarians who did not act fast enough. Their screams echoed even as the darkness swallowed them, but as their bodies were consumed, victers dived down to save the civilians from their demise.

Dagmey began to climb, pulling Jade with her. Streaks of blood began to trail out of the gouges in Jade's flesh, thick and hot. Jade gritted her teeth and reached for a handhold, her right fingers groping for—

A stab of pain rang through her right stump. She hissed out a breath as the bridge shuddered, shifting further towards the distant forest floor, cracking and snapping as the branch gave way. There was too much bridge left to climb. She was going to die.

Jade had wanted to, hadn't she? Wanted to fall and die and end the memories flashing through her head? Wanted to let darkness devour her, enter into the afterlife, ask Vix why he gave her green eyes and sent her into a galaxy that hated her. Yet the thought of it filled Jade with a burning dread. Her snake let out a frightened peep, and Chloe was rapidly processing possible means of escape in the lower right section of the visor. Dagmey was going to help Jade heal. They were going to live away from war, live peacefully and go to the market on mornings they were in town, eat food Jade had never tried and swallow egg drinks whole.

Tears of anger sprang into her eyes. She didn't want to die. She *wouldn't* die.

Victers leapt down the bridge and grabbed hold of the wood as they reached the two of them. They wore a single sash across their chest with a symbol on it, indicating some sort of loyalty Jade didn't understand.

"We're here to help!" one of them shouted, larger than Dagmey and with black and grey feathers striping their form. They and their companion grabbed hold of Jade, their talons carefully perched atop her skin without breaking the surface.

Dagmey looked down and nodded, releasing Jade's arm and allowing her to rest solely in the protection of the newcomers. Jade felt helpless as they quickly shambled up the crumbling bridge, and she grasped the terrace the moment they were close enough to pull herself back over the edge, cursing her lack of an arm, cursing the blood spilling from her left. She crawled away from the edge as the platform shifted, leaned downward, and the bridge's branch snapped.

It fell to obscurity, its collision with the ground concealed by wails and hissing fire which had fallen upon all parts of the city, chewing at homes and terraces alike.

"Are you two okay?" the larger victer asked.

"What's going on?" Jade shouted, holding her arm to her torn white shirt. Blood stained the fabric.

"Someone got the codes to our outer defenses and slipped in. We've been trying to call the other cities nearby, but we can't get a message through. We sent scouts," the victer said. "But we'll never know if they made it in time."

"Who's attacking you?" Jade pressed.

"It's a ship," the victer replied. "A galleon with one large flag on it. Some sort of bloody human hand inside a golden ring. It has lettering around it like…"

"We do not bow," Jade breathed.

"That's it."

Jade looked up towards the top of the tree, where the flames were full and red. Her heart sank.

They followed her here.

# Chapter 49

Aris watched from the portside as her ship grew closer to the landing pad above the trees. For a planet with no visitors, it was awfully accommodating. Flames leapt from tree to tree above the canopy, spreading across the densely packed forest that spanned further than she could see. Kuroda stood beside her, his mouth a wicked grin.

"Beautiful," he said.

Aris glanced at him. "So it is."

The landing pad was thick wood and the ship's engines grumbled as the hovering systems activated, keeping it a few feet off the ground. The plank was lowered. With a nod from their leader, the Blue soldiers, armored from head to toe, sprinted onto Ferges.

"You're sure she's here?" Aris asked.

A headache warmed the back of her eyes and Malkov materialized beside her. "I'm certain."

"Go with?" Kuroda asked, gesturing to himself and then to her hundred soldiers running off to make war.

"You'll stay with me," Aris said. "For now. Keep me safe, okay?"

Kuroda grumbled his compliance, dipped his head, and let her touch his mandibles. His scales were smooth beneath her fingertips.

"Keep safe," he murmured.

Aris smiled. *So obedient.* She pulled away and walked off the ship, resting her boots upon the landing pad and looking over the destruction her canons had caused. Yes, this would surely bring the self-righteous demon to light. Aris could be rid of it. Aris could finally get some sleep.

The travel here had been restless.

"She's coming," Malkov chimed, moving to hover beside her. "I can feel its friend reaching out into the network."

"Its friend?" Aris asked. The heat from the flames was enough to make her sweat. Her soldiers secured the landing pad and began to make their way to the other side, where a wrapping staircase led down the tree and out of sight.

"That's what she thinks she is," Malkov said. "She calls herself Chloe."

Aris scowled. *Of course she still has that stupid thing.*

Ahead, there was shouting, and as Kuroda came to stand near her, it grew louder. Aris frowned, squinting into the distance, through billowing waves of smoke and the flickering light cast by the blaze. And from the staircase came victers—dozens of them. At first, they held nothing but sashes across their chests, leaping at the nearest Blue with claw and beak, slicing throats and disemboweling chests.

But as her soldiers began to bite back, more arrived, with spears made of glowing crystals, with leather armor imbedded with gems over their vital organs, protecting them from harm. The birds screeched an ear-piercing battle cry that rose with the smoke, and it rallied those who were cut down by her troops. Injured avian monsters snapped at ankles. One with intestines pouring from his stomach pulled the pin to a grenade and sprinted into the wall of Blues.

"Friend!" Kuroda grabbed Aris and moved between her and the blast. The dock shook and her ears rang. Aris blinked a few times as her hearing relayed muffled sounds, disoriented by the explosion. Kuroda released her and she pushed him aside to see the damage done to her troops.

The harbor was not large, barely enough room for more than her galleon to fit. In such cramped spaces, the detonation had struck many of her troops, and sent some flying over the edge. Opes troops rushed to their companions' aid, trying to pull those up who were hanging on to lower branches, while others grasped holes in their chests and screamed. Her enemies did not fair much better, but there were less of them on the field. And as her troops struggled to recover, more arrived to stab spears through their skulls.

"Help," Kuroda growled. "Must help!"

Aris opened her mouth to respond but Malkov cut her off.

"And there she is," he purred as he vanished from sight. *The woman of the hour.*

From the staircase came the familiar form of the Green Demon. Aris blinked, her eyes growing wide. It was alive. Malkov had been right—the demon was *alive.* A helmet painted with a crimson skull sat over its head, it wore rags for clothes, and its right arm was gone. Blood dripped from its left and seeped from a wound near its stomach. Yet, as it stepped onto the dock, Aris saw it for what it really was. Its form twisted and changed. She grabbed Kuroda's hand and

361

stepped back as the helmet bled away, leaving nothing but a human skull without a lower jaw oozing blood onto itself; horns broke out from its temples, pointed out towards Aris; its left arm reached into the air and the flames around heeded its call, rushing to surround the limb with sweltering fire, burning away the flesh in thick chunks that fell in oily piles onto the wood beneath its bare feet; claws, like those of a victer's, dug into the pier as an arrow-tipped, thread-thin tail spilled from its spine to swing lazily behind it; and from her right arm, once a stump but no longer, a long, snake-like figure broke through the bandages. An okehesa, long, ivory, and drooling with desire for her flesh.

Aris stepped back. "Kill it," she breathed. "Kill it!"

And then there was lightning wrapped in shadow as the demon fell to its knees. It spread across the deck, killed everything it touched. Blues stumbled back, eyeballs popping in their skulls, blood vessels exploding in their hearts, most falling to their knees and choking on crimson gore. Those that managed to step out of its range looked to Aris for what to do.

The victers were untouched. The victers charged forward, grabbing Blues and yanking them into the killing electricity. Screams and blood and violence and fire. And within it all, the demon.

*This was a mistake.*

www.ingramcontent.com/pod-product-compliance
Lightning Source LLC
Chambersburg PA
CBHW030829110726
47900CB00006B/1812